THE TELLING TIME

THE TELLING TIME

P. J. MCKAY

POLAKO PRESS

COPYRIGHT

A catalogue record for this book is available from the National Library of New Zealand.
IBSN 978 0 473 52012 0 (e-book)
ISBN 978 0 473 52011 3 (paperback)

Cover painting by Catherine Farquhar www.catherinefarquhar.art
Cover design by Laura Becker www.laurabeckerdesign.com
Author photograph by Colleen Maria Lenihan
Published by Polako Press www.pjmckayauthor.com

POLAKO PRESS

In memory, of Gran, Phyllis Louisa Lamont,
who always said I would.

Children show scars like medals.

Lovers use them as secrets to reveal.

A scar is what happens when the word is made flesh.

— LEONARD COHEN

AUTHOR'S NOTE

The following family monikers are used throughout the novel:

Tata — Dad, father

Mam — Mum, mother

Dida — Grandad, grandfather

Baba — Grandma, grandmother

Ujak — Uncle

Teta — Aunt

A note on pronunciation:

Č/č as ch (like chalk)

I/i as ea (like east)

J/j as y (like yellow)

K/k as c (like cut)

Š/š as sh (like shut)

The Croatian terms of endearment — *Draga* (for females) and *Dragi* (for men) — are used throughout.

Dally (collectively Dallies) — a short-form for Dalmatian, describing the people who immigrated to New Zealand from the Dalmatia coastal region. Mostly an affectionate colloquialism.

GABRIJELA, 1958

KORČULA, YUGOSLAVIA

FEBRUARY

Sardines. We reeked of them — me and all the other women working at the Jadranka fish factory. Their stinking oil greased up our hair and our skin, and their flesh got wedged under our fingernails. I could taste them at the back of my throat. We sat jam-packed beside the conveyer belts, or on long tables, trussed up in our matching white uniforms and headscarves: preparing the sardines, sorting them and stuffing them into cans. There was no escape and complaining made no difference. I would be trapped there until I got married, and even then it wasn't a guaranteed thing. Some women never escaped.

My dream was to be a teacher but Tata said working at the factory was more important because I was doing my bit for the economy. Vela Luka and our family fishing business relied on me. Tata and Josip played their part by hauling in the fish on *Krešimira,* and I stuffed them into cans. My eighteenth birthday, in January, marked eighteen months at that prison. Most of the local girls did their time but that was no consolation. Men rule the roost in Yugoslavia, girls are second best, and throughout my childhood I'd been conditioned not to challenge this order.

All day I'd been stuck with two older girls who chatted between themselves with no interest in talking to me. We had no sooner emptied one tray of the lower-grade sardine chunks when someone loaded another pile on. Our job was to gather up the offcuts and pack them neatly around the higher-grade fillets in the cans trundling past. The offcuts made them look full without being the first thing you noticed. Our supervisor told us the job required judgement and dexterity but to me it required the patience of a saint. My head felt crammed with the clamour of machines, and the din bouncing off the walls and low ceilings rattled inside me. At times I felt it all might escape as a scream.

When the conveyer belts ground to a halt, I ripped off my head scarf, scrunching it into the front pocket of my uniform dress. I searched the room for my friend, Nada. She'd landed one of the better jobs that day, ladling olive oil into the cans before they were sealed. I hadn't seen Antica; she must have been late arriving. There was Nada, standing at the side, folding her headscarf into a neat triangle. As usual, her short dark hair sat perfectly around her pixie face. She waved and I signalled for her to wait. I never understood how she could always be so cheerful. Nada would never get into a war of words with our supervisors, unlike me. I was always saying things that got me into trouble — the same at home.

I joined Nada and we merged in with the trail of women, all in our regulation flat shoes, all trudging across the wet concrete floor towards the cloakroom. The men, in their rubber gumboots and over-pants, were already wielding their hoses, directing the debris to the sides in preparation for the night shift. I worried they might collect us up as well.

'Thank God that's over,' I said. 'Where's Antica?'

'Got the worst job.' Nada grimaced. 'Arrived too late again.'

Poor Antica. She would have spent all day at the first station, scraping off the scales with the razorblade knife. Her fingers and uniform would be smattered with sardine debris. I scanned the cloakroom for her.

'Had to go early,' said Nada, scrubbing her hands at the basin. She gave me a knowing look. 'Her mama was in charge of little Luci.'

I peered in the mirror at my washed-out face and greasy hair. Life was so unfair. 'That Marin better marry her soon,' I said. 'What a toss-up — babies or sardines.'

It was hard keeping the sarcasm from my voice but there was no point complaining to Nada. She got annoyed if I showed too much negativity. The three of us had been friends through school, and it always puzzled me where Nada hid her feelings. She let them out so rarely that sometimes I wondered if I knew her — if she even knew herself. I wished she would take a few more risks, open herself up more, but neither of us wanted to be like Antica. There were downsides to taking a rebellious nature too far.

'I hope her wages don't get docked,' said Nada. 'That would be the last straw.'

We finished scrubbing our hands and I checked my face again, still feeling unclean but knowing the worst of it would have to wait until my bath later on.

'Come on,' I said. 'Let's scat. We won't solve Antica's problems staying here.'

It was drizzling again outside. We were stuck in the middle of winter, February, my least favourite time of the year. Nada pushed up her lime-green umbrella and we huddled beneath it, joining the parade of nylon canopies, colourful contrasts to the grey of the sky and the stark hills looming over the town. I took the handle to make it easier. Nada only reached my shoulders and her legs were like thin sticks. Antica and I often joked that she might blow over in a puff of wind. All the same I envied her petite build. Antica begged to differ. She said men preferred something to hold on to — and she would know. Letting Marin fondle her breasts had led to little Luci.

Around the port there was a bustle of activity, boats coming and going, men shouting orders. I scanned the harbour for *Krešimira* but couldn't see her. I leaned in closer, shielding Nada, as we walked briskly away.

'And will you be seeing Branko tomorrow night?' asked Nada, glancing up with a sly smile.

'Depends,' I said, trying my best to sound candid. 'And you? Dinko calling by?'

Nada shrugged and laughed. Branko was Nada's older brother, and she often joked that one day we might be related. We were practically relatives anyway, having all shared a tent at the refugee camp in Egypt. I'd even been there, in that same tent, when their youngest sister, Ruža, was born.

'Sometimes I wish I could escape all this,' I said. 'Do you ever think it's strange that we lived in Egypt for two years, and yet now we never leave this small island?'

Nada frowned. 'That was horrible, though. Why would you want to leave? I'd much rather be here.'

'Just to see. There must be more to life.'

'You should be grateful for what you've got. Who would go back to all that?'

All that. Our camp stretchers lined up along canvas walls. Running barefooted and hiding behind the flapping canvas; jumping and sliding to soft landings in the sand hills on the perimeter of the camp. Mama sweeping and shaking and sweeping again, trying in vain to remove that endless sand. Snuggling against Mama and stealing her heat when the air froze at night. *All that*, plenty of memories, not all of them bad. Perhaps it was just the sardine factory draining me of any spark. I pulled my coat around me to hide my hideous uniform, hoping we wouldn't bump into anyone we knew — especially one of the boys.

The evening had closed in, but the oil lamps inside the houses added some cheer. We reached Nada's street and I handed her the umbrella. The rain had eased to a fine mist, and besides, our house was just up around the corner. It wouldn't matter if it rained again. I would be washing my hair anyway. It was always my routine at the end of the week; ridding myself of the sardines.

On the last stretch up the hill, I wondered what sort of day Tata might have had. I hoped the fishing had gone well. If the fish were running we were less likely to clash. Sometimes I wondered if he was disappointed I was a girl. That after the eight long years between Josip and myself — three baby boys lost in between — this was his way of punishing me. In his eyes I was nothing more than a helping hand for Mama. He never valued my opinions and I was constantly chasing his approval. Even back when we returned from El Shatt I'd noticed it. Tata was a puzzle piece plucked from my childhood — a piece that wouldn't fit snugly after our return.

Our house was in darkness except for the blurred light in the kitchen where the fogged-up pane sat ajar. My mouth watered at the aroma of freshly made bread as I shrugged out of my damp coat, cursing when my fingers bashed against the bathroom door opposite.

'Mama, I'm home!' I yelled, bursting into the kitchen but stopping short. It was deserted, and the light was so dim that it took a moment for my eyes to adjust. A loaf of bread was cooling on the rack, just to the side of the wood-burner stove. I checked through into the dining alcove.

'Is that you, Jela?' Mama's voice sounded strained. She was sitting with her head in her hands at the table.

'Are you sick?' I said, rushing forward and touching her shoulder.

Mama jerked her head upwards. A letter lay open on the table and I peered over her shoulder, trying to see who it might be from. It was typed and official-looking. My stomach churned. It was Mama's habit to twist and stretch her corkscrew curls whenever she felt stressed or unsure of herself. She stared ahead, the palm of her hand plastered against her face, her unruly mop of blonde curls hanging limp and stretched. It seemed that she might cave in on herself.

'Don't be worried.' She reached for the letter. 'This stirred up memories, that's all.' Her hands were ice-white and trembling. I rubbed her wooden back, still trying to check over her shoulder for clues.

'But who's it from?'

'Ivan, my brother. Half-brother.'

Ivan? We never talked of him. Mama's family story was complicated. Her tata had died when she was thirteen and just four years later, when she and Tata were engaged, her mama married Dida Novak. Ivan was their son. Both Baba and Dida Novak were dead now, killed in the war. I never got to know them. The last time they had visited I was just a baby.

'I feel so guilty, I haven't even visited their graves.' Mama's voice was low, as though wanting to hide from the thoughts that were creeping around, shadowing her.

'You couldn't,' I said. 'It was impossible. And it's best to remember them by your happy memories.'

'This letter's brought back all the horrors.'

I wrapped her in a hug. 'I'm sorry.' I didn't know what else to say. I kept rubbing her back.

Baba and Dida had been killed in the war. Along with Ivan, they were Partisan supporters. Ivan had been away fighting for the cause when it happened. Mama learnt about their deaths while we were in Egypt and when we returned a year later she couldn't face visiting their graves.

They were buried in Split, the place they had made their home, but it was a place that meant nothing to Mama. She always said she wanted to remember her mama on this island, Korčula. Split had always felt foreign to her, just like her step-father.

Mama picked up the letter and folded it back into the envelope then pushed herself slowly to her feet. She was a good head shorter than me now and so, so thin. Tata was always telling her to eat more, but Mama never put on any padding. Her stooped shoulders made her seem older than her forty-seven years, and if it wasn't for her white apron she might be mistaken for a black stick. People told me I had Mama's looks with Tata's hair. I'd also been *blessed* with Tata's build and next to Mama I felt hefty, just like I did with Nada.

'Perhaps light the lamps,' Mama said, 'and after you've changed you can help me with the dinner. I'll tell you about the good news then.'

I attended to the lamps in our small lounge and dining room, then made my way up the narrow stairwell taking the stairs two at a time. Ours was a three-storey house and our bedrooms were on the second and third floors: Mama and Tata's on the top and Josip's and mine on the middle floor. Josip shared his room with Mare now after they got married last year. It was weird knowing they were both in that room at night, so close, doing who knows what. I'd often hear muffled noises and laughter. It wouldn't surprise me if Mare escaped the sardine factory soon. I tore off my uniform and changed into my winter skirt and top. Branko and I never touched like that. We kissed, of course, but most of the time it was more a peck. If he ever tried to cuddle me, I always made sure that his hands didn't wander. It wasn't just because of what happened to Antica. If I was honest, I couldn't get past the feeling that I was canoodling with my brother.

Back in the kitchen, it was hard to tell whether the feelings in my stomach were hunger pangs or curiosity. Mama stood by the sink, the envelope now slotted between the slats of the shutter like a red alert. The wind had picked up and the window pane was rattling. I was itching to ask more but I knew better than to rush her. Uncle Ivan was a high-ranking officer in the Party. After all these years, why would he make contact? Mama had tried several times to reconnect after we had returned from El Shatt, but her letters went unanswered. Tata had said to forget him and it seemed Mama *had* given up. I scratched my brain, trying to remember the last time Ivan's name had been mentioned.

'Cut the cabbage, *Draga*,' Mama said, washing her hands. 'We're back to vegetable stew. Lord knows what Ivan will think.'

I stared after her as she crossed to the wood-burner stove. So Ivan was coming here? A large black pot sat on the stovetop. I knew it would contain her concoction of vegetables and beans for our evening meal. She struck a match to relight the fire.

'For how long?' I asked, still trying to make sense. 'And why now?' This was the most exciting thing to have happened in years — not only a long-lost uncle but a Party official too.

'A few months, apparently. He'll be leading a project upgrading the roads on Korčula.'

I chopped the cabbage. Many of the leaves were yellowed and I scrunched my nose at the sour smell but tried to slice them as thinly as I could. Branko had mentioned this project a week or so back, but I'd only half listened. He was always looking for ways to make money but most never came off. This might be an opportunity for longer-term work, and me having this contact might make it easier for him to apply.

'It's great news, isn't it?' I said tentatively. 'A chance for us all to reconnect.'

I was sure Mama would be thinking about Tata's likely reaction. At the time I'd only been seven or eight, but I still remembered Tata's scowl, his scathing words when Ivan had ignored Mama's letters. *Stuck in his Party ways, too good for the likes of us — his real family.*

'He'll be here in a couple of weeks,' said Mama, plucking a bunch of parsley from a jar on the window sill. 'He'll have to take us as he finds us. I imagine he's been used to better.'

Tata and Josip's voices boomed from the hallway and Mama and I glanced over, her forehead creased with worry. They slouched into the kitchen like weary giants, still in their old fishing trousers and checkered shirts. It was obvious they were father and son, although Josip's build was finer, more like Mama's. Both had jet-black hair, closely cropped, and both had a dark mat of chest hair, although more recently Tata's had sprouted tufts of white.

Tata crossed behind me, greeting Mama with a pat on her bottom and a peck on her cheek. Lately he had seemed to tower over her. Josip made a beeline for the dining table. This wasn't unusual, it was rare for him to pay either me or Mama attention. His chair scraped against the tiled floor and I heard the customary thump when he sat down. Through my childhood I'd looked up to Josip as my idol, but during my teenage years he'd become more of a disappointment. He was a solitary type, which frustrated me. I couldn't understand how he could shun people — my friends were the only thing that kept me sane. Mama defended him. *The world needs all types,* she'd say, describing Josip as like her tata, *a gentle soul with a quiet nature, nothing wrong with that.* He was her precious son, and so of course she wouldn't say a word against him. The way he repaid her affections made me fume, though.

'Busy day?' said Mama, glancing up at Tata.

'*Katastrofa!* Nothing in the nets.'

'Ah, well, you get those days. Tomorrow will be better.'

I wondered how Tata could be so blind. I wanted to shout at him — *Look at her face!* — but Tata seemed more intent on pouring himself a glass of water from the jug beside the sink. How could he not notice the letter? When he sloped off through to the dining area, Mama raised her eyebrows, her expression saying it all. I shook my head. We often shared a secret joke about how useless men could be, how much they missed by not paying attention to details.

'Where's Mare?' called out Josip.

'Back soon,' Mama said. 'She's stopping in to see her mama.' She turned to me. 'Set the table, please, Jela.'

I wondered when Mama would break the news but it wasn't for me to say. I went through to the dining area. Tata and Josip sat with glum faces, neither taking any notice of me. I gathered up the cutlery and mats from the old wooden sideboard and almost jumped when Josip spoke. 'Days like this make me think we *should* run the business as a collective. Tito may have a point about pooling resources.' He was leaning forward on his elbows, his hands either side of his face, a tactic I knew he was employing to avoid Tata's eye.

'Bah!' Tata exploded. 'Don't be an arse! That's their way of lining their coffers. Diluting ours. They want to see us struggle. Listen with your ears open, son.'

'But we're struggling anyway. Maybe it's a way to get ahead?' I wanted to cheer him on, it was so rare for Josip to share his opinions.

'I'll be damned if I'll hand over what I've worked so hard for.'

I reached around Josip, placing his mat and cutlery down. At school we'd learned about all the plans Marshal Tito had for our country. It annoyed me that Tata was always so negative.

'What about Jadranka?' I said, taking care to place Tata's cutlery down quietly so as not to jangle his nerves. 'That's run as a collective, and you make me work there.'

'If they pay fairly for our hard-earned fish, I don't give a damn how they run it.' Tata crashed his glass on the table, leaning back, his dark, muscly arms folded. 'You need to get your head out of the clouds and away from your books, Gabrijela. The secret to getting ahead in this country is to work hard like the rest of us. The dreaming days are over.'

My eyes smarted and I turned away, determined not to show him my tears. Why hadn't I held my tongue? Mama was always telling me not to interrupt their important conversations. She said it was disrespectful, but I knew it was more about keeping the menfolk happy. Mama came through then with the letter and the look on her face said, *Don't say I didn't warn you.*

'It came today,' she said, handing it to Tata then backing away to stand beside me. She pulled me in close. I wasn't sure if she wanted to reassure herself, or me. 'Ivan's coming to stay. The Party will be close to home for a while.'

Tata's jaw dropped. For a moment he seemed lost for words. 'To what do we owe the honour?' he said.

Mama explained about the road project. Josip looked to be all ears. I held my breath.

'But where will he sleep?' asked Josip, which was typical. He could never see past himself.

'Well, you and Mare could move in with her parents for a while,' said Mama.

Josip scrunched his nose and chewed at his fingers. I knew he and Mare felt comfortable here and he hated routines changing. My mind raced, thinking about the adjustments we would all have to make.

'How long have we got?' asked Josip.

'A few weeks. Plenty of time.'

Josip grumbled as though this was the most pressing problem.

'What did I tell you, son,' said Tata. 'The Party's itching to take us over. Your room's just the first step.'

Josip laughed then, and not for the first time I envied their relationship. Tata would never back down so quickly after cross words with me. He always made me work hard to regain his approval.

'Don't be ridiculous, Ante,' said Mama, crossing to stand beside Tata. She kneaded his shoulder. 'Ivan is family.' She didn't look convinced, though.

'When he wants to be,' said Tata. 'Means I'll have to behave myself, won't I?'

I hoped Tata was serious, and that Uncle Ivan might be able to both soften Tata's views and mend Mama's heart — be the glue to help stick our family back together again. Even Josip might benefit from having a male around who was closer in age to himself. I dared to dream for myself too — that Uncle Ivan might convince Tata about the need for good teachers, and the role they could play in reshaping our country. I was desperate to open my mind to a world of possibilities again, to reignite ideas I had crushed for so long.

GABRIJELA, 1959

AUCKLAND, NEW ZEALAND

FEBRUARY

I never wanted to move to New Zealand. It wasn't my choice.

Even on the day of my departure from Korčula, with the ferry looming like a white ghost at the end of the Vela Luka pier, I still half expected Tata to say he'd changed his mind. At nineteen I had no real concept of what lay ahead. All I knew was that I was travelling across the world to New Zealand, sponsored by an old friend of Tata's called Stipan Tomić. There I would live with Stipan and his wife, Marta, and housekeep for their grown-up son, Roko.

The journey was long: Belgrade, Athens, Cairo, Bombay, Sydney. On the last leg, the flight to Auckland, my world morphed into a pressurised cabin filled with the nauseating stench of cigarette and cigar smoke, and the well-meaning concern of my fellow travellers. My stomach was a messy tangle of unanswered questions. Would Stipan be there to meet me? What story had Tata fed him?

Through the shifting clouds I stared at the coastline far below; a long wriggling line filled with dense bush and cliffs, the sea lashing at the land. I thought it wild and rugged, hostile even, but I held onto the spectacular finish — the champagne spray of white foam — and flung another prayer skywards. When the plane bumped and thumped onto the tarmac at Whenuapai Airport, I felt a wash of disappointment. The terminal was tiny: a plain, flat, rectangular box parked at the edge of what looked like an open field — nothing like those other exciting places, cities touched down in but not explored, like pages given a cursory glance.

We filed down the steps from the plane to cross the tarmac. My first gulp of that foreign summer air and the strong blast of aircraft fuel nearly made me lose the contents of my stomach. It was the rush of heat after the cool of the cabin that surprised me — hot, fat air, expelled from the aircraft engines and woven through the humidity. The warm cross-breeze flicked at the hem of my full skirt, and I used my small suitcase like an anchor to flatten it. Somehow I managed to walk, clutching the case containing my paperwork and a few necessities for the flights: toiletries; a change of clothes; rosary beads; a book; my *dragi's* vest; and a stick of cherry-red lipstick, the one my friend Antica had given me for luck.

Closer to the building the air seemed to clear, with a waft of freshly cut grass. This, at least, was something I expected, as at school we had learnt about this country's reliance on agriculture — even so, it was disorientating not being able to smell the tang of sea salt so familiar from home. I pushed on through doors held wide by an air hostess with her pert little hat. It was these minor victories that propelled me forward on that day, and in the months to come. *Polako, polako* as we say at home, one step in front of the other.

The terminal was a hothouse. The man checking our paperwork had patches like valleys seeping from his armpits. 'Welcome, Miss Surjan,' he said, thumping his stamp down, the twang in his voice making my name sound all wrong. In the waiting area, a burly man waved, but I wasn't sure if it was Stipan. This man looked more like a businessman in his pale grey jacket and matching felt hat.

'*Dobro došla,* Gabrijela,' he boomed, rushing forward to take my hand, his brown eyes twinkling.

Up close he dwarfed me, a mountain of a man with comical ears jutting like flaps as though there to balance his hat. I expected his hand to feel rough, like Tata's, but it was warm and smooth. I couldn't manage a reply but my eyes watered at the sound of my language. In the strangest way I felt a sense of homecoming, a reassurance, just as I had when a kind Yugoslav man had taken me under his wing back in Greece to help me with the documentation. I had lost my language somewhere between Belgrade and Athens, having thought my grasp of English was better. When that same man waved goodbye and rushed for the departure doors in Sydney, I'd felt a keen sense of loss, a hollow pit in my stomach.

Stipan dropped my hand and took another drag on what was left of his thin cigarette. He lumbered towards the baggage area, leaving me to tail him, just as my goats at home would do while scavenging the hills for green shoots.

Outside the terminal, Stipan dumped my large suitcase and pointed to a pale blue car, its fat bottom encased by a shiny ring of metal hanging low to the ground.

The glossy red seat was burning hot when I sat, my knees pressed together with my small case at my feet. I didn't dare move and my head spun with waves of exhaustion. Stipan clambered into the driver's seat, wrenching around to toss his hat onto the seat behind. Flecks of silver peppered his dark hair that was shaved close above his ears.

Most of the trip was spent in silence. I stared out the window in disbelief at the variety of crops, light and dark green trees, and the rolling hills, burnished brown, that stretched as far as I could see on either side of the two-lane road. To me this country seemed ironed out, flattened, and in that moment, I would have given anything to see my homeland's stark limestone mountains that rise from the sea like giant monoliths.

'Home now,' Stipan said, pulling into a driveway off a wide street lined with a collection of timber houses painted in mostly lollipop shades, nothing like our brick houses at home. He cut the engine. 'Welcome to Ngaio Street.'

Their house was dreary in comparison, the colour of gingerbread, with dark-brown window trims. Spanning the front though, underneath the windows, were wide gardens bursting with rows of bright, spiky flower heads, all the colours of the rainbow, flowers I had never seen before. A drystone wall divided the house from the street, *meja* we called them on Korčula, but here the wall looked odd, out of place.

'Marta's inside,' Stipan said. 'Go on now.'

I hesitated, wanting to take in the place where I'd be living. It was as though I was carrying a boulder in my stomach; my tongue felt stuck to the roof of my mouth. From one of the front windows a lace curtain pulled back, and I worried again what Tata might have told them. How much they knew.

'Go on,' said Stipan, hauling my suitcase from the boot. He pointed at a pathway of jagged paving stones leading across the lawn. My legs felt wobbly and my feet disconnected from the ground. 'Don't keep Marta waiting.'

A tall, reedy woman dressed in a boldly patterned, pink, floral dress with dazzling white shoes bustled out. Her short hair was styled off her face in soft curls, and I wondered how, at her age, it could still be so black. She towered over me, and when she took hold of my hand her greeting felt as thin as her stiletto heels. 'Come,' she said, motioning me inside and stepping into a narrow, dark hallway. 'I'll show you your room.'

My new bedroom was small and plainly furnished but the curtains were a riot of colour, the same fabric as Marta's dress. The bed, with its pale green eiderdown, the colour of sea-sickness, was pushed up against one wall; a low wooden dresser with a round bevelled mirror sat against the opposite wall.

'We'll have afternoon tea in the lounge,' said Marta, peeling away from the door jamb. 'Once you're settled.'

When Marta clipped off down the hallway, I collapsed onto the bed, wanting only to close my eyes, to block out this strange new world and this woman who was so unlike Mama.

There was a nervous rap at the door followed by Stipan struggling in with my big suitcase.

'Oh,' he said, stopping short.

I scrambled to stand, embarrassed he had seen me like that. It felt too intimate, although I had no idea of his expectations as to how I should behave.

'Take your time,' he said. 'You'll be tired, but best keep yourself going. We'll be just across the hallway, in the lounge, but only when you're ready.'

His smile felt like a gift, a peace offering, as he eased out of my room and pulled the door shut. I cringed at my awkwardness, wishing I could transport myself back to the familiarity of home. But this was my new home. Stipan and Marta would give me my meals and a bed, and during the day I'd cook and clean for their son. They would pay me something called 'pin money' — not enough to send home, but enough for me to save.

I reached for the smaller suitcase at the foot of my bed and flicked its hinges, determined to do one thing. Cradling my lipstick and leaning in close to the mirror, I focused on steadying my hand to apply a shot of boldness. I hardly recognised the pale face framed by limp black hair.

The door across the hallway had been left ajar. I licked my lips, worrying that they looked too bright now. When I pushed at the door a smell of old blankets hit me first, and I blinked to adjust my eyes to the dim light. Marta and Stipan were sitting by the far window at a round table covered with a white lace cloth. I could barely breathe. *That lace.*

Stipan scrambled to his feet and beckoned me over. A milky strip covered the carpet, running like a pathway from the door, behind the sofa and across to the table, with hundreds of tiny raised air-bubbles on its surface that popped and crackled as I walked. I had the strangest sensation that I was back at the sardine factory with all the other girls, trundling along conveyor belts to our final destination: marrying a Luka local, bearing his children, and doing his housework. It was my *dragi*, my love, who had presented me with a different future, one outside of Korčula.

Not this one in New Zealand.

'Sit down, Gabrijela,' said Stipan, pulling out a wooden chair. Marta stared at me. Perhaps I looked different from the other young women here. I shifted on my seat, conscious of my own stale smell wafting upwards, and feeling shabby despite my painted lips. The table was set with pretty rose-patterned cups, saucers and side plates, bright as Marta's dress, crockery that seemed far too fragile to use. Just behind Stipan's chair was a tall stick topped with something like a fringed hat. It glowed with filtered light. At home we relied solely on oil lamps or the fire's warm glow, but this had a cord snaking from its base towards the wall. This must be the electricity we'd been hearing so much about, the reason for all the poles outside with their looping lines.

'Coffee?' It sounded like an order. I blinked, lost for a moment, before realising Marta was speaking English.

'Yes, please.' I sounded like a stranger even to myself.

Marta poured the coffee and pushed a small jug of milk towards me. I took my coffee black but still I hesitated, wondering if adding milk was common here. I scanned the table for something familiar, taking in the abundance and swallowing with relief when I saw our traditional pastry bows, *croštule*, piled high on a platter in the centre. The rest was a mystery: pale spongy circles topped with dollops of cream and cherry-red jam; a plate of golden pastry parcels stuffed with goodness knows what; perfect cubes of pink coated in white flecks; and a stack of neat rectangles, which I suspected must be *sendvič*, though they looked far too white and pretty to be made from bread.

'Sandwich?' Stipan passed the plate. 'Go on, try them, Gabrijela. Fresh eggs from my own hens.' We were back to Croatian and I felt a rush of warmth for him.

'Enough about your chickens,' said Marta, her voice stretched. She tapped my forearm and her eyebrow rose like an arch. 'Did Ante say *why* we needed a housekeeper, Gabrijela?'

'Tata said you needed help, that's all.' I ran my tongue over my lips. Was she implying I should know more? I glanced at Stipan sitting with both palms upwards. If he were a priest, *let us pray* would have followed.

'Gabrijela,' Stipan began then hesitated. 'Our Roko's had some bad luck.'

'Bad luck!' Marta chipped in. 'That what you call it?'

'Enough, Marta. Let me finish.'

Marta gave a disapproving sniff, crossing her arms and straightening her back.

'His wife's gone to the hospital,' Stipan said. 'She's an alcoholic. Too fond of the bottle. A hopeless case.'

I struggled to make sense of it all. Ever since Tata had announced his plan that I was to work as a housekeeper for Roko, I had tortured myself with images of this stranger. I imagined him as handicapped in some way, or with some dreadful personality flaw that had prevented him from marrying.

'I want that filthy woman scrubbed from my Roko's home,' Marta said. 'Cleaned to within an inch of its life. Understood?' She reached across and pinched me just below my elbow, applying just enough pressure to emphasise her point.

'It's a delicate situation,' continued Stipan, 'but when I discussed it with your tata, he said you'd be perfect. He said it would be just the start you needed in this new country. I hope it's the way you feel too?'

Marta tapped her index finger on the table, matching the dull thud in my head. 'You'll keep everything to the high standard I expect,' she said. Tap, tap, tap. 'My Roko's suffered terribly. These Kiwi girls are no good for our men.' She waggled her finger at Stipan and her eyes filled with tears. 'Told you, didn't I?'

'Now come, Marta,' said Stipan. 'Not all Kiwi girls are like our Pauline.'

'*Our Pauline!*' Marta scoffed. 'From the start I said she was no good for him, but there's no telling you men. Mama knows best — what our Roko needed was a nice Dally girl. One of our own.'

I nibbled at the corner of my egg sandwich trying to make sense of this new information. The bread dissolved like air in my mouth and the flavour was foreign. From somewhere deep in my mind I dredged back the smells which had tainted the Bombay airport terminal.

Marta made a hurried sign of the cross. 'I pray to our God for the annulment.'

Was this the real reason I'd been sent here? Did my sponsors think of me as a replacement wife? I knew about the proxy brides. Mama had spoken of them — girls from her village who had left between the wars, promised to men in America, Australia and New Zealand, men they had never met. Picture brides. If that's what they thought, they were mistaken. I wasn't going to marry any New Zealander.

I sent up my own quick prayer asking for my love to write soon and find a way to take me away from all this. The last time we were together, I'd snuck out to meet him in a secret cave high in the hills above Luka. 'To hell with the rest of them,' he'd said. 'We'll be together. I promise you, Gabrijela. I promise.'

All I had to do was wait. To get through my days in this strange new place as best as I could. *Polako, polako.*

～ ～

The yolks of two fried eggs stared up at me like knowing eyes. The dining table with its spindly metal legs and brown Formica top was pushed hard against the longest wall. We were crowded around the three remaining sides, Marta and Stipan at either end, and me on the long side. The one small window in the room, behind where Marta sat, had both panes thrown wide open but still the room felt claustrophobic, both a sitting room and dining room, and oddly shaped, as though a bite had been taken from the corner where the fireplace angled across. I estimated I could cross from one end to the other in five long strides, three crossways. I snuck a peek towards the open door behind Stipan, wishing I could escape. Stipan had given me a tour of the house the night before so I knew it led out to the back porch, off which was the wash-house and toilet. I shifted about on my chair with its scratchy fabric and the same spindly legs as the table, trying to get comfortable.

I had panicked over what to wear, settling in the end on a striped yellow blouse and a dark-blue flared skirt. Nothing from my meagre collection had seemed suitable, and on seeing Stipan lounging at the table in shorts and a checked short-sleeved shirt, and Marta in a simple black house dress, her bare feet peeking from under her chair, I felt overdressed, like a showpiece, one of those caged animals I'd seen pictures of in a book about the Moscow Zoo, shipped from their natural home and deposited in a strange land.

This was my first meal — I'd been too exhausted for dinner. Grace was a ritual that Mama insisted on, but Stipan was already picking up his knife and fork to eat. I followed his lead, feeling blasphemous as I made a hurried sign of the cross in my head. I hadn't realised I was so ravenous and although the eggs were delicious, the sound of our cutlery scraping against our plates felt like torture. I stabbed at my eggs, resentment building inside me like a knot, and focused my attention on one of the little white boxes on the wall. Stipan had explained these were for the electricity when he demonstrated how to switch the light on in my room. It was fascinating to see this new technology that we were still waiting for back home, but it was as though I was a child understanding things for the first time.

A small black cat, its tail a white tip, wandered in from the back porch mewing. When it slunk up next to Stipan's chair and wound its tail around one of the metal legs the air seemed easier to breathe.

'My *ujak* . . .' I started, but couldn't finish the sentence.

I wanted to boast that my uncle was a ranked officer in Marshall Tito's Party. That he'd been responsible for the project upgrading the roads on Korčula. That he was the one who had explained to me how the electricity would eventually flow. But what was the point talking about home, or the people I'd left behind? Neither Marta or Stipan seemed to notice I'd said anything at all.

'Ah, Mala. Meet our Gabrijela,' said Stipan, lounging back in his chair, his shirt buttons straining against his paunch. He patted his thigh and the cat jumped to settle on his lap. 'Lucky for Marta, she has a helper now.' He scratched the cat's neck and winked at me.

So, it was no different to home. It's the reason you have daughters, according to Tata, for the 'women's work'. Marta stood to collect the plates and I scrambled to my feet, doing what I knew was expected of me. I followed Marta into the tiny galley kitchen as though pulled along by an invisible string. My heart pounded in my ears. Did she want me to talk or remain silent? I doubted I could find words, let alone form a sentence. I wished Mama could miraculously appear and inhabit Marta's rigid body, to somehow pave the way and help me feel the ease the two of us shared while doing chores side by side — at least, until recently.

Marta turned a tap and I stared, transfixed, as the hot water flowed. 'We cook on electric stoves here. The same at Roko's,' she said, pointing towards a white appliance at the end of the room topped with three curly black rings. I would have to pray that using an electric stove wouldn't change the way I had to cook, that I would still know how.

'Welcome to the life of luxury,' Marta said, as though reading my thoughts. She rattled a metal cage under the water and pursed her lips, transforming what might have been a hint of a smile into a thin line. As the sink filled with bubbles, Marta thrust me a tea towel. It was bright, like a painting, with a picture of snow-capped mountains, and seemed far too pretty to be used for drying the dishes. 'We got a fridge last year. We share it with Roko. Did you see it in the wash-house?' She placed a plate in a wire rack.

I nodded and picked up the plate, trying to appear unfazed. I didn't want to admit to jumping back in fright earlier when I'd passed the humming, coffin-like box on my way to the toilet.

'I'll take you to Roko's later,' she said, piling more dishes in the rack. 'He likes to sleep in on a Saturday.' She stared out the window as though there was nothing more to say.

The flower beds edging the courtyard were an explosion of colour, contrasting with the staid brown paintwork of the back porch, and laid out neatly in front of two sections of wooden trellis that partitioned off an area behind. An ungainly timber structure with Y-shaped arms at either end and wires strung between reared up behind the trellis. A type of washing line, perhaps? At home we'd lean out the window to string the washing off the house.

The air felt heavy as though we were in a morgue rather than a kitchen. I consoled myself with anything that felt solid or true, even trivial things such as that minus her spiky shoes, Marta and I were the same height. My head was crammed with thoughts and questions but Marta's stillness made my words rise and stick in my throat.

After drying the last dish, I fled back to my room. Marta's curtains taunted me from the bed. Was this some cruel trick? Would I never escape this woman who was so unlike Mama? And then the reality. All that I had been pushing aside. That my confidante and rock had abandoned me. I squeezed my eyes shut but the images of those final days still played out. Mama taking to dusting our already spotless home with an unprecedented fervour. Mama a stranger, her face a blank canvas of resignation, who rather than pulling me closer had allowed the silence to stretch between us like a canyon. The days reducing to a handful before concertinaing into hours. And my anger and sense of betrayal that, just like those specks of dust, Mama found it simplest to wipe me clean off the family slate.

An hour later, Marta banged on my bedroom door and announced it was time to meet *our* Roko. I wrenched myself to standing, my head woozy from being hauled back from sleep. How long before this heavy feeling would pass? I dragged myself out to the hallway, joining Marta by the front door, the bell in my chest clanging like a warning. I stared at my old black pumps, awaiting her next instruction, taking strange comfort that she was wearing flat shoes as well. Marta opened the front door and motioned for me to follow.

Part-way along the jagged paving stones, I stopped. A large tree in full green leaf monopolised the lawn to the side of the path. How had I missed it the previous day? I stopped and stared like a halfwit, grasping for something familiar. It reminded me of our pomegranate tree at home, the fruit had the same orb shape and yet something was different. I cast my mind back a week. The tree at home was in its winter phase, the fruit not even set yet. This tree was laden with fruit but it looked unripe and the leaves were all wrong. Everything felt tipped on its head and suddenly my fears of coming to the Southern Hemisphere, having to live upside down and cling on for dear life, seemed founded.

'Persimmon,' said Marta, standing by the gate, holding it open. 'The fruit will ripen in May.' I shook my head, dragging myself back to the present before hurrying to join her.

After swinging the gate shut, Marta strode off down the street that crawled with children: riding bikes, running and chasing; clustered in small groups. I stared at the wooden houses, which to me looked temporary, as though having landed on their large kerchiefs of lawn they were poised to take off again. The brooding sun lurked behind the untidy mess of clouds and the heat invaded my every pore, making me feel clammy. At home I was accustomed to a dry heat, not this energy-sapping liquid cloak. Marta called to some of the children by name. I felt their intense stares, and the tears I'd kept hidden in my bedroom welled again. My *dragi,* Mama, my friends Nada and Antica, my brother Josip and his wife Mare, all the people I'd left behind. I hadn't known how different my life would be here, how unsophisticated my country was by comparison. I swallowed hard, trying to snap out of this strange dream world in which I was hurtling from one new experience to another, and felt relieved when a man mowing his lawn and a woman tending to her garden seemed too preoccupied to notice us.

Marta stopped and gripped my arm. She pointed at a house across the street and my stomach turned. I shielded my eyes against the flat glare. The weatherboards were painted white and the blue trim on the window sills was peeling in places. I forced myself to concentrate on the other features of Roko's house — the front fence made from white timber palings, rows of arrowheads pointing to the sky, and behind it, a scruffy browned-off front lawn with no flowers or trees. Perhaps Roko wasn't quite as house-proud as Marta made out.

'My Roko's suffered terribly.' She looked me in the eye as though searching for acknowledgement. 'You understand?'

I nodded, wishing she would let up. She dropped my arm and directed me across the street, pushing past me to stride through the gate and up the front path. I scurried along behind her, my heart still bouncing in my chest, wishing I was an ant who could crawl into the door's framework and hide. Marta rapped on the dark blue timber then burst inside, calling Roko's name. He emerged from a room at the side and

Marta spoke in English. All I understood was my name. Roko slouched further out into the hallway to lean against the wall. I edged up beside Marta, all the while feeling as though I was dangling centre stage.

He was a big man, like his tata, but whereas Stipan cradled his physique, Roko carried his. He wore a striped shirt loose over a white singlet and he'd rolled the sleeves up to his elbows. Rather than being good-looking in the clean-cut sense like my *dragi,* Roko was swarthy and fit, with a certain ruggedness, an unkempt, couldn't-care-less look. His jet-black eyebrows were distinctive and bushy, the same colour as his hair, which, like Stipan, he wore cropped on top and shaved close above his ears. I had no idea whether he noticed me. It was easiest to look away.

Marta spoke again and I stared at the floor, trying to find answers to the questions racing through my mind. I'd expected Roko to be older but he didn't look any older than my brother. Marta was still prattling and beckoning for Roko to move closer. He scowled, but Marta seemed oblivious.

'Hello, Gabrijela,' he said, cutting off Marta mid-stream. He stepped away from the wall to face us. His frown lines pushed his eyes back under his brows as though they were seeking protection, making him appear tough but vulnerable at the same time.

'Pleasure to meet you, Roko,' I said, using my best English, determined to keep my voice strong.

For the briefest moment his eyes met mine. They were caramel-coloured, a mix of serious and sad. He glanced away and I dragged my eyes to the ground. He was barefoot, with marked tan lines part way up his calves, making his feet look stuck on, like two white boots. I was so nervous I almost giggled. Marta saved me, this time in my own language.

'Gabrijela will start on Monday. I'll show her everything. Will we see you over the weekend?'

Roko didn't answer. He was already retreating to the room he'd come from. Marta shrugged and rolled her eyes. I wasn't sure if this was an apology for his rudeness or an acknowledgement that their relationship was strained. As I followed her down the hallway, she explained how the layout of Roko's house was the same as their own: two bedrooms either side of the front door, a small bathroom down the hallway with the equivalent of my bedroom alongside, and the formal lounge opposite. She opened the door to the small bathroom and I felt a secret thrill again. How long until I was offered the luxury of having a bath with no need to boil the water first?

At the doorway to the formal lounge, Marta pulled at my sleeve and leaned in close. 'Hardly used,' she said, opening the door. The furniture sat at haphazard angles, and unlike her own lounge, there was no carpet on the floor. 'Pauline wasn't much of an entertainer.' She snapped the door shut and strode off to open the door at the end of the hallway. Marta of the spiky white heels was back.

Poor Pauline. It can't have been easy having Marta as a mother-in-law. But was alcohol a habit in this country? What were the rules? I wasn't so naive that I had never drunk *the poison*, as Mama called it, but it was only on rare occasions and then, mostly watered down. I knew its dangers. Maybe Marta had been half Pauline's problem? I wouldn't let her get the better of me.

Inside the sitting-cum-dining room I did a double take. Not only was it the same odd shape as Marta's, but all the furniture, even their placement, was identical: a dark-green, padded bench seat running along the far wall beneath the window; to the side of the fireplace, the same low-slung, pale green armchairs jammed into the space beside the dining table; the fire-grate stacked with pinecones. Had Marta already started to wipe Pauline from the house, or had it always been set up like this, and Pauline felt she couldn't change it?

'My Roko needs a cooked breakfast,' Marta called from the kitchen. 'Plenty of energy for the heavy stonework at the quarry. He takes a packed lunch and you'll prepare him an evening meal. Keep him company, but you must judge when enough is enough. Understood?'

I joined her in the tiny galley space, nodding to appease her. The view from Roko's kitchen window provided the most striking contrast between the two houses. There were no flower beds, just a concrete pad behind which was a huge lawn and a jumble of weeds along the fence lines. The same timber structure loomed like a prehistoric monster. I looked to Marta, my panic rising again. She was busy opening the cupboards and tut-tutting.

'Empty!' she whispered, her eyes flashing wild. 'That woman wasn't fit for domestic purpose. Thank God there were no babies. ' She looked me in the eye. 'A bottle in the bed's never a good recipe. But you can't tell these men, can you?'

'No,' I mumbled. 'Same at home.'

Marta's face relaxed into a smile. It was only for a moment, but I took it as a small victory.

Later that afternoon Stipan called me from my bedroom. He wanted to show me his garden, but how could he not understand that my head was reeling and my body clock was still stuck on the other side of the world? Again I hauled myself from the fringes of sleep to join him in the rear courtyard. The sky had cleared to bright blue and the sun was searing hot.

'Dahlias,' Stipan said, pulling a giant crimson starburst forward. 'Aren't they spectacular? And these tall orange ones are gladioli.' He stooped to touch some low silver clumps with leaves like fur. 'We call these little beauties lamb's ears. Feel them, Jela.'

Hearing my nickname, the one used by my friends and family, felt like another gift from Stipan among all this newness. I bent to rub the leaves between my fingers too. Their softness reminded me of my goats. I felt a sharp ache remembering the way they would nuzzle up against me with their liquid eyes. I took my time pulling myself to standing. Stipan flung his arm towards the gap in the trellises and smiled broadly. 'I grow everything from seed,' he said before striding off.

I followed, but it was the wooden monster my eyes were drawn to. Closer up it seemed even more ungainly. I imagined the Y-shaped arms like semaphore signals sending pleas to the sky. My forehead felt clammy and I turned back to Stipan, envious of his floppy hat. He was standing in the garden, beckoning me over.

'Only grow the Italian ones,' he said, cradling a tomato in his palm. 'Some things I won't compromise on. And there's plenty of silverbeet and *kupus*. Dallies can't survive without cabbages! You won't go hungry, Jela.'

That much was obvious. Stipan's garden stretched the length of the backyard and overflowed with plants laid out in neat rows, so different from our small patches at home. Two black birds with white pompom tufts at their throats swooped low. I followed their flight, watching as they landed on one of the monster's high lines.

'Aren't they beautiful,' I gasped, squinting my eyes against the sun as they fanned their feathers and whipped away into the trees, their calls tuneful, like songs.

'Tuis. Native birds,' said Stipan.

'But Stipan? That thing. Is it for the clothes?'

'Bah! That eyesore,' he said, with a wry grin. 'Great for the drying. Or so Marta tells me.'

One of the timber beams had ropes tied off like fishing knots and I realised it might work by a pulley system. I hoped what Tata had taught me on *Krešimira,* might be useful. But how would the clothes dry in this air that seemed laden with moisture? Our winds at home were dry and heavy with salt, the same ingredient we used to draw out the moisture when preserving our meat and fish. My head swooned. It was as though the multiple layers of green, not just from Stipan's garden, but collectively, from the texture of the surrounding trees and bushes, were crowding in to envelop me.

'What made you come here?' I asked, blinking to help stave off the giddiness, cursing Tata again for being so vague.

'Like everyone. To make a better life. They were calling out for the stonemasons and I knew the craft well, of course. It was 1926. Our Petra was just a baby. Marta's sister Kate was already here and happy to be our sponsor.' Stipan's face clouded with sadness. 'You know I had to lose my name? Bah! They changed it to Tomich. With an ich! I wouldn't live anywhere else now, but the homeland . . . it still holds my heart.'

I doubted this place could ever be home, and I vowed to keep a clear picture of my Yugoslavia, the smells and the sounds, to not let those pictures fade. A scramble of clucking and flapping erupted from behind a thatched fence at the far corner of the section.

'My chickens,' Stipan said, puffing out his chest.

'But how do you have time to care for it all?' I asked.

'Easy. I retired from the quarry late last year. It was when Marta and I travelled to the homeland. Our first time back. What a shock. But it was incredible to meet up with your tata. We met in our late teens you know, when I moved to Vela Luka for work.' He patted me on the shoulder. 'You'll be missing your family and friends now, Jela, but it gets easier.'

Tears stung again and I turned towards the courtyard. Marta and another woman were looking our way.

'Ah well, it's time to meet our Petra,' said Stipan. 'Do you remember me pointing out where she lives, on our ride from the airport?' I shook my head. He had pointed out so many places but they had all blurred into the other. 'Henderson, remember? Our Hana lives there too. And our youngest, Zoran. I told you, he makes the wine there.' He strode off, calling out, 'This is good! Petra, you can meet our Gabrijela.'

His use of my full name came like a jolt, as though all the friendliness we'd just shared was gone. I followed Stipan on auto-pilot, wondering how much else I had missed on the trip from the airport. Petra was a good head taller than Marta and cut a striking figure in her lemon frock patterned with white daisies. It had cutaway arms that complemented her bronzed arms. As Stipan made the introductions I wished I'd had the chance to freshen up. Everything about Petra seemed toned and taut.

'Nice to meet you,' said Petra, in Croatian. She tilted her chin, jerking her head so that her ponytail flicked from behind. 'Let's hope you do a better job than Pauline.' These last words seemed charged with scorn.

'I'll do my best.' There was a drop of perspiration teetering on my forehead.

'Please tell me you don't drink alcohol,' she said.

'Rarely,' I replied, holding her stare, all the while thinking, *It's none of your business. I'll do whatever I like.*

Marta was pulling on Petra's arm. 'Come, *Draga,* help me get the eggs.'

Petra's judgement came before they disappeared behind the trellis screen. 'She's rather pale. A little scrawny for a Dally, don't you think?'

I swiped at my brow. Stipan had moved back to his dahlias and was snapping off the dead-heads. Even after that brief encounter I could see that there was something invincible about Petra, that I would have to watch myself around her. I made it back to my room before the tears took over. Tata was to blame and I would never speak to him again. I reached for my *dragi's* vest and wrapped my arms tight around it as though cuddling him, wishing myself back into his arms.

MARCH

I peeked around the kitchen doorway. Roko sat at the dining table, a block of stone, reading the newspaper and eating his breakfast. I pierced his stiff back with my dagger stare. He can't have been blind to my distress, but over the past two weeks he hadn't said a word to reassure me. We could be in the same room and he'd stare right through me as though I were a genie who had magically appeared to prepare his food and scrub his clothes. I leaned against the doorframe, sapped of all energy. *If things don't improve, I'll get out and take my pin money with me. Why should I pander to him? I've had enough of being told what to do.* But even as these brave thoughts formed in my head, I knew I was stuck: a young girl with no money and no contacts other than this family. Even if I could return home I'd be viewed as fickle, ungrateful for turning down the luxuries, foolish for turning down a better way of life. I thought back to my parting limpet-like hug with one of the local ladies who had travelled on the same ferry from Vela Luka to Split, the one who made sure I boarded the right bus to Belgrade airport. 'You're one of the lucky ones,' she'd said, matter of fact, prising herself away.

Roko pushed himself to standing, and I scrambled, peeling myself off the doorframe to busy myself in the kitchen. The fact he hadn't communicated his expectations added to everything else I felt unsure of in this country. A man's gruff voice on the radio taunted me as Roko passed. At times, that small brown box with its leather pinhole cover had been my only companion, but now I felt an urge to throw something at it, to silence the static. I snatched up Roko's packed lunch and crossed to the dining table, slapping it down.

Back in the kitchen, the monster stared back at me. At least this was one thing I had conquered. Not that it was any consolation. How much had Tata known about what I was coming to? At the time I'd been too incensed to ask questions, too bewildered when he shouted his decision at me in December, the same time that our sermons were filled with 'forgive and forget'. If my *dragi* and I ever had a daughter, or a son for that matter, I would never restrict their opportunities or take their freedom away. I would teach them to make good choices so that they didn't end up like me, compromised, having risked everything. Perhaps I should be grateful: it was clear that Roko was hell-bent on his own plan and even if it was Marta and Stipan's idea to snaffle me, a nice Dally girl, then at least their son was uncooperative.

He passed by to collect his lunch and slammed the porch door as he left. I thumped my fist on the bench. *Katastrofa!* No manners, not even a thank you. I waited until he'd swung off down the driveway on the black bike with its rusty handlebars, then crossed to the table, slumping down beside his dirty dishes and pulling the envelope from my pocket. It had arrived the week before, my first letter from home. I'd been carrying Mama around with me ever since, rereading her words and savouring the sound of her as though willing her into the room. This was my real Mama, not the distant Mama I'd left behind. She had news about Josip, Mare and the newest member in our family, baby Jakob, about my naughty goats, and our annoying neighbour, and my friend Nada.

I lay my head on my forearms and let my sadness wash over me in waves. Why hadn't my *dragi* written? I'd sent a letter most days. Surely he must have received at least one by now? I ached for his reassurance, to know that he was coming to get me. The Dally picnic on the weekend had been the final straw. While I'd enjoyed the familiarity of the Mass, I'd hung back afterwards, unsure of the games they were all playing, and feeling on show as though judged by my own people. My insides had felt like cotton wool and I'd stood to the side, sizing up what the girls my age were wearing and how they wore their hair. They all seemed to know each other — and worse, they all seemed to prefer speaking English. Marta had pushed me towards some annoying older women, the only ones who seemed happy to speak my language. They drilled me with endless questions: who did I know from home, who was I related to? I felt like screaming, 'What does it matter? Can't you see I have to make friends here?'

'Good *morning* everybody!' I jerked up my head and stared at the radio on the mantelpiece. It was Aunt Daisy, the lady I'd discovered on my first morning who always entered the room at nine a.m. with her cheerful greeting. I'd got into the habit of keeping her beside me wherever I worked and letting her barrage of happy words wash over me.

'Come on, girl,' I muttered, pushing back my chair and shaking my head to clear the mess, annoyed at myself for wallowing. I must have been sitting there for at least half an hour. One of Mama's favourite sayings was back and I forced a smile. 'Life's for the living. Tears are for the dead people,' I muttered, mimicking Mama's voice. 'Get yourself moving.'

The clothes were already soaking in the copper, and I placed the radio on a shelf in the wash-house. There was something about Aunt Daisy's voice that wasn't intimidating, and while I still understood so little of this strange *Engleski* tongue, I challenged myself to recognise at least some of her words. Each day, with Aunt Daisy's help, I was understanding a little more and recognising words from my school days. I stirred the washing with a big stick. Aunt Daisy chattered while I lifted the clothes then rinsed them in the concrete double sink to the side. I thought about Mama bent over the bath at home with her washboard, how I'd travelled half a world away and ended up with the same chores. I twisted the clothes to wring out the water. At least some jobs were easier here — having a copper connected to electricity, for one — but still I felt cheated.

When I stepped onto the porch with the loaded wicker basket, the rattle of the cicadas was almost deafening. Would the lady next door already have her washing out? I'd seen her a few times but I'd felt too self-conscious to introduce myself, embarrassed about my lack of English. I paused, taking a deep breath, always hoping for a whiff of the sea. I hadn't realised how the smell of a place could ingrain itself, how desperate I would be to hear the sea, to smell it, and to feel the salt stinging my skin. If only Roko lived in one of the seaside suburbs Stipan had driven me to on my first weekend. His pride had been so obvious when he'd shown me the Tamaki seawall and explained how he'd helped construct it all those years ago. I'd been more intent on drinking in what was behind his stone barrier, imagining that sea washing over me.

She was there, pegging up the last of her washing, tiny beneath her line laden with sheets and towels. The call of the cicadas now seemed like a congratulatory cheer. She must be cutting corners, I thought — her washing couldn't possibly be as clean as mine. I stalked over to my own monster and untied the knot. The timber arm creaked and groaned as I pulled on the rope, lowering the beam until the line was within reach, then tied it off again. *I'll have to be more organised*, I lectured myself, jabbing the pegs on the washing.

'Hello there!'

I straightened, holding a pair of Roko's Y-front underpants by the waistband. She was looking over the fence, her forearms resting on the top, beckoning me over. I dropped the underpants in the basket and crossed the lawn to join her. She looked immaculate: lipstick even at that early hour and not a hair out of place. I smoothed back my hair, certain it must be like a bird's nest given how I'd been raking my fingers through it earlier.

'Hello, I'm Joy,' she said. Her hair was like fine strands of beautiful copper-coloured wire, moulded into a stiff bob and framing her face.

'Jela,' I replied, my hand at my chest, determined to keep my voice strong. It struck me how she was a little like my friend Nada — her compact features, her tidiness.

She rattled off a string of words I had no chance of understanding. She must have noticed my blank expression because her hand went up like a stop sign. 'Woah! Okay,' she said, smiling. 'Slowly, slowly.'

There was something about the way she scrunched her nose, and the freckles peppering her face, that lent her a mischievous look. It was as though she was transformed into someone younger, less regal. I hoped she might be the type who didn't take herself too seriously. '*Polako, polako,*' I said, signalling downwards with my palm and grinning, hoping she might see that I too had a sense of humour. That I would be fun to get to know.

'Welcome,' she said. 'Your country?'

'Yugoslavia,' I said, feeling proud to have understood her words.

'Dally? Like Roko?'

'Yes.' I nodded, my mind racing to think of something else to say, to keep this conversation going. '*Lijep dan.*' I pointed to the sky. 'No. No.' I waved my arms skywards, frustrated I'd slipped back to Croatian. 'Bootiful!' But as soon as the syllables left my mouth I knew they sounded wrong.

'Yes,' she said, nodding enthusiastically as though wanting to reassure me, her hairdo sitting fixed like cement. 'Nice . . . dry . . . washing . . . today.' She sounded out each word, gesturing from her line to mine.

'*Šampion*,' I said, opening my palms as though handing over a prize. She looked puzzled, and I pointed at both our washing lines, the English words suddenly there. 'Number one!' I said, giving her the thumbs-up sign.

Joy rewarded me with her own thumbs up and clapped with delight. 'Okay. I can teach. Help you. With your English.'

'Yes.' I nodded, feeling fit to burst. 'Yes, please.'

She reached over the fence and we shook hands as though making a business deal. A baby cried out close by.

'My little boy,' Joy said, dropping my hand. 'Bye, Jela. See you soon.'

Her baby was sitting in what looked like a sling on a metal frame. He was throwing his arms about, jiggling and squawking. My eyes pricked with tears, memories of my little nephew Jakob, and Antica's little Luci. When Joy turned back the child was on her hip and seemed calmer. She waved before disappearing down a narrow pathway to the side of her white house with its cheerful red roof.

I crossed back to my line with a buzz of energy. *This might be the start of a new friendship.* I'd never had to make new friends before: there had always been people who had been part of my life from the start. A fantail danced close, flitting from the fence over to the line and back again as though dancing to the cicadas' tune. It fanned its tail, flashing its white underside. I untied the rope and hoisted the line. Roko's washing soared high like my own trophy.

Much later that afternoon there was a knock at the front door. Had I heard right? It wouldn't be Marta: whenever she came she would barge in unannounced. I opened the door a notch, hoping it might be Joy from next door, but it was a man and a woman. He was smartly dressed in a dark suit and grey felt hat and she was all in navy, hanging back as though lurking in his shadow.

The man stepped forward.

'Hello?' I said, almost a whisper.

He responded with a torrent of words and I shrank back as the woman pushed forward, tapping him on the shoulder. She carried her handbag like a shield, looped over her arm and close to her body. From it she dug out a photograph. 'Here,' the man said, thrusting it at me. 'Pauline. Our sister.'

That name. I held the thin picture with both hands, focusing on keeping my face calm. I was on the verge of uncovering Roko's secret, one I was certain he would be furious I'd been privy to. I held it to the light, making sure to inspect it properly, heart pounding in my chest. There she was. Roko's mystery wife. They were lounging on the sand in front of one of Stipan's stone walls. Roko was perched on his side facing in towards Pauline. She wore a striped swimsuit cut straight across the bust with a halter strap. A pretty face, heart-shaped. She wasn't stick thin, but neither was she scrawny — a little slimmer than me. Roko was puffing out his chest, his smile confident, a proud rooster. Pauline had her leg cocked towards him, and it didn't take much imagination to see how they felt about each other. My face turned to flames. It seemed that Roko was staring at me, challenging me, making me think about the times I'd seen my *dragi* like that.

'Come.' I thrust the photo back at the man, turning to hide my embarrassment. I ushered them down the hallway towards the end room and gestured for them to sit in the easy chairs.

'Thank you,' said the man, motioning for me to go first.

I felt proud that I'd taken charge and squeezed past them to sit on the window seat. The man twisted and placed his hat on the dining table. The woman sat staring at her handbag that was balanced on her lap as though it contained something heavy. She coughed a little, shifting about and gripping the hooped handles. The man leant towards me, his hands clasped. A new thought grabbed at my insides. *Do they think I am Roko's new woman?*

'Justine and Peter,' he said slowly.

'Gabrijela,' I replied, feeling their stares. Their judgement. 'I am house lady. Helping Roko—'

'Yes, yes,' the man cut in. 'But Pauline. Her belongings, please.' He swept the photo in a wide circle as though asking Pauline to scan the room.

'Rings!' Justine chimed in, tapping at her own finger. 'Her clothes.' She patted at the sleeve of her dress.

'We collect them,' Peter said, staring at me to check I had understood.

I had, but I wasn't sure where these things were or, more importantly, whether they had the right to take them. I nodded, trying to give the impression that I was taking everything in slowly. 'I get Marta.'

'No!' Justine cried. 'Police.'

She dug in her handbag, producing a letter and waving the official-looking paper at me. On it was a picture of some scales within the printed header, and a stamp at the bottom. Justine tapped, tapped, tapped at the paper.

I assumed Pauline's things were in the master bedroom, but I only went in there to make Roko's bed, dust and vacuum, or to put a pile of folded washing on his bed. I hadn't seen anything belonging to Pauline. Besides, it would feel wrong to snoop.

'Roko home soon,' I said, pointing to the clock on the wall.

Justine and Peter exchanged tense looks and talked in hushed voices, their words spilling out so quickly that I couldn't make sense of them.

'We will wait,' said Peter finally. 'Here, for Roko.'

He seemed grateful when I handed him the newspaper. I scuttled into the kitchen and set about preparing Roko's favourite sandwich: egg mayonnaise with a dash of curry — the secret ingredient I'd tasted in the sandwiches on my first afternoon; the first thing Marta had taught

43

me how to make. The comforting aromas of onion, tomato and beef stock were already settling around the kitchen from the osso buco bubbling in the oven. Marta had handed me her recipe that morning along with some beef shanks — substitutes for the veal. I hummed as I mashed the eggs with a fork, partly to ease the silence, but also because the kitchen was my domain and someone else was the outsider for once.

Roko swooped down the driveway at his usual time, 4.30 p.m. I snuck a glance towards the visitors. Their backs were still turned. I crept around the corner and out the back door. Roko sat on the porch pulling off his work boots. 'Visitors,' I whispered urgently, pointing inside. 'Peter. Justine.' I scanned his face for a reaction.

He frowned and scratched the top of his ear. 'Ach! Wait here,' he said curtly, heaving himself to standing.

I edged back against the house. Roko brushed past me but left the back door wide open. I ducked into the wash-house, snatched up a broom and made myself busy clearing the quarry dust off the porch but peeking through the door. They were congregated in the centre of the room. Justine was shouting and shaking a piece of paper in Roko's face. Roko stood stock-still, hands on his hips. I moved on to sweep the small courtyard area. Peter was rubbing Justine's arm as though trying to calm her.

Roko threw his hands skyward. 'All right! All right!' he yelled, storming from the room. I brushed the debris into a pile. Peter and Justine were whispering, their heads bowed close. Roko returned clutching a collection of bags, some overflowing, and dumped them at Justine's feet. I didn't need to understand more than a few words. 'Take everything. Don't come back!'

When the front door slammed, Roko retreated up the hallway too.

. . .

Roko was still bristling when we sat down for dinner. It was as though we were thrown back to how it had been in my first days at his house: strangers casting dark shadows, and me conscious of my every move. I hadn't appreciated until then the small progress we had made. Roko had his head cast down. He seemed intent on shovelling his risotto and stew into his mouth.

I grabbed at the confidence I'd felt earlier, unable to bear the silence for one minute longer. 'I met the lady. Next door one,' I said, my cutlery poised as though floating above my dinner plate.

'Joy Johnstone,' Roko replied tersely. 'She's one who likes to know what's going on.'

I lowered my knife and fork, waiting for him to say more. He took another mouthful and chewed noisily. Again, I felt worthless in his eyes, desperate to be seen as a real person, someone worthy of conversation, a person others wanted to meet. We continued to eat in silence and a loud rap at the door came as a relief. Roko swivelled around. Hana, Roko's other sister, popped her head around the door.

'Surprise!' she said, stepping inside and flinging her arms wide. 'C'mon, give your big sister a hug.'

Roko scrambled to his feet, his face creasing into a smile. He wrapped Hana in a warm embrace, and his shoulders seemed to relax as though a weight lifted off him.

I had met Hana at the Dally picnic. She seemed kinder than her older sister but I couldn't be sure as I'd only talked to her briefly. They were both much older than me — Petra by fifteen years, and Hana, eleven — and both had husbands and children. I was envious of their looks, their beautiful olive skin offsetting their dark eyes and hair. If it wasn't for the way they wore their hair they might have been twins. Hana wore hers short and styled in soft curls around her face, much like Marta's, whereas Petra's high ponytail made her brow look stretched and taut.

'Where've you been hiding?' Hana said to Roko in Croatian as though making sure to include me, which gave me confidence that my initial impressions had been right. 'It's been ages. I brought the boys to see Mum and Dad. Dida's got them busy in the chook house. Thought I'd take my chance to escape.' She raised her eyebrows. 'Petra's there with Mum.'

Marta was always saying, *Petra leads such a busy life — three teenage daughters, you know.* Was Hana inviting me in on a joke? Petra always had time to visit her mama, and I suspected she was the type who liked to *look* busy. Regardless, her effect on me was always the same: anything I tried to say always came out in a jumbled mess.

Hana took the seat at the far end of the table so that Roko was opposite and I was in between. 'Yum, dinner looks good,' she said.

'Would you like some?' I made to get up from the table, embarrassed I hadn't offered sooner.

'Should have saved room,' said Hana, brushing me off. 'No, I've eaten. You carry on. I wanted to make sure I met you properly. I feel terrible I got dragged off at the picnic. How are you finding things?'

'It was a day for visitors,' I said, smiling, wanting to show my appreciation that she was taking an interest, that she was bothering to speak to me. 'I met the lady next door and this afternoon we had some other visitors.' I stopped short, sensing Roko's glare. Why did I always speak without thinking? But my tongue felt loose, as though all the exciting things wanted the chance to escape.

'Don't mind him,' said Hana, her smile reassuring. 'Must have been Joy. She's great fun. Who were the visitors?'

'Peter and Justine,' Roko cut in, rubbing at his face as though even saying their names was exhausting.

'Really?' said Hana, flicking me a worried glance. 'Must be a relief to have that over.'

Roko was balancing on the rear legs of his chair. He took a deep breath. 'Had to happen, I guess. Been dreading it though.' He closed his eyes.

I looked to Hana for guidance and mouthed, *Should I go?* But she flapped her hand, signalling for me to stay. 'What did they want?' she asked, after what seemed the longest time.

'The last of her things.' Roko opened his eyes and crashed forward on his chair. 'Damn it!' He thumped the table. 'I wanted to hold on to something small. A reminder . . . despite everything.'

'That's understandable,' said Hana, hands on the table, pushing herself to stand. 'But it's important to let go as well. You were too wrapped up in her, even you've admitted that.'

I stayed seated, frozen to the spot while Hana went to comfort Roko. I knew what he meant. I had just one photo of my love, but it wasn't as important as his knitted vest, which over the past weeks had helped me through the lonely times. At night I'd breathe him back into my room, holding his vest up to my face, recapturing his smell. Each morning I would reach for it again and cradle him to my chest. His vest was all I had to hang on to. That, and his promises. Roko's head was down. Hana kneaded his shoulders.

'From the photo, you both looked happy,' I said. 'Seems such a shame.'

Hana rolled her eyes at me. 'Our Roko was like a puppy dog. Pauline cast a spell on this tough-nut brother of mine.' She squeezed Roko's shoulder. 'That's right isn't it?'

Roko glanced up with a faraway expression. 'She's a great girl. Just couldn't beat the booze. It changed her. Changed everything. She's better off in the hospital. But it's over for us.'

'It's better,' said Hana. 'We all tried our best but it's time to move on. Put it down to experience.'

'How long were you married?' I asked, my heart like a drill in my chest. It seemed we were conversing on a knife edge and I didn't know how deep I could go.

'Four years. I was just twenty-two. She was twenty. Both too young.'

I didn't think they were too young. My *dragi* and I had talked about marriage.

'Do you still see Pauline?' I asked.

Roko looked startled. Perhaps it was me mentioning her name. 'At the start. Not now,' he said gruffly, as though he was flicking the switch on our conversation and the old Roko was back.

'It's good to talk about these things,' said Hana, her voice business-like. 'You know the family's been missing you?' She tapped her brother's shoulder. 'I'd better get going. Mum will wonder where I am.'

'Time for the dishes,' I said, standing to gather the plates, pleased to have an excuse. 'I'll leave you two to say goodbye. Lovely seeing you again, Hana.'

I stood at the kitchen sink with the dinner dishes strewn about. It seemed Roko had been cloaking his sadness with surliness and deep down, despite everything, I was pleased that he and Hana shared a close bond. I thought about my brother Josip, how he had failed me by swallowing Tata's concocted story, how over the years we had grown apart. Even though Josip had his sights set on taking over our family's fishing business, I suspected he was frustrated that it was me being sent away on what he thought was a big adventure. We were so different, but how had he not realised that I'd envisaged a smaller step to escape our hemmed-in life on Korčula, maybe to one of the bigger cities on the mainland, somewhere like Split, Dubrovnik, Zagreb even — not this place half a world away. He was too caught up in himself, too short-sighted to see, but that was no excuse.

I hung the tea towel on the oven door to dry and collected my things. Roko was nowhere to be seen, but I left feeling certain there would be a letter waiting from my love back at Marta and Stipan's. After a day which finished so differently from how it began, this would be the perfect finish. But it wasn't to be.

APRIL

F riday was bathroom day. It didn't start well. When I hung my towels out, Joy's washing was already flapping and she was nowhere to be seen. True to her word, Joy had become my language teacher, conducting our classes most mornings over the back fence. Without this bright point my day would drag even more. Joy was my yardstick for all that I aspired to in this new country — her busy life and the way she dressed, just like the well-groomed ladies smiling at me from the magazines. At first I'd hoped for more, that we might become friends like the regular stream of ladies who visited her home, but I'd had to console myself with being grateful for what we did share, and on this of all days, I was denied.

I stomped back inside, forcing myself to voice the words, to issue my ultimatum. 'Still no letter. No more chances. He's finished!'

Instead of feeling empowered, my voice sounded unsure. Desperate. But after all these weeks, ten in total, I could not play this tortuous game for one day longer. My excuses for my *dragi* had worn as thin as the blue aerogramme his words should have arrived on: he must be busy in his new job; his letters have got lost; Tata has intercepted them.

I carried the radio through to the bathroom, grateful for Aunt Daisy's distraction but feeling jittery. It was as though my body was dosed on nervous energy, the kind you get when you wish so hard for something that might just as likely end in disappointment. How had my *dragi* pushed me to this? He'd promised me he would come, *to hell with the rest of them,* and I'd believed him, trusted that he loved me as much as I loved him. How could he have loved me like he had, if all he was doing was spinning me lies?

Aunt Daisy prattled on but I couldn't focus. Even when 'Splish Splash', one of my favourite songs played I couldn't summon the energy to sing along, let alone hum. It was as though I couldn't get comfortable with how I was feeling: anticipation, fear, annoyance? Perhaps I was just hungry? I scrubbed at the bath, thoughts of my *dragi* pushing this way and that.

'Gabrijela!' Marta called from somewhere at the rear of the house.

Could her timing be any worse? I was always wary of her popping in, certain she was checking up on me. My mind traced back to the kitchen, trying to remember what state I'd left it in.

'I'm here,' I called, determined to keep the exhaustion from my voice.

'Just passing,' said Marta, closer now. 'You mentioned fish for dinner. You could join me for a walk to the shops. Come on then!'

Fresh air might help, I thought. I retrieved the red zipped purse containing Roko's housekeeping money from the kitchen then unhooked the jute shopping bag from its spot in the porch. After clicking the back door shut, I hurried to catch Marta, who was already halfway down the driveway, her black shopping trundler an extension of her arm. Marta did everything at speed, with a focus on efficiency. I clutched the jute bag close, enjoying the sun on my face. The autumn sky was cloudless, the clearest of blues, a stunning backdrop to the bronzed gold, yellow and orange tones surrounding us. Surely my *dragi* couldn't ruin this day. But even as I willed it to be so, a shiver traced my spine. We'd been enjoying a spate of warm, sunny weather throughout April, and yet still there had been no letter. Tears pricked my eyes. *Soiled goods,* Tata yelling those same words. *Please God, make Tata wrong.*

I drew alongside Marta and we walked in silence. I had come to accept this, conceding that I would have been lost without her in my first weeks. Not only had she introduced me to the local shop owners and helped restock Roko's pantry, but she'd gone out of her way to set me up with personal necessities: sanitary items, toiletries, and a large stash of aerogrammes and stamps. I sensed that, underneath her brusque exterior, she understood how I was feeling, that perhaps she remembered what it was like when she'd come here herself, how much she had found strange. Regardless, I knew how to play her game: Marta fulfilled her duty to look out for me provided I understood I was a nuisance. If she felt talkative, we talked, but if she didn't instigate conversation I knew to remain silent.

We passed by Joy's white picket fence and I glanced across, wondering what jobs Joy would have on her list for the day. A low bed of red and orange flowers licked the base of her house like a ribbon of fire. Was it the bright sunlight or had those flowers bloomed overnight? I had passed by so often and yet never noticed them before. Perhaps there was only so much newness a person could absorb. Perhaps this was God's way of cushioning the change. A sleight of hand. By revealing the novelty, piece by tortuous piece, new immigrants might be tricked into thinking their world hadn't morphed into something more shocking. It might be the colour of a house that I could swear had been painted overnight, or a street sign with words I felt certain I'd never seen before. Even the shape of the streetlights or the markings on the roads could differ from one day to the next. At times, over the past months, I had become a master of masquerade too, but perhaps this element of trickery is the same for anyone moving to a country where the language is not their own?

'You look pale. Everything all right?' she said, matter of fact. I snapped my head to catch her eye. 'You seem distracted, that's all.'

'Just a little queasy,' I said.

'Make sure to wash your hands. Can't afford germs spreading.'

Once we rounded the corner at the end of the street the cries from the school playground echoed from further ahead. A short woman behind a pram moved towards us. Joy? At once I was on quicksand where nothing felt certain. Having not told Marta about my friendship, I worried she might not approve, that like Roko she might consider Joy nosey. As she drew closer, Joy's hair was a flash of copper, the sun glinting off the tips and curtaining her face in a warm glow.

Marta's face gave nothing away. I worried what Joy might expect. Whether she would think it rude that I hadn't waved out as I would usually do, or whether, like me, she was worried about Marta being there, given how she shied away from talk about Roko or his family. Would she want me to pretend we didn't know each other? Joy jolted her pram to a halt, the black-and-cream carriage jouncing on the small spoked wheels.

'Mrs Tomich, Jela, lovely to see you,' she said, but her worried crease told me she felt as uncertain as me.

'Joy,' said Marta with a curt nod.

For the briefest moment we all faced off like wary cats. Joy gripped the curved chrome handlebar, her eyes refusing to find mine. I was relieved when Marta stepped forward to peer into the pram. 'How's the little man?' she asked, her voice still stern.

I sidled up beside Marta. Her baby, David, had wrestled his legs free from the blankets. He was kicking upwards, arching his back.

'He's fine,' said Joy, leaning in from the opposite side, cocooning him again with his blankets. 'Just been to see the Plunket nurse.'

'He's sick?' I asked, forgetting my nerves.

'All fine,' said Joy. 'Just a regular check for his height and weight. Did you use Plunket when the kiddies were little, Mrs Tomich?' Even though she was speaking slowly, it was torture to keep up compared with our lessons across the back fence.

'Couldn't have survived without them,' said Marta, straightening and squinting towards the shops. 'Gabrijela, we should go.'

'Yes,' I said, looking to Joy, my mouth set like an apology, willing her to see my discomfort and not blame me for Marta's rudeness.

'I'm off too. Wee David needs a drink. See you next week, Jela.'

I edged up beside Marta, anticipating her outburst. 'You want to be careful,' Marta said, quickening her pace. 'That girl's not to be trusted.'

No wonder Joy hadn't invited me to her place. It was likely she would never get to know the real me. Would she even want to? My heart sank at the thought of returning to the isolation I'd felt in those first few weeks, the possibility that I might always feel like a paper cut-out of my former self, someone with no substance in this country.

Marta waved and called out to a lady across the road. She looked dressed to go to town: white gloves; shiny black handbag, and her pièce de résistance, a purple ruched hat, velvet perhaps, gracing her head in the softest of folds like whipped cream. The lady waved and climbed into a car beside a man who waved too as they drove off.

We reached the school, and the children's cries filling the playground sounded like a discordant band of trainee musicians. Marta waved to a group of girls gathered by the fence who jiggled about returning her wave, seeming both shy and excited. It was the primary school which Roko and all the Tomić children had attended, so Marta always knew someone. It still baffled me how Tata could crush my dream of further education, how he could reduce me to a life of drudgery. Every time I passed this school my disappointment felt double edged; my *dragi* had rekindled my dream to become a teacher. I focused on the collection of shops at the end of the street. Surely those hopes wouldn't be dashed again?

'Cross,' Marta said, her trundler crashing off the kerb. I nearly bumped into her. There was no need to cross for Simun's shop?

Then I saw them up ahead. The two women. One pushing a pram back and forth, the other grasping the hand of a toddler. They were always together, these two, as though one couldn't exist without the other. Over the weeks I had tried to be friendly, saying hello, smiling, but they seemed determined to snub me.

'Nothing better to do with themselves,' grumbled Marta, her pace slowing as though she was reluctant to walk past them.

I snuck a glance across the wide street, still trying to fathom Marta's reaction. Both women had their heads locked together and then one shouted, 'You lot should be ashamed! Disgusting, that's what!'

Marta winced as though she'd been struck by their venom. I looked behind, wondering who else might have heard but the street was deserted.

'I'll give you what!' Marta cried, shaking her fist. '*Katastrofa!* You know nothing!' She brushed past me, gripping my arm to tug me along. 'Idiots! You're not to talk to those girls, understood?' Her face twisted in a scowl. I nodded, still too shocked to speak. Marta dropped my arm. 'Good-for-nothing busybodies. They think our Roko's to blame for Pauline and they're determined to make my life hell. They won't succeed, though! I could wring Pauline's neck for all the trouble she's caused our family.'

Marta set off, unleashing her fury, the wheels of her trundler bashing against the pavement. Simun's fish shop was our target and I struggled to keep up with her, not daring to look behind. I took a strange comfort, knowing it wasn't me or my looks or the way I dressed that had caused those girls to avoid me. I had been tarnished by association. But what did she mean, *disgusting*? What had happened between Roko and Pauline? How well had Joy known Pauline? Had they been friends? I wished I could ask Joy, but any time Roko's name came up she clammed up or changed the topic, as quick as a sprat dancing in the shallows.

Marta pushed at Simun's shop door. The bell tinkled, a welcome to safe ground. Simun emerged from the rear of the shop, his navy and white striped apron tied around his wiry frame. I let my breath go and checked the wall clock behind the counter. One hour until Mr Postie.

At the gate I sent up another prayer. *Please God, let there be a letter and I'll never disappoint you again.* Like Simun, I counted Mr Postie as a friendly face, and I was grateful to him for delivering my letters directly to Roko's over the past month. In the corner of Joy's garden, a tui hopped among the spindly limbs of a tree laden with red berries. As the bird alternated between feasting and singing, the white tuft at its throat bobbed and the sunlight showcased its iridescent bronze, blue and emerald feathers. I craned my neck down the street to where Mr Postie was rounding the corner, his bright red saddle bags hanging like targets. The letters came regularly: from Nada and Antica; Mare who wrote with news of Josip and Jakob; and Mama, bless her, who wrote without fail each week. It was always a relief, as though for a fleeting moment my friends and family were beside me. My hands felt clammy watching Mr Postie, who seemed to stop at every letterbox. The tui flew off, a noisy flurry of flapping wings, singing its goodbye.

'Greetings, missy,' Mr Postie said, drawing alongside Roko's gate, touching his hand to his cap. He dug into his bag. 'Three today.'

I flicked through the mail. The brown envelope on the top was for Roko. Antica's messy scrawl was on the blue aerogramme beneath. I knew it before I'd even uncovered the last one. A white envelope. Another letter for Roko. I stared at his house unable to move, swallowing down the last of my self-esteem, burying my sob as a gulp.

The pretending was over. My *dragi* had led me on like a lapdog. I'd known it for weeks but I'd insisted on playing my stupid game.

Somehow I dragged myself back to the house and closed the front door before slumping against the wall, sliding until I was seated on the bare floorboards, my legs outstretched. My thoughts crashed inside me, all-consuming waves which left me reeling and dizzy. A wave of nausea hit, impossible to contain, the bile rising in my throat then onto the floor beside me. Again and again I heaved. When I had nothing left to give, I edged away, inch by slow inch, pools of my vomit trailing me. I mustered the last of my reserves to turn my back on my stinking mess, curling into a tight ball, crushing my nose and mouth into my armpit to avoid the terrible stench. My head throbbed so hard I worried it might burst.

When I forced myself to move it was as if I had aged twenty years. Stiff and sore, I set to cleaning up my mess. Then I forced myself out to the washing line, reasoning that it was best to regain some routine. I untied the rope and lowered the creaking wooden beam, but as I wrenched the towels off the line, piling them higher and higher into the basket, all I saw was a mountain of despair. What I had thought was love was no more than a cheap transaction. I had been seduced by that man's charms and the lure of escape, a fool who refused to acknowledge the facts. Facing Roko would be impossible. I left him a note explaining that I was sick, and somehow made it back along the street to Stipan and Marta's. By God's grace, Marta didn't question me but shuffled me into my bedroom instead.

Once I lay down, my dreadful thoughts gelled. I'd been clinging by a thread — one foot still on Korčula, the other teetering in *Nova Zelanda* — now I was cast adrift without an anchor to ground me or a map to guide me forward. I had lost everything. I unhooked my rosary beads from the headboard and touched the gold crucifix to the top of my head, making the sign of the cross. Usually my fingers worked quickly, dancing over the stanzas, ballerina steps taking me through the opening prayers and onto the five longer decades, but I couldn't progress past the first short row of glass beads. There was Tata standing over me, yelling, *Stupid girl! You're a disgrace to this family.* My fingers worried the beads and my hurt felt as sharp-edged as it had on that day. *Who will want you now?* His fists raised. And me, defiant — still so sure of my *dragi*'s love.

MAY

J oy's simple invitation, would I join her for morning tea, Friday, at ten, set my heart racing. Nearly four months in and this was my greatest achievement yet. There was a spring to my step when I pushed her white picket gate open and strode towards her front door. It didn't matter that the trees were skeletons with emaciated branches stripped of all colour. It didn't matter about the pelting rain ricocheting off my umbrella. I sheltered my plate of *fritule* and pinned the bag, holding the picture books and some freshly picked persimmons, tighter under my arm. For once I wasn't forcing my feet forward, one step in front of the other, *polako, polako*. I was off to see Joy and, with any luck, another step closer to building a true friendship in this country.

Her front porch was no more than an indent reached by a narrow set of concrete steps. Juggling everything proved difficult. I managed by placing the doughnuts on the small concrete slab then turning outwards to collapse my umbrella, the bag still pinned under my arm. I faced her front door again, a pane of textured glass, rippled, as though a storm had blasted through leaving raindrops as permanent markings. It was odd seeing into her house, the shapes and colours at least, but not the full picture. My worries returned. None of my winter shirts matched the smart burgundy and black panelled skirt Marta had given me and I'd been determined not to resort to my tatty grey cardigan. But did I look ridiculous in short sleeves? I rapped on Joy's door feeling jittery. She emerged from the rear, blurry around the edges, a mix of mustard and cream.

'Hi, Jela!' The usual string of pearls clutched at her throat and her lips flashed orange. She wore a cream twinset and a mustard A-line skirt. Joy took my plate as I stepped inside. 'What a dreadful day! Don't you look smart. Quick, come through to the kitchen where it's warm. These look delish.'

I deposited my worries and followed her up the hallway. Opposite the entrance to the lounge was a collection of framed photos. A picture of David hung among them, his one tinged with colour.

'Where's the little man?' I asked.

'Shhhh.' Joy gestured down another hallway to the right. 'Having his morning sleep. Come.'

Inside Joy's kitchen there was none of Marta's clutter. Instead of lace curtains, modern slatted blinds were lowered around a small dining alcove and concertinaed up over the kitchen sink. I liked how they lent the room a bright and airy feel despite the gloomy day. Joy crossed to a glossy red bench, an island set at right angles to the stainless steel kitchen bench, and fussed about slipping my *fritule* under a fine gauze cloth. I hung back, unsure whether I should join her. Despite mastering our conversations over the back fence, and whenever we met on the street now, everything felt at odds.

'I feel terrible it's taken so long to invite you,' said Joy, spinning back, her arms hanging slack by her sides. 'It's difficult with Roko. Did he know you were coming today?'

I hesitated. Even after so many months I wasn't sure how well they knew each other, and I didn't want to be drawn on Roko's insinuation that Joy was nosey.

'No, but it's none of his business.' I scrambled for another topic. 'Has Mount Wellington always been your home?'

A look of relief crossed Joy's face and she smiled. 'No. And Dad wasn't happy either. But wait. Let me get you a cardigan. That weather's turned you to ice.'

I objected, scrambling to uncross my arms at the same time, not realising I'd been hugging myself tight. My protests were fruitless and when Joy rushed from the room I wondered whether she too was grateful for the chance to gather her thoughts. We would have to tackle the subject of Roko at some stage, but any mention of him was always a sticking point, a full stop, a topic Joy had been a master at avoiding.

I crossed to the red island to unpack the books Joy had lent me to help with the language, leaving the persimmons in the bag. Everything was so orderly, from the stack of letters propped in a rack at the end of the island, to her glossy white cupboards and black-and-white checkered floor. I loved the splashes of colour tying in with her island: the red figurines on the ornate cuckoo clock hanging above the stove, and the white wooden calendar surround decorated with a red filigree pattern. I made sure to stack the books neatly, placing the larger hard-covered one on the bottom, its little foxes racing about in cars, trucks, even a crocodile car, and the smaller *My ABC* book, with its comical lion surrounded by alphabet blocks, on the top. *You can do this*, I reassured myself, grateful that the rain was no longer lashing at the windows, making everything feel calmer. But when I looked at that lion again he might have been mocking me, so assured he was, lounging back while balancing a stack of ABC blocks on one talon. The kitchen door banged, startling me.

'I can't,' I said, as Joy pushed a beautiful crimson-coloured bundle into my hands.

She waggled her finger as though scolding me. 'There, that's better,' she said, after I slipped the cardigan on. The wool was so soft and luxurious I felt a million pounds. 'Keep it. It's one Mum knitted and it's always been too big for me. The colour's spot-on with your lipstick. You look beautiful.'

'Thank you,' I said, stepping forward and hugging her. Joy squeezed my waist and I made a show of parading up and down her kitchen as though I was a model in a magazine. Joy clapped with delight. For the first time in this country I was being true to myself, showing the fun side of my personality, the real Jela. 'You didn't finish telling me about your tata,' I said, still buzzing with adrenalin.

'My *dad*, you mean?' Her teasing brought us back to familiar ground. 'Let's just say he thought I was making a mistake marrying Roger. He can be a bit of a snob.' She tapped the side of her nose and lowered her voice. 'Is Roger *really* the man of your dreams? Plenty more fish in the sea. All because I was moving from Epsom to Mount Wellington.'

We collapsed into giggles and it felt liberating — it had been a long time since I'd joked like that. Joy grabbed hold of my arm. 'I want to show you something. Quick, now the rain's stopped.'

She led me out the back door and we hurried along a side path towards an outhouse, a miniature version of Joy's home, with white weatherboards and a red-tiled roof. Even though it was a short distance, the wind whistled through the narrow gap, tangling my hair. Joy pushed the door open, flinging her arm in the direction of the concrete tub. A circular drum sat beside it, supported on four black legs like miniature stilts, a gleaming white version of a copper. Embossed on its side were large gold letters, and a separate arm with two rubber rollers angled back over the tub.

'What a beauty,' I said, moving closer to peer inside. A black propeller sat in its base.

'Close!' Joy said, crouching to trace her fingers over the letters and sounding out the name. 'She's BEATTY, but I call her Betty. That's how I'm the *shampion!*' I laughed at her mimicking my accent and at the way she was thumping her chest, looking so pleased with herself. 'She's my secret weapon. I've been dying to show you.'

'Incredible,' I said, still grinning and running my fingers over Betty's smooth white metal as though it were a gemstone. When I looked up, Joy was edged back by the door.

'So,' she said. 'How much do you know about what happened next door?'

'A little,' I said. 'Were you and Pauline friends?' Even asking the question felt dangerous, as though I might upset the balance, put all that we'd gained at risk.

'I wanted to tell you, Jela. I'm sorry it's taken so long to invite you. It's just—'

I waved my hand, batting away her apologies. 'Don't be silly. But can you tell me what happened? Slowly. *Polako, polako.*'

Joy's face relaxed again. 'I love that saying. All right, I'll try my best. But you mustn't say anything to Roko, and especially not Mrs Tomich.' She searched my eyes. 'Let's go inside first.'

Joy got busy plugging in the kettle and spooning the Nescafé powder into the cups. I made myself useful by ferrying the plates and food to the table in the dining nook with its rectangular table surrounded on three sides by a padded black bench seat. Joy's dinner set was the same one we used at Marta and Roko's — their *everyday set* — with its autumn-leaf design. I scanned the array of food: pikelets, as I knew to call them now, with jam and cream; tiny skewers with chunks of cheese, pineapple and a wedge of dark onion; some little brown biscuits topped with chocolate icing and a walnut; and my *fritule.*

Joy switched on the lights so that the room glowed warm. 'There, that's better.'

I hadn't noticed that the black clouds had collapsed even closer, dredging all the brightness from the room. 'Maybe Marta might buy one of those Bettys,' I said, raising my voice against the wind batting the windows. 'We could share her like we do the fridge.'

Joy called back from the stove. 'Good luck! That was always Pauline's dream, but Mrs Tomich was like a brick wall on the idea.'

'Oh,' I said, taking a seat at the dining nook, the rattling windows behind me, confident that it would be a matter of picking the right moment.

Joy set down a tray with our coffee cups and took a seat at right angles to me with the island at her back. 'We saw a lot of each other,' Joy said, handing me my cup. 'We were all good friends, Roko included. It's terrible what happened.'

She looked me in the eye, and I nodded for her to continue.

'Things came to a head at a party Roger and I held late last year. Everyone was tipsy but Pauline was really bad — the worst I'd ever seen her.'

'Was she always drinking too much?' I still struggled to reconcile the image of a drunk Pauline with that face in the photo.

'Not always. She was often tipsy, but I'd never seen her rolling drunk — not like that night.' Joy leaned forward and touched my arm. 'I wonder if she'd got clever at hiding it. Poor Roko, it must have been dreadful for him. He would usually take Pauline home, but on that night he didn't notice until too late and when he tried . . . Well, Pauline exploded, swearing like a trooper and hitting out at him — his chest, his arms — making him lose his temper.'

'What did he do? Did he hurt her?'

'No, nothing like that,' said Joy, shaking her head and lowering her voice. 'He told her to go to hell. That he'd had enough.'

My memories flooded back to our lounge at home when Tata found out about me and my *dragi*. Tata shouting, me cowering behind Mama.

'Are you okay? Do you want me to stop?' asked Joy.

'No. I'm fine, honestly,' I said, desperate to push those other thoughts aside, feeling guilty I couldn't confide the real reason I was sick to my core.

Joy shuffled to the end of her seat and reached inside a cupboard at the end of the island. She pulled out something that looked like a mirror, laying it on the table between us. It was her wedding photo, a beautiful black-and-white studio portrait centred within a bevelled mirror mounted on a hexagonal-shaped wooden board — but a crack ran through it, severing Joy's dress like a fault line.

'What happened?' I picked up the photo, which was much heavier than I expected.

Joy shook her head. 'End of the day it's just a photo. I doubt it can be fixed. I still can't believe she threw one of my precious Hummels, though.'

'Wait,' I said, waving my hand. 'What's this hum-thing?'

'An ornament. Quite a heavy one — like a rock. It was on the mantelpiece in the lounge and Pauline grabbed it to throw across the room. She was aiming for Roko and luckily he ducked but this photo was the casualty. Honestly, it was like a gun going off. You can imagine the shock.'

'Must have been dreadful.'

'Next thing Roko was exploding again. He dragged Pauline kicking and screaming from the house. That was the end of the party and it's the last time I spoke to either of them.'

She was quiet then as though lost in thought, sipping at her coffee.

'Was it then that Pauline went to the hospital?' I dared to ask.

Joy scrunched her face. 'A few days later. They took her in the ambulance. We heard Pauline yelling from here. Dreadful. I tried my hardest with Roko, leaving him notes, inviting him for dinner, but he seems determined to ignore us. It's awkward and now we've got into the habit of avoiding each other.' Her face looked on the verge of collapse.

Determined to lighten the mood, I pointed to the chocolate biscuits. 'What are these ones?'

'Afghans,' said Joy, pushing the plate towards me. 'Try one. I can give you the recipe.' The mix of light and dark chocolate crumbs was divine. Meanwhile, Joy popped a doughnut into her mouth. 'These are sensational,' she said. 'Did you know they're my favourite?'

I wanted to pinch myself. Was I really sitting there watching Joy savour my treat from home? 'I can teach you how to make those, but anything else I'll need lessons for. Marta's already given up on my baking skills. Oh,' I gestured to the bag on the counter, 'I hope you like persimmons? I brought you some from their tree.'

'What a sweetie. Thanks! With Pauline gone I thought I might miss out on that treat this year.' Joy reached for another doughnut. 'How are you getting on with Mrs Tomich?'

'Difficult,' I said.

'It was the same for Pauline. That woman made life impossible. I feel like rattling her cage, making her see how she drove Pauline to the drink.'

'Were you and Pauline good friends?' *No wonder Marta was wary.*

'The best,' said Joy. 'We shared everything.' She frowned then, wrapping her hands around her cup, eyes downcast. 'If I'm honest, Mrs Tomich wasn't the only one to blame. I could have done more to stop her and I feel so bad now.' She glanced across, crestfallen. 'Pauline and I would share a drink most afternoons once our jobs were done. It was fun swapping stories, and for me it felt a little wild, risqué, a break from all the drudgery. Sometimes I knew she'd already been drinking, but I didn't do anything to stop her. If anything I encouraged her and now it's too late.'

'You can't take the blame.' I didn't know what else to say so I reached for a pikelet, folding it like a crescent to contain the cream.

Joy took a cheese stick and bit off the onion wedge. 'That's enough sad stories,' she said. 'There's other important things to ask. No more secrets.' Her eyes gleamed wicked and the light above caught the copper in her hair. 'Tell me, someone must have been giving you the eye back home? I can't imagine with your gorgeous looks there was no one.'

I looked away, the combination of cream and tart jam still singing in my mouth.

Joy reached across to rub my arm. 'Oh, Jela. I'm sorry. I didn't mean—'

'It's no worry,' I said. 'Really. I'm fine. I miss him, but he'll be coming soon. I just need the . . . How do you say it?' I scoured my brain for the right word, aware of Joy's puzzled expression and of how much I couldn't tell. '*Strpljenje* is what we say at home.'

Joy's laugh exploded. 'Stir-pee-yay-yay. What a great word! I wonder what you could mean? Come on, try and explain.' She leant forward on her elbows, her chin resting on her hands, back to being my teacher again.

'It means he's coming but I have to wait, be happy, because nothing moves fast where I come from.' I scanned her face, hoping I'd reassured her. I was certain the questions were racing across her mind, as many as the freckles tracing over her scrunched-up nose.

'Maybe you mean patience. Could that be it? You mean he's coming to get you but you have to wait. Not complain?' I nodded and she rubbed her hands together. 'How exciting! Yay-yay — what a perfect word. You're not here for Roko, then? To be honest I thought you probably were.'

'No! I'm here as his housekeeper. It's a family favour. Our tatas were friends.'

'Well, it's good there's someone at home. Is there a chance you'll go back?'

'Not sure yet. Have to wait and see. But can you keep it a secret? I don't want Roko's family worrying.'

Joy squeezed my arm. 'Of course. I love secrets. What's his name?'

'*Moj dragi.* What's in a name? Far better to show the emotion. We Yugoslavs, if we love someone, it's the *only* name we use.' My guilt felt as obvious as my new crimson cardigan but I couldn't backtrack.

Joy pulled back, still puzzled. 'Well, I guess that makes sense. You mean, like "darling" here?'

In the distance there was a high-pitched cry. David. Perfect timing, I thought. Almost simultaneously, the cuckoo called his tune, popping in and out on his perch. 'Cu-ckoo. Cu-ckoo.'

'That'll be his majesty,' said Joy. 'Oh my goodness, where did the time go?'

'I best get going too,' I said, making to move. 'For my own jobs for the majesty next door.'

Joy waved me a hurried goodbye from her front door. I huddled under my umbrella, making a beeline for her white gate, my guilt contained under the nylon canopy. After a morning of such honesty I had misled Joy when I should have been my most truthful.

Throughout the afternoon I pushed aside my worries about fudging the truth to focus on the positives of my morning. All that we had shared, Joy's honesty about Pauline and the part she had played in the terrible story. Ironically, I took some comfort from this — that someone I held on a pedestal had taken risks and made mistakes too. It provided some reassurance that my secret might stay safe with Joy, but as for her pushing me for further answers about my *dragi*, I resigned myself to keeping my lies going. My limitations with the dreaded *Engleski* gave me no insights into this country's moral compass, no sense of the reality, the word on the ground from the younger ones. And even if Joy had strayed, I doubted she would have been so stupid to risk everything like I had. If I was to keep Joy as my friend, she could never know the extent of my story and the shame I was living with now — no one could.

At dinner, with the fire crackling in the hearth, Roko was relaxed and talkative. Over the weeks we had made small progress, falling into a pattern where we were both more tolerant of each other but still careful to skirt around topics that might cause friction. My improving ability to converse in English helped, but it was as though we had also come to an unspoken agreement, each carrying our hurt like the jagged edges of broken china with neither pushing the other to explain. Perhaps he recognised the fragility in me too.

'Those hailstones were freaky,' he said, recounting the story of his bike ride home. 'Someone upstairs was shooting at me. You saw how soaked I was coming in.'

I laughed, recalling the bedraggled mess that had come through the door, too frozen to speak at the time. 'I had to brave it going over to Joy's. She invited me for morning tea,' I said, not stopping to think. I scooped up some lemon instant pudding and a wedge of Marta's preserved peaches, feeling carefree for the second time that day.

'Oh?' he said. 'And how was that?'

I scanned his face for signs that he might explode. This is good, I reassured myself, no more secrets. Perhaps he wondered why it had taken me so long.

'Good,' I said, looking him in the eye. 'Joy told me about growing up here. I wondered what it was like for you.' A small lie couldn't hurt.

He paused for what seemed like an age and I worried I'd pushed him too far. 'Trips to the beach,' he said. 'And the Dally picnics, of course. Riding my bike around the local streets . . . Tip-Top ice cream.' He smiled as though remembering the taste, then frowned. 'Petra got teased at school. The kids called her "stinky" — all the garlic and onions. By the time I got there, there were more Dallies and they weren't so mean, but I always felt different.'

He glanced up, seeking confirmation that I had understood. I made sure my face didn't betray my surprise. Despite our progress, and his efforts to speak slowly, it was rare for him to link so many sentences.

'But why did you feel so different?' I was intrigued he could feel out of place in his own country.

'Dally parents, I guess.' He opened his palms as was Stipan's habit, as though God might have the answer. 'Mum refused to speak English for a long time and her rules were always strict. Petra and Hana were hardly allowed out as teens.'

'Same as home,' I said, thinking about my own upbringing and how Branko might as well have been hand-picked for me.

'Petra tells the story about getting a right telling-off. One of the neighbours asked Mum how she was coping with her teenager, and Mum thought "teenager" meant "bad girl".' Roko tipped back his head and laughed. 'Easy to see the funny side now but it must have been hell on my sisters.'

I laughed, too. This was easily the most relaxed we'd ever been. I was surprised how interesting I found him and how handsome he looked when his eyes crinkled in a smile. He'd been hiding his sense of humour under all that gruffness.

'By the time I got to be that age I'd worked out how to get around Mum, using her language gap to my advantage, choosing which words I'd teach her. Half the time she had no idea what I was up to. I'm always telling Zoran I paved the way.'

I'd only met Zoran, Roko's younger brother, a couple of times. Like Roko, he seemed to steer clear of home.

Roko was looking at me, smiling, with a glint in his eye. 'And you? How was your childhood?'

'Ah, well, very different.' I looked away, struggling to find the words to explain. 'When I was four, I lived in a refugee camp in Egypt. They shipped us by boat towards the end of the war. I didn't see my tata for two years. He had to stay home, to fight if he was needed.' I stopped, realising I'd slipped back to Croatian, but also the irony given Tata and I weren't talking now. The way Roko was staring made me lower my eyes, but I wanted to continue, to tell him about myself, to share something beneath my surface.

'The sand was so hot. It whipped around our legs sending us running for cover to our tent — one that we shared with a number of families. For meals we'd line up with our tin plates. Everyone ate the same which meant we all shared the same bugs. Some people died from the sickness.' His brow was creased, as though he was already thinking of more questions.

'They set up a tent as a school room. I was so proud when I finally got to join Josip, my big brother. Until we returned home I didn't realise that living like that was anything out of the ordinary.'

'What happened when you got back home?'

'The war was over and the whole country got busy — everyone working to a plan to re-build Yugoslavia under Marshall Tito. You must know this, though?'

It was clear, by the way he hesitated, that he had no concept of what we'd all been through, despite my country being part of his heritage. Perhaps living so far away meant he hadn't needed to know. How could I convey in a few words how it had been? I felt disgruntled when I stood to clear the dishes.

'You've led an interesting life,' Roko said as I reached to collect his plate. His eyes seemed focused and kind. 'I'd like to hear more some time.'

Hemmed inside the kitchen and scrubbing at the dishes, I couldn't reclaim my lighter mood. Nothing could change the fact that New Zealand was so unlike my homeland or that I was stuck here. I wiped the dishes dry, stacking the plates to the side, my spirits sinking further. Even though Roko and his family were my closest links to home, our lives couldn't be further apart. And what of that flicker of interest I had just felt? I scrubbed harder at the remaining pot. How could I ever trust my judgement again? Besides, there was no comparison between these feelings for Roko and how I'd felt about my *dragi* — even knowing now how misguided they were. But would second best always be my lot? I slapped the wet tea towel against my leg, blinking hard, seeing the mess for what it really was.

JULY

Roko and I were squeezed into the back seat of Stipan's car, our knees stacked behind the front seats, both holding ourselves like wooden pegs. I was conscious of my extra bulk with Joy's champagne-coloured mink stole wrapped around my shoulders. Along with Marta and Stipan we were headed for the Yugoslav Club Ball and whereas I'd felt like a queen wrapping that stole around me earlier, I now felt as nervous as I had at sixteen for my first dance back home. I fiddled with the diaphanous chiffon layer of my dress, the palest shade of aqua that floated on top of the satin underskirt. Joy had reassured me it would be perfect, but I was still nervous about fitting in and doing the right thing at these club events. The dress had been Mama's, one she'd altered for me, and I'd worn it to all the dances back home. Everyone said it matched my blue-green eyes perfectly. When I'd checked myself in the mirror earlier, I'd swallowed a lump thinking about all the other times I'd twirled around the dance floor with my *dragi*, and others, that same skirt swishing like a whisper.

Marta, in her emerald-green party dress, was prattling away and for once I was grateful. When Stipan swung around the corners, Marta reeled herself back, determined to keep the plate of smoked-fish savouries balanced on her lap. It was the kind of joke Roko and I might share at his house now — Marta attached by an invisible fishing line — but not in that car, not when we felt so on show, especially now that Roko was gracing the family with his presence. To me it seemed that everyone in the family was on tenterhooks, as though by acknowledging Roko's presence at Sunday lunch and the like, they were fearful that he might realise his mistake and disappear again.

Stipan pulled up to the curb and Marta, Roko and I peeled ourselves from the car. A steady stream of people merged towards the club entrance, and Hobson Street buzzed with a mix of English and my own language. Marta had confided this would be Roko's first club event since Pauline, and I wondered how he was feeling. Earlier, when he'd arrived at Marta and Stipan's in his dark suit and bow tie, I'd been taken by how handsome he looked. Now, standing alongside Marta, he looked hesitant and half of me wanted to reassure him, as any friend would. Stipan drove off to find a park, but I hung back, frustrated that the ease Roko and I shared at his house disappeared the moment we were outside those four walls. We might as well have been strangers again. A young woman, a bundle of energy in a bright red shift dress, pushed forward, pulling along a tall man in a dark suit. Her blonde hair was wound in a coil and her lips flashed a sparkle of red. Marta waved them in beside us.

'Marta, Roko,' the red woman gushed, 'lovely to see you both.' Her eyes darted, up and down, as though sizing me up. The man turned to talk to Roko.

'Sara, meet Gabrijela. And you too, Davor,' said Marta, tapping the man's shoulder. Davor raised his hand, acknowledging me, before returning to his conversation. Sara was still scanning me and I pulled my stole closer.

'Jela's come to help our Roko,' said Marta, then turned to me. 'We've known Sara from when she was a little girl.' Her head flicked back. 'How was your trip to the homeland?'

Marta and Sara chatted and we inched forward. Most of the women wore heels, and I felt like a little girl in my flat pumps. I'd already decided that once I'd saved enough pin money I'd buy a new pair of shoes. My tongue worried at my painted lips, grateful at least for this small luxury. The clear mid-winter sky was threaded with purple and black, not yet dark enough to showcase the stars. Not long after I'd arrived in this country I'd confided in Stipan that I couldn't find *Polaris*, the star Tata had told me about, the one he used to guide *Krešimira* home safely after a long day on the water. Stipan had shown me how to pick out the pattern of stars making up the Southern Cross, but it wasn't the same, and I still felt disorientated.

As we neared the entrance, Marta pushed forward to join Roko and Davor.

'I love your dress,' Sara said, dropping back beside me. 'How're you finding it here?'

'I'm managing,' I said. 'Easier when I can speak Croatian.'

'There'll be plenty of young men with their eye out, and they won't care what you speak.' She arched her eyebrow. 'Our Roko will want to keep a close eye.'

'I love the dancing but I *won't* be returning the looks,' I gabbled, my hand at my mouth.

'Really?' Sara's eyebrows lifted again and she turned away, back to Davor.

I felt certain she thought me a prude. Mama would say, *ispeći pa neći,* bake it, then say it. Of course I was interested in meeting people, the men included, I just had no need for love. I had accepted my fate: romance was a privilege I had squandered and the only way to safeguard my secret, and my self-esteem, was to remain single. Deep down, in my darkest place though, I was still making excuses for my *dragi*. His broken promise was the sharp point of a knife twisting at my heart, yet I was still holding out hope he would come. There had been no arguments. No word of warning. Perhaps my *dragi* had been tricked somehow, cajoled into thinking that he could bury our love alive, hide away all that we'd shared, bide his time until Tata's anger subsided. Even though Roko and I were both lost souls swimming against the tide, he at least might have the option of finding someone else — that's if the annulment Marta kept talking about ever came through. I wondered if any of the girls would be giving him the eye, even though he wasn't available, not really. Why was it so much easier for the men? I rubbed at my gold locket, the one Mama had given me on my eighteenth birthday. At the time she said it had special powers, that it could ward off adversity, as it had during the war when she'd hidden it from the looting soldiers by sewing a secret pocket in her dress. The weight and shape of it were reassuring, but it couldn't change the facts: men were the ones holding the power, and I would never be free to return the looks.

Davor pulled Sara forward at the entrance to the club and handed their ticket to a man sitting at a small desk. Marta and Roko had gone through already. My heart pounded but the man waved me on, directing me to the small cloakroom at the side, explaining that I could leave my stole there. Passing this to the lady behind the desk made me feel exposed, as though I was shedding a piece of my armour. She handed me a number on a piece of paper and I panicked for a moment, twisting it in my fingers, unsure what to do with it. A Maori lady beside me was dropping hers inside her purse and I turned away, tucking mine inside my bra. How long had it taken before *this* lady felt accepted amongst our people? Stipan had explained how this group of New Zealanders, with their coffee-coloured skin, had a special link with our culture: both languages shared the same phonetics, and many of our Dally men, especially during the early gum-digging days, had married Maori women. I turned back, wanting to connect with this lady, even with just a smile. But she had already moved on, the noise from the double entrance doors spilling forth like a blast as she swept through.

I inched my way over. There were hundreds of people inside, at least three times more than at the Vela Luka dances. My heart ached for Nada and Antica, and all the evenings we'd spent at the dances together back home as I scanned the sea of unfamiliar faces, looking for Hana, wishing that Joy could have been born a Dally. The decorations were magnificent, flash compared with home: twisted strips of red-and-white paper streamers floating in criss-cross formations across the rectangular hall, bunches of red balloons clustered at points around the sides.

A mural depicting a typical village scene spanned the far wall, and the images that I'd been pushing down all day flooded back. Memories of home that were so hard-hitting, and of that last, very special ball I'd attended in Dubrovnik, back when all my troubles started: fortified sea walls and crenellated towers; whitewashed buildings and church towers piercing the sky; Italian-inspired domes popping above terracotta roofs; sheer mountains hemming the village in; pelargoniums and oleanders in shades of pink and red and cerise and bright green; and the sea, shimmering in front of it all, the bluest of blues, cradling the fishing boats like babies.

Stipan tapped my shoulder and nudged me forward, his hand at my back. 'Come, Jela. Let's find you a friend.'

Closer up I recognised many of the faces of the young girls I'd first seen at the Dally picnic and then many times since at Sunday Mass. They were gathered at the side, leaning in towards each other and giggling. I suspected they might be swapping stories, like we used to do, of which boys would have snakes in their pants, and which ones they wanted to dance with. It was my habit now to join this group outside the church after Mass. They always welcomed me but it was annoying that I never had the chance to speak to anyone individually, to find some common ground. Many of the girls were related, or had gone to school together, or socialised within their family groups. They seemed to operate as a package, a bulk deal, and I craved the chance to pull someone aside and tell them more about myself. Instead my place seemed to be on the fringe of their group, listening in on their chatter, trying to make sense of it, pretending I was a part of things. I wondered if everyone had to go through this trial period before being officially welcomed into their ranks.

'Valentina, take care of our Jela,' said Stipan, his voice sounding too loud. A number of the girls turned but Stipan was already backing off.

'Come,' Valentina said, holding out her hand to pull me into their huddle. 'Your dress is lovely. Pretty colour.'

'Thank you,' I said, glancing around, wanting to catch the eye of the others, to say more, to tell them all how nice they looked. They were already back to their conversations, a hive of busy bees, speaking too fast for me to keep up. Two large flags draped from the ceiling — the Yugoslav alongside the New Zealand one — and right then I would have given anything to have my time again. To be held close and have him lean in close, whisper in my ear and have my heart pound. To feel at home.

Hana waved out, a bright white spot close to the mural. She was already moving forward and I raised my hand, feeling a wash of relief. I tapped Valentina's shoulder, signalling that Hana wanted to see me. Valentina shrugged then turned back to the group as though it was of no consequence whether I stayed or went. Hana and I met part-way and I complimented her on her dress: a white satin number, full skirt with a violet sash, and lime-green trim around the neck and cutaway arms.

'Your dress is fabulous too,' she said, tugging on my arm. 'Can you believe Roko's actually come? You've been good for that brother of mine, you know.'

'Nothing to do with me,' I said, but I don't think she heard. Her mission seemed to be to drag me to the far end of the hall at speed. I didn't mind. I kept my eyes fixed on her sash as though it was some regal force pulling me along and catching me in her whirl.

Hana stopped short. 'Talk about surprises! Zoran's dating a Kiwi girl,' she whispered, leaning in close. 'He's keeping her well away from Mum, though.'

'Can't blame him,' I whispered, thrilled I was a confidante. Hana took a step back, frowning, and I rushed to make amends. 'Just thinking about Pauline and what happened.' I cringed inside, wishing I had more space.

'Pauline was always trouble,' Hana said tersely, the silence pounding between us. 'Roko was just too blind to see it. Come.' She grabbed my arm again, leading me off as though that conversation had never happened.

When would I feel at ease with this family? To know when to say it and when to bake it. I should have learnt from Marta's reaction after mentioning Joy's new washing machine. She had snapped: *You still need to boil the clothes, Gabrijela — those new machines only do half a job.* Up ahead, Sara and Petra were among the group we were heading towards — resplendent red alongside cool sapphire blue — but when we closed in Petra turned her back, blocking us out. Hana seemed oblivious, squeezing in and wedging me between herself and Petra. Their extra height, broad shoulders and strong arms made me like the cross-link on the letter H, insignificant, a girl with no right to be at such a party.

'Ah, there you are, Jela,' said Sara, craning forward. 'I've just been telling Petra you're not interested in our men.'

'Not good enough?' said Petra, a blue flash drilling me with her stare. She flicked her ponytail and turned away.

It seemed everyone else in the huddle was staring too. Hana leaned in close. 'Don't worry about her. It takes a while to break the ice. Give her a chance.'

I wanted to scream that I had been interested in someone but what would that prove? They would all likely think I was reacting, making an excuse. The band was setting up in front of the mural, a group of seven men: one hefted a piano accordion, another a trumpet, and a couple of the men held tamburicas. They were dressed alike in crisp white shirts, black trousers and red cummerbunds. I wondered where Roko was, if he might ask me to dance. It was strange to think it but anything would be preferable to dealing with Petra and Sara. A folk tune started up and Petra and Sara wandered off. Hana's husband, Franjo, was beside us, tapping Hana on the shoulder. 'I'll send a partner over soon,' she called back.

Across the hall some women were laying out food on two long tables, and I wondered where Marta might be. A lady serving drinks from a hatch just behind waggled her finger at some men gathered out front, tipping back her head and laughing. Roko and Stipan were close by, holding glasses of red wine. The music was catchy and I tapped my foot, itching to dance, to feel a part of things, all the while scanning the room and wondering who Hana might send my way.

A young guy was skirting the dance floor and it wasn't long before he approached. We were about the same height but his tuft of curly hair made him appear taller. His shirt was so ill-fitting that I wondered if it had been passed down, or maybe he still had to grow into his body. He bowed formally, introducing himself as Clem, then led me to the dance floor mumbling something about working for Franjo. We joined in on a rock and roll number, 'Wake Up Little Susie'. I recognised it from Aunt Daisy's programme. Clem's eyes darted this way and that, anywhere but my face, and his dance moves were clunky. I wasn't bothered. I realised how much I had been itching to dance, to lose myself in the music. I was already hoping that Clem might want to dance again, but when the song finished he led me to the side, and I barely had time to thank him before he scuttled off.

Two men were slouched against the wall just along from me, neither of them looking capable of standing. I inched away, not wanting to draw their attention.

'I'm sorry, *Draga*, I didn't mean to startle you.' It was Kate, Marta's older sister. Her hair, like white spun silk, was styled neat as a cloche hat.

I'd met Kate a few times. Even in her heels she was a head shorter than me. She was always immaculately turned out — tonight in a floral blouse and trim, straight skirt — and the sheen of powder on her face reminded me of the scones with their flour dusting that Joy had been teaching me to make. I held out my hand but Kate pulled me into a hug, kissing me. Her skin was soft as rose petals and sweet-smelling, like Marta's Nivea face cream, the one I'd snuck open to try in the bathroom a few weeks back.

'You realise how brave you are, don't you? Coming all this way by yourself.'

Something about Kate's tone caught me off-guard — Mama, her reassurance, how much I missed that. Kate drew me close, her hand around my waist. 'Mind, I know how that feels. I was only nineteen when I came out myself. Everything will work out. You wait.' Her eyes twinkled. 'I still remember my adventure. Not easy, is it? All history for me now. I made my life here and I hope you have the same luck, dear. You will.' She squeezed my waist. 'Come, sit with us.'

She herded me towards a group of women, more like grandmothers, all seated at a table to the side. Memories of the Dally picnic crowded back, but when Kate motioned for me to pull up a chair it felt different. She was so full of confidence, and even though I was certain she had Marta's feistiness, there was also a warmth about her. I knew some of her story: she'd been the first of the family to come, six years before Marta and Stipan; she and her husband Nick had been successful growing grapes. They had organised a job for Roko's brother, Zoran, and Marta was always telling me how he was destined to be the best winemaker.

'Bet you're still tired,' she said, patting my arm when I sat beside her. 'It took me months to get over that journey. How long has it been now?'

'Five months already,' I said, not needing to think. It felt more like five years.

'Lucky you, coming by plane. In my day, of course, the boat was our only option.'

I nodded, thinking how it was my uncle and his Party connections that Tata had used to sweep through all the necessary paperwork and pay for my fare. Ironic, given Tata's disparaging views of my uncle and the Party.

'We were stuck on that boat for weeks.' Kate's voice dragged me back. 'By the end of the journey, I knew these girls so well.' She smiled and waved her hand at her companions. 'We were thrown together. All proxy brides as naive as each other. Weren't we, ladies?' A few of the women rewarded her with a smile, and I thought how lucky they were to have come as a group. 'But that sickness. Ach! You couldn't escape it, only temporarily when we leant over the railing and let go of our stomachs.'

I scrunched my nose. My nausea on the plane had been nothing compared with that day, three months ago, when my resolve had been pushed to the limit. I could still taste the acid in the back of my throat.

'What silly dreamers,' Kate said, her face bright, not noticing my discomfort. 'Most of us were only nineteen or so, the same as you, clutching photos of those dreaded men. We'd never met them, of course, even though we were already promised to marry them.' She let out a peal of laughter. 'We believed we were coming to the land of opportunity.'

She was a natural storyteller and I sat back, allowing her story to wash over me. It was my own determination to escape my small life which had pushed me to take the risks I had. Mama had told me about the girls who left as proxy brides. Perhaps forty years ago it was no different. Perhaps when you're young the risks always seem worth it and the problems surmountable.

Kate nudged me. 'Ah, well. I clutched that photo of my Nick so tightly that his face was no longer recognisable. When I scanned the wharf I worried I wouldn't find him. His real face was no match for the photo anyway. Those men were all scoundrels and my Nick was no exception. We can laugh now, but they'd all sent their most flattering photo — taken when they were in their prime. Some even sent photos of a completely different person.' Kate laughed again. 'A photo's no match for the real thing. What do you think, Jela?'

My face coloured. I could feel it like a slow burn.

'Nick and I made a good life for ourselves,' Kate continued. I compressed my lips, worrying that she might sense my relief. 'Well, you've seen our land out west, and the grapevines. Look.' She pointed across the room. 'Here's our Hana, and Roko. You two will make a lovely pair, dear.' She gave me no time to protest. 'How *is* Roko? It's lovely to see him here. You've been like a breath of fresh air for him.'

'Roko's keen to show off his dance moves,' said Hana, beside us now, turning and grinning at her brother.

'Aunt Kate,' Roko said, stepping forward to kiss her cheeks.

'Come on. Let's see how you Kiwi men dance,' I said, my words tumbling out, determined to escape before Kate said anything further to embarrass me.

'Hmmph!' he muttered, his look suggesting he would be happier showing off his escape moves. 'I'd rather watch.'

'Would be terrible to forget how,' said Hana, her eyes pleading.

'Off you go, you two,' said Kate, and Roko reluctantly gestured for me to join him. We walked towards the dance floor like strangers, me trailing behind him. 'Enjoy yourselves,' Kate called, and I prayed I was doing the right thing, worried it might set us back again.

'That'll Be the Day', a Buddy Holly song, started up. Roko shuffled from side to side and I was relieved to lose myself in the catchy tune. He was light on his feet but, like Clem, reluctant to catch my eye. I sensed that it wasn't so much inexperience but because he was feeling as much on show as I was. When I snuck a glance, Roko was still looking to the side. *Tears are for the dead people*, I thought, throwing myself into the music. 'That'll be the day when you make me cry-hi,' I sang, stamping my foot and twirling around. It felt cathartic, as if I was setting my inhibitions free, but I didn't dare look at Roko in case he was scowling. Shaking my arms and twisting my hips I sang, 'You know it's a lie,' wiggling my index finger as though scolding Roko. I wondered how he felt. If, like me, he was enjoying our dance. Our eyes met and he grinned, just a fleeting twitch of his lips.

The song finished and Simun, whom I hardly recognised out of his fish-shop apron and black woollen beanie, tapped Roko's shoulder. 'I've been waiting for the pleasure all night, Miss Jela. Can I steal her, Roko?'

'Of course,' said Roko, already backing off towards the bar.

Simun placed his hand on the small of my back. I felt a small rush of confidence thinking how I had progressed in this country. Joy was now someone I counted as a friend, and here I was with Simun, another local who, just like the postie, was a familiar, friendly face. He guided me around the floor to 'Bye Bye Love', twirling me at arm's length then pulling me close. It was exhilarating, but I was grateful I'd avoided this song with Roko. 'I'm through with romance' and 'hello emptiness' were topics we could dodge at home, but there would be no hiding from those lyrics on the dance floor.

The music came to an abrupt halt due to a commotion beside the bar involving the drunken men I'd seen earlier. They were yelling and jostling each other beside the food tables. I wasn't alarmed. This kind of kerfuffle was common at home between men who'd had a skinful. Simun excused himself, dashing over to help, leaving me stranded along with many other women.

'Likely they're all relieved to be let off the hook,' one lady said with a wry smile, heading off to join her friends. I smiled too, wondering if Roko felt that he'd been rescued by Simun. There he was, alongside Stipan and many of the other men, all like human winches trying to pull the drunk men apart. I felt certain someone would land on the food table the way their arms and fists were flying. Had I really been that relaxed dancing with Roko? It was as though I'd finally had the chance to show him what I was really like, to be my true self. I wondered if he liked what he'd seen, then shook my head to lose the thought. Of course we were more relaxed. We'd spent so much time together getting over our differences, nothing more, and that was all it could be.

There was a sharp ripping noise. Someone waved a piece of white fabric high in the air like a flag as the drunken men were hauled towards the door. One man's shirt sleeve was in tatters. The music restarted, just like at home, as though nothing had happened. The dance floor became crowded and I moved off for some food. My earlier conversations with Kate and Hana spun in my head as I piled calamari onto my plate. I needed to be wary. If only there was someone here that I could call family of my own. With Marta and Petra I was always on my guard, but even with Hana I'd been caught out. It was exhausting having to side-step around when conversing with this family, let alone others in this tight-knit community.

The calamari rings were delicious, comforting, a reminder of home and my thoughts returned to Mama. If only I could see her again, hear her voice. Stipan returned through the main doors, rubbing his hands together like cymbals as though he'd just disposed of some rubbish. He beckoned me over. 'Have some more to eat. We'll be off soon.' He lit a cigarette and took a deep drag. '*Katastrofa!* Always someone to ruin the evening.'

Roko joined us. 'Ready for home? Go find your mother.' Roko rushed off and Stipan turned to me. 'Fools, hard on their luck.'

Stipan was rarely so short-tempered. Was he reminded of Pauline? Had she embarrassed the family here? I felt sorry for those men and wondered how many others had left Yugoslavia with a dream, only to have it crushed in this place which had promised so much more. I didn't let myself dwell on the only time I had drunk alcohol at full strength — the start of all my troubles.

OCTOBER

J oy and Roger were hosting a pot luck dinner, *not a party*, Joy was quick to point out. It was a celebration for the start of summer, given that Friday marked the beginning of Labour weekend. Roko swung in on his bike an hour later than usual. I waved to him from the kitchen window as he crossed to the porch to remove his boots. His dark-green overalls, always clean in the morning, were now scuffed up with markings from the quarry dust and chips. The back door clicked open, and I cocked my head from the kitchen as he slumped at the table, pulling the newspaper close.

'Here you go,' I said, placing down his mug of tea and sandwich with last night's lamb. 'There's not much time. Joy's expecting us there around seven.' Neither Joy or I had believed it when Roko accepted and all week I'd been expecting him to pull out.

'I haven't forgotten. Stop your fussing. Let a man unwind.' The look on his face was pure Stipan and it seemed this was all he would say. It was the kind of response that had annoyed me earlier, before I understood he was a man of few words.

'I'll run your bath, then.'

'It'll be the first time, you know. Since Pauline.' I was at the door to the hallway. There was a strained edge to his voice and I turned back, half of me wanting to wrap him in a hug and tell him everything would be all right.

'Ah, they won't bite,' I said, my feet stuck to the floor, my voice too matter-of-fact. 'One step at a time. *Polako, polako*, eh?'

When I returned he was sitting in one of the easy chairs facing the fireplace. 'Bath's run,' I called from the kitchen. I hoped the evening would go well for him. He deserved a fresh start.

The moussaka I'd prepared earlier, and my platter of *fritule*, sat on the stove top ready to take next door. I filled the sink for the dishes, watching the bubbles form as though matching the mix of excitement and nerves brewing in my stomach. Joy had borrowed a dress for me from her sister — the one who got all the height genes in her family — and I was busting to put it on.

'Got some news this week,' Roko said, so close that I jumped in fright.

'*O Bože!*' I said, my hand at my chest, my heart still racing. Mostly, unless we were sitting at the table, he'd call out from a distance. But there he was, so close, leaning against the kitchen doorjamb, wringing his hands as though trying to contain what he wanted to say, stop the words from spilling out. I edged back to the sink, focusing on the suds, my cheeks still burning.

'My annulment's come through,' he said after what seemed an age. 'Today. From the Church. Thought you should know.'

I gripped the rim of the dish, determined that he wouldn't see my hands trembling. This was such a personal revelation, so out of character. 'Ah, well,' I said. 'Means you can move on, eh? Marta will be pleased.'

'Another reason to thank God,' he said, one eyebrow raised and a silly grin wrinkling his face.

'Never hear the end otherwise,' I said, scrambling, worried at once that he might think me disrespectful.

Another flash of a smile. 'Time for my bath, then,' he said, heading down the hallway.

I returned to the dishes, my thoughts still a jumbled mess. What did this mean? Was he inviting me to celebrate with him? To show some compassion or understanding? Of course I felt happy for him. He was a single man now. Free to start again. I scrubbed at the last dish, my resentment building. *But what about me?* I realised then that I'd taken some comfort in the knowledge that we were both dealing with a full stop in our life. That it wasn't only me with past mistakes. Over the months I'd come to see us as on a joint pathway. Now, by the stroke of a pen, the Church had wiped Roko's slate clean, leaving me with no such reprieve. Even if I was brave enough to tell the priest in the confession box it still wouldn't change anything. There would be no holy rule to annul what I'd done.

I slipped into the side room, the match for my bedroom at Marta's. The dress lay on the bed and I tried to rekindle my enthusiasm, taking a moment to rub a triangle of the fabric between my fingers, tiny checkered squares of cherry-red and white. After pulling on the dress then cinching the waist with the red belt, I twirled and inspected myself in the mirror. Earlier in the week, Joy and I had admired how the skirt floated. *Shows off your impeccable curves,* she'd said and we'd both collapsed in laughter. Now, I felt self-conscious. Would he think I was making an effort to dress up for him? It was as though the wall of protection surrounding us had tumbled, leaving me exposed. Pushing aside those thoughts, I curled my fingers around the eyeshadow compact that had made a small dent in my pin-money savings. I leant close to the mirror, steadying the tiny wand, and brushed a thin smear of blue powder onto my lids. Joy was back: *Try not to be heavy-handed.* Don't be a fool. I thought, peering closer, applying my lipstick that was close to the nub now. Why should anything change? When I reached for my old pumps, I took a deep breath, my fingers at my locket, reassuring myself: *Tears are for the dead people. Get going, girl.*

Roko was waiting in the living room, his hair still wet and slicked back. He'd changed into his smart steel-grey trousers with the narrow leg. The shirt I'd never seen before: it was in burnt-orange tones and for once he'd buttoned the sleeves at the cuff. The colour suited his tanned face and he looked younger somehow, as though the news of his annulment had lifted a weight off his shoulders. I couldn't help thinking about my *dragi,* how he always took pride in his appearance — crisp pressed shirts, shiny shoes — and how even dressed casually he looked refined.

I dragged my eyes down, patting the front of my dress. Roko's feet stuck out like milky white icebergs. 'Those white boots stop the stones biting your feet?' I blurted, my laugh erupting like a snort. I grinned, remembering the first day we'd met and how I'd been too afraid to say what I was really thinking.

He pointed at his feet. 'Ha! They'll do won't they? Spent years hardening these up.' He made a show of biting his fingernails, reminding me of my brother, Josip.

'Might look better with shoes.'

'Shoes?' he said, in all seriousness. 'No one wears shoes to parties here. Not in the summer. Didn't Joy say?' He let me stew for a moment before laughing heartily. 'Ah, don't be worried, Jela. I wouldn't do that to the neighbours. Being there be shock enough.'

I laughed too. 'Pays to check. Who knows with you Kiwis?'

He raised his eyebrows. 'Is that a new dress? Stylish.'

'Joy lent it to me,' I said, not knowing where to look, wanting to get next door, away from ourselves, among other people.

Roko hung back at the base of Joy's front steps, holding the moussaka as though he was a mannequin in a department store display. I knocked and a flash of bright yellow appeared.

'Look at you!' I said, 'Don't you look smart,'

Joy's hair was pulled back from her face by a wide yellow headband, the same colour as her dress but patterned with white dots. A mix of stunning and risqué, she might have just stepped off the latest catwalk. She hugged me as I squeezed past and then pecked Roko on the cheek, him stooping, angling the heavy dish. 'Thanks for coming,' she said, as Roko twisted and righted himself.

'Great seeing you again,' he said in all seriousness, as though he hadn't been living next door for the past year.

An awkward silence followed. I was still stunned by Joy in that dress, that she'd been brazen enough to wear something so short.

'Here, let me take that,' Joy said, reaching for the moussaka. 'Roger's in the lounge, Roko. You remember your way?'

She made a cringing face as Roko made his escape. 'That was awkward,' she whispered. Then, louder, 'Come on through. Let's get rid of these plates.' She pushed past me at speed, heading for the kitchen. The lounge was already noisy with laughter. *This will be fun*, I reassured myself.

It made sense now why she had been so secretive about the dress. I'd made a passing comment about one just like it in the *Woman's Weekly* a few weeks before, saying I'd never show off my knees like that. *We'll see*, Joy replied, with a knowing look that left me feeling prudish.

'Oh my goodness, I definitely need a drink now.' Joy bent to put my moussaka in the oven. She held out her hand for my platter. 'Thanks, Jela. You're such a sweetie. These look amazing.'

'So does your dress,' I said.

'Mum whipped it up.'

Before I could answer, she was rushing for the door. I worried my *fritule* would go flying. 'Let's join the others,' she called back, leaving me in her wake.

I hung back at the lounge doorway feeling stranded, watching as Joy crossed to a table set up at the far end of the room. Roko was opposite, amongst a cluster of men in front of the fireplace. Brown beer bottles were strung along the mantelpiece, and I thought about where Pauline might have been standing at that last party and wondered whether Roko remembered this too.

'Trust you'll have another?' a man with red hair said to Roko, raising one of the brown bottles.

Roko held out his glass. 'Go on. Pour me some more of your poison.'

'C'mon!' the man said. 'Better than that Dally plonk.' Most of the men laughed.

Davor was among them and I scanned the room for Sara. My heart had sunk when Joy told me she'd invited them. I'd seen Sara a number of times since the ball, at other Dally events, and once at Marta and Stipan's, but I still felt wary around her. Joy didn't know Sara and Davor well, but she'd thought it might be easier for Roko if she invited them. There she was, at the other end of the room from the table, seated among the women on the smaller of the two couches: sleek Sara, neat black dress, her hair a soft blonde curtain around her shoulders with the ends flicking neatly under. Patsy, a friend I'd met through Joy a month or so back, sat beside her, wearing the dress she and Joy had gone shopping for. Patsy had confided how she struggled with clothes: *If only I could lose a few extra pounds.* The simple white shift dress with its lime-green flowers was a perfect choice. Marg, an old school friend of Joy's whom I'd met only once before, was perched on the larger couch, her knees angled towards the others. She waved me over. 'Look at you, Jela!' Her booming voice matched her boldly patterned dress in pink and orange tones. 'Don't you look a treat.'

Sara glanced up, rewarding me with a smile. 'Love the colour with your dark hair.'

'Style's perfect too,' said Patsy, smiling.

'And look at all you lovely ladies,' I said, feeling on show but pleased at my display of confidence. I still found it strange, especially when addressing a group, to hear myself speaking *Engleski* out loud. Marg patted the seat beside her. 'Joy lent it to me.' I whispered, relieved to sit down but still revelling in the praise heaped on me.

'Looks like your kind neighbour's bringing you a drink,' said Marg, motioning at Joy who was like a bright yellow canary flitting over. Perhaps that dress was Joy's answer for a shot of courage?

'Try it,' said Joy, thrusting a tall glass filled with an amber liquid and topped with a wedge of lemon at me. 'Pimm's and ginger ale. Our summer drink. Isn't it, girls?'

Marg nodded, raising her glass.

'First things first, though,' Joy said, pulling me to stand before I had a chance to take a sip and leading me towards the group of men. 'Jela hasn't met our lumps yet,' she called back over her shoulder.

'Steady on,' someone called out.

'Jela, meet Roger,' Joy said. 'Otherwise known as my darling husband.' She looped her arm through his. I knew he was a good-looking man, but close up he was even more striking: ice-blue eyes contrasting with dark hair and a tanned face.

'Great to meet you finally,' Roger said, holding out his hand. 'Joy's told me plenty about you.'

'And, as for everyone else,' Joy said, throwing her arm wide at the group, 'this is Marg's husband Peter.' The man was a good head shorter than the others, his face peppered with freckles. He acknowledged me with a wave and I thought how Marg must dwarf him.

'And Paul, Patsy's husband.' He was the red-haired one I'd seen earlier. He gave me a cheeky grin. 'And you've already met Davor. And Roko, of course.'

Roger moved off to the side to flick through his record collection, and Joy led me back towards the ladies. We sat on the couch, me sandwiched between Joy and Marg, and I snuck another glance at Roko. He was laughing and slapping Davor on the back, the most animated I'd ever seen him, and I conceded that perhaps Joy was right.

Marg nudged my shoulder. 'Roko looks relaxed. You must be good for him.'

'It's thanks to Joy that he's finally out,' I said, sipping at my drink. 'Nothing to do with me.'

'I'm sure it's got plenty to do with you,' said Marg, as though she couldn't be more serious. 'What do you say, Joy?'

'Happiest I've seen him in a long time,' said Joy. 'Time's a great healer though. Can't have been easy for him. They struggled getting out towards the end.'

Marg shook her head. 'She was a mess.'

It surprised me how many people knew about Roko and Pauline. Everyone I came across seemed to know something or have an opinion. I tried not to sip my drink too fast. My preference was still for wine mixed with water, but wine wasn't popular here, at least not with the locals. The Pimm's was refreshing but a little sweet for my taste. It was the first time I'd drunk alcohol at Joy's, and I couldn't help thinking about Pauline and the reason I needed to be wary myself.

Roger turned the music up. 'Blue Suede Shoes'. I knew music was his passion and that he was one of the first in the neighbourhood to own a record player.

'Roko keeps checking across the room for you,' said Marg, shimmying away in her seat to the music. 'He's been doing it all evening.'

She was starting to annoy me and I edged away. If she had been one of my friends back home I would have given her what for, but I was still so conscious of appearing rude here.

'Give her a break, Marg. You're reading into things,' said Joy, placing her hand on my knee. Marg scrunched up her nose then spun around to speak to Patsy and Sara. I wanted to hug Joy who was leaning in. 'You do look great in that dress. Roko say anything?'

Maybe it was the Pimm's, but I felt a rush of boldness. 'Told me I looked stylish.'

'Knew it would impress. The eyeshadow looks fab too.'

Marg saved me from having to say more, turning back and switching the conversation to summer holidays. Sara and Patsy joined in too. I couldn't add much, and keeping up when more than one person was speaking English was still a struggle. Besides, I'd never been on a real holiday. Rather, our family had relied on day trips to the beach for family picnics. The closest I'd come to a trip away was the refugee camp in Egypt and that one time I'd gone to Dubrovnik for that special ball.

I sipped on my drink, edging back into my seat, tapping my foot to Elvis. The men were getting louder. How did Roko feel about the drinking? And what of those strange conversations we'd had earlier; the compliment he'd given me? I glanced across, catching his own fleeting glance. Could he be attracted to me? It was difficult not to make comparisons between him and my *dragi*. Roko wasn't as socially assured: he seemed happiest standing back whereas my *dragi* loved being the centre of attention, a show-off at times. Maybe Pauline had forced Roko into the limelight too often? Or perhaps, like me, he was finding it odd, us being at Joy's house together? How would my *dragi* fit among these people? It was infuriating not being able to forget that scoundrel, but could Roko ever match what my *dragi* had meant to me? I worried that Roko and I had simply learnt to tolerate each other.

Joy nudged me. 'Roko *does* seem relaxed,' she said, breaking into a smile. 'You sure you're not putting something in his food?'

All of the girls were looking my way. 'He has been more chatty lately,' I said, trying to brush her off. 'Takes a Dally to know one, I guess.'

'You would know.' Joy slapped my leg. 'Help me with the food. You too, Patsy.' She was on her feet, clapping her hands. 'Right, folks. Grab a plate.'

'Not before time,' Pete called out. 'Our throats have been cut over here.'

'Can't see why. There's been no shortage of liquid refreshments!' Marg retorted.

'Don't take what I just said the wrong way,' I said, leaning in to Joy. 'You know I'm waiting for my *dragi*.'

'Relax,' Joy whispered. 'Always best to keep your options open.' She grabbed Patsy's hands. 'Come on, girls, let's make a train.' Patsy put her hands on Joy's hips and I followed suit behind Patsy. 'We're off!' cried Joy, her bright headband and fiery hair like a beacon up front. She wove us past the men, Patsy and me bouncing and bopping behind to the music. 'Toot, toot!' Patsy cried, as we disappeared out the lounge door all the way into the kitchen before collapsing in a heap of giggles. Joy gripped the red bench and it was an age before any of us could speak. 'Oh my goodness, that was fun!' she said, her face glowing. I hugged her, charged by the burst of energy.

Joy got busy, handing the moussaka to me and a casserole to Patsy. She led the way back to the lounge carrying a potato dish. Just before the doorway, Patsy leaned back. 'Your man at home must be pretty special. Hope he's worth the wait — you could do far worse than Roko Tomich.'

She strode off and I paused, all my fizz drained flat. It was Joy who had spilt my secret to Patsy a week or so back, letting a comment about my *dragi* slip. I should have owned up then. All I needed to say was that I'd been dumped. There would have been no need to admit I had lied, or to disclose the worst parts, but somehow I justified keeping up my charade. In part I worried about answering their questions and feeling embarrassed about my naivety, how trusting I had been. Even after eight months I was none the wiser as to how they would view me. Joy had been cryptic of late, at times joking about men and their expectations, sharing magazine articles with titles like, *How to Keep Your Man Happy*, then nudging me while referring to Roger's "appetite" as though holding the word between her index fingers. And yet, when Marg had joined us for afternoon tea, Joy nodded as though approving of Marg's comment, *serves her right,* while discussing their old school friend who had been forced to give up her baby for adoption.

But it was also my ploy to keep Joy's teasing at bay. She had been quick to pick up on the fact that the tensions between Roko and me had eased and that we were getting along much better. She loved nothing more than to make comments about how great it would be if I could stay and be neighbours for ever. I reasoned that if there was even the slightest chance Roko felt something for me I didn't want Joy's meddling — good-hearted as it might be — to frighten him off. This was all the more important once the thaw between them was likely. But now, with Patsy on my case too, I would have to tell them both the truth, but not until after the party — the last thing I needed was a scene in front of Sara.

It was difficult to find a spare inch on the table for my dish. Even after nine months, the abundance of food, especially meat, still took me by surprise. Our food at home had been basic, and Mama had done her best, but there are only so many ways to change up cabbage stew. The men piled their plates high, pulling up chairs to sit close to the table. Elvis was still playing and we women took our plates back to the couches and balanced them on our knees. The compliments flowed as we ate but I struggled to concentrate. My favourite was Sara's crayfish and prawn casserole. I told Marg I loved her pavlova, but in truth it played havoc with my churning stomach and I found it overly sweet.

After dinner, Joy and Marg insisted I go back and join the others once I'd helped take the dishes through to the kitchen. Roger was still sitting at the table, laughing raucously with Peter and Davor. Roko was chatting in a huddle by the fireplace with Sara, Patsy and Paul. I decided I'd feel braver holding my glass of Pimm's and went to retrieve it.

Davor waved out as I turned, joining me and gesturing towards the couch. 'I've been wanting to ask you more about the homeland,' he said. 'Sara and I went earlier this year. My folks are from Markarska. Sara's are from Tucepi.'

'Oh, they're beautiful places.' I was embarrassed to admit that I'd never visited either, despite their proximity, just north of Korčula, on the mainland.

'What are your thoughts on Tito?'

'What do you want to know?' I said, stalling for time, wanting to consider my answer. I looked back to the fireplace. Paul's face was ruddy, almost the colour of his hair. Roko had rolled up his sleeves, and I thought he seemed more at ease, that really he was happiest in a crumple.

'Don't worry, I won't report you,' said Davor. 'I'm interested if you think the country is better or worse off under Tito?'

Before coming to New Zealand, I would never have said a word against Tito. When Tata criticised his policies and the Party I felt embarrassed. Now I realised how much our country was still struggling.

'Well, he's a great leader,' I said, trying to read Davor's expression. 'They say the country's going from strength to strength under his rule.' I wasn't sure whether Davor would have an opinion, given Roko's reaction whenever we talked of the homeland.

'To be honest, we were surprised at how backward it was,' said Davor.

'Where did the night go?' said Sara, squeezing in beside him. 'I hardly got to talk with you, Jela.' She patted Davor's leg as if he was a dog. 'You go off and say your goodbyes while Jela and I have a chat.'

Davor moved off and Sara inched closer. 'I hear Marta's got her wish. Petra called me to say the marriage has been annulled.'

'Great news, isn't it.' I was pleased that I knew.

'Good news for you. Just the one hurdle, I hear?' She leaned in closer, staring at me as though the answer was written across my forehead.

I wrenched back. 'What do you mean, hurdle? I work for him. Nothing more.'

'Oh, come on, Jela, don't be so naive. Why else would Marta and Stipan bring you here?' She lowered her voice. 'How much do they know about this other boy?'

I blinked hard. It must have been Patsy. They had been talking for most of the evening. Joy wouldn't have said anything. She knew how I felt about Sara.

'It was just my silly way of getting the attention off me. My way to stop their teasing about Roko. There's no one else.' From Sara's expression it was clear this all sounded like excuses.

Davor returned. 'How did you think Roko was tonight?' Sara asked him.

Davor looked puzzled. 'Good. Yeah. Happy? Come on, *Draga*, we should go.' He held out his hand and pulled Sara to standing. 'Nice seeing you again, Jela.'

'Marta's been singing your praises, by the way. All the Dallies are talking. Hope it's all not in vain,' said Sara, turning back.

I watched them leave, straining to hear when they left the house. Only then did I make my move. Roko and Paul were back with the other men at the table. There was no sign of Patsy. I called from the front door, 'Thanks, Joy. I have to get going.'

Joy rushed from the kitchen. 'Are you okay, Jela?'

'Got a headache. I'll be fine.'

'Only if you're sure?' said Joy, closer now, her face concerned.

I was already at the base of the steps. 'Thanks. It was great. I'll see you next week.'

Without looking back I wrapped my arms across my chest then walked like a whip, cracking along the footpath towards Marta and Stipan's. The wind had picked up and the sky looked heavy, threatening to rain. Word would surely get back to Roko and the rest of the family, that I'd been in love with someone back home. There was no knowing how they would react or the questions they might ask, but I was certain Marta and Stipan would not be happy. My mind felt crammed with Sara's comments. Keeping close the reason I had been sent away was now even more important. Damn Tata! If only he could have been more flexible, less judgemental.

Mala darted from somewhere across the front lawn to greet me, winding her tail around my legs, purring as I hesitated on the front porch. When I opened the front door, she scurried up the hallway, a black streak.

My rosary beads felt like rocks between my fingers, and no amount of polishing could rub the problem away: Sara would spill my secret. The only remaining question was who she would choose to tell first. My secrets and lies were fake pearls set to unravel from their cheap string to leave me exposed and my life in tatters again.

Throughout the long weekend following the party I existed in a state of dread, listening out for visitors, certain that at any moment Marta might pull me aside and insist on a phone call home.

At Sunday Mass I snuck furtive peeks sideways, scanning the pews up front again, willing Sara away. Somehow I was saved, although it felt as though my discomfort was reflected for all to see by the whitewashed walls in the modern spare space. The high row of windows at the sides were unadorned squares of glass through which light entered without allowing a glance outside. I would have given anything to be back in our church at home where the stained-glass windows and intricately carved stonework spoke in pictures, encouraging your mind to wander. At St Patrick's, Panmure, there was no such respite. For the hour-long duration of Mass I squirmed, forcing my mind to the prayers and rote routines: standing, sitting, kneeling, the long march to take communion, habits which saw time pass. Afterwards, when we gathered in huddles on the concrete pad outside the church, I hung off the usual bunch of girls, forcing my eyes away from the flight of steps leading to the cemetery. Those gravestones were a line-up of bishops, each dignitary topped by a gleaming white cross, each one seeming to pass judgement.

~ ⚮ ~

I made seeing Joy my first priority on Tuesday morning. She was in the outhouse bent over Betty, slotting the clothes through the rollers like letters through a post box. At first, she didn't hear me and I hung back, determined not to startle her. That machine could eat fingers given its efficiency at squeezing out water. Joy wore another new dress, as short as the one from the party. Perhaps her mama had been busy over the weekend? I wiped my hands down the front of my new dress, another of Marta's hand-me downs, knowing I should feel grateful. I knocked and Joy straightened and turned, flicking the switch on the wall to silence the whirr of the rollers.

'Jela! What a nice surprise. I was worried. You seemed rattled on Friday. Is everything okay?'

'Don't worry about me,' I said, before realising I was patching things over again. 'But I need to tell you something. Something I'm not proud of.'

Joy frowned and brushed her hair from her forehead, resettling the strands into the neat shape of her bob.

'It's silly,' I said. 'But I lied. About my *dragi.*' I hid my face in my hands. 'There's no one coming. He let me down and I was too embarrassed to admit it. I'm so sorry, especially after all the fuss I made.'

Joy pulled me into a hug. 'Jela, don't be silly. I'm not surprised, you know. I had my doubts. Why didn't you say? That must have been dreadful. What a wretch! Has he only just told you?'

'No, a while back,' I said, fudging the fact that he'd never written once. I pulled back and looked her in the eye. 'I couldn't admit I'd lost him. That there was no one. I felt less attractive, like I wasn't good enough to have a boyfriend. And now with Roko . . .' I hid my face again.

Joy pulled me close. 'Are you finally admitting you and Roko are sweet on each other?'

'Maybe.' I took in the laundry shelf behind Joy's head: the pack of Rinso washing powder, a cake of Sunlight soap on a chipped saucer, a scrubbing brush on a stack of David's nappies. 'Not sure.'

'It's perfect!' said Joy. 'Don't know why it's taken you so long.'

'But it's not that simple. And now I'm in trouble.'

Joy scrunched her nose, frowning, her freckles worked into a hard line.

'Patsy must have said about my *dragi*. Sara asked me about him at the party. She'll definitely tell Marta now.'

'But what's the problem?'

'They'll think badly of me. I don't know if Tata told them, and they might think me untruthful. It's difficult to explain. They won't be happy I've had a boyfriend. What's the English? *Na povratak u ljubavi* is how we say it at home, that I'm bouncing back, settling for second-best. That's the last thing they'd want for their precious son.'

'You're reading too much into things. Your *dragi* was just your boyfriend and you've been here, what?' Joy counted the months on her fingers. 'Gosh! It's over eight months already. Marta will understand. She was young once. These things happen. They'll be fine.'

'I hope you're right. Dallies can be over-protective about matters of the heart — especially the parents.' I paused, searching Joy's face. 'To be honest, I'm not sure how Roko will react either.'

'Roko will be fine, trust me.' Joy's face turned serious. 'He'd be the last one to worry. Take it one step at a time. *Polako, polako.*'

I hugged her. 'I'm sorry for lying, and thanks. I wouldn't have survived here without you.'

'Well, it's time for my best advice yet.' Joy's expression was impish. 'Go catch that Roko. He's a good one. Worth the chase.'

NOVEMBER

I t took another two weeks, into November. Roko and I had been skirting around each other, perfecting our strange dance. It was as though, having crossed to a place of greater familiarity before Joy's party, we had lost the knack of feeling comfortable, neither of us knowing the rules any more. Our conversations had reverted to the banal, but each exchange carried an undercurrent, a suggestion that we were on the cusp of change.

Roko instigated this change, surprising me after our Friday night meal. 'I've been meaning to ask,' he said, from the chair in front of the fireplace. 'Dad's loaned me the car. Can I take you for a drive tomorrow?'

Somehow I managed to answer as though this was nothing out of the ordinary. 'I'd love that. What time shall I be ready?'

'I thought about ten, if that fits with your plans?'

'Ten should work fine,' I said, smiling at the absurdity and moving into the kitchen. Mass on Sunday was the only fixed plan I ever had.

After tidying the few remaining dishes I made to leave. 'I'm off. See you tomorrow. Don't be late!' My heart felt as though it was perched on my chest, pounding at my own front door so hard I worried Roko might hear it.

He waved his arm, not bothering to turn around. 'I'll be there. Make sure you're ready.'

I bolted for the back porch, desperate to get some fresh air. The moon floated high, a luminous ball with clouds stretched across its face. The evening was mild but even so, shivers travelled up my spine. I reassured myself: the danger period had passed. Surely Sara would have already said something to Marta or Petra? Perhaps Tata *had* told them about my *dragi* and they were relieved it was over?

Closer to Marta and Stipan's, I allowed myself the luxury of feeling excited about what the next day might bring, smiling as I reflected on some of the funny moments over the past weeks: his hand brushing mine as he handed me his dinner plate; both reaching for the salt shaker then hiding behind a gabble of words with no meaning or context — saying plenty and yet nothing at all. I did a little dance up the pathway but at the front porch my stomach gripped and gnawed. Why should I assume everything had smoothed over? Marta could just as likely be waiting, ready to drill me with questions. I pushed at the door, trying not to make a sound.

'That you, Gabrijela?' Marta peered from around the bathroom door. 'How's our Roko?'

'Fine,' I said, my voice a little too sharp.

'Hmmph! Stipan tells me Roko's taking you for a drive in the morning. You'll do well to get your beauty sleep. *Laku noć.*' She closed the door with a sharp click.

'*Laku noć,*' I whispered, opening the door to my bedroom, my prayers ready to flow.

My fingers danced over my rosary beads as I spoke with God: *Please give me strength for what lies ahead; let me know that what I feel for Roko is true and that I can trust my feelings — that I'm not settling for second best.*

～ ～

After breakfast I kept my bedroom door ajar, listening out for Roko. I wished I had something new to wear, something fresh like the trim three-quarter-length pants Joy's mum had just made her — pedal-pushers, Joy called them. My navy-and-white-striped dress would have to do, the one I'd worn on the plane coming over, the one with the flyaway skirt. I pushed aside the Marta curtains — not enough wind to cause problems — then crossed back to the mirror to touch up my lipstick, cringing at my reflection, remembering how wide-eyed I'd been during my first dreadful days here.

'Jela,' Marta called. 'Our Roko's waiting.'

How had I not heard him? I gathered up the handbag Hana had given me recently and made him wait another minute. Marta, Stipan and Roko were crowded close to the back door when I joined them. I hung back by the kitchen and Roko flashed me a nervous smile. He had taken care with his appearance too. His hair still looked damp and he wore the smart shirt from Joy's party, loose this time over a singlet and shorts, the sleeves rolled up. His milky-white feet were in clunky brown sandals, the same type Stipan wore.

'Ah, Jela,' said Stipan, his face breaking into a kind smile. 'You're off on a special trip today?'

'Lucky me,' I said, eyes down, unable to look, my mind cartwheeling.

Would those feet ever darken and catch up? There must be hope. Stipan had worn the heavy quarry boots for years and yet didn't flaunt the same tan line.

'Time to get going. Don't want to waste this weather,' said Roko, breaking the awkward silence.

Marta stared at me. 'We'll still be here. Did you forget about food, Jela?' There was no time to answer. 'Lucky I've packed a picnic. It's in the boot.'

I wanted to be grateful, but why was she always so difficult? Pauline dashed across my mind again.

Roko pecked Marta on the cheek. 'Thanks, Mum. Let's hit the track, Jela.'

From Mount Wellington we skirted around the outskirts of Ellerslie and Remuera, across the Orakei basin, past the Hobson Bay boat sheds lined up like toy sheds and onto Tamaki Drive. The Waitemata Harbour sparkled like a jewel and the landmarks I was accustomed to seeing on my Sunday drives with Stipan and Marta looked different, as though I was seeing them with new eyes: Rangitoto, the city's most distinctive volcano, was now a hump-shaped lizard lazing in the harbour.

'You okay?' Roko's right arm was bent out the window, his hand guiding the steering wheel.

'Yes,' I said, smiling. 'Always happiest by the sea.'

Roko stared ahead and we drove in silence. I gazed out the window at the city bursting with colour. Joy's summer had arrived. People were strolling along the waterfront, some with pets. Families gathered on picnic rugs on the beach, or in the parks — children running, chasing balls, making sandcastles, some out swimming. Perhaps I should have brought my bathing suit? No. The embarrassment of getting changed. How would he look at *me*?

I focused instead on all the boats making the most of the slight breeze. The harbour was a playground of sails, and I felt that same deep-seated ache whenever I remembered the sights and smells of my homeland. It felt like such an age and I worried what I had forgotten, whether my memories were true.

We wound our way towards St Heliers, past the stone sea walls that bore Stipan's signature, his special pattern of rocks. I'd come to think of them as his stake in the ground, his claim on foreign soil, in this country he now called home.

I was pleased I'd had the sense not to wear nylons when, at the beach, Roko suggested we take off our shoes. While he found a safe place for them up by the bank, I waited on some flattened black rocks, fixing my eyes on the water, drinking it all in. The rocks were pitted with crevices and small holes, rough under my feet, reminding me again of home.

'Beautiful, isn't it?' Roko called out. He was flapping his arms at a seagull that was strutting towards our shoes. The bird swooped off with an angry caw.

'Meanie,' I called, watching him pick his way back over the short flow of rocks.

I nudged him with my hip when he drew alongside. He held out his hand and I took it as though this was the most natural thing, feeling as free as the bird circling above us now. We stepped onto the sand and wandered down to put our feet in the water. The waves crept in, quiet little rolls, retreating with just the gentlest of tugs. I dropped Roko's hand and ran ahead, splashing and kicking the water into a spray. He picked up some stones and skimmed them across the flat water. When I joined him again, I threaded my fingers through his and we walked on towards the cliffs at the eastern end of the beach. There was no need to fill the silence with talk but every so often he reassured me with a smile.

A few families were gathered on picnic rugs at the sheltered bay. Buckets, spades and beach paraphernalia strewn about. 'Achilles Point's just around there,' said Roko, pointing past some children who were clambering over the rocks to the side. 'If the tide's right, we can get around.'

We picked our way past the children, some bent low inspecting rock pools. We needed to take care because some of the rocks were sharper there. I pointed towards some small caves up ahead. 'There were hundreds of caves in the hills around Luka. Exploring them was one of our favourite games when I was younger.'

'Mountain caves?'

'I guess. They were set into the steep cliffs. We tried to find a new one each time. Who knew what you might discover. Sometimes it was things left from the war.'

'Like guns?'

'Occasionally. Josip found one. But more likely it was scraps of ammunition. Sometimes old clothing, or an empty food can.'

'We made do with sticks shaped like guns,' said Roko. 'Dad always said we were lucky living here. To be honest, I had no idea.'

'Before coming here, I didn't realise what we'd gone without. It wasn't all bad, though, and there's still so much I love. It wasn't until I was older that I wanted to escape. I miss it.' I turned to stare at the sea.

Roko pulled me close. 'You're a brave girl, Jela,' he said, caressing my cheek with his finger.

I could barely breathe. His lonely mole, just below the line of his jaw, twitched as he bent to kiss me; a delicious kiss, a taste of what might be possible. Afterwards, I buried my face into the warmth of his shoulder. It felt like an eternity since I'd been held close like that but I couldn't relax. Feelings of shame pricked all the way down my spine and I edged away.

'I want to take you to a secret place for our picnic,' he said, not seeming to notice my discomfort, his eyes bright like caramel toffee, his expression playful.

He took my hand and led me back over the rocks and along the beach to collect our footwear. I forced my mind back to the present, determined not to ruin the moment again. When he gestured towards the car I stared at him, puzzled, having assumed our picnic would be somewhere on the beach. Roko drove the car up a series of tight bends and no matter how much I badgered him, he remained silent.

'We'll walk from here,' he said, pulling over and flashing me a mischievous grin. From the boot he took a small case and a crimson-and-green tartan rug. 'We're off to Dingle Dell. Coming?' He handed me the rug.

I followed him, ducking my head to squeeze through a gap in a small copse of trees. A gravel path bordered by palms and ferns wound its way uphill; there was a densely planted area either side. I paused to examine a bright green fern frond, pulling it close, intrigued by the tight coil close to the trunk. It was as intricate as Mama's lace work.

'Our koru,' said Roko. 'The beginning of a brand-new fern. The Maori people say it's a symbol for life. How life changes but stays the same.'

I nodded, impressed by his knowledge of nature and was about to ask more, to test his know-how on some of the other plants, but Roko was striding ahead, the little suitcase so at odds with his bulky frame. I followed, clutching the rug close, feeling as though I was being drawn into a magical world. It was cooler in there. The sun's bright disc was no longer in command. Instead, the light was whittled down to threads that pierced the tangled canopy to paint dappled shadows on the path. I had the strong sense that nothing would have the luxury of drying out in that place. The air held a tang of dampness, not an unpleasant smell but one that brought to mind saturated moss, or moisture beads clinging to the undersides of the fern fronds. I was transported back to that cave, to those final moments with my *dragi. No!* I squeezed my eyes shut, determined to banish those memories, rushing to catch Roko just a short distance ahead.

'What is this place?' I asked, puffing a little as I drew closer.

'Patience.' Roko turned back and grinned before pushing on up the hill.

At the top, the path opened onto a small grassy clearing that was bathed in sunlight. There was a peep out to the cornflower-blue sea and we were the only ones there.

'It's perfect,' I said, 'but tell me the story. How did you find it?'

Roko smiled. 'Dad liked bringing us here. He was asked by some of the locals — men he worked with while building the sea walls — to help with the project of replanting it. It was nothing more than a swamp originally and it's a place he's proud of. He also used to say that the view was a reminder of home. I thought you might appreciate it too.'

I dropped the rug and flung my arms around him. Suddenly I didn't feel homesick and being here with Roko felt perfect. He laid out the rug and unclipped the hinges on the case. Everything was in order: plates the colour of butter and a selection of cutlery with bone handles all held by some leather straps in the lid. A thermos, cups, and containers of food were packed into the base: ham sandwiches, a selection of fruit and thick slices of gingerbread loaf. Marta had thought of everything, even small containers of butter, milk and sugar.

As usual, Roko was intent on devouring his food and we enjoyed our picnic with little need of conversation. When a fantail danced close, landing on the suitcase lid before flitting away again, I confided how I'd thought of those little birds as friends when I'd first arrived, how they were a reminder of the swallows that used to nest in the eaves of our houses at home. Roko smiled and I revelled in this new ease between us. After eating he lazed back on the rug, his arms crossed over his stomach. He reminded me of a contented cat, like Mala stretched in front of the fire. I assumed he had dozed off and for a fleeting moment considered stretching out alongside him but then cautioned myself, *polako, polako*. It would feel too intimate, a step too far. My hands felt clammy, and I smeared my palms on the rug as though to wipe away my disgust. I knew so much about the ways of love, or lust, and yet I had lost all sense of appropriateness. Would I ever regain this? Regain my sense of self-worth? That man, in robbing me of my innocence had also thrown away the rule book.

I gazed out to sea, feeling the heat from the sun and forcing my mind towards things I could control. Anticipating telling Joy my news, and writing to Nada and Antica, Mama as well. I pictured their reactions, Mama's smile. How wonderful to share something positive — to make her proud again.

'Jela?'

I turned to him, surprised at the strained note to his voice. He was propped on his elbow now but facing away towards the bushes. I leant across to touch his shoulder but he flinched, and I withdrew my hand as though I'd been burnt. It was some time before he spoke and when he did he was still turned away, his back rigid.

'Does it worry you about Pauline? That I've been with her?'

I took a moment to answer, weighing up whether this was also my moment to confess, whether I felt courageous enough. The little fantail danced close and I stared out to sea, knowing I had everything to lose. Even though I would have to broach the subject eventually I didn't want to ruin this day.

Roko turned to face me, looking worried, as though he was the one needing rescuing. My words spilled out. 'It makes no difference to me.' I reached across again, my fingertips feathering his forearm with whisper strokes. 'But how would you feel if I had stories of my own?'

It was done. I made sure not to draw back, to look straight into those eyes which had often held such sadness, to make certain he understood me, that there could be no misunderstanding. He blinked as though puzzled before hauling himself to sit, shaking his head as if to clear away any thought of me with someone else. Perhaps he thought of me as another problem? Maybe I had shocked him? I inched my arm back, staring at my hands cradled now in my lap as though nursing a bird with a broken wing. His stare felt too intense. I hadn't felt this exposed since Tata found out about me. Perhaps Roko was no different? Perhaps he thought of me as soiled goods too.

'You've surprised me, that's for sure,' he said, after the longest time. 'Knocked the wind out of my sails. Hadn't thought you the type.' He leant over and made a clumsy effort to pull me close, but I shrugged him off, holding his eye, fuming inside. A look of shock crossed his face. 'C'mon, Jela. Of course it doesn't matter. I'd be a right arse to criticise, wouldn't I?'

I snapped my head towards the water, still seething. *Not the type!* Perhaps he thought I had no spark? That photo — Pauline's leg cocked towards him, his look, her smile — was I so different? My eyes smarted, my confidence feeling rocked to its core. But how did I want men to view me? What would Roko's reaction have been if I had been brazen enough to lie beside him?

'*Katastrofa!*' I said, under my breath, swiping my hand out towards the horizon, as though giving that other man a slap across the face too. Again, I begrudged the bubble surrounding me. The thin iridescent film distorting my perceptions, keeping me at arm's length from the subtleties and nuances of this country. But Roko must realise how difficult my confession was? How could he show so little compassion given what he had been through too?

The sea was blurry now but I continued to stare, furious about life being so unfair, about double standards and how much easier it was for the men. I thought about Branko, my first boyfriend, the one I'd sent packing when he thought he had the right to tell me what to do, to keep me in a box, contained. Tata was the same and perhaps Roko was no different. Surely I hadn't come all this way, sacrificed so much, to end up with the same small-mindedness? With my *dragi* it could have been so different. The thought was no sooner out when I realised how warped it was, how that man had twisted my perceptions. I punched my clenched fist onto the rug.

Roko inched closer and squeezed my shoulder. 'Come here, you,' he said. 'Get off your high horse and tempt me with another kiss. I'll listen to your story properly then.' He rubbed my back. 'I'm sorry, Jela. I was an arse.'

I was still bristling when I turned to him. He brushed his lips against my forehead. 'It pays to be totally sure about these matters,' he murmured, before kissing me properly.

He asked no further questions. I wanted it to feel right but the magic had vaporised and all my fears which I had kept hidden for so long wrested their way to the surface. I knew it. Of course it was true. This curse was mine to bear, my penance, God's punishment. And any shot at happiness would always be plagued by it.

We wasted no time in packing up and returning to the car. On the drive home the very air we breathed felt laced with peculiarity. The spell had been broken. Even if there was a chance of me breaking this jinx, I would be a fool not to be cautious about being let down again. Worst of all, I couldn't erase Roko's expression of disappointment, the sense that I'd failed him, that I should have been stronger.

DECEMBER

It was my first public date with Roko and my first time at a race meet. I was with Roko's family, and together we took up several rows near the back of a huge grandstand at the Ellerslie Racecourse. With all the finery surrounding me, I felt nervous, on show, conscious of his family watching my every move as though I might behave differently now that I was Roko's girl. We were packed into the stand, a sea of hats, our knees at each other's backs, a riotous ripple of colour, like stacked dominoes poised to topple forward down to the race track. Simun had told me earlier in the week that he would be coming with his family. Most of Auckland must be here, I thought, scanning the stand, grateful for Joy's advice: *It's a day not to miss, a social event on the calendar — everyone will be dressed to the nines.*

I was so proud of my new cream shoes with the smart bows that Joy had helped me pick out with my saved pin money. She would be in the crowd somewhere, *enjoying a flutter.* I searched the sea of faces again, desperate to catch a glimpse of her, thinking how Mama would love to be here. If only I could transport her, even for a day, and see her eyes open wide like saucers. There was one face I didn't want to see. I still worried that my luck was about to run out, that the curse was real. I'd only seen Sara once since Joy's party — at Mass, where she had ignored me. One day at a time I reassured myself, *polako, polako*.

Roko was seated directly behind and I turned, aching for a smile. His nose was buried in his race book. Petra and Marta chatted at the end of my row, Petra waggling her hands in her white gloves. She wore a shiny black-and-white polka-dot dress, one I'd never seen before. Marta was all in red, her new hat with its thin rim was like an upturned saucepan. A single ruched flower, the size of one of Stipan's dahlias, was stuck where the handle might have been and it bobbed about as she talked.

Hana, in her fresh mint-green sundress paired with white gloves, sat beside me. I thought those gloves so luxurious, something that a queen might wear. Having never imagined myself owning something so frivolous, I now coveted them, secretly adding them to my wish list. Tracy, Zoran's mystery girlfriend, sat on the other side. I'd been informed by Hana that she was just two years older than me, but she seemed sophisticated and much older than that. Her short orange shift dress, one like Joy's, was sure to draw comment from the rest of the family.

As though on cue, Hana leaned close. 'Take a look at Tracy's hairdo. What do you think?'

'Very modern,' I said, keeping my answer neutral, trying to read Hana's face.

'Enjoys being the centre of attention,' said Hana, nodding as though to affirm her knowing look. 'No wonder Zoran kept her hidden for so long.'

I glanced behind again. Roko's nose was still buried. Like all the other men in the row, he was dressed in his suit. Stipan wore his smart felt hat and even Hana's two young sons were like mini businessmen with their grey serge shorts tightened with fabric belts, shirts tucked in and grey socks pulled up to their knees. Petra's three daughters were all dressed in pretty party dresses teemed with white ankle socks with lacy frills. Both Kate and Nick had joined us. Kate, in her smart lemon-coloured jacket and skirt, had one of Petra's girls either side of her.

Tracy nudged me. 'Marta's the stop sign and Petra's the conductor,' she whispered. 'Won't get much past them.'

I stifled my laugh with my hand. Secretly, though, I coveted Marta's hat. My head felt so bare and plain, and I had already decided a hat would be my next purchase, before the gloves. I flexed my ankles remembering my new shoes, a perfect match for my navy striped dress.

Roko tapped me on the shoulder. 'You okay?' he mouthed, beaming when I nodded yes.

I turned to face the track again, feeling lightheaded. It was a month since our picnic, but I still sought his affirmation, his assurance that he hadn't reconsidered. I found it impossible to push aside the fear that I was a passing convenience, a fad. If the way Roko kissed me was anything to go by, then 'soiled goods' couldn't have been further from his mind, but then my *dragi* had been no different. It was obvious Roko found me confusing at times. He couldn't hide his hurt expression when I put up the shutters and closed him out. I had no warning when these feelings might strike to ruin a tender moment — me turning away, becoming matter-of-fact — and every night I prayed that Roko would focus on the beautiful moments, the times when I felt free to be myself and send my fears packing, the times when our love felt right.

All the same, I knew it was madness not to have a contingency plan. The niggle about how much his family knew of my past life was a constant worry, and with the prospect of Sara still lingering close, I'd been trawling through my options, even though the thought terrified me. I could trust Joy to help me find somewhere else to live but getting a new job would be difficult. If it came to it, though, I would have to find a way.

Again I took in all that was new: The streams of well-dressed people, the complicated patterns of gleaming white rails and manicured flower beds, the cars and umbrellas and yet more crowds of people, many jammed inside the centre of the track — some racing from one set of rails to another, cheering their horses on. The race master spoke so fast that I couldn't understand a word. I had asked Roko about the miniature men and he'd been unable to hide his amusement when he explained they were jockeys. I loved how their vibrant silks contrasted with their constrained white jodhpurs and shiny black boots.

There had been a number of races already. The horses, all tagged by numbers, had thundered around the track, hooves flying, their jockeys perched like flies. I struggled to tell them apart and their colours, so distinctive close up, blurred on the far rails. It was never clear to me how many times the horses would go around the track before finishing. I'd made a fool of myself in one of the earlier races, clapping and cheering, thinking the race was finished, when in fact it was only partway through. Hana and Tracy had teased me, but I'd learned now to gauge where the race was at from the fervour of the crowd, or by how many words the race master tried to cram in, or by the way the jockeys lifted their white bottoms in the air, tensing their knees while urging their charges on.

Roko tapped me on the shoulder again, flapping his race book. I expected he wanted to explain more of his secret information about the horses and their form.

'Time to try out your betting skills,' he said. 'Shall we go see the horses up close?'

I picked my way past all the knees to join Roko at the end of the row. He guided me down the central concrete steps, his hand at my back. The morning haze had burned off to a blue-sky special. I shielded my eyes against the flat glare, and we weaved our way through the crowds towards the birdcage enclosure for a last look at the horses before they went off to race. We leant against the white railing, and Roko held his magic race book out front, pointing at each horse and at the information on the page. The trainers, all turned out like businessmen in suits and hats, paraded the ten or so horses around the ring. Their charges were brushed to a high sheen and up close they looked powerful, lean and keen and strong. It seemed to me that those horses held all the cards: it was them leading the men to a business deal, not the other way around. I had no need for Roko's details.

'You can tell a lot from looking,' I said.

Roko raised his eyebrows and I could tell he thought me naive, that I knew nothing about horses and betting. I didn't let on that I'd chosen my horse the moment she entered the ring — a chestnut mare with a lustrous coat and a white streak running down her nose like a lightning bolt. I'd noticed the way she pricked up her ears and nodded when the trainer leant in to pat her neck. She was strong and ready to run the race of her life. I could just tell.

'I like the look of number fourteen,' I said.

Roko checked in his magic book. 'Red Glare. No past form.'

'That's the one. You'd better show me how to place a bet.'

Roko frowned. 'Keep your money in your purse. Might as well back a donkey.'

I said nothing. Fourteen was the sum of five and nine and having nearly made it through 1959, if this horse could overcome the others in the race, it would be a sign. Roko led me over to the stand of totes in the area behind the grandstand where we waited in line at the row of small windows. I clutched my money in my hand, and when we got to the front the woman behind the counter leant forward, close to the glass window.

'What'll it be?' she said through a cut-out hole.

I pushed my ten shillings under the slot. 'Number 14. For a win, please.'

She pushed a ticket back. 'Good luck, Missy.'

We walked down to the front rails to watch the race. The starting pistol cracked and the horses launched forward. I strained to see Red Glare but it was impossible. The noise was deafening and it was only when they came down the final straight that I picked out the race master's words: *And, number fourteen. Number fourteen, Red Glare is ahead by half a length. Red Glare . . . Red Glare . . . she wins!* I jumped up and down pumping my fist in the air.

'Looks like I should keep you on,' said Roko, grudgingly. He pulled me into an awkward hug.

I rubbed my hands together like an excited child, knowing that his pride would be dented. 'Goes to show you shouldn't be too calculating. That gambles can pay off. Horses are a lot like men.' The look in his eyes told me he understood my meaning.

My winnings, twenty-five pounds, were a fortune. With that much money I could buy the hat of my dreams, something much nicer than Marta's. Best of all though, Red Glare had thrown me a lifeline. If things didn't work out, I could afford to rent a room somewhere, take my time finding a new job.

We re-joined Roko's family. They had laid out picnic rugs under the shade of some lacy silver birch trees in the car park. Petra and Andrew's car was parked up close to shield off the spot and a large brown bottle of DB stood like a trophy on the car's roof. The men, suit jackets and ties off, shirtsleeves rolled up, leant against the car, each holding a picnic glass of beer. Stipan and Franjo puffed on cigarettes. The five children were sprawled on a tartan rug, the boys with their socks off. They were in fits of laughter at Hana's youngest, Peter, who was wiggling his arms and legs in the air like a beetle on its back.

'No more giggle juice for you lot!' Stipan called.

'We've got a winner,' Roko announced. 'Seems Jela can pick 'em. She's just won twenty-five quid.'

The children cheered and raised their colourful plastic cups.

'Bravo!' called Tracy who was chatting with Hana beside one of the rugs. Hana clapped too.

'Keep her on, then, Roko,' said Franjo, raising his glass.

'Who was your pick, Jela?' Stipan asked.

'Red Glare,' I said, turning to the children and giving them my best impression of an angry stare. Peter let out a peel of laughter. My sense of empowerment felt wonderful, as though my winnings were a cloak of armour.

Marta, Petra and Kate were busy unpacking containers of food from the picnic baskets. 'Well done, Jela,' Kate called out.

I walked across to help with the food. 'Beginner's luck?' said Petra, stretching out her white-gloved hand to pass me a plate of ham sandwiches.

'A little luck goes a long way,' said Kate, winking.

'Luck and good judgement,' I said, flashing Petra a smug smile. I pointed to the empty rug beside the children. 'Shall I put the food there?'

'Thanks.' Petra's voice was clipped.

I'd offered to make food, but Marta had insisted *it's all covered.* Her comments from a few weeks back still stung: *Baking's a skill you either have or you don't. Better to focus on getting the language right.* I wondered if Marta would ever allow me to contribute. It was no consolation that Tracy hadn't been asked to bring anything either. Regardless, there was an impressive selection: Marta's gigantic bacon-and-egg pie, Petra's shortbread and slab of fruit cake, punnets of fresh strawberries which Hana had collected from a stall in Henderson, and a mountain of sandwiches made by Kate.

'Come and eat before the sun ruins it,' said Marta, clapping her hands like a school mistress.

'Would any of you ladies like a shandy?' Stipan called over.

'Yes. Lovely, Dad,' said Petra.

I didn't know what a shandy was. Normally I would have asked Hana, but she was engrossed talking to Tracy. I decided to risk asking Petra. Maybe Hana was right in saying that sometimes Petra felt left out, that I should give her a chance.

'What's a shandy?' I asked in a low voice.

'A mix of beer and lemonade. It's refreshing — why not try it?'

She sounded pleased to be asked, and after getting my food I made a point of sitting next to her on the rug. I was still feeling charged from all the adrenalin racing through me. Roko delivered our drinks and I flashed him a smile.

'Živjeli!' I said, clinking Petra's cup with mine.

'And to you,' she said.

I took a sip of the drink. Petra was right. The combination of cold and sweet was refreshing and I hadn't realised I was so thirsty.

'Our Roko seems happy,' she said.

'I'm happy too.' If this was all it took to get Petra on my side I'd been a fool for waiting so long.

'I trust he's not playing second fiddle?' she said, under her breath, wagging her white index finger. 'Sara told me you're stringing along someone else back home.'

My heart raced, and my cheeks started to burn. Why had I sat next to her? 'I'm very fond of your brother,' I said, willing my voice not to waver. My nerves jangled as though electricity was pulsing through me. What would it take to be accepted by this family? Petra gave me a withering stare and I wanted to throw my shandy in her stony face. I might as well have handed myself on a plate for her to cut me up into tiny pieces.

'Do Mum and Dad know about your secret man? I can't imagine they would've subsidised your living here if they'd known the truth.'

Red Glare was back and I felt a rush of determination. I could either accept the curse or fight it. Now I had the wherewithal to live wherever I might choose, there was no need to pander to Petra. 'Why don't you ask them, Petra? In fact, why don't you ask Roko what he thinks?'

For a moment she looked shocked, then the old Petra returned, making it clear she couldn't bear the sight of me, her ponytail flicking like Marta's fly swat as she turned away.

I scrambled to my feet, desperate to escape, knocking over my drink. The pale amber liquid dribbled in slow motion across the rug and seeped under Petra's polka-dot skirt.

Moments later, Petra was on her feet as well. 'Oooh! Yuck,' she said, patting at her wet skirt. She pulled off her gloves and threw them on the ground like rubbish.

Marta rushed across with a pile of serviettes. 'Has our Jela been a little clumsy?' said Marta, dabbing at Petra's bottom. 'Too excitable after your big win? Don't worry, *Draga*, it will dry in a flash. I'm sure we can get the stain out.'

'Who cares about the stain?' said Petra, lowering her voice. 'How much did you know about *our* Jela? Apparently, she's stringing a man along at home.'

For a moment there was silence. 'Come over here, please, Roko,' I said, my voice sounding loud and brave although my legs felt like jelly. 'Your sister's got something to say.'

Petra shook her head. Everyone stared our way but nobody talked, not even the children. Roko placed his picnic tumbler on the roof of the car and stepped forward.

'Really?' said Marta, her voice high-pitched. 'I didn't know this. Is it true, Jela?'

It was too late for stories. The truth was my only option. I shuffled close to Marta and Petra and said under my breath, 'There was someone. I thought he was coming, but it's over. He let me down.'

'How well did you know this man?' said Marta, outraged. She glanced towards the children and when she turned back her face was twisted into a scowl. 'I hope not *too well*,' she muttered.

Roko was beside me now, his arm around my shoulders drawing me close. Having felt so brave I was now close to tears. 'What's the problem?' he asked.

I stared at the trampled buttercups and daisies feeling certain that now the Tomić family suspected it, they would want nothing more to do with me.

'I was just telling Mum about Jela's *other* man back home,' said Petra, pleased with herself. 'I thought you should know before you took things further. It's not the best way to start off again, is it?'

'And,' Roko said, 'what's the problem? What makes you think I wouldn't already know?' He squeezed my shoulder but I didn't dare look up.

'You want to be careful, Roko,' said Marta. 'Don't settle for second best.'

'Jela is the best thing that's ever happened to me, so stop your meddling. Both of you.'

I couldn't look at Marta and Petra, but I squeezed Roko around his waist, feeling a rush of pride. Another of Mama's sayings played in my head: *doće maca na vratanca* — the cat always comes to the tiny door. *What goes around comes around, Petra.*

Without another word, Roko ambled back to join the men by the car. Marta and Petra bustled off to the picnic baskets under the trees. Kate joined me, pulling me to one side. 'Your story's not so different from mine. I wish you all the best. You seem a great match.'

Our stories were similar although I doubted Kate would have a chapter to forget like my own. But unlike Kate, I was grateful to have been given the opportunity to get to know Roko *malo po malo,* little by little. I thought again how Kate must have felt when she first arrived, and about my own first impressions of Roko. It was strange thinking about Tata's role in all of this. But even if my coming to New Zealand had been a setup, and Tata *had* been complicit in the tangle of mistruths which had led me to Roko, it made no difference — I would never, ever, be able to forgive him.

I thought about my winnings, that wad of possibility, the freedom they could buy me. Ever since my picnic with Roko I'd been tossing around the same questions. Was I settling for second best? Rushing into another bad decision? Choosing a life that was the same as what I'd been running from on the other side of the world? I hadn't yet told Roko the full story, and I wasn't sure if I'd ever feel brave enough. And what if my *dragi* did show up with an explanation? How would I feel? It was as though at times, that man still had me under his spell.

There were too many questions and only one certainty. Roko might not have all the charisma of that other man, but he had just stood up for me in a way my *dragi* never had, even when I had needed him to most. I thought back over the year that had been. How that persimmon tree was heavy again with bright green leaves. How, despite autumn wreaking havoc that tree had flaunted its bounty like beacons of hope through into winter. If I could let my doubts fall away, let them wither to dust, then just as spring predictably follows winter with new life, everything might set hard and fast in its rightful place — even by the next summer.

LUISA, 1989

AUCKLAND & YUGOSLAVIA

JANUARY

L uisa storms onto the front porch of Mike's flat, a dilapidated Grey Lynn villa. *He won't get away with this.* She pounds her fist on the wooden door which now feels more like a barricade. *Where the hell is he?* She's hardly slept all night. If he was out training he'd be back. It takes all her self-control not to yell out. It wouldn't do for the neighbours to hear. Gossip's the last thing Luisa needs. A childhood spent at the Dally club educated her on that. She learnt early on to keep her personal life close and not disclose any tantalising titbits to be shared among the well-meaning ladies, many of whom are Mum's friends. Mike hasn't been to the club. She couldn't bear the raised eyebrows — Dally boys are tops and any others are likely to be trouble. She pounds her fist again. *Maybe it won't come to that.*

A fat blowfly bombs into the porch to begin an agitated dance, sheering past her ear and ricocheting between the peeling weatherboards in the confined space. *This heat is making us all half-mad.* Luisa slams her fist into the door again. *Where the hell is he?* The fly goes quiet, maybe knocked itself out. She checks her watch, it's just before midday. Surely he can't still be in bed? But then again . . . You can do this, she reassures herself, although she's not quite sure just what 'this' even is.

Footsteps. Luisa collapses her arm and smears both palms down the front of her hot-pink boob-tube dress. The towelling fabric soaks up her nerves, a positive she hadn't considered when pulling on the dress.

Mike's flatmate, Geoff, stands at the door. 'Luisa! Come on in.' It sounds like a wary question rather than a greeting.

'Thanks,' she says, stepping into the gloomy space where the bedrooms are lined up, two on each side, all the doors closed. Geoff heads down the narrow hallway and raps on Mike's door. This feels so odd — that bedroom she knows so well.

'Hey, mate, Luisa's here,' he calls, glancing back.

She feels on show, a pink warning sign. It's a few moments before Mike's muffled call comes from the opposite side of the hallway. The hairs on Luisa's neck prickle and a shiver runs through her.

'I'll go put the jug on,' says Geoff, scurrying off.

So, Amanda hadn't been telling tales. They had bumped into Geoff and his girlfriend outside the movie theatre last night. Luisa was there with her best friend Niamh, and Bex, a new teacher at Niamh's primary school. Luisa had invited Mike, but he'd declined. *Babe, I'd rather be home sticking pins in my eyes.* She'd known *Rain Man* wouldn't appeal — Mike preferred action over drama — besides, it was a good chance to catch up with Niamh and meet her new friend. Well, it was, until Amanda pulled Luisa aside.

Luisa hadn't said a word to Niamh, making her excuses to head home rather than join them both for a nightcap. Bex had protested but Niamh, bless her, knew Luisa wouldn't be swayed. Niamh's one of her oldest friends. They went right through primary school and McCauley Catholic College together. Niamh knows Luisa as well as anyone.

Luisa closes her eyes as the grim facts settle. Mike emerges, bare-chested. He's so careful to close Fleur's bedroom door that it sounds like a whisper. When he moves towards Luisa it's with the same cocksure swagger that over the months she convinced herself she was comfortable with. What a fool she's been.

'Guess we've got some talking to do,' he says, pushing the door to his room wide. He dredges his hands through his shaggy black hair as though ransacking it. So, it's confirmed. Fleur, the spunky new flatmate, has replaced her.

Luisa brushes past him, turning on him the moment he shuts the door. 'How could you?' She shoves him in the chest with both hands.

'Steady on,' Mike says, stumbling backwards, raising both hands as though surrendering. His deep brown eyes flash a look of confusion. 'Jesus! Hear me out.'

'You're a shit!' she yells, not caring who might hear. 'A two-timing bastard! How do you think I feel?' She scrunches her eyes against the tears but they sting at the corners.

Mike rubs at his face. 'Jesus, Loobs, I fucked up. Sorry.' He shakes his head as though hoping the right words might settle. 'What else can I say?' And in that instant Mike Turipa is back. Those beautiful eyes, brown pools. It all feels so wrong. Only a few days ago he was drawing her close. He points towards his bed with the scrambled sheets. 'Maybe sit down. I'll try and explain.'

His room smells so familiar, hints of aftershave doing battle with the mustiness left hanging from the damp towels. Luisa has an urge to fling the window open as she would usually do, but then the reality of what's happening settles over her.

'What's there to explain? You've ruined everything.' It's a struggle to get her words out. Mike moves forward, reaching out. Luisa flinches. 'Don't. Just don't.'

His arms are left hanging as though he's just dropped a parcel. 'I didn't mean to hurt you. Trust me. It's the last thing I wanted, and I was going to tell you today.' He's tracing circles on the bedroom floor with his bare foot as though trying to solve a puzzle.

'How long have you been carrying on?' She's asking but she doesn't want to know. It's over. And there's no way she'll have him back. What more does she need to know? Luisa regrets being so nice to Fleur now.

'Give me a break!' he says, hands on his hips. 'It's just this minute happened. I was about to tell you. We'd organised to catch up later, hadn't we?'

'Yeah, right.' Amanda's words are loud and clear in her ear. 'You said you couldn't see me this morning because you were *training*. I guess it depends on the context. Bloody hell, Mike!'

She can't bear it. The room feels as though it's caving in. She doesn't have a boyfriend or a travel mate now. She needs to escape, and she does so, like a whirlwind, slamming the door to his bedroom and then the front door. She's determined it will be the last time she ever sets foot in that house again.

Kermit, Luisa's Ford Cortina, the car she scrimped and saved for after starting work at Slaughter and Co. a couple of years ago, is parked haphazardly to the kerb. *For God's sake, get a grip. What does it matter you've parked so badly! Your boyfriend's just dumped you. Is it any wonder you've lost him?*

On the drive back her thoughts race: they're still on the Christmas break and so she won't have to cope with seeing Mike on Monday; it will be two weeks before they're both back. She grips the steering wheel tighter. Why did she let her guard down and fall for someone at work? It was never going to end well, but then the details: at least the law firm is spread over four floors and she and Mike work in separate departments. Ironic, given that she used to find excuses to go down to his floor.

Back at her Epsom flat, Luisa makes a beeline for her bedroom. Inside her ordered space, away from prying eyes, she collapses on her bed, fists clenched at her sides, staring up at the pink art-deco light fitting. It's as though having kept her tears at bay she can't release the tension now. Her mind flogs her options, but this problem can't be solved by logic. She thumps her fists down and finally the tears well then run like rivulets, streaking her cheeks before breaking like a dam so that she has to crush her fist against her mouth to stifle her sobs.

What now? She and Mike planned their overseas trip together: they were to leave in April and backpack through Asia. Most important for Luisa, their plans took them through Yugoslavia to meet up with Mum's estranged relatives on Korčula, the island where Mum was born. Ever since her teenage years Luisa has been positive Mum's hiding something. Too many things don't stack up — the disconnect with her tata, the way she's cut off her own brother.

Mike was on board. After all, she was the catalyst for him reconnecting with his family. He used to joke about his quarter-strength blood, saying he was better shrugging off his Maori cloak. He'd even gone as far as anglicising his given name, Mikaere, changing it by deed poll the day after he turned eighteen. Luisa could never fathom why he wouldn't embrace his culture; she worked on him for months. Last November he had reconnected with his Uncle Mikaere on a marae just north of Gisborne. Luisa still remembers the hongi Mike exchanged with his uncle, how they embraced. Mostly, though, she remembers how they made love that afternoon in their motel room, as though a weight had lifted from Mike and some tenderness had crept in over the bravado. It was then that she realised he'd changed for the better from knowing her. That she'd been a positive influence in encouraging him to dig deeper, past the surface layers. When they returned to Auckland she made it her first job to contact Uncle Josip and Aunt Mare.

The phone rings.

'Coming,' Luisa groans when her flatmate taps on the door. It takes all her strength to drag herself off the bed and out to the hallway. 'Hello. Luisa speaking.'

'Lulu.' Niamh's cheerful Irish lilt sings down the line. 'Just checking in after last night. I was worried. You okay?'

'Hang on a tick,' says Luisa, cradling the handset in the crook of her neck. Niamh is the one person she can tell but she needs privacy. She will tell her flatmates, but not yet, not until she absolutely has to. She picks up the telephone base unit and returns to her room, the cord snaking behind. Closing the door she collapses to sit cross-legged, cradling the base in her lap. 'I'll explain more later.' She focuses on the flame tree outside her window. 'Long story short, Mike's dumped me.'

Niamh's reaction is immediate. 'The fecker! Eejit! Oh, hon. Listen, I'm on my way over.'

'No! You know me. I need time.' Luisa keeps her voice steady, determined to hide how much she's hurting.

Niamh's never seen her fall apart, not in all the years they've known each other. They've shared plenty of happy moments, but sadness is something Luisa prefers to deal with alone. It's been years since she's let anyone see that, even her family.

'I'm fine. Let's catch up early next week.' Niamh is still protesting but Luisa cuts over her. 'Honestly. And no, you don't need to worry. I just need time to think.'

'Well, only if you're sure.' Niamh sounds a little miffed. 'I'm worried about you, hon. Promise you'll call if you need.'

'I will. And don't worry.' Tears threaten as she pictures Niamh's kind face. 'Hey, thanks. I'll call next week. Promise.' She replaces the receiver in a rush. *One step at a time, polako, polako,* as Mum would say.

Back on her bed, the phone returned to the hallway, Luisa stares at the ceiling. Mike was her first true love. With him she felt she could be a different person, be less worried about what other people thought: he challenged her to be less rigid, to take risks. She makes an effort to unclench her fists but still feels worthless, as though she's the one that's failed. Luisa's not used to flunking at anything, not unless you count her dismal past record with guys. Niamh so often teased her,

You're like a hedgehog Lulu. Get rid of those prickles. Mike had succeeded, though, as Luisa had always been confident the right guy would. He simply pounced, taking her by surprise at the firm's Christmas party just over a year ago. In her mind she lists the reasons why she's a good person. *Stop it, Luisa. Just stop!* She clenches her fists tighter and curls on her side to stare out the window.

And what of her trip? There's no way she can contemplate doing by herself what she and Mike had planned. Not when she's never been out of New Zealand — the extent of her overseas travels has been down to the South Island, to Dunedin, to study law at Otago University. It was her way of gaining some independence, escaping the cauldron of home. There are too many stories in the newspapers about the Moonies and those other weird cult groups. About girls going missing. She's brave but not stupid. There will be plenty of others heading off for their 'overseas experience' but Luisa knows from flatting that you want to be choosy who you travel with. Some people would be a disaster. Maybe she could fly straight to London. Get a job and travel to Yugoslavia as planned in September, once she's met some new friends. Wouldn't it be fantastic to show Mike he's dispensable. That she can travel without him. *Damn Mike!* That's another thing Luisa hates — plans changing. What the hell is she going to do?

～ ～

Niamh surprises Luisa early the next morning, auburn hair piled high, tennis racquet in hand. Luisa doesn't think she'll have the energy, but Niamh insists, driving them down to their local club. It's a passion they shared through school, having worked their way up the ranks to make the top team. Niamh was right: bashing a ball helps. The mid-morning sun is biting, despite their choosing the far court to take advantage of the shade. Luisa returns the ball, the sound so satisfying as it curves off her racquet's sweet spot to land deep, close to Niamh's baseline. Niamh scrambles to retrieve it, her hair flying like a bunch of spring carrots tethered to her scalp, but her return smashes into the net.

'That's it!' Niamh stamps her foot. 'I'm letting you win. But only this time.' She's already moving towards the net. 'Damn you, girl, I won't make it so easy next time.'

'That's what you always say. Besides, I haven't beaten you in ages. Must be my frustrations coming out. Hey, thanks. I needed that.'

'No worries.' Niamh rewards her with a beaming smile, her face the colour of beetroot. 'But get me out of this heat unless you're wanting to scrape me off the court too. How do you stand it? Must be your continental blood.'

It's true. Luisa feels as though she has hardly broken a sweat, but there's a sheen coating her arms, intensifying her nut-brown complexion, which over the summer break has hit its full bronzed straps.

'Come on. There's some shade at the clubhouse,' says Luisa. 'Can't have you flaking out and using more excuses.'

They collapse on a wooden seat that's shaded by a deck above. Luisa stretches out her legs.

'Look at the state of ya,' says Niamh, slapping Luisa's thigh. 'How do those greyhound legs hold you up?'

Luisa laughs at the familiar joke, but then the reality of how everything else has changed hits her. Over the past twenty-four hours it's been the same; there's been no warning, as though her emotions are riding a tidal wave.

'Come on, Lulu, I know you too well,' says Niamh. 'It's time you told me the full story. You've got to admit I've been more than patient and here's as good as anywhere.' She places her hand over Luisa's. 'Come on. No more excuses.'

Luisa confides and Niamh listens, all the while rubbing Luisa's back. A young kid saunters past, one hand in the pocket of his stubby shorts, the other swinging his racquet. He lets himself into the caged volley-wall area and his shots sound like gunfire — *crack, smack, thwack.*

Niamh pulls her close. 'You poor hon. What an absolute fecker.'

Luisa shakes her head. 'Worst thing is, what to do about this trip? I still want to go. And I'm determined I won't give him the pleasure of seeing me fail. But I'm shit-scared of heading off alone. I don't think I can do it. Getting on a plane and heading half a world away will be challenging enough.'

'You're right there. I'd be worried myself.' Niamh sits quietly for a moment. 'You know, I've been thinking ever since our call yesterday. I wish I had the money to drop everything and go.'

Luisa goes to protest, but Niamh taps her on the knee, cutting her short. 'Hang on, hear me out. Look, this might be a dumb idea, but you've met Bex, right? She wants to head off. It wasn't going to be until the end of the year, but perhaps you guys should talk? She might leave earlier. Could be worth a shot?'

'I guess,' says Luisa, her mind racing, already dismissing the idea. She knows so little about Bex. That she's a good friend of Niamh's says something, but she can't rely on that. Friends aren't always transferable. 'I was thinking more that I could fly straight to London. I'll get a job for sure. Seems there's plenty of options for lawyers and I might be able to sort something before I leave. If I got myself there, and settled, I could travel once I've met some new friends.'

'But what about your family in Yugoslavia? All your plans? You've already contacted your uncle. He's expecting you, isn't he?'

'I could leave that for a while but still work it so Mum doesn't get a whiff. It might be easier to fudge if I was working. Besides, Mike and I weren't planning to get to Yugoslavia until September. I could stick to the same plan but just leave from London.'

'Seems a shame to miss having a holiday and to travel on the way over. You've worked so hard for this. Why wouldn't you ask Bex?' Niamh looks intently at Luisa as though searching for the answer in her eyes. 'How about I mention it? There'd be nothing to lose, surely?'

Niamh seems so certain and her intuition is usually spot on. Besides, Bex does seem fun. 'I guess there's no harm in asking.'

'Leave it with me,' says Niamh.

'Only if you're sure.'

'Couldn't be more certain. But come on, this wrecked body needs a shower.' Niamh nudges Luisa. 'Hey, I'm glad I got you out — even if you did thrash me. Cross fingers my idea will work.'

Luisa feels lighter somehow as they climb the steps that wind up to the parking area. The bank is planted with sweet-smelling jasmine. It's as though her best friend has just held out a silver tray and lifted the cloche lid on a new possibility. And wouldn't it be fantastic to show Mike he's dispensable. That she can make her own plans. Travel without him. But even as she's thinking this, the worries creep back. She hardly knows Bex. But then again, she'd thought she knew Mike and look where that's left her.

APRIL

Ordinarily Luisa would race up the stairs, any opportunity to build fitness into her day, but tonight her feet drag and the echo sounds ominous. The thrum from the boardroom collides with the quiet of the stairwell. Her first instinct is to bolt, but she chooses the bathroom at the side as a temporary sanctuary and checks herself in the mirror. Her hair needs some attention, nothing that a rustle and scrunch with her fingers won't fix. Lipstick could do with a touch-up. She fishes in her satchel for her latest favourite, Clementine Burst, perfect for that shot of boldness. She flies out in two weeks and she wants Mike to see that she's back in control. He's sure to be there. Her workmates tell her he's had no qualms, always a regular at Friday night drinks. Whenever she saw him over the past weeks she avoided speaking to him. It feels as though she's been hiding herself away. Her gold hoop earrings catch the light, matching the sun-kissed tips of her spiral curls. *You're good to go, Luisa Tomich. No excuses.*

Even so, she hesitates at the wide doorway of the corner boardroom. A bank of windows face the harbour and the suburbs south. Free drinks are always a drawcard so her colleagues are packed shoulder to shoulder, probably seventy-odd people. An occasional shriek or lower-gauge laugh pierces the din. Luisa feels as if it might engulf her, that she might be swallowed up.

Sharp dark suits, a mix of trousers and skirts cut off at the knee; business shirts; flowing blouses; a few dresses scattered throughout. Most of the women jiggle on dagger heels. Luisa flexes her toes, conscious of the tired ache. She's tall enough to see over most of the heads and scans the room for her friend Kath. Her mop of blonde hair and bright purple suit should be easy to spot but it's Mike her eyes fix on. He's in the centre of the room with his back to her. Kath is off to the right, close to the windows, purple arms flying while chatting to James and Tony, two of Luisa's fellow litigation lawyers. Luisa collects a glass of bubbly from a table just inside the doorway and weaves her way around the outside of the room.

'Good to see you back!' says Kath, waving Luisa over and pulling her into their huddle.

'Hey, Luisa,' says James, pushing his big red-framed glasses further up his nose as if to take a better look.

'We were worried,' says Tony. 'Glad you've got your mojo back.' His striped shirt is open at the neck and his tie is stuffed in his trouser pocket. He raises his bottle of Steinlager.

'Here's to that,' says Luisa. 'Cheers!' She raises her glass and takes a large swig.

Luisa lets their patter about weekend plans wash over her and flicks a glance towards Mike. He's still there, back turned, talking with his supervising partner. Luisa doesn't have a hope of blending in beside Kath, but wasn't that the whole purpose of coming? Out to the side, Auckland sprawls from the dense city cluster to the suburbs, a view Luisa is sure she will never tire of. Having grown up in Mount Wellington, she always dreamed of getting off ground-level and would gaze up and wonder about being inside these high-flying spaces. She still feels privileged to be working here. Mum and Dad joined her in this same room last year after the ceremony for being admitted to the bar. Luisa was embarrassed by her mum's wide-eyed reaction and her comments to one of the senior partners: *All this tiny food! It's a lot of money to spend!* It took all Luisa's self-control not to bundle Mum up and get her outside. Dad wasn't a problem, but then he knows how to hold his tongue. Luisa doesn't doubt Mum's proud of what she's achieved, but it's also increased the distance between them, as though her mum can't relate to the world Luisa now lives in.

Kath touches her elbow. 'Earth to Luisa, come in.'

Luisa makes a show of laughing it off. 'Shit, sorry. I'm not the best company.'

'Nothing that a few drinks won't help.' Kath turns to James, who's tapping her shoulder. 'What? Go away, pest.'

Tony leans in. 'How're you feeling, Luisa? Pleased to escape all this soon?'

'Nervous and excited. Bex and I are having another planning session Sunday night. You've met her, eh? At the pub for our combined farewells.'

'Bex. Yeah, couldn't forget her,' says Tony. 'Party girl, short blonde hair. A teacher right?' He lowers his voice and leans in closer. 'Have to admit I more than noticed her. Felt a bit down when I realised she was heading off. Lost opportunities and all.' He tips his bottle and takes a long swig.

Niamh had laughed when Luisa mentioned it, how Bex attracts so much attention. Luisa knows there's no one at the moment, but how will Bex cope when it's just the two of them travelling? It still niggles her how little they know one another. But then as Niamh says, *It's the perfect opportunity to get to know each other.*

'Refill?' Kath reaches for Luisa's glass. Tony turns away.

'One more, then I'll get going.' Luisa rolls her eyes. 'Family dinner tomorrow and Mum needs help with the prep.'

'Stay put,' says Kath, already moving off. She calls back over her shoulder, 'All my mates are deserting me. Got to make the most of it while you're still here.'

'Go,' Luisa mouths, swishing her hand.

Niamh was a lifesaver suggesting Bex as a travel mate and they've negotiated a new plan. Bex was desperate to get to New York and see some of America. It wasn't Luisa's first choice, but then she'd had to convince Bex about Yugoslavia, a country Bex knew nothing about. Luisa wasn't surprised: she's got used to it over the years. For many Kiwis, Yugoslavia's socialism is a step too far, and even she has to admit the history is confusing — too many broken and changing borders, too many wars won and lost. After the US they'll spend time in Turkey and Greece before finishing with Yugoslavia. Not that Luisa's family know anything about this last part, and Bex has been sworn to secrecy.

Someone touches her on the shoulder and she turns.

'Hey,' says Mike.

He looks so relaxed and he's wearing that tie she bought. *Does he even remember?*

'Hey.' Her voice sounds too cheerful, like she's happy to see him. Luisa narrows her eyes, tries to look as though she doesn't care. Her face colours; she can feel it. It's ridiculous he still has this effect on her.

'Don't want to harass you,' he says. 'It's just . . . we haven't spoken, since, well, you know. First time's always the hardest. I want us to move on, be friends.'

'Don't!' She shrugs him off when he touches her arm. 'Leave it. I don't want to talk.'

Kath shoves herself back into the circle, thrusting another glass of bubbles at Luisa. 'Hey, Mike. Sorry we won't get to catch up — hear you're leaving.'

Luisa's grateful. Kath's the master of the one-liner. She jokes about honing her skills by having to keep her four smartarse brothers in line.

Mike gives Luisa a resigned look and shrugs. 'Catch ya, then.'

Luisa watches him move off. It still baffles her that she's lost him.

'Sorry if I was a little blunt,' says Kath. 'Did the trick, though.'

'Perfect rescuer, unlike these morons.' Luisa points her glass towards James and Tony, who are still deep in conversation. 'Cheers, my friend! And here's to life getting less complicated.' She drinks, but the wine tastes cloying now, far too sweet. 'Hey, I think I'll shoot off. Small steps still. Have an awesome weekend and see you Monday, eh?' She forces a smile and squeezes Kath's arm.

The room and its occupants are a blur as Luisa rushes for the door. She feels her colleagues' eyes trained on her back and imagines their comments. Mike said people don't hold onto stuff, that gossip is a passing fancy, snippets tossed about like petals then forgotten. He was right about the talk when they first got together. People moved on quickly. Still, she's relieved it's not often that she's the headline act. When the lift pings she's grateful she doesn't have to share the space. She can breathe again. What still baffles her is the way she let her guard down, relaxed her rules. The physical attraction helped, those eyes, that broad, toned chest, but it was also his intelligence and wit. Deep down, she admired his laissez-faire attitude — his willingness to let things happen and to hell with the consequences. Even so, she backed herself to tame him. And in a sense she had, given she was the girlfriend who lasted longest. *Still feels like failure, though.*

Outside, the Friday night crowd bustle past. The evenings are getting cooler, but it's nothing that a brisk walk won't fix. She steps into the crowd and strides up Queen Street towards the town hall and her bus stop. It feels good to clear her head. There's an electric energy and she can't help feeling recharged. The bright yellow moon-face of the Town Hall's clock tower glows like a beacon. She's always imagined this historic building like a displaced ocean liner. A piece of neo-Renaissance architecture cast off from Italy and wedged in the middle of Queen Street. Soon, she thinks, she will walk the streets of countries where buildings like this are common, taking in the sights Mum so often reminisces about. Luisa smiles. It was the reason Mum insisted on the spelling of her name, Mum's way of keeping a connection. Her older sister, Anita, was named after their Baba Ana, Mum's mother — a name Kiwis are more familiar with — now that Luisa's older, and past the frustrations of always having to spell out her name, she's grateful for this nod to her European roots.

At the post box, Luisa digs the aerogramme from her satchel. This will be her last letter to Uncle Josip before they leave. It explains that Bex is coming now and reassures him that she will send an update from Turkey. All in all they've been communicating for the past six months. Uncle Josip has sent his replies to her work address. Mum's the type who visits without warning, making it her business to check the flat letterbox on her way in. She says it's a habit of old but Luisa calls it nosiness. Either way she can't risk Mum finding out. She holds the latest thin blue letter to her lips before dropping it through the slot. *There, another secret on its way.*

A young woman, spiky bleached hair, black eyeliner, sits midway along the bus. Luisa refuses to catch her eye as she slips into the seat behind her. Across the punk's denim jacket, the words 'Nut Kicker from Hell!' are emblazoned in red. Luisa stifles a laugh. Kath's short shrift of Mike pales in comparison. There's just a scattering of other passengers, a couple of young guys in suits up front, and a middle aged Polynesian woman sitting opposite. She wears a pristine orange hibiscus flower nestled in her thick, ropey hair. It pushes forward from her ear, a nod to her culture, the place she hails from.

Even though Luisa was born a New Zealander and feels proud to call herself a Kiwi, she's a *Croatian* Kiwi: this is her point of difference, what sets her apart. Niamh feels the same about her Irish blood. The bus turns into K' Road, past where the Dally club used to be and along Symonds Street towards New North Road where it's located now. Luisa wonders: if she was to total the time spent in both buildings, what it would amount to. Maybe years? As a teen she scoffed at some of the old-fashioned rituals, the traditional dances, the music and the annual club picnic which for years her parents insisted she and her siblings attend, but now she wants to deepen her understanding of her culture — which, despite all that, feels at arm's length. She wants to live and breathe and see for herself what she's heard so much about. It's a special part of her, hard to describe, but she gets emotional thinking about it, what it means deep down.

The bus meanders up to Newmarket and along Broadway, the neon shop signs blazing even though the shops have closed. Nut-kicker waits beside the driver until the bus pulls over then stalks off, her bleached hair tinged blue by the street lights. An elderly man in a hat shuffles on, behind him a woman with a toddler. The man hacks into his handkerchief, his shoulders rattling.

Dida Stipan. It's six years since they lost him. Baba Marta went five months earlier. *At least I've got to know Dad's family though.* Mum's relatives have only been introduced through photographs and penned birthday messages, or phone calls where you had to fight the static and time lapses. From the photos, Baba Ana is the one Luisa most closely resembles. Baba had the same wild crop of spiral curls and sculpted face.

A group of rowdy teens only just make it on before the bus pulls away. They bump and swagger past Luisa towards the rear seat. The bus trawls along Manukau Road, within striking distance of Luisa's flat which she moved out of three weeks ago in preparation for heading away. How long will she be gone? She hopes she'll be lucky enough to last out her two-year working visa. If she plays it right, and fits plenty of travel around her work, she might even be able to stretch her time away to three or four years. Who knows how long she'll need to mend the rift between Mum's family, let alone get to the bottom of what her mum's hiding away.

It wasn't Mum's dry eyes when Dida Ante passed in 1975 that alerted her to something being amiss — it was a couple of years earlier when Baba Ana was slipping into Alzheimer's oblivion. Baba was Mum's conduit, and as conversations became more difficult Mum became increasingly distraught. It was then that parts of the story emerged, along with lashings of venom: how Dida Ante had sent Mum to New Zealand against her will. Luisa is certain there must have been a love interest, but knows that Mum won't let on. She admires what Mum's achieved, coming out here and making a new life, but her old-fashioned attitudes are frustrating. They've come to an unspoken agreement since Luisa left home to skirt around the important topics instead of arguing. Mum drilled into both Luisa and her sister, *Wait until you're married.* Luisa suspects Anita complied but Mike took Luisa by surprise. One minute they were kissing on the balcony in full view of the other staff, and two weeks later she had joined him in bed. Even now she doesn't regret it. It's frustrating that Mum puts up these barriers. The supposed scandal is likely to be trivial anyway, given how strict the rules would have been then.

After Dida Ante died things became more complicated. When Uncle Josip told Mum he was putting Baba Ana in a rest home, Mum was outraged, yelling down the phone at him, *Locking Mama away, sramotno!* Afterwards she refused to talk to her brother. It's been nine years since they've heard from Korčula: the inevitable call to say Baba Ana had passed. Mum was inconsolable for weeks, but then she picked herself up and got on with life. Not that it changed things with Josip. *Mum's stubbornness is impressive,* thinks Luisa. *You have to give her that.*

The Polynesian lady's stop is close to Mount Smart stadium. She looks a lonely figure, lugging her shopping bag along the street and Luisa hopes she doesn't have far to go, gets home safely. It's been three years since Luisa attended her first music festival at this stadium — the Greenpeace Rainbow Warrior concert to mark the bombing. It was also perfect for celebrating Luisa's 21st birthday: partying with her friends, singing along with Neil Young, 'Hey, Hey, My, My'; pogoing to Split Enz, 'I See Red'; sharing her first joint and drinking too much, then throwing up on the pavement outside — not the ideal ending, but memorable, a story she laughs about now even though it's one she's not keen to repeat. Niamh was delighted: *You're finally human!*

Luisa's still smiling when they reach her stop. She has fond memories of this neighbourhood, of Ngaio Street. Many of the houses in Epsom are more salubrious, but this part of Auckland will always be special. She passes the gingerbread house with the rock wall that used to be Baba and Dida's. It holds such special memories: Dida Stipan's stories; the meals they all shared. Now that she has the opportunity to travel to the other side of the world, if she wasn't to visit Yugoslavia it would feel as though she was splitting herself in two and ignoring one half. It's like a calling. Baba and Dida made a better life for all the family by coming to New Zealand, but they never downplayed the hardships, or the sacrifices. Luisa feels it's her duty to visit the homeland, to acknowledge their sacrifices, to pay homage. She's still thinking about this as she lets herself through the front door.

'That you, *Draga*?' Mum calls from her bedroom. 'Come quick. I need the help deciding.'

'Hang on,' says Luisa, suppressing her irritation. 'Be there in a tick.'

She ducks into the other front bedroom, the room she used to share with Anita, and pulls out jeans and a T-shirt. Marko, despite being the youngest, was lucky getting a room to himself and Luisa has always envied him having a space to call his own. She and Anita clashed as teenagers: her sister was messy and yet so damned compliant. She made Luisa seem rebellious, which was laughable. Marko was the one to push the boundaries but then he also had the knack of flying under Mum's radar.

'Luisa! I'm catching the cold.'

'Coming!' says Luisa. Two more weeks, she reassures herself.

The master bedroom is strewn with clothes. Mum stands beside the bed in her underwear, arms and legs toned from all the time spent outside in the garden. Her tanned limbs are a striking contrast to the sheath of white hugging her torso — full knickers, V-necked sleeveless singlet tucked in at the waist, and a peep of lace frothing at her cleavage. There have been many times Luisa's wished she'd been gifted even half Mum's impressive bust. Valentina has worked her magic. Mum's hair has been restored to jet-black and styled into soft curls. She's a fine-looking woman, thinks Luisa, and still shapely despite middle age adding a heft to her hips. Mum's beautiful skin has always been a joking point between Luisa and Joy — that it's thanks to Mum applying the Nivea cream with religious fervour.

'I was hoping you'd be home,' says Mum, flinging her arm towards the pile on her bed as though everything is hopeless. 'How can I decide?'

Luisa picks through the pile and selects the ruby-coloured dress, the one Mum wore to Luisa's graduation. 'I've always loved you in this.'

Mum frowns. 'Not too flashy?'

'No. It's perfect,' says Luisa, holding firm. She wants to avoid spending the evening toing and froing between multiple choices. Mum will be worried about looking over-dressed, or out of place, among the other Dally ladies coming to the party. It is frustrating that Mum's so concerned about doing the right thing, that she can't be her own person. Take Valentina. Despite Mum's criticism of the gold dripping from her hairdresser's wrists, *makes her fortune off her own community,* she refuses to go elsewhere, insisting you have to be loyal, *support our own.* Luisa realises this was a new country for Mum and that sometimes she struggled to fit in, but after thirty years, surely she's earned her place? She's made her family here. And it's not as though she's made any effort to hold on to her family back home. She's never returned, despite all her talk of missing her precious homeland. Sometimes Mum is like a pack of mismatched playing cards where there's no chance of logic. It's Dad Luisa feels sorry for. Everyone else in his family has made the trip back, and Luisa's certain he'd love to do the same. When she pressed him on it he brushed her off: *Better things to spend our money on.* He was probably protecting Mum, but who would know? He's a man of few words and never been one to cause a scene.

'What's for dinner?' asks Luisa. 'You get dressed and I'll give you a hand.' She wants to stay on side and any offer of help is like gold to Mum.

'Takeaways. Your tata's picking up the fish and chips.'

'I'll tidy up here. You go put your feet up. *Idi dalje.* Go on!' Luisa swishes with her hand. 'Start planning tomorrow's jobs.'

Mum makes a show of saluting before pulling on her clothes. She pauses by the door. 'Thanks, *Draga.* You know I'll miss you.'

Luisa shoos her off, smiling at how sentimental Mum's been of late. She makes sure to put everything back the way Mum would expect. Maybe it's why Luisa feels best when her own life is orderly, everything in its place with no surprises. She runs her hand over the intricate carved top of the kauri glory box, cleared now of clutter. It was a wedding present from Aunt Kate and Uncle Nick, and it's always sat at the base of her parents' bed. Mum's filled it with fine linen, crockery and a few pieces of jewellery, her box of treasures with sentimental things that she plans to hand down. Luisa doesn't care for glory boxes: *Better to use things while they're half-fashionable.* Why would Mum want to hide things away, especially treasures with a connection to her former life?

Back in the small dining room that doubles as their family room, Mum's in her La-Z-Boy, feet outstretched. The room is crammed with furniture but their family have always preferred gathering in this tight space rather than the formal lounge. That room is used only for special occasions and large gatherings, like the party they're holding tomorrow evening.

'Turn that silly man off,' says Mum, waving her arm at Paul Holmes on the television.

Luisa obliges then collapses into the other recliner. 'Everything's back to normal in there.'

'I'll be pleased when this party's over,' says Mum. 'Get the whole place back to normal.'

'You'll love it once tomorrow comes,' says Luisa, although Mum does look exhausted. 'It's an impressive milestone, twenty-eight years married. Perfect timing for me to see everyone, too.'

Luisa rubs her hand over the La-Z-Boy's arm, a comforting habit of old. The short Dralon fibres bristle as she works her fingers against the fabric's grain. 'Guess what,' she says, checking Mum's face, her fingers still stroking the upholstery. 'I made it up to work drinks.'

'Was he there? *Da svinja*?' Mum's eyes flash with something close to distaste. 'I could thump that boy. Box his ears!'

Luisa grins. Mum's so black-and-white. Mike was welcomed like family when she finally introduced him, but since he dumped her Mum refers to him as 'the swine'.

'He was. And I survived. First time's the worst.' She can't believe she's resorting to Mike's patter.

Mum tears up. She's been doing this a lot lately. It's because she's worried about Luisa heading off without Mike. 'I'm sorry, *Draga*. I still can't believe he did that to you. Things have a habit of working out, though. Just promise you'll be careful.'

'You know I will.' Luisa reaches across and pats Mum's arm. 'Come on, we've talked about this. It's worked out fine already. You've met Bex and you've said how much you like her. I think we'll be a great combination.'

'I just wish . . .' Luisa can guess what Mum's thinking. The same topic that's caused so much heartache over the last nine months, ever since Luisa started planning her trip. The silence settles between them, a slow simmering stew of unanswered questions.

'Don't look like that, *Draga*. I'm not the only one to blame.'

Luisa thought she'd kept her face expressionless. She wants to steer clear of all that. 'Don't be silly,' she says. 'I'm disappointed in Mike. I'm not thinking about you and Uncle Josip.'

'That's okay then,' says Mum, still huffy. 'But you know I feel guilty the way things fell apart. You can never understand.'

Luisa's frustrations from the past weeks threaten to boil over — *Make me understand, then* — but she clamps her mouth shut. What's the point? It's difficult walking this precipice. Why is it with Mum that she finds it hardest to contain her anger?

'If I could change things I would,' says Mum, heaving herself out of her chair and heading towards the kitchen. 'But that brother of mine will never understand.'

Luisa lets her go. Bex stepping in was a lucky break. If she hadn't, there was every chance Mum might have pushed to join Luisa earlier rather than stick to their agreed plan: her parents will join Luisa in a year's time once she's done the travel she wants to do and is settled in London with a job. Luisa's promised that they will all travel to Korčula then and she won't pressure Mum to contact her family. *It'll be fun*, she reassured Mum. *Just let me do my own thing first.*

Mum bustles about in the kitchen and Luisa reminds herself of the need to tread carefully, to not jeopardise what's been set in motion. Only then will there be a chance to pave the way for a reunion, to fix things without Mum mucking things up. *Two more weeks, just two more weeks.*

AUGUST

TUESDAY

Yugoslavia feels so close now. It shares a border with Greece, and Samos is an island just like Korčula. Mum so often described the colours back home — the vibrant blues, pinks and greens — and these same colours are here, colliding with the way of life based around the fishing villages. There's the Mediterranean flavours too, lashings of olive oil and garlic, the way Mum cooked at home. Luisa can picture herself on Korčula now. She can almost taste the country she's waited so long to experience. Earlier in the day, she and Bex made the most of the morning cool, visiting the Roman ruins at the temple of Hera. Now, with the sun blazing, they while away their afternoon on Kokkari beach. Tomorrow they'll catch the boat to Athens.

It's only the tourists who remain, lizards lazing on bright blue sun-loungers strung out along the beach. The row of umbrellas behind them, matching blue-and-white striped petals, are like exotic poppies in full bloom. The locals have retreated indoors, except for the beach hawkers. Bex lies on her stomach reading her book. Her cute turquoise bikini she picked up in Turkey is a perfect tonal match with the sea. Luisa is in her sleek black one-piece. She wishes she could borrow

Bex's curves to fill out a bikini. Bex jokes that a string-bean body is preferable to a perfectly condensed pear, but Luisa's not convinced. The sun is a warm, weighty blanket on her back and the steady swish-swish of the sea tumbling forward and back over the pebbly shore merges meditatively with the hum of conversation drifting along the beach. Only the occasional shriek from a seagull, or caustic shout from a beach hawker, pierces the relaxed mood.

Luisa will go for another swim later. Right now it feels too exhausting: even reading saps her energy. It's been fun getting caught up in Bex's bubble, and easy, given the condensed time they've spent together to fast-forward their friendship to a place that would ordinarily take Luisa much longer. Some of the confidences they've shared — embarrassing drunk moments, losing their virginity — are the kind Luisa often hesitates to disclose. The opportunities for talk have been endless, on buses and trains, while walking and exploring new places, and it's a skill Bex has honed. There's an energy about her, a directness that's refreshing. Luisa's joked lately that Bex could be her secret weapon: meeting new clients at work has always been the 'must try harder' point on her performance review. There's been the odd niggle — Bex does like getting her own way — but it hasn't been a major and mostly Luisa's been happy to go with the flow.

The closer they've drawn to Yugoslavia, the more Luisa has been thinking about Uncle Josip and how maddening it is that Mum's made this so difficult for her. Until she finds his reply at her next poste restante address in Belgrade she won't relax.

Bex's lounger creaks and groans and Luisa drags her head upwards to squint across at her. Bex is sitting now, replacing the cap on the sunscreen tube. Luisa's hardly broken a sweat but there's a sheen coating her arms, intensifying the colour of her tan.

'Luisa, we need to talk.'

'What?' Luisa says, the effort almost too much.

'I feel terrible . . . but I have to change my plans. Go straight to London from Athens.'

Luisa pitches up and her own lounger squawks. How can Bex be so selfish? There's been no hint of this. Just the other day when they were posting the letter to Uncle Josip Bex said how much she was looking forward to Yugoslavia.

Bex's head is cast down with her arms wrapped around her knees. The afternoon sun feels overbearing.

'What do you mean?' Luisa tries to keep her voice calm but inside she's churning.

'I need to be sensible. I'm nearly skint and September's the beginning of the school year.' Bex's voice is clipped.

Luisa's thoughts race back to Mike. He's the reason Bex is here. That they're even having this stupid conversation. Surely she's not going to be let down again. Bex signed up. No one forced her. It's rich to change her plans now.

'That's bullshit, Bex! You won't even need money when we're with my rellies.' Despite the familiarity they've gained, Luisa has been cautious about holding her tongue to keep the peace. She can't believe she's venting now. A couple who were happily canoodling glance across. Is Bex even blinking behind those big white sunnies? Luisa can't tell. She looks rigid, as though by moving she's afraid she might cause more upset.

'I thought you'd understand,' says Bex. 'You know money's tight. And we're so close to your rellies now, it's not as if you'll need me.'

Yeah, right. Luisa's head is spinning. *It's great to be logical when it's me you're letting down.* Luisa's been so careful to keep their spending in check: sharing meals, limiting alcohol, sticking to a budget that would work for Bex. A scraggy cat approaches and Luisa flicks her hand. It slinks off towards the shoreline, taking an exaggerated path as though knowing to give them a wide berth. What hurts is that Bex has conveniently ignored the one thing that's most important to Luisa. Only a couple of weeks back she'd opened up to Bex, really opened up: her worries about meeting her relatives and whether they'd accept her; her quest to understand why Mum's father sent her away. Luisa's stomach churns. She and Bex have been so comfortable with the routine of moving from place to place, country to country. She pictures herself sitting alone in a hostel, asking directions, seeing the sights and having no one to share them with.

'It's not just about the money,' says Bex, cutting in to Luisa's thoughts, her head resting on her knees.

'Then what else?' says Luisa.

Silence. Just the swish, swish of the waves, creeping onto the shore.

'Come on. We had a plan. It feels like you're ditching me. Looking after yourself!'

The couple are openly staring now. Luisa glares at them and they hunker back down.

'I've had enough. Want to unpack. Start living normally.' Bex's voice, which is usually so forthright, sounds tiny.

'How can you say that? It's just an extra month. You can unpack at my rellies. Shit, Bex, you owe me.' The couple are still leaning on every word but Luisa doesn't care. 'We've done all the things *you* wanted. It seems convenient to take off now.'

'It isn't what I want, but I have to be sensible.' Bex rubs at her face, eyes still hidden behind her sunglasses. 'I'm worried about London. How I'll cope. If I get there before the school year starts I'll have the best chance of finding a job.'

'But the school year's *always* started in September.' Luisa only just stops herself from throwing her hands in the air. 'How come this wasn't a problem when we were planning?'

In slow motion Bex swings her legs to sit facing Luisa. She removes her sunnies and her face is all angles, like cut glass. 'There's something I need to explain, but it's something I haven't told anyone else, not even Niamh. Can we walk? It'll be easier to talk.'

The vulnerability on her face reminds Luisa of the spidery crazing lines on Baba Marta's old china teacups. This is important, Luisa thinks, scrambling to stand, as though she's about to be let in on the real Bex.

They wrap and tie their sarongs and bundle their gear into daypacks. Luisa thinks of popped balloons. She feels guilty, as though she's failed Bex, missed the signs. Along the beach the line of lizards are as they were. The inquisitive couple have slotted back like spoons, their backs turned.

'Hey, you. I'm sorry.' Luisa pulls Bex into a hug. 'Don't worry. We'll work this out.'

Bex is quiet again as they wander up the beach. Luisa's eyes smart and she's thankful for her dark glasses. The crush of small pebbles is replaced by the clipped flip-flap of their jandals on concrete and Luisa slows her pace, flicking her arms to shake out the tension. She's like her dad on a mission: arms swinging like rotors, fists clenched into tight balls.

Further ahead two older Greek men amble, deep in conversation. One has a newspaper folded under his arm, the other holds a laden shopping bag. A bougainvillea splays over a wall, a blast of shocking fuchsia. Bex still hasn't said a word. A woman sits on a wide step in front of a turquoise door, shelling some kind of nut. Her hair is a shock of white, contrasting with her black dress. She glances up, her square-cut jaw set.

A dog, the colour of Russian fudge with a bushy tail, crosses the street and pads alongside them. They've grown accustomed to this escort service, available most mornings and evenings when it's cooler and the dogs have the energy to shake themselves up from the patches of shade they've been slumbering in. This dog has broken the mould.

'Hello, you,' says Luisa, grateful for an excuse to speak. The dog slows, and Luisa wonders if its eyeing the hill ahead, weighing up its energy levels. It turns and slopes off.

'No staying power,' says Bex, staring after the dog. Luisa wonders if she's registered the irony but then a wry look crosses Bex's face. 'Come on, this hill's not going to beat us.'

Bex strides off and Luisa is left feeling like one of her school children. She is already partway up the rocky slope before Luisa catches her again.

'You're probably wondering why I chose to come away with you.' Bex doesn't give Luisa the chance to answer. 'The chance to travel felt like I'd been gifted a solution at just the right time. I admired your determination to follow your dream. You seemed so sure of yourself. It was the kind of stuff I wanted to see in myself. What I'd been talking to the counsellor about.'

A counsellor? Niamh described Bex as the most upbeat and motivated person she knew. Until now, Luisa's had no reason to question that.

'Amazing what you can hide,' says Bex, as though sensing Luisa's confusion. She pulls ahead again, scaling the hill like a mountain goat. Luisa tries to ignore the burn in her lungs as she picks her way up, still trailing behind.

'Towards the end of last year I realised I needed to face up to some things about myself.' Bex turns to offer her hand and pulls Luisa up to stand on the ledge. Luisa is relieved when Bex collapses onto a bench seat tucked into the hillside at the rear.

'There's so many things I'm not proud of. Everyone jokes about my string of boyfriends, me included, and some of the choices I made were shockers. I've been using guys like a crutch, bandaging over what I couldn't face. The counsellor helped me understand that it goes back to Mum and Dad's divorce. Hardly rocket science.' Bex grimaces, and counts off the reasons on her fingers. 'Only child. Dad distancing himself. Mum so distraught I couldn't trouble her. Having a boy at my side saved me from focusing on my troubles. After so many years all it's meant is that I've wound up feeling used and disconnected from who I am. By the end of last year I'd backed myself into a corner. I'd lost the essence of what I really wanted from life.'

Luisa puts her arm around Bex's shoulders, drawing her close.

'Being able to come away with you and leave all that behind, felt positive, a step forward.' Bex leans her head on Luisa's shoulder. 'But I can't ask Dad for more money, and I don't want to fail or make things harder than they need to be. I thought I'd be okay, that I'd be happy to wing it. I was looking forward to breaking free of all the routines, but I guess it's something else I've learnt — I'm not much of a risk-taker.' Bex lifts her head and frowns. 'Unless it's men we're talking about. My counsellor would say, *be kind to yourself.* I need some security, and teachers don't have the luxury of a big pay-cheque.'

Luisa turns and focuses on the view. The difference in what they earn has come up a number of times already, and she knows to steer clear of that topic. Even with Niamh she's never been comfortable, but it's not something she can solve.

'You've been through the mill,' she says. 'Hey, I understand, honestly.' She rubs Bex's back and they both gaze across the mix of flat and terracotta rooftops towards the azure sparkle. Luisa drinks it all in. For Mum, New Zealand must have felt so foreign.

'I'll definitely miss these stunning views,' Bex says eventually. 'That sea's like a jewel.'

'Easy to take for granted.'

Bex nods in reply, seeming content to sit and absorb it all. Luisa wonders what she's thinking. Most likely the obvious, that London will feel a million miles from all of this. A few clouds stretch like soft, twisted scarves along the horizon, tone upon tone of muted coral mixing with the blue sky. Luisa pictures her mum, hands on hips, pontificating the way she does. *Bog će ti pomoći* — find the inner strength. Luisa grins. God's got a lot of work to do, but of course she'll cope. She's made it through law school, succeeded in a high-demand job, and she's comfortable with this travelling drill now. Mum travelled to New Zealand by herself, after all.

She sneaks another glance at Bex, whose face is turned to the sun, her sunnies a white figure-eight racetrack perched across her nose. There's still a niggle, though. How much money has Bex got left? If she doesn't have a buffer, arriving in London by herself could also be madness. The irony of Luisa's letter to her parents isn't lost: *We're taking a boat across to Italy, then winding our way up through Europe, to London.* Not a lie, just a small shift in latitude to the left. Perhaps she should ditch her plans and travel to London with Bex — make sure she's settled? She can always visit Yugoslavia later. But then, how responsible should she feel for Bex? She's already made concessions. At what point does she stop owing her? Mum's back in her head: *Life is full of compromises.* Perhaps there is a better way.

'Hey, you. Being young isn't always about being sensible.' Bex rewards her with a cheeky grin. It's the same advice Bex has flung her way over the past weeks. 'I don't want this to sound selfish, but how would you feel if we pooled the money we have left? I've still got travellers cheques and you could pay me back. You know as well as I do that you'll get a job. We can re-think things and shorten the trip. Get to Korčula in a couple of weeks, or however it works best. Just imagine unpacking, and being in a home, experiencing the culture. Take your time, though. You don't need to decide right now.'

Bex's forehead creases with a frown. 'It's tempting. And I can see why you're a gun lawyer.' She quietens for what seems like an age. 'Okay,' she says finally, her voice more determined. 'Can I think about it? But only if you're sure you don't mind and I can pay you back. Can't have you becoming my substitute crutch.'

Luisa pulls her close. 'Of course I don't mind. I'd be stoked. You should know that.'

Bex wriggles backwards to look Luisa in the eye. 'I'll let you know tomorrow. You know I'd be gutted to miss out.'

As they pick their way back down the slope, the sky turns a burnished orange, the scarves now transformed into licks of fire. Luisa feels she may have just negotiated a minefield — that the balance might be restored. Of course she could survive by herself, but it wouldn't be nearly as much fun. Besides, if Bex does agree, the added bonus will be that Luisa can help settle her in London later. Keep an eye on her.

AUGUST

MONDAY

Six days later, needing to escape the cauldron of Athens, Luisa and Bex are in Thessaloniki. Their backpackers is close to the beach, away from the city centre. They wander along the sea wall looking for a taverna to dine at and a waiter pounces, greeting them as though they're the catch of the day. He leads them to a corner table set with a checkered green-and-white cloth overlaid with a thin plastic sheet secured around the table legs by an elastic band. The plastic cover allows for a quick turnaround of the tables — the Greeks are slick at this — but tonight they won't be rushing. They need time to finalise their plans for travelling into Yugoslavia.

The waiter hands them the menus and lights their candle in the iron holder before racing off to chase down some potential patrons who have had the gall to pause at his blackboard menu then wander on. Bex laughs when he leads them back. 'Got 'em! They're masters at it, aren't they?'

Luisa laughs. The light reflected from the candle stub is pathetic, but the coloured paper lanterns beneath the canvas canopy cast a cheerful glow against the night's blackness. Another waiter sidles over and Luisa and Bex order the grilled swordfish and a salad to share.

'Maybe some of those fava beans too,' says Bex. 'They were delicious the other night.' Luisa casts her a sideways glance. It would be petty to quibble, but she's surprised Bex isn't pulling back on her spending now that she's agreed to the new plan.

'The drinks?' asks the waiter.

'Water,' they both chorus, then splutter with laughter.

The waiter backs off and Luisa thinks how she could kill for a beer. She wouldn't have hesitated a week ago and with Yugoslavia so close she feels like celebrating.

'Decision time.' Luisa pulls out the map and spreads it on the table. It's been tougher than she anticipated, poring over the guidebook these past few days. It's brought home just how little of Yugoslavia they will get to see before arriving on Korčula. There's no point nit-picking, it's a small price to pay and she can always return. What's important is completing what she set out to do with her family.

Bex opens the guidebook at a marked page. 'Here's what I think,' she says, and Luisa feels like one of her pupils again. Not that she'd ever say — there will be something Bex finds annoying about her too. 'If we take a train through to Bitola,' Bex continues, pointing at the map, 'at this part of the Macedonian border, we could make it on to Lake Ohrid in the afternoon.'

'But why go all the way over there? We talked about heading to Skopje, and then on to Belgrade. Don't we want the most direct route?'

'This will still be direct,' says Bex. 'And look.' She points to a photo. 'Ohrid's a Unesco World Heritage site.' She rubs her hands together. 'The mosaics are meant to be a-mazing.'

'You and your bloody mosaics,' Luisa laughs. 'Haven't you seen enough by now?' Through Turkey and Greece, Bex has become obsessed with them as a teaching tool. Still, Luisa is impressed that teaching is a vocation for Bex, not just a job.

Bex is adamant. 'Never! But I can list all the other good reasons. One, it'll be cheaper to stay out of the city. Two, it'll be far more interesting going this way, and three—'

Luisa chimes in with what has become their catch-cry: 'The route less travelled is always the most interesting.'

'Exactly,' says Bex.

'Still,' says Luisa. 'I wonder if we should keep it simple this time. There's a train from here that takes us straight through to Skopje. How do we even get to Lake Ohrid?' She looked at this option a couple of days back and the information was sketchy.

Bex stares at her. 'From the train we take a bus. It's in the book.'

'Okay,' says Luisa, thinking she should recheck, but Bex's research is usually spot on.

The waiter returns and Bex pushes aside the paperwork to make room for the food. Luisa divides their meal. Thankfully the portions are generous: Luisa is so ravenous she could easily devour a full meal. The fish is a little dry, but the feta and black olives in the salad have the perfect balance of salt and sharp. As usual there's a small pile of olives building at the side of Bex's plate which Luisa will savour later.

'Hang on, we know those guys, don't we?' Bex points to the street. 'Oh my God, it's definitely them! The Dick and Dan show.' Bex is on tiptoes now, waving. 'Hey, Deek! Over here!'

When they first met back on their first night in the Big Apple, Bex had teased Dick about his Aussie accent. The international hostel was on Manhattan's Upper West Side. An old brownstone where Luisa had half expected to find Bert or Ernie from *Sesame Street* lounging on the wide front steps, or welcoming them at the front door under the grand portico entrance.

Luisa feels a flash of irritation. She would rather focus on their planning, and these guys will be a distraction. There's no mistaking them. Tall and spindly Dan, sporting his distinctive Lennon-style glasses, and Dick, a beer can of a guy with muscles to match. Nearly four months on, Dan's hair is an unruly ginger thatch. In New York they discussed the possibility of meeting, knowing their paths might cross in Greece, but the guys were going to London first and then travelling south. Luisa had forgotten about them and besides, everyone's plan could change on a whim or a train timetable. But then, travelling had been all about turning expectations on their head.

'Deek's wearing his tan well,' whispers Bex.

'I thought you were changing all that?' says Luisa under her breath. She means it as a joke but she worries it sounded like an accusation.

'Lighten up. What's wrong with looking?' She grins. 'You should practise more often.'

Luisa shrugs off the snide. She hasn't been brave enough to broach again what Bex told her on Samos, but she's seen no evidence of her changing. She might as well be a chameleon disguising her convictions under a light-hearted shell. This is the first time Luisa's pushed back but she won't do it again in a hurry. Maybe Bex's man-radar will always be fine-tuned. Mike is back in her head and she blinks him away. She and Bex will have to differ on this point — chopping and changing isn't the solution either.

'You girls look great,' says Dick, and Bex welcomes him with a hug. 'No jet-lag this time, eh?' Luisa scrambles to her feet and Dick raises his hand to acknowledge her.

'Small world,' says Dan, smiling across at Luisa. Bex wraps him in a hug too. Luisa hangs back, thinking, *We hardly know these guys*, but says, 'Why not join us? Have you eaten yet?'

'Yeah, down the road,' says Dick.

'A beer, then?' says Bex.

'Now you're talking.' Dick pulls out a chair.

'Round of ouzo?' says Dan. 'To celebrate running into each other again.'

'Let's stick to beer,' says Luisa firmly, catching Bex's eye. 'We've still got some planning to do.' *Bex will thank me later.*

The waiter returns. 'Amstels?' says Dick, glancing around the table. Bex gives Dick the thumbs-up. 'Four please, mate.'

The waiter nods and smiles but Luisa wonders, not for the first time, what the locals really think, if they get tired of the banter from the invading backpackers.

'Hey, remember the last time?' Luisa picks up her fork to finish her meal, determined to lighten the mood again. She uses her best American drawl. 'Dollar for a slice, miss.'

'Jeez, that's right,' says Dan. 'Don't want those problems tonight.'

They last ate together in a pizza joint. A dishevelled man crashed in beside their table demanding a slice of pizza. Luisa felt both repulsed and sympathetic.

'And remember that guy who just about mowed us down, Lou? *Fook New York.*' Bex has the knack of getting the intonation just right.

Dick and Dan laugh. 'There were some crazy people, all right,' says Dick.

The waiter returns holding the beers high on a tray. He clears the girls' plates.

Dick raises his bottle. 'Here's to all the mad, bad experiences. Been a blast though, eh?'

They clink bottles and Dan takes a swig. 'New York was a shocker. I honestly believe murders did happen every day. Couldn't wait to get out. Where's next for you girls?'

'Yugoslavia,' says Luisa. 'Mum was born there. We're staying with my rellies.'

'Yugoslavia!' says Dick. 'Just been through.'

'Really? What did you think?'

'Crazy place. Didn't see much. Stopped in Belgrade and what was the other place, mate?'

'Sarajevo,' says Dan. 'Where the First World War started. Hey, your money goes a long way. Economy's a joke — prices go up every Thursday.'

Luisa tries to figure out what this means.

'To cheap travel then,' Bex says, raising her bottle and smiling at Luisa.

Perhaps shortening our trip wasn't necessary. Luisa wonders whether Bex feels any trace of guilt.

'Seriously, though,' says Dan, clinking his bottle against Luisa's. 'You're lucky to know someone there. We had a blast in Holland at my aunt's.'

It's the same argument Luisa threw at Bex but she's frustrated. Dick and Dan are shining examples of backpackers catching a *glimpse* of a country. There have been a number of times on this trip where she's felt like they've all been stuck outside, looking through a window, a bunch of foreigners talking about themselves and their own experiences. She wants to feel a connection in Yugoslavia.

The guys convince them to have another round and Luisa relaxes. She needs to do this more often, to go with the flow. Since Mike dumped her it's been too easy to lose the knack. She enjoys the banter as they catch up on the places they've been, and when it's time to leave it's like seeing off old friends. Dan picks up the bill from where its propped between the salt and pepper shaker then places a collection of drachma notes and coins on the table. Luisa itches to check the bill. *Stop it!* she warns herself.

'Great seeing you girls,' says Dick, hugging Bex then Luisa. 'Good luck with the planning.'

Dan does the same. 'Look after yourselves,' he says.

When they sit back down, Luisa checks the bill. Dan's contribution more than covers his and Dick's share of the beers. Bex reaches for the guidebook but Luisa doesn't hesitate. 'No more planning needed,' she says, and Bex's mouth drops open.

Luisa grins back. 'Being young isn't about being sensible, you know.'

Yugoslavia, of all places, should be where they opt out of the travel-worn routes. The Dick and Dan show has put this in perspective. Lake Ohrid will be the first step to exploring the true heart of the country she's longed to embrace, not just the 'flimsy wrapping', as she's come to think of the popular tourist routes. One more day and what she has dreamed of will be a reality.

AUGUST
WEDNESDAY

The no-frills train pulls into Florina station. The simple wooden building is scuffed at the edges and spattered with graffiti. A lone guard paces the platform. Even the tracks have reduced to a single line.

'Jeez, check out the station,' says Bex. 'What a dump.'

'Give it a chance.' Luisa's voice carries a sharp edge. She's disappointed but determined not to admit it. 'A lick of paint would do wonders.'

They haul themselves out onto the platform from where the smattering of passengers left on the train have rushed off already. The guard looks away. It's just after midday but the furnace-like temperatures of Greece feel much further than a morning away. It's as though they've shrugged off summer and stepped into autumn. Luisa glances further up the track. Yugoslavia must start somewhere up there but it's nothing like the pictures she's been carrying in her head. The mountains are dark and deeply forested with thick clouds hugging their tops. She reassures herself that what Mum described is in a completely different part of the country; the Croatian coast is miles away and Macedonia's a separate republic. It would be like comparing Bluff with the Bay of Islands at home. Bex is still looking unimpressed and Luisa forces a smile.

Inside the tiny station the waiting room is deserted. They dump their packs against a wall and Luisa checks the timetable. The journey from Thessaloniki was meant to have taken five hours but took six. *Bloody 'Greek-maybe' time!* The next connecting train to Bitola is at 2 p.m. but they could have caught one half an hour ago if their first train had run to time.

'Just over an hour to kill,' says Luisa.

Bex rummages in her pack. 'Jeez, where're my trackies? What's happened to summer?' She digs deep and the black pants with their distinctive three stripes emerge like a snake. She glances around before slipping out of her shorts, down to her underwear.

There's the sound of shuffling at the door and Luisa turns. A young guy, his face like a fox, leans up against the doorjamb, leering.

'Jesus!' says Bex, twisting around with a jump and scrambling to pull up her pants. She backs up against the wall.

The fox makes a clicking noise with his tongue. They've got used to this blatant attention through Greece and Turkey but there's always been more people around.

'Must be the local come-on,' says Luisa under her breath, glaring at him. 'How're we going to lose this sleaze-ball?'

'Click. Click. Click.'

'Just ignore him,' says Bex.

'Piss off!' Luisa says, waving her fist, but he doesn't budge.

Without taking her eyes off him, she reaches back and unzips the flap at the top of her pack, groping around until her fingers curl around her Swiss Army knife. Disguising it in her palm, she draws out the longest blade. Everything feels like slow motion as she takes a step towards the fox. 'Don't mess with us!' she growls, stamping her foot and aiming the blade at his head like a miniature gun, looking him in the eye.

How long does she stand there? It feels like minutes. The creep backs out of the room, his hands held high as though in surrender. It's not until she hears him driving off that she relaxes her arm and snaps the knife shut.

Bex dissolves into laughter. 'What was that about? I've never seen you so tough. Genius!'

Luisa's hands shake now. She leans against the wall for support and laughter takes over. Every time she attempts to speak she erupts in hysterics. 'Oh my God, he was probably harmless,' she finally manages to splutter. 'But I wasn't taking any chances.' The laughter takes over again. 'Was I?'

'Nope,' says Bex, wiping away her tears. 'I'll keep you on my side.'

'Imagine if I'd had to face that guy on my own!' Luisa hugs her. 'We're a good team.'

It's not the first time she has relied on that little red knife, tucked away in the pocket of her daypack or under her pillow at night. Dad gave it to her as a leaving present and although he wouldn't have thought of it as a weapon, she's been relieved to have it on a number of occasions. Especially in New York, a city itching with agitation where the warnings followed them around: *Be careful girls, murders happen every day. Stay safe.*

Luisa searches for her own warm clothes, pulling out the same Adidas tracksuit pants and a sweatshirt. 'I'm going to find the bathroom.'

'Good idea. I'll mind our packs,' says Bex.

The bathroom smells like disinfectant. Luisa wants to make this quick but it's an effort to wrench up her pants because the fabric's so stiff. She tries to remember when she last wore them. Once she has hooked the stirrups under her heels, the three stripes run like tracks at the sides of her legs. She pulls her red woolly socks over the top, folding them down at the ankle like leg-warmers. *That's better.* The fabric clings against her legs as though giving them a mini-massage. There's something about the elastane that makes her feel in control, just as she was with that creep. She swallows another explosion of laughter as she returns to join Bex.

The battered local train sits waiting, and the ruddy-faced guard paces the platform looking officious and eyeing them with contempt. His blue uniform looks shabby but the row of brass buttons running in a line up to his neck gleam. A pen pops out from behind his ear underneath his conductors cap. 'Passports!' he demands, holding out one hand and twirling an ancient-looking stamp contraption in the other.

Luisa hands hers over and he leafs through each page with painstaking care, licking his tobacco-stained forefinger. Luisa wonders what he's looking for, if he's surprised by the number of stamps crowding the pages. When he checks Bex's passport it's with the same raised eyebrows.

'Open!' he orders, pointing at their backpacks. He gives their possessions only the most cursory of looks before thumping his stamp down on their passports. 'Okay, okay,' he says, waving them on.

Welcome to Yugoslavia, Luisa thinks. She had hoped for so much more. She wonders what Bex is thinking. Of all the places they've been this is definitely the most disappointing.

Inside, the tiny train is like a tin shack on wheels. They sit opposite each other and use their packs as padding against the corrugated sides. There's just one carriage and only seven other passengers, all of them male. The train is so slow to get going that Luisa doubts they'll even struggle up, let alone conquer, the mountainous terrain ahead, but the rhythm kicks in, and they rattle and lurch forward. She stares out the window. Are these peasant farms they're passing? There are hay stacks everywhere, tepee shapes with pitchforks sticking out the top. They look like they've been rolled by hand. A woman at the side of the tracks puts down her slops bucket and waves. Is that hessian sacking she's dressed in? None of these images match the pictures she's been carrying in her head.

'Hi,' says a lanky guy, leaning on Bex's seat back. 'I can practise my English? My name is Nikola. I am pleasure to meet you.'

He slides into the seat beside Bex and when he flashes Luisa a smile his brown eyes twinkle. He looks about their age but wears old-man serge trousers teamed with a tan corduroy jacket. His shoes look like the type they used to wear to school — regulation black and just as scuffed up. His hair seems slathered with wax and crinkles back in waves like an inky skullcap. *I am pleasure to meet you too*, thinks Luisa — very cute. Somehow he reminds her of Mike, not just his olive skin and dark eyes, the way he moves perhaps? Mike had the same sureness. The fact she's lost him still sticks like a dagger. Bex gives Luisa a raised eyebrow: *What about this for luck.* She's quick to introduce herself, then Luisa.

'Where you come from?' he asks, beaming again, as though this is the best thing to have happened to him all day.

'*Nova Zelanda*,' Luisa replies, sounding out the syllables.

'Ah, Amerika. My friends go. Nice place.'

'Not Americans. Kiwis,' says Bex, nudging him.

'Ah, Kiwi girls.' Nikola smiles.

'And you. From Bitola?' Bex asks. 'It's good living here?'

Luisa cringes at Bex's pronunciation, her pure Kiwi accent.

'Bee-tola.' Nikola corrects her, then frowns. 'Our country is no good. I want to get out.'

Luisa's tempted to try out her Croatian but she knows the Macedonian dialect will be different. 'Your English is good. You learn it here?'

'Ah,' he says. 'A little at school, but most from the TV. And your very good pop songs.' He smiles. 'I'm learning to be the mechanic. For the fast cars.' He gestures towards the rear of the carriage. 'Florina has the good pieces for the cars. Greece is the very wealthy country.'

Could have fooled me, thinks Luisa, wondering what they might be heading towards. Bex does her best to convey the story about the creep and soon they are all laughing. Luisa acts out the moment with the knife.

'So, I am to be frightened of you,' he says, grinning.

'Very,' says Luisa, her voice like a warning. She checks her watch. 'Nikola? We want to go to Lake Ohrid. There's a bus?'

He frowns. 'Now? I'm not sure. Maybe just morning. We can see. Not long now.'

It's just after three p.m. when they pull into the Bitola station. Luisa and Bex hoist their packs.

'Come,' says Nikola. 'We can find the bus.'

The air reeks; nearly every chimney belches smoke. Piles of rubbish are strewn about and the footpath is no more than broken slabs of concrete parked either side of the dusty road. They are forced to walk down the centre of the road between the groups of men, a patchwork of ages, perched upon the slabs. Their eyes feel like drills and Luisa is grateful to be trailing after Nikola. Some sit on ramshackle chairs, others directly on the concrete. A few gather around small tables, their heads lowered, playing games. She wonders if some might be playing briškula, the card game the men play at the Dally Club at home. Most puff on cigarettes and the smoke hovers, a thick shroud in the still air.

Nikola strides ahead. Luisa quickens her pace and Bex manages to fall into step beside her, taking two steps for every one of her loping strides. In New York they had been the ones staring, taking in the crowds of people, faces that were a melting pot of features and colour where nothing seemed to gel. The streets there were filled with noise: sirens mixed with the growls from brash tin-can cars cruising low to the ground and flaunting ostentatious number plates. Buicks, Fords and Chevrolets ruled the streets while bright yellow taxi cabs swarmed like locusts. Here, the buzz of the men's conversation hushes to an eerie silence then returns like disconnected static once they pass by.

'It's like we're movie stars, or models, someone famous,' says Luisa.

'Pity about the catwalk,' says Bex under her breath.

'Where are the women?' whispers Luisa. Somehow, it feels better filling the void with chatter.

Bex pulls a face and shrugs. 'Anyone's guess. We might as well be back in the Dark Ages.'

Bex is right. This place does feel like a step back in time. Perhaps the men think them flashy, profligate, spoilt even? Maybe their sweatshirts seem too bright? They're probably wondering how two young foreign women even got to this remote part of the world. How they would have the money. What a joke — if only they knew.

Nikola is waiting up ahead. He leads them down a tiny side alley that's too narrow for vehicles. The seal is too pot-holed and rutted anyway. This feels more comfortable, in this back street where there are some women. It's impossible to tell their age. Most are dressed simply in black dresses, with headscarves hugging their round faces. One woman stands out, parading patterns of bright orange and yellow on her black skirt and wearing her white headscarf loose, like a bonnet. Perhaps they're Muslim, thinks Luisa, but she's not sure. It's no wonder the men stared at them. Luisa glances across at Bex who rewards her with a smile.

'This is cool,' she says, and Luisa feels a rush of relief.

The women are all busy with some form of domestic chore: sweeping their front yards, tending to their gardens, hauling buckets or bags loaded with who knows what up the street. Most stop and stare but their looks don't seem hostile or accusatory — perhaps they're intrigued to see two young women with packs loaded high on their backs. Another side of life, a possibility. One flashes them a gummy grin and waves. Bex waves back. The woman's grin widens and Luisa wonders if these people have access to a dentist.

At the end of the alley, Nikola points ahead to the main town. People stand in clusters, muted shades of black or grey. Luisa is appalled by how utilitarian the low-rise apartment buildings look. Everything in this place seems worn out and there are so many who are idle. Bex was right. It does feel as though they've turned back the clock to an earlier decade. Luisa thinks about pictures she's seen from the war years and tries not to stare, but she can't help it. Closer, it seems that the only shot of colour comes from the odd headscarf. Across from the bus station a group of young men point and jeer. Nikola yells at them, shaking his fist, and they scuttle off. Inside the terminal Nikola checks the timetable. Bex has gone quiet again. When he turns back his face says it all: there is no late bus.

What now? Bex was so certain and Luisa wonders if she even bothered considering transfer times. But then, the buses and trains have run at all hours elsewhere and they've got used to travelling on a whim. The lack of information in the guidebook should have been a warning. It seems the rules are different here.

The place Nikola points out looks more like a hotel. Luisa's thankful for the bankcard tucked securely in the money-belt around her waist. This might be the time she has to step in for Bex and dip into her reserve funds. A dusty ochre car pulls up to the kerb and the driver leans across to yell at Nikola through the open passenger window. He's gesticulating, both hands waving, and Luisa smiles. This feels familiar, like the club at home or family gatherings with Dad and Uncle Zoran.

Nikola loops around to the driver's side and leans in the car window. The two men seem deep in conversation.

'Check out the make of his car,' Bex whispers. 'Zastava. I reckon it might be straight out of Russia.'

'Close rellie of the Lada for sure,' says Luisa. She looks across to the building again. Definitely not a hostel. On the cracked sign over the porch the few lights still working reveal the shape of a beer tankard. 'Come on,' she says, tugging at Bex's sweatshirt. 'Help me check this dive out. It's definitely a job for two.'

'Hey! Kiwis. Wait!' Nikola calls out when they are halfway across the road.

He catches them before they head up the short pathway. A flight of steps leads to the double entrance doors where a light is shining behind the glass panes. Two old men sit either side of the steps. One can't stop scratching himself: behind his ear, his crotch, his chest. The other stares vacantly. A terrible stench of urine hangs in the air. The twitching man jerks his arm and Luisa jumps back, the weight of her pack throwing her off-balance so that she almost loses her footing. Bex grabs her and the man cackles as they rush past.

Inside, the dark panelled walls of the foyer sap any available light. The reception desk is unmanned but the bar behind is crammed with customers. Bex pulls a face, and Luisa can't believe they're even contemplating staying in this dodgy-looking place. Nikola hangs back by the door. The sign behind the desk advertises rates in both dinars and American dollars.

'Is this right?' she asks Nikola. 'One room costs fifty US dollars?'

'What a rip-off,' says Bex, scrunching her nose. 'We've never paid that sort of money. Anywhere.'

'Maybe I have the better idea,' Nikola says, motioning, already half way out the door.

They give the men on the steps a wide berth. Nikola points across the road to a thick-set, stocky man leaning against the ochre car. 'My friend. He can help.'

As they draw closer, Luisa double-checks that it's not fur coating his forearms. Even his feet clad in clunky brown sandals are super hairy.

'Kosta,' Nikola says. 'My friend. He has room. At his house.'

'Please. Come,' says Kosta, his arms still folded like a Cossack dancer, his voice booming.

Nikola claps his hands and babbles. 'His mother. His sisters. Everyone's there. I come too. For the language help.'

Kosta shifts about as though he can't get comfortable. Luisa wonders if his clothes might be a size too small. He seems older than Nikola — thirties, even? His eyebrows sit heavily and his thick beard curls around his chin and mouth.

Luisa pulls Bex over to a quieter spot on the street. 'I'm not sure,' she says. 'I can pay, honestly.'

'For God's sake, don't be a ditz. It's a no-brainer,' says Bex. 'Why waste our money? We should be grateful. I don't want to piss them around.'

Nikola and Kosta are staring and Luisa gives them a cheery wave, still feeling torn. This is the kind of experience she's been wanting, but she would feel more comfortable going to the home of two strange women.

'Come on. It'll be fun,' says Bex. Luisa thinks this will be another one of those times when she'll look back and kick herself for hesitating. 'We've struck it lucky. At least it'll be a cheap night.'

Bex grabs Luisa's hand and pulls her back to the car. Mum's back in Luisa's head: *Life's for the living, tears are for the dead people.* Bex is right. Why would they spend a fortune staying at that horrible hotel? It's a no-brainer.

All the same, when Nikola instructs them to leave their packs beside the car, Luisa watches closely as he loads their packs into the boot. All their worldly possessions are inside and without them they'll be snails minus their shells. She clambers into the back seat behind Bex, scrunching her nose at the pong of stale cigarettes. The fawn-coloured lining is fuzzed with layers of grime and they perch either side of a slit running down the middle of the back seat. The sagging brown vinyl exposes stained foam and springs. Nikola turns and gives them the thumbs-up as the car takes off, the engine sounding like gunshot.

Nikola gives a running commentary on the local landmarks but Luisa can't concentrate. Outside, ramshackle fences built from sticks or wooden posts divide the land. Sunflowers are jammed against corn and cabbage fields, and towers of watermelons are stacked outside makeshift stalls. The mountains behind everything form a stark backdrop, some capped with snow. Luisa wonders how far out of town Kosta's family live. How much time they should allow in the morning for the bus. Nikola has turned his attention to Kosta and they are talking non-stop. Luisa wishes she could understand, but the dialect is so different.

'Amazing,' Bex says, turning back from the window. 'I didn't imagine it would look so different from Greece. It's obvious we're in another country. *Your* country.' She slaps Luisa's thigh. 'Exciting, eh?'

Luisa forces a smile. She knows Bex is trying to get her to relax but it's hard to dampen her disappointment. Even though it's well after five p.m. people are still toiling, some bent low slashing sickles, others standing behind cumbersome ploughs. Groups of women struggle along the side of the road with loads of firewood strapped high on their backs. They straighten to glance at the car then lower their heads and trudge on. Surely these woman are too old for this type of work? They all look like grandmothers. If Baba Marta was alive, she would be getting dinner ready at this time of day.

Maybe she's got Yugoslavia all wrong? New Zealand seems so full of hope in comparison. It makes more sense now why so many Dally families send their hard-earned cash back home, often going without themselves. A worrying thought catches her. Could her relatives be putting themselves under strain by having them to stay? Uncle Josip is a fisherman so probably is not a huge earner, and she is unsure whether Aunt Mare works. Her family would never be considered well-off but from what she's seen today, and through Greece and Turkey, she has a new perspective. For the first time in months, she feels a pang of homesickness. It's as though all the colour has bled out of the pictures she's been carrying in her head.

Nikola turns and claps his hands, pointing to a gap in a tall hedge. They pull into a gravel driveway curling around in front of a white clay farmhouse and Nikola instructs them to wait by the car. The row of trees cast long shadows and Luisa leans against the car, wrapping her arms tight across her chest, watching as Nikola and Kosta head off towards the house. Bex busies herself pulling their packs from the boot, dumping them down and snorting with laughter as clouds of dust explode.

'Check your arse,' Bex says, as Luisa goes to help. 'Car's not the only thing needing a wash.'

It feels cathartic to laugh, but Luisa clamps her mouth shut at the sound of footsteps rounding the corner of the house. Kosta and Nikola stride out in front of four women in plain black dresses. Nuns minus their headgear, Luisa thinks, as the women draw close. Maybe headscarves are an accessory for town? Whatever the reason, she is relieved Nikola wasn't lying. Kosta tugs at the sleeve of the stout, older lady and pulls her forward. Her hair is beautiful, snowy white and caught behind in a neat bun. If they hadn't just been in Bitola, Luisa could have been fooled into thinking she had just stepped out of a hair salon.

'Please. My mama, and my sisters,' Kosta says, sweeping his hand to indicate the three younger women, a clique of twittering birds hanging behind.

Kosta's mother is a similar height to Bex. She takes her hand. 'Welcome,' she says.

The sisters look to be close in age to Luisa and Bex. They are taller than their mother but still a head shorter than Luisa. One wears her jet-black hair loose while the others have theirs pulled into ponytails. It's obvious they're sisters — same almond eyes, same sharp noses. She glances at Kosta, checking for the resemblance, but she can't see past his facial hair.

Kosta's mother drops Bex's hand and turns to Luisa. 'Welcome,' she says and her hand is a mixture of soft and sandpaper. 'Come.' She gestures towards the house.

Luisa reaches down for her pack.

'No! No!' The sisters flap and squawk, pointing at the men.

Kosta's mother herds Luisa and Bex into a dimly lit room. There's a slight musty smell and the festival of lace reminds Luisa of Baba Marta — the crocheted doilies on the coffee table, the elaborate curtaining on the windows behind. A grandfather clock ticks loudly in the corner, the dark walnut veneer polished to a high sheen. Kosta's mother gestures towards the plump sofa.

'Thank you. Thank you so much,' says Luisa, conscious that she's gushing.

For a moment, Kosta's mum seems stuck in the spotlight, then someone calls from

another room. She turns and marches off, barking orders, the gruff sounds seeming at odds with the mild-mannered woman who's just been with them.

Luisa and Bex perch either end of the couch. Somehow it feels wrong to talk. Luisa fingers the stuffing oozing from the rolled arm rests and runs her hand across the seat. The fabric is beautiful: pale hydrangeas on a worn linen weave.

'Nailed it this time,' whispers Bex. 'What a privilege.'

Luisa eases further back into the deep seat and closes her eyes. There's so much she doesn't know about Mum growing up here. She would often say, *You don't know how good you've got it in Nova Zelanda,* but Luisa never appreciated what she meant, never bothered to ask. She feels guilty. Travelling has shone a light on what Mum must have glossed over: the stories of her childhood, spending time at a refugee camp, growing up under a new Communist regime. Mum focused on the positives, but Luisa's certain there must have been hard times. Perhaps her mother's life wasn't too dissimilar to the lives of the women they've seen?

'Come! Come! No sleeping time.' Nikola startles her when he enters the room and crashes into one of the low-slung chairs opposite the sofa.

Kosta is there too, thrusting a pack of cigarettes in their faces. He shrugs as though mildly disapproving when they decline, then heaves into the chair beside Nikola, leaning over to offer him a cigarette and lighting it from his own. His chair sags as he reclines further back. The buttons on his checkered shirt strain against the mound of his stomach. He pulls hard on his cigarette and it seems that he's trying to hook his sandals under the rim of the coffee table. When he stretches again he succeeds. Now he's a convex banana, incongruous alongside Nikola, who is stretched out, relaxed. Kosta's trouser legs have crept up and cling to his thick calves. Luisa dares to glance at Bex. She's smiling too and Luisa's laugh erupts like an explosion.

The women file in carrying plates of food. Kosta's mother carries a glass bottle filled with a strawberry-coloured liquid she pours into tall glasses. Luisa searches the older woman's face. Surely she wouldn't be plying them with alcohol? She takes a sip but can't work out the flavour that's like summer with a sharp tang.

'Her special,' Nikola says. 'From the cherry tree.'

'Yum! Delicious,' says Luisa, raising her glass. Kosta's mother claps her hands as though delighted.

The sister who looks the youngest sidles close to Bex. Nikola beckons her over and she whispers in his ear. 'She wonders to touch your hair. It's okay?' he says, grinning.

'Sure. Wish I'd washed it though,' says Bex.

Soon all three sisters are alongside Bex, touching her smooth blonde bob. 'So soft. So white,' Nikola translates.

'You want to see?' Luisa says, noticing one of the sisters staring at the gold locket Mum handed down to her on her eighteenth birthday. The sisters crowd around but before she can show them the enclosed photo of Mum as a child, Bex retches and whips her hand up to cover her mouth. Luisa slides her glass towards Bex who snatches it up, sipping quietly, her face colouring. Kosta's beard can't mask his smirk.

'That feta,' Bex mouths. Luisa's not surprised — it's the most pungent cheese she's ever tasted.

Kosta's mother bustles back through the door and motions for her daughters to gather around her. Kosta extracts himself from the coffee table to join them. They speak in hushed tones, then all four women wave goodbye and file from the room. Luisa glances towards the grandfather clock. It's close to seven p.m. She looks to Nikola for an explanation.

'They go to work,' he says. 'Back at midnight.'

'Really?' Luisa stares at Nikola. Her mind races and all she can think about is how stupid they've been. 'Where's his tata? On the farm?'

Nikola jerks his head towards Kosta. 'We don't talk of him.'

'Come,' says Kosta, gesturing for them to follow. He leads them down the hallway, past the kitchen, and flicks a light on in a small bedroom. Luisa lets go of her breath upon seeing their packs propped in the far corner, to the side of a wide bay window. 'See, all good,' says Kosta, patting his stomach.

High up by the ceiling, the wallpaper peels away in places but the wooden floorboards gleam. Luisa smiles. She wonders whether they use methylated spirits, like Mum does, *my secret weapon.* Heavy brown curtains hang either side of a lace screen and two single beds are lined up with just the narrowest gap between. Luisa knows which bed will be hers — the one furthest away by the bay window. She prefers a wall alongside and it makes no difference to Bex.

'We go to the cafe now,' says Nikola. 'In the town.'

Kosta smiles and stretches his bear arm to drape it around Nikola's shoulder. Luisa and Bex exchange looks. Luisa feels conflicted but maybe it will be safer with others than alone in this house in the middle of nowhere.

'Five minutes to freshen up?' says Bex, holding up her hand, her fingers spread. 'See you back in the lounge?'

'Yes. Good,' says Nikola, turning to leave with Kosta.

Once they've gone Luisa crashes onto her bed. Bex sits beside her.

'What job starts this late?' Luisa whispers. 'And what's with the dad?'

'Not exactly the story they spun us,' says Bex. 'Those poor women! What a crap life having to go to work now. I'm embarrassed they had to run around after us. Come on, though. It'll be a chance to party with the locals.'

'Don't expect too much.' Luisa is still annoyed that Bex decided for them about going out. 'Do you think we should bail now? Go back to that hotel?'

'Don't be so paranoid. They're harmless. Really. And Nikola is gorgeous, don't you reckon?'

Luisa shakes her head. *Typical.* 'I did give him a second glance,' she says. This conversation feels so unreal.

Bex nudges Luisa with her shoulder. 'Impressive! About time Mike's knocked off his perch. Come on, then. We better get ready.'

They change into their jeans but Luisa feels as though she has lost all control. Her mind races, wondering why Nikola and Kosta are friends since their personalities seem so different. There's the age gap too, but perhaps she should cut Kosta some slack. It's clear he's had a rough time with his dad. She peers in the mirror, scrunching her spiral curls. She could do with freshening up, but a smear of lipstick will have to do. She doesn't want to over-do it and give these guys the impression she's made an effort.

A wave of emotion catches her by surprise. Being in Yugoslavia among these strangers, the women on the street, Kosta's mother with her manicured hair. It cuts at her heart. Luisa has lost the opportunity to meet Baba Ana, Mum's mother, Luisa's lookalike. She tried forging a connection with Baba on the phone but the combination of her thick accent, together with all the static and gaping time lapses, conspired against them. All that's left are Baba's birthday and Christmas cards — second-rate substitutes for what might have been.

'What?' Bex says, leaning in close to apply a touch of eyeliner. She's wrapped the pretty scarf she bought in Turkey around her neck too, the one Luisa had spotted first.

Luisa lets it go but the thought gnaws: if Mike was here, it would be so much easier.

The streetlamps cast a warm glow over Bitola, and the sharp grey lines of the buildings seem softer, less austere. The damp air clings to Luisa's face. It isn't raining but fine droplets of mist dance in the suspended pockets under the streetlamps. She tails behind the others, crossing the pot-holed road to the cafe, a plain square building with huge windows stretching close to the pavement streaming with condensation.

Kosta pulls open the heavy door. Here we go, thinks Luisa as a blast of hot air slaps her in the face. She's wedged behind Kosta but can just see over his shoulder through the layers of smoke clutching the air like clouds, suspended over the Formica tables. The room heaves with men, drinking, laughing and shouting. A sole middle-aged woman wearing a bored expression seems to be responsible for the bar. An old-fashioned tape-deck blares beside her, competing with the cacophony. Kosta signals he's going for some drinks.

'This way,' Nikola says, pointing towards a spare table at the rear of the room.

They weave their way across with Nikola stopping to exchange greetings at nearly every table. Most of the men just stare, but one, an older man, his chin covered with a thatch of white stubble, leaps to his feet.

''Ello, 'ello,' he says, bowing deeply and waving his black woollen cheese-cutter cap like a toreador. He clasps Luisa's hand, pumping it up and down.

'Please. My uncle Boris,' says Nikola, slapping him on the back. Uncle Boris' grin broadcasts a gaping hole where his front teeth should be.

'Bootiful! Bootiful!' he calls as Nikola herds them off.

Luisa's face is red-hot when they reach the table. She's relieved to wriggle out of her sweatshirt but pulls back in disgust when her elbows stick to the tacky table-top. The built-up layers of grime are a vivid reminder of the student pubs at Otago University. Revolting. Kosta leans over to place a jug of beer and glasses down, the overflow adding to the grunge. He shoves the person seated behind him who moves, allowing him the room to sit. Nikola pours the beer and Kosta raises his glass.

'*U Zdravje!*' Kosta says, gulping down the contents and slamming the glass down. He pours himself another then reclines in his seat, lighting a cigarette. Luisa takes small sips. The beer's too bitter for her liking: she much prefers a lighter style. Bex doesn't seem to mind; she's already knocked back most of her first glass. Nikola and Kosta lean their heads together, whispering.

'Kiwi girls, they like the good time, no?' Kosta raises his glass. '*U Zdravje!*' He slugs back his drink again.

'Cheers!' says Bex, draining her glass. Nikola refills their glasses. Luisa just needs a top-up.

'So you party on your travels?' Nikola asks. 'Here, we love to make fun.'

'Why do you think we're party girls?' Bex rubs her fingers and thumb together in the universal money symbol. 'Not enough of this to go wild but we've had some fun nights, eh Luisa?'

'Plenty,' Luisa replies, with a warning look.

They haven't eaten enough today and what they had at Kosta's was just a nibble. Bex's face is already colouring close to the shade of her coral T-shirt — not a good sign. But then, she seems to have her sparkle back. Luisa feels torn. Why not relax and have some fun? Ever since Samos, she has felt they've been holding back, that things have changed. 'Tell one of your stories,' she says. 'The bathtub girl in New York, or that time we hitchhiked in Turkey.'

'Tell Kosta about your special knife,' says Nikola, beaming.

Bex needs no further encouragement, throwing in actions to help. Kosta appears to be all ears and Nikola can't keep his eyes off Bex. He seems entranced. No wonder, Luisa thinks, the way that scarf makes her eyes pop a brilliant blue. She tries to keep track of how often their glasses are being refilled and makes a point of covering Bex's glass but she shoos her hand away. Bex seems totally engaged, laughing and chatting, but Luisa can't get in the mood. Bex throws her the odd pointed look. It makes what Bex said back on Samos — about admiring Luisa and wanting to make changes — seem like filler, just empty talk.

Luisa's not sure what to believe but she envies Bex in this situation. It's not just her spontaneity. Even if Luisa *had* been interested in flirting with Nikola she wouldn't have stood a chance; it's obvious he only has eyes for Bex. Sadness washes over her. These times. This ache. It still catches her by surprise. If only she and Mike were still together. Being principled is well and good but she worries she might never get over him. Nikola is cute, but what would be the point?

Bex snorts with laughter over something Nikola has just said, then leans across to whisper in his ear. Luisa checks her watch: 9.45 p.m. Kosta seems to be contemplating something. Perhaps he's making the same frustrating comparison between himself and Nikola? A folk song breaks through the din and everyone has started singing. Nikola and Kosta are up on their feet, clapping each other on the back, their voices booming forth.

'Up, up!' Nikola hauls Bex out of her seat.

They signal for Luisa to stand too. She's relieved to feel included, to be participating again rather than sitting back and observing. Kosta encourages them to clap along, and they do their best. Bex beams at her. This feels better, thinks Luisa, draping her arm around Bex's shoulders. They sway and clap to the music, trying their best to join in on the chorus. Another popular song follows and Bex throws in some dance moves. Luisa follows her lead. Nikola and Kosta, and some of the men at the tables close by, encourage them. It's fun, even in that confined space, to embrace the sense of freedom she always feels when dancing.

Bex asks for water when they take their seats again. It's still stifling hot and the dancing hasn't helped. Luisa signals for the same. Bex turns her attention to interrogating Nikola and Kosta about their lives here. Luisa helps with the questioning and this feels better, as though she's on an even footing. They learn that the connection between Nikola and Kosta is through their mothers who were school friends. Nikola's dad died a few years back and he lives in a small flat with his mother. Kosta has been like a big brother to Nikola. Nothing more is mentioned about Kosta's father, but his mother and sisters often work night-shifts at the garment factory to earn overtime rates — the bonus money is worth it when they meet certain deadlines.

'Does your mother come out to the cafe?' Luisa asks Nikola.

'During the daytime. Yes. But our women are different to you western girls.'

'What do you mean? They'd love it,' says Bex, in all seriousness, patting his forearm, as though encouraging him to think more about the idea 'You should ask them.'

Nikola looks sceptical and frowns. Bex places her hand on top of his which Nikola then turns into a game, drawing out his hand and placing it over hers again. Bex whips her own hand from underneath and lays it on top. Challenging him. Laughing. A fast-paced game of who can slap their hand on top the fastest ensues. Bex gives up, dissolving into giggles.

'Stop! Stop!' she splutters. 'Enough. You win. Drink time.'

Luisa feels like thumping her to bring her to her senses. Kosta smirks at Bex then turns to Luisa. 'You think the same? That my sisters would enjoy to drink here? For me they are best at home.'

'They must get tired of that. Everyone enjoys a change,' Luisa answers, not quite believing she's even having this conversation.

'It would make problems,' says Kosta. 'Life is different in your country. You are different.'

A chill runs down Luisa's spine. Bex will have to watch herself — this doesn't feel like harmless banter. She tries to catch Bex's eye, send her a warning look, but she seems determined to ignore her. Again Luisa questions whether she's reading Bex correctly but it's as though she's lost the rational part of herself, her ability to judge and know what's best. She tries reassuring herself but it's hopeless. Nikola and Kosta have made their views clear and the TV shows would only perpetuate the myth that western women hold a different set of values. After all, they didn't hesitate asking them along tonight. Luisa scouts the cafe again. There's definitely just the one lady behind the bar. She remembers how those men on the street stared. Perhaps it wasn't just the way they were dressed? Luisa feels like a scarlet poppy in this roomful of men.

Luisa still feels completely sober when they head back outside at the end of the evening. It's just after eleven-thirty and the street is deserted, making the others' laughter feel too loud. Kosta's mother and sisters should finish work soon, Luisa thinks, relaxing a little. The air stings her face and arms and she scrambles to pull on her sweatshirt. Kosta and Nikola stand to the side, their voices booming, their arms waving. Bex is in her own little world, dancing around, mimicking their movements, not seeming to notice the cold. She skips over to Nikola and reaches up on tiptoes to plant a kiss on his cheek. He smiles down and takes her hand. Everything feels out of place. Kosta points in the direction of the car before striding across the road. Bex and Nikola follow, still hand in hand.

'Bex, wait!' calls Luisa, hurrying to join them and desperate to sound some form of alarm. 'He's had way too much to drink! Maybe I should drive?'

Even as her words spill forth she knows they are pointless. It's the same at home where the men insist it's their place to drive. Kosta stands waiting by the car, glaring. What choice does she have?

'Lighten up! We'll be right,' says Bex, opening the back door and pulling Nikola in behind her.

It feels odd climbing into the front seat. Luisa turns to check on Bex, who is snuggled next to Nikola, her head on his shoulder.

'I don't see any traffic,' says Bex, holding her hand to her mouth as though stifling a laugh. 'You?'

Kosta grunts and turns the ignition. The Zastava roars to life, and Luisa stares out the side window trying to ignore the muffled noises from the back seat. She should have made more of an effort to slow Bex down on her drinking. It's just as well they stuck to beer. The car is so tiny that her shoulder nearly touches Kosta's; it doesn't help he's so broad. When he moves the gear stick, his hand brushes against her leg and she angles towards the car door. He huffs, and she worries again about the impression they are giving these guys. Bex isn't helping. It's all gone quiet in the back. Luisa sits rigidly, willing the farmhouse to appear, grateful that Kosta doesn't appear to have difficulty driving although his breathing is deep, like a snort sometimes. When they turn into the driveway, the house is still in darkness. Kosta cuts the engine.

'Will your mama and sisters be home?' asks Luisa, still searching for any sign of light.

Kosta shrugs. 'I think so.' He lumbers out of the car and points towards a building looming as a shadow to the side of the main house. 'They sleep there.'

Perhaps there is a pinprick of light? When she saw this building earlier she thought it was a long shed.

'This mine house now,' Kosta says, before striding off.

Luisa hangs back until Nikola and Bex climb out of the car. The wind is cutting, sharp daggers of ice, and Luisa wraps her arms close to keep in some warmth. Nikola draws Bex close and Luisa follows them, their feet scrunching against the gravel path towards the back porch. It's where they left from earlier. The kitchen leads off it, and a small bathroom. Luisa excuses herself, relieved to escape into the tiny bathroom. She can't wait to get into her bed, can't wait for this day to end. Even so, she has to force herself to walk back inside the house.

Nikola and Bex are beside the Aga stove warming their hands. Kosta has planted himself midway along the narrow galley kitchen space, leaning against the bench, his feet jutting out blocking the through-way. It's as though she's being asked to walk the gauntlet to get past him and down the hallway to their room.

'So, now,' Kosta says, a smug look on his face. He rubs his hands together and beams. '*Viski* and cards?'

Luisa is sure he realises it's the last thing she wants. 'Not for me, thanks,' she says, conscious that her voice sounds clipped. She makes an effort to soften it. 'Hey, thanks for a great night, but I'm shattered. Bex are you ready for bed too?'

'*Viski* and cards sounds like fun,' says Bex, grinning up at Nikola. 'Come on, Luisa, stay and enjoy yourself.'

'I'm knackered,' says Luisa firmly. 'Will you be okay, though?' She wants to give Bex another chance to see reason and opt out.

'I can look after myself. Don't want these boys missing my card shark shills.' Bex giggles and corrects herself. 'Skills. I'll be in later. See you in the morning. Sleep well, heh.'

'Okay then. But only if you're sure?'

Luisa steps over Kosta's legs, determined not to stumble. 'Night, everyone,' she says, turning back at the door, grateful she got through without incident.

Luisa's guilt prickles. She shouldn't leave Bex by herself with these guys. But she gave Bex the choice and she's chosen not to listen — just like the other times this evening when she blatantly ignored Luisa. Bex can fend for herself.

She flicks the light switch in their room and pushes the door firmly shut. Seeing her pack propped in the corner fills her with a strange sense of homecoming, and when she kneels on the bed to draw the heavy brown curtains, this routine of preparing for bed calms her. Rustling through her pack she pulls out her toothpaste — her forefinger will have to be her toothbrush tonight — and the long T-shirt that doubles as a nightdress. After changing, she finds some tissues in her daypack and uses them to spit out the excess paste. Nearly there. She clicks the buttons on her digital watch to set an alarm, then uses the glow from her watch to guide her back to the bed. There's no way they want to miss that bus. Still, she can't settle. Will Bex be all right? Florina pops into her head. She wrenches herself back out of bed then inches alongside it until her hand finds her pack and the knife. It may be stupid, but it will help ease her brain. Back in bed she tucks the little red knife under her pillow.

AUGUST
THURSDAY

Luisa awakes to footsteps, or maybe the door squeaking? She feels groggy, and her mind twists around the question of whether she even managed to nod off. The last thing she remembers is lying curled up, listening out for Bex. The light from the hallway shines in and she glances across. The other bed is still empty and for a split second she's relieved — this must be Bex coming in now — but it's Kosta's bulk, backlit by the hallway light, and his distinctive shambling footsteps crossing the room. Luisa edges herself back against the headboard, her mind still fogged.

'Kosta. What? What time is it?' All she can manage is a whisper.

He stumbles, knocking against her bed, and she wrenches the covers up closer to her chin, her eyes still trying to adjust.

'Go! Get out!' Her voice is stronger this time.

His breathing sounds laboured, as though his mouth is set like a saw and each intake of air is rubbing against his sharp teeth. She's crammed in the crease of the corner, her shoulders bridging the right angle.

'Nikola. Bex?' she calls out, her voice pitiful.

She hoped by hearing their names it might bring Kosta to his senses but it's as though he's in a trance. A disgusting sound explodes from him. A guttural snort. Her instinct is to scream but she worries this might make him angry and instead clamps her mouth shut. She tries flattening herself further against the wall but the room has run out. Instead, she pulls her knees to her chest, hugging them. Kosta turns his head towards the door; a sudden movement. *Oh God. Please let it be someone coming.* Maybe it's Bex, or his mother? Maybe someone has heard. He shambles back down the length of her bed then over towards the door.

Now. You have to move now. She reaches for the knife under her pillow. The snap as she extends the blade coincides with the door clicking shut. Her mind is frantic, mapping out the route to the doorway. First step, crawl to the foot of the bed. Her throat feels dry. It's now or never if she's to get past him and out that door. Her eyes strain against the coal blackness as she crawls towards the foot of the bed, desperate not to make a sound. There's a rustling sound and a metallic thud when something hits the floorboards. Luisa freezes before easing herself off the bed, heart pounding, certain that Kosta is standing close to the other bed.

Luisa feels her way as the curtain fabric gives way to the wall. Her foot bumps one of the backpacks and she grips the knife tighter, blade pointed in front, searching with her free hand for the rear wall. It's a relief to feel it against her palm, and she pauses for a moment, taking a breath, straining her ears. Keeping to the wall will be her best chance to skirt past and escape. With her back pressed close she shuffles, tiny steps, her other hand cutting at the air with the knife. His laboured breathing is closer now. It happens so quickly. She senses his movement, tries to duck to the side, shrieking when he catches her arm and jerks it upwards. The knife flips from her hand and clatters to the floor. Kosta has a vice-like hold but with her free arm Luisa swings wildly, using all her force. He manages to intercept this arm too, catching her forearm and tipping her off balance. In one motion he seems to wrench her forward then backwards onto the bed.

'Kosta. No! No!' she screams.

Her heart drills her chest. Her mind won't keep up. All those fearful nights walking home alone rolling into one. She tries to wrestle free but his fingernails dig into her shoulder, pushing her back. One hand closes around her leg, and all she can think of are his furry arms, that bear's paw crushing her calf. He jostles her backwards. *No!* She refuses to be a limp rag doll. *Fight!* But she's pinned flat on her back. She can feel his bare legs. The bulge of his penis. One leg is still free and she arches it, determined to find some leverage to kick, up, out, anywhere she can connect. It's hopeless, she's like a flimsy stick insect, flailing and Kosta has manoeuvred his body to lie on top of her, all his weight now pinning her lower half with her arms forced behind her head. *Make him go away!* But the screaming is only in her head, her voice paralysed because she's run out of options.

His face looms close and his cloying breath is a mix of alcohol, garlic and cigarette smoke. Luisa squirms and twists her head, this way and that, taking ownership of the one body part she can still move. His weight feels suffocating. *Think!* She lies quietly, turning to stare at the wall. *Think.* There's no time; his snort is a bestial animal sound, so close to her ear that she startles, jerking her head back and screaming in fright.

'Stop! Oh Jesus, please. Bex!'

For a brief moment it's a relief to hear her own voice, as though she's succeeded in reconnecting, but then his hand clamps over her mouth, severing her plea. Somehow, he manages to keep both her arms pinned. She tries wrenching one free but it's no use. Why hasn't anyone heard? Luisa's heart sinks. Bex can sleep through fire alarms and with alcohol she's ten times worse. But Nikola? It dawns clear that this was a set-up. They would have likely put drugs into Bex's *viski*. The flat of Kosta's palm presses against her mouth but his fingers still roam, stroking the side of her face. He whispers, she has no idea what, then that same guttural snort. She tries another tactic, forcing herself to smile, and maybe he senses the movement because he lifts his hand away. Luisa gulps at the air and he brushes his fingers against her face, his words still slurred. She tentatively moves an arm, just the tiniest of movements, but he plasters his palm back over her mouth and pushes down harder with his body.

'Let's find the others. Please. I won't tell.' She pleads with him, the words leaking out from behind his palm like gurgles under water.

His hand is between her legs now, wrenching them apart and even though his weight has shifted a little he still has her pinned. She's repulsed by his stiff penis prodding and pushing against her leg. Closer and closer and she tenses, an attempt to transfer energy into her pelvis so that she might catapult him off.

'Get off! Oh my God. No!' she screams but her cry is pulverised as he clamps his mouth on hers.

There's no air, but she feels compelled to shut her mouth like a clamp, against the mess of hair, his beard rasping her cheek and the side of her mouth. Her lip sears with pain when he bites it and drives his tongue in. Luisa gags, biting down hard with her front teeth. His roar forces her mouth to yank open and a panicked sob escapes. Turning her head towards the wall is a way to keep at least one part of her body away from him. There's no point in crying. This is happening. Her most dreaded fear has finally caught up with her.

All that remains is a sickness in the pit of her stomach as he searches with his fingers, pushing the flimsy fabric of her underwear sideways. He shoves against her with his penis. She feels so raw. All she wants is for this to be over now. He thrusts into her, again, and again, and again, and she yelps out in pain, sobbing now, big gasping sobs. *Just make it end. Please make it end.* He still has her wedged and she worries that if she moves, he might hurt her even more. The thought makes her whimper and she goes quiet, so quiet, holding her breath to not make a noise.

He continues to thrust, arching his back, and moaning. Then his strangled cry. She feels completely overpowered by him and that hideous sound. Her chest hurts from holding her breath so tightly and she releases it as a gasp. Her heart quickens and without warning her body shudders. At first she doesn't recognise the groan as coming from herself. But it is her. Her body convulses. *Oh, Jesus. No! Make it stop.* Repulsed, she tenses her body, desperate to regain control. Kosta's body shudders and he collapses, all of his weight, his breathing deep, and heavy.

Tears pool and then dribble down the side of Luisa's nose. When Kosta finally rolls off her he lies at her side. Luisa lies stiffly, determined not to make a noise, her face still turned towards the wall. It takes all her effort to breathe. It's as though she's been opened up, drilled into, cutting deep to where her anxieties have lain in wait. But now they are flowing, leaching through her eyes, crawling over her body like an army of ants. There is no cathartic release, just emptiness. She wills him to go, still worrying that by moving even an inch she might encourage him again.

Kosta curls off the bed and looms over her. Luisa lies quietly, very quietly, feigning sleep. After pulling up the covers and patting them around her, his breathing sounds calmer. She's determined not to flinch when he strokes her face, but when his bristly hair brushes against her ear she can't help moving away, just a nudge. He whispers something, she has no idea what, but he seems oblivious as to whether she's awake or not. It's only when he shuffles towards the foot of the bed and back towards the door that she feels she can breathe. He stops and picks up something from the floor and Luisa remembers that thud — the sound of his belt buckle hitting the floorboards.

Luisa holds onto her sobs until the door closes shut. She's a felled tree but it's his detestable, stinking sap, leaching from her, slicking her thighs like glue. Her tears flow, giant gouts of disgust and vulnerability, but she's too frightened to make a sound.

Somehow the night passes. The light filters under the curtains and brightens the room. Luisa's tears have shrivelled inside her. She hasn't slept, nor dared to leave the room. It's too much of a risk. Every time she moves the cloying smell from that bastard animal's semen rises to taunt her. And so she lies still — she might as well be a stone except that her mind is still alive. Thoughts twist and tumble, a tangle of contradictions which seem impossible to unravel. How could she have thought this was the country of her dreams? She worries about Bex, but in the next instance her mind lashes out. How could Bex have deserted her? She has no choice but to wait. If Mike were here, he would know what to do. If Mike were here, she would be safe.

The click of the door sets her heart racing again. Luisa's body twitches and shakes uncontrollably from head to toe as though she's frozen, so incredibly cold. Bex tiptoes in and pads across the room. Luisa huddles down into herself, curling up like a koru.

'You awake?' whispers Bex. 'Fat chance me sneaking in. Busted, eh?' She giggles and touches Luisa's shoulder. Another spasm attacks Luisa's body. 'What's the matter, hon? Shit. You're angry, aren't you?'

Yes! Luisa wants to scream, but all she can manage is a moan.

'Oh my God! What's the matter?' Bex rubs Luisa's arm. 'Are you sick?'

'He. Raped. Me.' Luisa's words spill out like grey dishwater.

Bex thumps down beside her and wraps her in a hug. 'Kosta? Oh my God. No!'

Luisa scrunches her body into a tighter curl. Bex is speaking but her words mean nothing. All Luisa cares about is feeling the warmth of Bex's arms. Safe arms, wrapping her close. She's so exhausted. All that's left are tiny sniffs — shadows of tears.

'Luisa, listen. You need to listen. It'll be okay, but we need to get out of here. I'm going to find Nikola.'

'No! Don't!' Luisa grabs at Bex's sweatshirt.

'I'll be straight back. Five minutes. Don't move.'

Bex pulls away and hurries across the room. Gone. Luisa's arm is left dangling and she pulls it into her huddle, her hand a tight ball against her heart. She won't let this beat her. And then the clarity. The horrible realisation. Bex is safe. Bex abandoned her. Luisa thumps the mattress but there's no release from the anger contained in her tight fist. How could Bex do that? It's been their unspoken rule to stick together. She should have let Bex go and fend for herself in London. Bex was the reason they came this godforsaken way and Luisa is the one who's paid. None of this anger helps. She has no choice but to wait. The numbness creeps back.

When Bex returns she switches on the light. Luisa tries to hide her head. She can hear Bex rummaging through a pack.

'Quick,' Bex says, tapping her on the shoulder. 'Nikola will drive us into town. He's got the keys.'

'But Kosta?' Luisa groans.

'Nikola's keeping a lookout. You get dressed. I'll sort our gear.'

Luisa forces her legs out from under the covers; placing her feet on the ground counts as small progress.

'Here, I'll help,' says Bex. 'You stay sitting.'

Luisa might as well be a puppet. Bex undresses her then feeds Luisa's arms through the straps of her bra, leaning around to hook the clasp behind. She helps Luisa into a clean T-shirt and sweatshirt. Luisa can't bear to look down. Not at that other part of her body.

'Maybe keep those on, hon,' Bex says, as Luisa tears at the waistband of her underwear. 'For the evidence.'

'No!' Luisa snaps, scrambling to her feet to wrench her underwear down, wincing. She refuses to be a puppet. *No!* She pushes through the pain and makes it to her pack, pulling out a clean pair of knickers along with a plastic bag. 'This will do.'

'Good idea. These now.' Bex hands Luisa her tracksuit pants and takes the plastic bag. She picks up the discarded knickers by their waistband and drops them inside. Luisa's sneakers are lined up beside the bed, the socks already tucked in. Bex points at them. 'Hurry, hon. We have to go.'

Luisa slumps back on the bed. 'Ouch!' Her eyes well. That reminder. That change in movement. She scans the floor and finds her knife lying against the skirting board, its blade still snapped out. Everything feels like slow motion as she pulls on her shoes. Without thinking she has reached across to retrieve her watch from the small table between the beds and is fixing the strap around her wrist: 7.25 a.m. The routine feels strange when everything else is at odds.

Bex is dressed. This feels right. Bex is always first to get ready. She brushes past Luisa and leans out the door to the hallway. 'Hurry,' she whispers, beckoning. 'Take Luisa's pack. The red one.'

Nikola scurries in and Luisa averts her eyes and stares at the knife. Bex crosses to the same spot and her knees crack while bending to retrieve it, startling Luisa. Bex snaps the blade shut, and Luisa feels that same sense of hopelessness — failure on a sharp edge.

'I'll take this,' Bex says, cradling the knife in her hand.

Nikola has Luisa's pack slung over his shoulder, her daypack looped over his arm. Bex hauls her own pack onto her back and clutches her daypack to her chest. She motions, *Quick!* Luisa makes it to the door but hesitates, holding on to the frame, scanning the hallway, left then right.

'Go,' Bex whispers urgently. 'Follow Nikola. Through the kitchen.'

They slip down the hallway, through the tight galley kitchen and out onto the back porch. A chill wind catches Luisa when she steps off the porch and she lifts her fist to her mouth. Bex urges her onwards, towards the Zastava, the gravel crunching under their feet, far too loud. Nikola closes the door behind Luisa and she sits, tucked in behind the front passenger's seat, her knees wedged shut, her hands like wringers on her lap. She edges away from the slit and dares to glance out the window. Bex and Nikola climb into the front seats. The house in the early morning light is less white and more a dirty cream. The sun colours the tops of the terracotta roof tiles, a sly kiss. Luisa shudders and stares at her white knuckles. It's only once they ease out of the driveway that she lets out a dry whistle.

'I'm sorry, Luisa,' Nikola blurts.

Arsehole, Luisa thinks, drilling the back of his head. 'Get me out of here,' she says, through clenched teeth.

Nikola flicks his head as though shocked to hear her speak. He turns back again and the only sound is from the wind whistling against the car.

'The police station, right?' Bex says, turning to Nikola, her voice snarky.

It's the last thing Luisa wants. She doesn't want to see anyone. Doesn't want to tell. 'No!' she says, determined.

'We have to, hon,' says Bex, and Luisa feels powerless again.

'Please,' says Nikola, raising one hand. 'I feel guilty. I didn't know. Didn't know he could do that. My place is small. But now, I wish . . .' His voice trails off.

'You *should* feel guilty!' says Bex. 'How can you be friends with that monster?'

'He is friend of my family.' He thumps at the steering wheel. 'I don't know him like friend, more like . . . older brother. I trusted him.'

'He was an animal,' says Bex. 'Look what he did!'

Luisa shudders. She can't control the shakes.

'Luisa, I tell you,' says Nikola, catching her eye in the rear-vision mirror like a startled animal. 'I keep saying I'm sorry. I cannot believe this. I don't know this side of him.' His fingers tap at the steering wheel.

'You know now,' Luisa mumbles, staring out the side window to the mountains in the distance. Home feels so far away. It's as though she's on quicksand and being pulled under.

'I know,' Nikola says. 'And I'm sad, very sad.' He shakes his head. 'You are our guests. We mean to look after you. Now I am all wrong.'

'How can we be sure this wasn't a set-up?' says Bex. 'How many others have you caught in your web; you the charmer and he the monster?'

'Bex, please! Believe me! I have no idea. Trust me, I feel shame to admit this.'

Bex jabs her finger onto the dashboard. 'So, what will you do?' Her voice is shrill, indignant.

'I must leave to police. They will know. For me, I will be angry.'

'You have to speak to him. To his family. You must tell them.'

Jab, jab, jab. *Please, make this stop.* Luisa tries to ignore the flow of words. She would give anything to have her family around her now. She looks to the mountains, feeling emptied out, then jumps when her watch erupts. Nikola jerks his back. Luisa slaps at her wrist to silence the shrill beep. Pointless now.

'I try,' says Nikola. 'But I'm scared too. I'm wanting to hurt him. I have no trust in myself.'

'You should throttle him,' says Bex. 'Give him back his own medicine.'

'First we go to police. Then we find a way to get you Kiwis out. Then is his turn. Only then.'

This shuts Bex up. Perhaps she is thinking through the next steps. Luisa concentrates on taking deep breaths. The danger is behind her but she still can't order her thoughts. She doesn't want to think. Can't.

The police station is a two-storey concrete building, with rows of square windows half-covered with roller blinds. An ugly air-conditioning box sits to the side of the main doorway. Two large flags droop from poles cast at an angle midway along: one is the Yugoslav flag, but Luisa doesn't recognise the other. A flat roof slab that looks glued on, an afterthought, covers the porch.

Nikola leads them up the small flight of stairs to the double entrance doors. The air-con box clatters and rattles. The policeman at the front desk rubs at his eyes and speaks to Nikola in hushed tones. Perhaps he's been awake all night too? He motions for them to follow him past the front desk, through the room with four desks, and out through a rear door. Down the corridor he pushes open a door and switches on a light. They gather inside a tiny room that resembles a packing crate, ply-thin walls and no windows. A bare bulb dangles spider-like from a long cord, and a small ornate crucifix hangs from a nail on the wall. The policeman speaks, and Nikola translates.

'He will call the doctor. Luisa. Your clothes, from the waist down please. You must lie on the bed. Bex, come now for the paperwork.'

'I'll come soon,' says Bex curtly, 'after Luisa's settled.'

Nikola and the policeman leave the room and Bex bustles around, gathering up the sheet folded at the end of the bed. 'Last step, hon. Get yourself undressed. Use this sheet to cover you.' She sounds like a nurse and Luisa does as she is told. A means to an end. All she wants is to have a shower and wash that bastard away. When Bex drapes the sheet across her half-naked body it seems farcical. She's never felt so exposed. Bex leaves, and Luisa lies there — tired, sore, scared. How could Bex leave her again?

She needs air so wrenches herself up, causing the mattress to crackle. Leaning back on her elbows she studies the crucifix on the far wall.

Plastic comfort. It's the Greek Orthodox style, all four arms rounded off, and brightly gilded with religious icons. Mum is in her head — the prayers she would recite — but Luisa won't tell her. This is something she must deal with herself. Mum has led such a chaste life and this would break her heart, rock her to her Catholic core. Worse that it's happened in her beloved homeland. Besides, Mum would be far too quick to fire the shots at Uncle Josip, linking what's happened with him being a conspirator and laying blame for encouraging Luisa to visit. The venom would fly, given Mum's reaction when Uncle Josip decided to put Baba Ana in a rest home — trivial compared with this. Luisa couldn't do that to her uncle. She wants to heal her family, not increase the rift by dragging them further apart.

She shifts again, trying to get comfortable. Even this slightest movement makes the mattress complain, taking her back to the many times she's slept in tramping huts back in New Zealand, back when she still felt clean. She slams her fist into the bed. There's no point in letting her mind wander — she can't escape her disgust. Why can't she have a shower? Is that too much to ask?

Minutes tick by. *Rape.* Always her worst fear, carried secretly once she understood what the horrible word meant. She had dodged the reality until now. How many times had she left the pub, or a friend's house, keys clenched ready for attack and walked home alone? She was always relieved to push her door open. Always lucky. But not anymore. At least she's done something right by staying on the pill. Regardless, she counts back to her last period. Antalya. How many weeks since they were there? Turkey feels a lifetime ago. Three at least. Past the danger zone, but is there a chance she forgot one of those tiny tablets? She's so careful but there's always a risk. *Oh, God — that dodgy stomach in Turkey.* Her mind is muddled and she can't remember the timing. She can't deal with that now. Only one thing is certain: they won't have the morning-after pill in this place.

A short little man, thinning hair, tired brown suit, the doctor, Luisa presumes, strides into the room shadowed by Bex. He taps her brusquely on the shoulder, indicating with a rolling hand that he wants her lying on her back. She complies, and the mattress crackles again. Her body aches, as though all the stiffness has been carried through her on spidery threads, a giant web transporting the dull pain to her furthest-away nerve endings. The smell is back.

Bex sits and squeezes her hand. This doctor has no interest in pleasantries. He lays his suitcase on the other bed, clicks it open and rummages through the contents, muttering to himself. Luisa shudders at the rubbery screech as he pulls first one hand then the other into disposable gloves. He turns back towards the bed, sniffing loudly as he approaches.

Luisa stares up at him and it's as though she's glued inside a movie. He takes her by the chin and shines a bright light at her face, twisting her head from side to side. With a stethoscope he listens to her chest, then lifts the sheet and pushes on her stomach, listening and muttering to himself. When he moves to the foot of the bed he taps at her ankles then moves his arms as though they are held by an invisible elastic band. She knows the smear-test drill: slide your ankles up, bend your knees, splay your legs wide.

The doctor sniffs and extends his index and middle fingers, holding them like scissors. Luisa tenses. Her breath escapes in short, sharp bursts and Bex squeezes her hand. It all happens so quickly. He inserts his fingers inside her vagina. The pain is hot and searing, and she squirms. Her eyes fill with tears and she yelps, a small animal sound. The doctor doesn't seem to notice her discomfort, continuing to poke and prod. When he withdraws his fingers, he speaks but it's like a bark. 'No married?'

Bex shakes her head. 'No. No.'

The doctor leans in close, staring at Luisa, frowning. He enunciates each word. 'Not. First time. Then?' Not a hint of compassion.

'Bloody hell! What's the difference?' Luisa erupts. 'He raped me!'

Bex leaps up. 'You're here to swab for semen. Get out!' She points at the door.

The doctor rips off the gloves and tosses them on the floor. He snatches up his bag and marches from the room. Luisa turns towards the wall.

'Hon, I'm so, so sorry,' says Bex. 'I thought it was for the best. I should have stopped him.'

Just words. Fruitless, futile words. 'Get me in the shower,' Luisa snaps.

As the warm water courses over her body, she stares at the evidence washing down the plughole. She doesn't care. It's the price of feeling clean. All she wants is to bury this experience — the memory of it, together with her shame. When she steps from the shower box she expects to feel some change, but there is none.

Bex is still treating her like a child, handing her clean clothes, helping her dress. Luisa's body feels disconnected, as though she's made up of disparate parts. Bex tugs on her hand and Luisa focuses on not shuffling but the stiffness is worse now. Her mouth feels dry and she runs her tongue over her lips, flinching at the patch of raw at the side, remembering his bite.

Back in the office, Nikola straightens from his slouched position over a desk where he's talking to a policeman. Luisa is not sure if it's the same policeman they saw earlier. They all look the same, these officials in their blue uniforms. Maybe that's what Kosta's mother and sisters roll out on demand at the factory where they work? Overtime rates for hierarchy.

'We have no choice with the doctor in Macedonia.' Nikola says, resigned.

The policeman stares, looking baffled. Uncomprehending.

'When's this disaster going to end?' says Bex, sounding exhausted. 'Is the paperwork complete?

'Not to worry,' Nikola says. 'I have asked. A few more details. Coffee now. Please. Come next door.' He plucks a piece of paper from the desk.

It is the same place: a cafe by day, and a bar at night. It's deserted now except for a table of four middle-aged women in the centre of the room. Nikola leads them to a table by the window. Bex pulls Luisa into the seat beside her. Nikola sits opposite. Luisa can't bear to look across at where they were sitting last night. She gazes out the window instead and Bex reaches for her hand but Luisa pulls away. She's had enough of people touching her.

'What happens next?' Bex asks Nikola, her voice low.

'I'm not sure. First you must complete the papers. Then the policeman speaks to Kosta.' He pushes a piece of paper across the table, pointing at the gaps on the form. 'Here. Please.'

Luisa glances at the form. Only some of it is in English.

'What's this?' Bex asks, pointing to a scrawled note at the bottom. 'Is that the doctor?'

Nikola turns the paper and translates. 'It says, patient healthy, no injuries and . . .' He squints at the paper. 'No virgin,' he says uneasily. 'Luisa must write here. Kosta here,' he rushes.

A burst of laughter explodes from the group of four women. Luisa looks across, and the one wearing a bold red headscarf turns away, back to her group and their laughter. They seem engrossed, the pitch of their voices rising and falling in sync with their moving heads. Luisa can't help comparing them to Mum and her friends at the Dally Club. If only Mum was here . . . She blinks hard. Perhaps she's now the latest juicy morsel of gossip? She snatches at the officious form, screws the paper into a ball and tosses it across the room. How dare they reduce her harrowing experience to this? Red headscarf moves to get up, but the others pull her back, returning to their huddling and whispering.

Bex launches in again. 'With doctors like that I'm not surprised this happens. He should be banned.' *Enough. It's too much.* Luisa's shoulders slump and the tears are back. Bex puts her arm around her, pulling her close. 'He should be shot for the way he handled that examination.'

The waitress approaches with their coffees and Luisa feels compelled to cover her face with her hands, to disappear.

'My mama says the same but we must make do. This is the small town. We have no choice.' Nikola sounds exhausted.

Bex scrunches Luisa's shoulder. 'You should ring your parents, hon.'

'No,' Luisa snaps, shaking her head. 'They don't need to know.'

Bex pulls back and stares. Their silence might as well be broadcast from a loudspeaker. 'You can't just carry on as if nothing's happened,' she says. 'That's crazy talk, even from you.' She rubs Luisa's back as though she wants to push her opinion in. Make it stick.

What would it achieve? Luisa's mum is one issue, but there's also her dad. He doesn't need more heartache. She knows about his alcoholic first wife — not that he confided in Luisa, Mum told her when Marko was going through a rebellious phase and drinking too much. Dad's heavy-handed reaction to her brother had seemed so out of character. Dad is such a gentle man and it made sense when Mum explained. Why can't Bex understand? This is yet another example of Bex only scraping the surface. No wonder she felt justified in changing her plans back on Samos.

Nikola reaches across and touches Bex's hand but she scowls at him, pulling away like a spring recoiling. *And yet they were so close last night.* It is all just a game, thinks Luisa, Bex selling her heart for short-term gains. She must feel guilty, surely? This wouldn't have happened if Bex had listened to her last night, if she'd been true to her convictions about the way she relates to men — but perhaps it will always be a problem for Bex. Some people never change. Luisa learnt that lesson with Mike, and she should have trusted her instincts about Bex, resisted when Niamh was making such an effort to convince her that it would be okay. But then, how well do you ever know anyone?

'I have the idea,' Nikola says. 'My aunt Helena. She is the teacher of English at the university. In Skopje. Maybe she can help. First I must telephone. Everything is possible from there.'

'What do you think, Luisa?' Bex asks.

'Anything. Just get me out of here.' She's grateful to Nikola for taking control.

'I do what I can,' Nikola stammers, scraping back his chair. He's nearly out the door before he calls out again. 'I come back, when I know. Wait here.'

The group of women push back their chairs too. Red headscarf stops outside the cafe and stares through the window, a mirror perhaps? Luisa can't help wondering how many of these women have experienced the same.

'What is it with these people?' says Bex.

Luisa doesn't answer. She's thinking about Mum again, and whether red headscarf knows Nikola, or Kosta's mother. She hopes Nikola won't tell his aunt about what's happened, that he'll be discreet. She takes a swig of coffee, trying to protect her sore mouth. It's stone cold and she swallows hard, flinching at the bitter aftertaste.

A crowd of flapping, head-scarfed women closes in as their bus pulls up to the terminus. Even from inside the bus Luisa can hear their squawks. She and Bex have spent the afternoon travelling from Bitola to Skopje. Nikola returned to the cafe just before midday having organised everything: tickets for the bus, and the promise of accommodation with his Aunt Helena. Luisa and Bex have sat side by side in prickly silence for the duration of the trip — four long hours.

The acerbic cigarette fumes saturating the air did nothing to improve their mood. It seems they've run out of things to say, lost all common ground. Bex spent most of the trip reading her book. It baffles Luisa how she could concentrate. All she could manage was listening to music on her Walkman: Tracey Chapman, Billy Joel, Toni Childs, but with each new tape the lyrics gained new meanings: problems, it seems, are what songs are inspired by. She scans the faces below and wonders which one is Helena, whether there will even be an Aunt Helena.

'Come on,' says Bex. 'Time to move.'

They step onto the platform and the women rush forward, tugging at their clothes. 'Best room! Best price!' they shout, each trying to out-yell the other in their frenetic bidding war. 'Six US dollars! Five! Five!'

Bex nudges Luisa forward. 'Keep moving,' she says, sounding hassled.

Luisa grits her teeth and hugs her daypack close. Her big pack is in the hold and she shoves her way towards the rear of the bus, flicking her arm at the women and raising her hand like a stop sign. A diminutive woman with dark brown hair, cut short like a skullcap, pushes her way through and tugs at Luisa's sleeve.

'I'm Helena,' she says, just as Luisa tries to shake her off. 'Nikola is my nephew. Come.' Her button eyes gleam behind her gold, wire-rimmed glasses.

There's something reassuring about this woman who they follow without hesitation. In a no-nonsense manner, and with a few harsh-sounding words, Helena shoos all the vultures away. Thank God for Helena, in her tweed suit spliced with olive tones, and her sensible brown shoes and thick nylons. She leads them out of the station and over to a white car. The same box shape as the Zastava. After loading their packs into the boot, Luisa takes the front passenger seat — she's had enough of second-best — and Helena pulls away from the kerb.

'I'm truly sorry,' says Helena, turning to Luisa. 'The bus was early. Unusual for here.' She grimaces. 'Could have saved you from all that rabble.'

It's a relief to hear English again. Luisa has a strong sense that Helena will take control.

'And which one's Luisa?' Helena asks.

Luisa puts her hand to her chest and Helena responds with a warm smile. It doesn't feel necessary to speak and Luisa is grateful.

Helena turns towards the rear. 'Hello. Then you must be Bex?'

'Hi, and thanks. Jeepers. That was full-on back there. Is there always a welcoming party?'

Good old Bex, doing her job, smoothing the way. She's so bubbly now and yet on the bus she couldn't manage more than a few words.

'Afraid so,' says Helena. 'I apologise. It's happening more and more with the inflation. God rest Tito's soul. Our great leader must be turning in his grave. People offering their homes as hotels for the price of bread on the table. I wonder what this country's coming to.'

'We didn't realise it was so bad,' says Bex. 'Thanks so much for having us to stay.'

'Nikola tells me you are his friends and need my help. I'm happy to do this. We can talk through what's needed at home. Please know that you are very welcome. It's just me, so you won't be disturbing anyone. You can stay for as long as you need.'

Luisa's relief feels like stepping into a cosy house on a blustery day, but the irony is not lost. If only they had paid one of those head-scarfed women back in Bitola for their accommodation. Even on the bus Luisa was labelling some of the men as potential thugs. She stares out the window at the grey concrete buildings.

'I'm not sure what you know about our history,' Helena says. 'We had a major earthquake back in the Sixties. Our city's almost completely rebuilt.' She sweeps her arm as though she's throwing away her words. 'We got rid of the old, and the city's more organised now — modern shopping malls and the like — but I fear we've lost some of our charm.'

They pull into a wide street with no footpaths. Most of the houses sit close to the road behind low concrete fences. Helena stops outside a small rectangular house with a flat roof. Two large square picture-windows sit either side of a bright yellow wooden door. Underneath the front windows are garden strips of massed pink pelargoniums, their pretty ruffles and white centres a welcoming sight. It's a clever way of brightening an otherwise austere exterior. That same tug for home returns. Dida Stipan had a knack for making things grow and he would have approved of Helena's efforts, thinks Luisa.

Helena insists on carrying Luisa's backpack and although Luisa feels guilty, she's grateful. How much has Nikola told Helena? Perhaps it's the sight of this house and Helena's kindness but Luisa feels as though she's wearing an overcoat and carrying rocks in her pockets — one for every trauma over the past twenty-four hours. Helena leads them through her front door, past the two front rooms, and into a small bedroom. There's just enough room for two single beds covered with pretty patchwork quilts in cerise and grey.

'There's just the two bedrooms,' Helena says. 'Are you happy to share?'

'Of course,' says Bex.

Luisa's too tired to speak. She thinks about the collection of rooms they've walked into over the past four months, staying for one, two nights, three, at the most. She wishes this was just one of those times, but nothing will ever feel normal again.

'Join me in the kitchen at the far end of the hallway,' says Helena. 'Just when you're settled.'

'Helena?' Luisa says, struggling to find the right words. 'I'm feeling a little sick. Would it be rude if I went straight to bed? I'm so sorry.' All she wants is to crawl into the bed and make this day end.

Helena doesn't hesitate. 'Not at all. You must do what's best.'

'I'll come with you,' says Bex. 'Give Luisa some space.'

Luisa's relieved. Any other time they would enjoy setting up their beds and reflecting on their day, but everything's wrong now. She pulls the quilt cover up, balling a corner in her tight fist. She rubs it against her chin just like she did as a little girl. And then her mind casts back further, back to that place where love was unconditional, Mum sitting on the bed beside her, tucking her in tight, a snug bug in a rug. *Idi spavati moja draga djevojka* — go to sleep, my darling girl, go to sleep. Mum's hand brushes her forehead and although sleep comes quickly, it is fitful and the night passes slowly.

AUGUST

FRIDAY

Bex isn't there when Luisa opens her eyes the next morning, but she'd seen the mounded shape of her in the night. Luisa finds her in the kitchen, sitting at the table studying a map. The table is covered with a white cloth and breakfast is laid out: bread rolls, slices of ham, cheese, fresh figs, strawberry jam, and a carton of juice. Luisa's lips feel so dry, but every time she licks them is a reminder. Her stomach turns and she's unsure whether it's hunger or nerves.

'How did you sleep, hon?' Bex asks, glancing up.

'Good. I guess.'

'You must have been exhausted, poor thing. You were dead to it when I came in. Helena said to make ourselves at home. She's gone to work. She'll be back mid-afternoon.'

Poor thing. Is that the best Bex can manage? Luisa might as well have just stubbed her toe. The wooden chair is heavier than she expected and she uses two hands to pull it out. She eases herself down, wishing there was a cushion to sit on. Bex is still studying the map and Luisa takes in the room with its black-and-white lino floor. Yellow chintz curtains line the window above the stainless-steel bench and sink. The stove is similar to the one at home with the curly elements. A noticeboard above the table has a collection of items, pinned at all angles: five or so postcards, a scene from London, another from Paris; pictures of flowers and a cute tabby kitten torn from a magazine; a white card inlaid with a gold cross, maybe a mass timetable; and pinned neatly in the right hand corner, a photo of Nikola with his arm around a middle-aged woman, both of them laughing. Despite everything, Luisa smiles. In this country of strangers, his face is familiar now and he had the compassion to help them.

She reaches for a plate, taking a roll and smearing it with jam. If she can forgive Nikola, why can't she do the same for Bex? But even looking at Bex's face makes her feel like shouting, bringing Bex to account, listing all the reasons why she's culpable. And she had expected more, an apology, more guilt. Bex should have protected Luisa but instead she let her down and now, it seems, wants to skim over the surface of what's happened. How could she have ignored her on the bus? *Poor thing*. It seems she wants to wipe her hands clean, pretend it didn't happen. *Maybe that's how she deals with all her relationships when shit happens.*

'Helena's suggested we talk about a plan,' says Bex, not meeting Luisa's eye. 'She can help organise bookings. I've told her we'll probably fly straight to London.'

'Stop it!' snaps Luisa. 'Just stop your stupid plans!' It's unbelievable Bex can be so business-like, disregarding her dream, dumping it like trash. How could she not understand that her leaving will mean Luisa has lost everything?

Bex stares as though in disbelief 'I'm only trying my best. I assumed that's what you'd want? You were the one who wanted to come here. I'm just trying to get us out.' Her eyes well and she presses her sleeve against them. To Luisa it seems she's hiding.

'And what about what I want?' says Luisa. 'Have you thought about that? Or don't I count anymore?'

Luisa takes a bite from the roll but it hurts to eat. Bex turns away and Luisa chews slowly, turning the bread over in her mouth. But what *does* she want? Back on Samos she was convinced she needed Bex — thought the whole experience would be reduced somehow, be less of a celebration without her. She thinks back to the choices they made in Thessaloniki, how she pandered to Bex, how dearly she's ended up paying. She needs to look after herself now. No more compromising.

'We should make our own decisions,' Luisa says, feeling as though she's cutting the tension in the room with a knife. 'If you want to head to London, fine. But I want to stay and meet my relatives. Put this behind me.' She's surprised at how strong and calm her voice is.

'You really want to stay?' says Bex, turning back, blinking hard. 'Even after what's happened?'

'Yes.' Luisa has never felt so sure of anything.

Bex is quiet but after a moment says, 'I can't stay. Really. Not after this.'

It's a pity you didn't say *can't* the other night, thinks Luisa, but it's Mum's voice in her head. 'You made your choices in Bitola,' she says instead. 'I need to make mine now.'

'Come on, Luisa! That's not fair!' Bex thumps the table. 'You can't blame me. You know I feel like shit. That I'd turn back the clock if I could.' She covers her face with her hands and her voice is like a whisper. 'Jeepers. I need your forgiveness. I can barely live with myself as it is.'

And there it is. The shield that Bex has been carrying to deflect her emotions — at the police station, on the bus, arriving here, her greeting this morning — has finally been let down, the barrier that's been niggling Luisa. But it's those last words, *I can barely live with myself,* that stop Luisa short. What will more bitterness achieve? Bex is sobbing now but Luisa doesn't move to comfort her, doesn't have the energy. Time apart will be the only healer.

'He's not going to dictate to me,' says Luisa, amazed at the certainty in her voice. 'Korčula will be a new start. It's what I came here for. If I don't go, I'll feel like I've failed, let him win.'

'How will you get there?' says Bex, peeping through her fingers. 'I'm worried about you.'

'Not sure, but maybe Helena will have some ideas.'

Luisa wonders if this will be the end of their friendship. Whether Bex will always be a reminder, a dark shadow. She can't think of that now. What's most important will be keeping what has happened from her family, Uncle Josip included. She will have to be strong. Her family have been experts at shelving conversations, and now it's her turn.

AUGUST
MONDAY

Saint Helena of Macedonia, that's how Luisa has come to think of their hostess. She has been the one positive in this struggling republic. Someone should cast a bronze bust of this woman so she can be placed on display like the one on Helena's mantelpiece of Tito, only hers would be cast with a smile. She's been so discreet, not probing for more information on what happened in Bitola, just ensuring that Luisa and Bex have what they need. Yesterday she helped organise Bex's flight to London. She's provided nourishing food — soup, rustic bread and hearty stews — and even though Luisa eats sparingly, it has helped to restore normality.

It's their fourth day here. Luisa's spent most of the day in the lounge, avoiding Tito's cold stare by tucking herself away on an armchair in a sunny corner. Over the past couple of days, in this same chair, she has fought off fitful sleep. Horrible images of Kosta rear close, that beard, those hairy arms and feet, and the only way to be rid of him is by waking. It's easier to keep her eyes forced open. To stare straight ahead. It's been the same at night. Thoughts of her family, even Mike, help temporarily, but inevitably she's left feeling emptied out.

Each time she passes Tito his metal eye seems to judge her. Maybe it's the way she walks, still a little tenderly, or perhaps he can see right into her heart? Tito wouldn't approve of the disunity that's built between Bex and herself. Bex has been out for most of the day, *having a look around*, which Luisa knows is code for avoiding her. There seems nothing more to say, and any exchange invariably ends up feeling like a pot boiling dry: good intentions to start with but reducing to nothing. It's sad, but it seems they've run out of solutions: the promise of a new friendship slashed just as surely as a daffodil bloom hammered by unseasonal hail.

Luisa knows she's partly to blame. She's made no effort, no concessions, to allow Bex back in. She's always found it difficult to hand out second chances when someone has hurt her. If anything, with Bex she's been more lenient. Mum's the same, and Anita. You can push so far but once breaking point is reached, that's it. Why gloss over it? But it's still hard to disguise her disappointment. Having been there for Bex in Samos, it feels as if Bex has copped out, fallen at the first hurdle. It will be a relief when she's gone. Bex will be one less thing to worry about.

She's been rolling the problem of the phone call around in her head. Both Helena and Dex are adamant that she can't travel by herself. Helena was insistent over breakfast, *You must ring him tonight.* Luisa knows she doesn't have a choice. She confided in Helena that she's worried how Josip will react, but Helena told her, *Any uncle would come.* Luisa couldn't explain that this uncle might wish she'd never made contact in the first place. Each time she passes by the telephone table with its tapestry seat, half way down the hallway, she gets a queasy feeling.

Helena joins Luisa in the lounge after their evening meal. Bex has headed off to bed with the excuse of needing plenty of sleep before her flight to London. Helena's matronly cream blouse is tied with a floppy bow at the neck. Luisa is reminded of Mrs Dooly, her favourite teacher from college, who had a similar dress sense and no-nonsense personality.

'Something to help you sleep,' says Helena, handing Luisa a glass of red wine. 'It might help with the phone call too.'

'Thanks,' says Luisa, taking a sip. The wine tastes of summer berries, light and smooth, easy to drink. 'Have you ever been to Korčula?'

'Only once as a child. I remember it as a beautiful place. It was summertime, and the water was the clearest and most enticing colour. Bluer than blue — a match for the sky. I'd love to go back but how things are heading in this country, well . . . I don't know.' Helena glances over to the mantelpiece where Tito sits and takes a sip of her wine. 'Our leader would likely be very disappointed.'

'Because of the inflation?' Luisa asks, thinking back to the comments Dick and Dan made, and the bus terminal with its mob of women. She isn't sure whether they should be offering to pay Helena for their stay, and if so, what she would expect. She makes a mental note to speak with Bex about it in the morning. At least it will be something concrete to talk about.

'The plummeting dinar's one problem. But no, I'm talking more about our nationalistic hotheads, Slobodan Milosevic and the like, the people who want independence for their republics and greater power over others. They're probably taking their cue from the other countries where Communism's under pressure. They want to erode our common identity — all that Tito worked so hard for. I fear it will all go to waste.'

'I'm not sure I understand.'

'Too much greed and past hurt,' says Helena. 'When Tito died, no one could step into his shoes. Now, we have a system where the leaders from each of the six republics take turns to rule on a rotation basis.'

'Do you think it's still safe for me to travel here?' Luisa can't get her head around what this might mean: there's no reference point. The politics at home seem like child's play; the legal system here would be a nightmare in comparison.

'You'll want to keep an ear out. Be sensible. But most likely, you'll be fine. We're experts in this country at jumping from one crisis to another.'

Helena gives her a warm smile. Luisa is certain Helena wouldn't put her in any danger, that she has good judgement. Besides, one of Luisa's reasons for coming was to understand more about Yugoslavia's past, how it functions. Until now, her knowledge has been limited to the opinions from those at the Dally Club, or from within her family, and mostly she has let this talk wash over her. Mum always called Tito a saviour but Dida Stipan, Baba Marta and Aunt Kate disagreed. None of Dad's family could fathom why the rest of Mum's family had stayed put.

'You thought Tito was a good leader?'

'The best. He rebuilt our country from the ashes of war. I was just a baby at the time and growing up was tough, but I also saw incredible progress. You can't have that without good leadership. Tito led our people for thirty-five years until his death. He was a master at pulling together a nation divided by past power plays. Yugoslavia's been in mourning ever since — grief on a national scale. I worry that our country died with him.'

'Mum was born here during the war years. She left when she was nineteen.'

'Many of our people left, but those of us who stayed have had a good life. As I say, we had a great ruler.' Helena leans over and pats Luisa's arm. 'I'm sorry you've had problems here.' She scrunches up her face. 'There are many who are dissatisfied, even those living in the furthest corners, away from all the main tensions.'

Luisa goes to take another sip of her wine, but she's already drained her glass.

'Right, young lady.' Helena pats her arm. 'Enough talk of the past. Time to make this phone call.'

'I'm worried my Croatian will be scratchy. Could you double-check what I want to say?'

'I'll do my best, but first you must tell me *what* you want to say.'

Luisa has no choice but to trust Helena. 'I don't want to worry him,' she says, 'but here's what I thought.' She takes a deep breath. 'We had some bad luck. I was hit by a flu bug and was too sick to move on from Macedonia.'

'Go on.' Helena's expression gives nothing away.

'Our money ran out because of the expensive hotel. Bex has chosen to fly straight to London, but I still want to visit them on Korčula. Would it be possible for him to meet me in Skopje and take me back? I'll pay him back, of course.'

'That sounds sensible,' says Helena. 'Now let's work on the right words.'

Luisa shows Helena what she's written and Helena takes her time reading it through.

'This looks fine,' she says. 'You've obviously had a good teacher.'

'Mum spoke Croatian at home, and we got some extra tuition at the local club — not that I appreciated the lessons at the time.'

'Well, it's time to put them into practice.' Helena stands and pulls Luisa to her feet. 'No time like the present.' Helena opens her arms and it feels comfortable stepping forward into her embrace. 'I'll stay close, in case you need my help.' She rubs Luisa's back. 'Go on now.'

Luisa lifts the handset of the black, rotary telephone and listens for the dial tone. Her hands shake, but there's something reassuring about fitting her finger into the correct numbered hole on the plastic dial, swinging it to the right, and watching it flip back. Even the clacking sound calms her. She listens for the connection to be established, twirling the spiral cord connecting the handset to the base on her finger like she used to as a child. For some reason the safety spiel from the airline hostess crowds her head: *In an emergency, place the bag over your nose and mouth and breathe normally.*

'*Zdravo.*' The tone of his voice reminds her of Mum.

'*Ujak Josip. Ja sam Luisa.*'

There's just the slightest pause, then in Croatian he replies, 'Luisa, we've been waiting for your call. Are you in Yugoslavia already?'

Luisa looks down at her scripted notes and starts to speak.

AUGUST

WEDNESDAY

L uisa stands alone in the Skopje terminal, a sullied statue, concrete limbs at her side. The airport crowd mills around her and she wonders if they even notice her. They are nothing but a blur of faces. Young, old, male, female — these are the only distinctions. The man's voice over the loud speaker is an urgent stream. Luisa recognises only a few words: *British Airways, JAT Yugoslav, Swissair.* Now that the day has finally arrived she's numb, but she forces herself to feel something: the kindness and warmth Helena has shown them over the past six days, and her sense of loss when Helena waved goodbye, her tail lights blending into the dirty night. They can't have been the easiest of guests but their hostess held Luisa tightly, kissing her on both cheeks, *Go well and stay strong, Draga,* she said, pressing a piece of paper into Luisa's palm. *Don't hesitate to call me.*

Behind her are rows of check-in counters and above, suspended from the ceiling, are departure boards with venetian-blind slats that flick and clack as though someone is shuffling giant playing cards, over and over. Luisa is searching for an update on Bex's flight when Bex returns and dumps her overstuffed daypack at her feet. Luisa turns her attention to the stark bank of full-length windows that look out to the car park and drop-off area.

'Sorted?'

'Yep,' says Bex, flicking her boarding pass from hand to hand.

Luisa reflects again on how sad it is: their relationship boiling down to this. Throughout their travels it has been as though they were hitched by a bungy cord — one where they could stray only so far before being flung back together again. It was in Bitola that their cord snapped. In Bitola, Bex strayed too far.

A noisy band of young guys approach from the side and both girls startle. Bex goes to wrap her arm around Luisa's waist but Luisa shrugs her off and edges away. *It's a little too late for that now.* But she can feel her face starting to crumple. *Be strong, don't let it show.* Luisa concentrates on scanning the main entrance doors for Uncle Josip. He could be here any moment. She wonders if he's an early type, like her dad.

The announcement for Bex's flight punctures the air. Luisa lets out a slow dry whistle. Bex's face looks stretched with exhaustion; her arms hang limp by her side. It's infuriating that Luisa still feels some responsibility for the way Bex is hurting too. They've both been guilty of putting up barriers over the past days. Luisa stares down at her feet, unsure of how to finish, how to say goodbye.

'I'm sorry,' Bex whispers, touching Luisa's arm and pulling her close. It feels awkward. Staged. 'I know you'll be fine, go—' Bex swallows hard, struggling with her words. 'Go finish what you planned.' She kisses Luisa on the cheek, a kiss that doesn't linger.

Luisa tries to answer but nothing comes out. Now that the moment is upon them her mind races, questioning whether she's made the right decision. She reaches out, scrambling to hold on to something and catches Bex's sleeve. But Bex is pulling away and everything feels as if it's moving in slow motion. Bex bending to pick up her day-pack, backing away, waving — a stiff forced wave — like a small child learning how. It feels so wrong. Bex turning and heading for the departure gate. Luisa watching her go. It's impossible to tell whether she looks back because Luisa's eyes have filled with whorls of blurred light.

Upright. Stay upright. Luisa's backpack lies on the floor beside her and it takes all her willpower not to collapse on it. For now, she must keep a lookout for Uncle Josip. She rocks on the balls of her feet, the tiniest of movements from side to side, wanting to regain some control over her body. Tiny threads of pain still serve as a reminder and she winces, stilling her body, forcing her mind away from all that. It's back. The worry that her period hasn't come. Again she rationalises that it's the stress, all the upset and trauma, of course that's the reason.

The rain slaps against the terminal windows. All day it's been claggy, the sky overshadowed with dirty threatening clouds. The lighting from around the building's exterior reflects inside as a harsh glare. Luisa is mesmerised by the headlamps of the cars swooping in, the soft glow of their amber circles. She thinks about climbing into Uncle Josip's car soon. How it will be them flaunting their red tail-lights as they crawl away, leaving Macedonia far behind.

Waiting. Waiting. She feels dizzy and so tired, as though Bex's departure has drained her last ounce of energy. She glances over to the double entrance doors, pulling her jacket closer. For the hundredth time she justifies her decision to stay, ticking off the reasons. Then she sees him. A man wearing a burgundy beret, lingering inside the double doors, scanning the room. He points in her direction and rushes forward, and as he draws nearer she's reassured by his smile. He's twirling a small New Zealand flag on a stick above his head. She wants to run towards him but her feet remain stuck.

'Loo-ee*za*! Loo-ee*za*!' he calls out.

Her legs shake. The man seems worried now. It's in his eyes and in the arch of his bushy eyebrows. She blinks, trying to focus, but all she can manage is to crumple into his outstretched arms, to stare over his shoulder towards the windows and the lights behind. Why are they so blurry? He's saying something, but she can't make out his words. The lights spin as she buckles towards blackness.

When she comes to, her head rings with strange noises. It's a struggle to open her eyes and she twists her head, this way and that, blinking. Josip's face comes into close focus. He's kneeling beside her. She feels so groggy and she blinks again, trying to clear her vision. A woman places a hand on Luisa's forehead. They are pulling at her from both sides, under her armpits, hauling her up to sit. The woman hands her a flimsy plastic cup and Josip leans in, encouraging her to drink.

'*Popij*,' he says, tipping the cup. 'Are you hurt?'

Luisa takes a tiny sip, still nauseous, but the thunder and lightning in her head have quietened.

'Come, *Draga*,' Josip says.

Draga. Dida Stipan. Her child-hand enclosed in his giant paw as they collected the fresh eggs from the hen house. Dida's eyes like warm caramel.

'Let's get you over to the side. Away from these crowds,' he says, a gentle voice. 'Don't cry, *Draga*.'

They're everywhere. The crowds of people. The lady is talking loudly but Luisa can't understand her. She seems agitated, tapping Josip on his arm.

'Do you think you can walk?' Josip leans in, his breath warm against her ear.

She's doubtful she can stand but nods. The woman is on her other side, hitching her up under her arms. Josip supports Luisa too and somehow they walk, half-dragging her, towards the bank of windows.

'Move it, move it!' says Josip, swishing his free hand sideways at a group sitting on a bench seat.

They scramble to their feet and move away. It's a relief to slump down. Luisa's forehead feels clammy and instinctively she reaches for her stomach as her body is racked by spasms. She retches but there seems nothing to bring up. The lady rests her hand on Luisa's forehead. It takes all her effort to breathe deeply, stop the giddiness. The faded linoleum comes into sharp focus with its deep cuts and dirty scuff marks. The woman mutters something to Josip.

'My pack,' Luisa groans, suddenly remembering.

'Bah! First the precious cargo, then the old knapsack.' Josip pulls a large handkerchief from his pocket and hands it to the woman.

The woman yells out instructions then dabs the handkerchief against Luisa's forehead. Someone lugs Luisa's pack over and rests it against the seat just along from them. All the while Josip sits beside her, rubbing her back. The lady offers her the cup of water again and she manages tiny sips. It takes an age, but the nausea passes. The lady touches her cheek, a gentle fluttering tap. She says something to Josip then waves goodbye and eases away. Luisa and Josip are alone now. The air feels cold at her back.

'I'm sorry,' she says, her voice croaky.

'Ah well, it's one way to introduce yourself,' says Josip. His lined face seems etched with concern but he smiles. 'I was worried, *Draga*. But you've got your colour back now.'

'I'm sorry.' Is this all she's able to say? 'I'm hardly ever sick,' she adds trying to sound strong.

'Bah!' he says, as though hitting her apology away. 'Mare will get you better. But there won't be any detours. I'm taking you straight home. Sorry, *Draga,* but I hope you don't mind a long drive.' Josip sits quietly as though thinking, chewing on his fingernails.

It doesn't matter how long it takes. All Luisa wants to do is leave Macedonia far behind.

'There's something else.' Josip's face is stern now. 'When we get home I must telephone your mama. No arguments.' He shakes his head. 'Gabrijela would never forgive me.'

She doesn't have the strength to answer.

AUGUST
THURSDAY

Luisa's head throbs. Would Josip have made the call yet? The question has been rolling over and over in her mind as she's drifted in and out of a restless sleep. She forces one eye open and glances towards the window. Threads of sunlight slip through the slats. What time is it? Mum would be furious, and her razor-sharp tongue is the last thing Josip needs after the shocks of the past couple of days. She curls herself into a tight ball and cringes. Her surprise phone call. Fainting at the airport, having to make the long drive here — could it be any worse? Luisa knows she can't hide away despite every fibre of her being wishing she could. Poor Josip and Mare. She scrunches her eyes again, trying to ignore the mess in her head.

Curiosity wins and Luisa eases out of bed. Her sweatshirt lies discarded at the foot of the bed on top of a crocheted blanket, a riot of colourful squares. She cringes at the memory: Mare tugging at her sleeve, Luisa insisting, *No, I can undress myself*, acutely aware, despite feeling so ill, of the need to hide the gruesome yellow-green bruise on her upper arm. She pulls on her sweatshirt. Her body is stiff but the cool tiles beneath her feet feel refreshing, soothing. At the window, she pushes open a pane and leans forward to unlatch one of the shutters, wincing as she folds it against the house. The salt-laden fresh air rushes in, and Luisa scans over the terracotta roof tiles strutting down to meet the harbour nestled at the bottom of the steep hill. The water is the most intense shade of turquoise. Boats cruise, and much further away, behind them all, the mainland's sheer mountain backdrop crashes into the sea.

Luisa wonders where Orebić is. The place from where she and Uncle Josip crossed on the car ferry that morning. All she remembers of that horrendous drive is lying on the bench seat, pillow tucked under her head, her fingertips tracing the crackled lines in the leather over and over. Somehow it helped block out the fishy smell that was playing havoc with her stomach. Getting to Orebić, stepping outside, and catching a true whiff of the sea was a welcome relief. The dawn sunlight played on the paintwork of Uncle Josip's pickup truck, nostalgic, a strange sense of homecoming. The cheerful burnt-orange colour reminded Luisa of the brightly coloured Fun Ho! toy trucks her brother Marko played with as a small boy. But then reality returned and with it, embarrassment: catching Aunt Mare off-guard with their early arrival; retching at the breakfast table; Mare trying to help her undress. Gazing out at this scene, in this country where she'd expected to embrace her culture and feel at home, Luisa feels emptiness, as though she has lost her anchor, been cast afloat.

A flapping noise distracts her. High up to her right an assortment of laundry is precariously suspended. Would it be possible to lean out from one house and pass something to your neighbour across the way? A small gang of children, their voices pitted one against the other, as though filling a bubble of excitement threatening to burst, commands the narrow street leading up from the town. The end of a school day? Luisa has lost track of time. They are all dressed similarly in maroon and white. Has she really slept for most of the day? Despite all that's happened she wonders how Bex has coped getting to London. Hopes she's all right. It feels odd not having her here.

Turning back, she takes in the plainly furnished room with its whitewashed walls and muddy-green tiled floor. It's a comfort seeing her pack propped next to a plain timber chest of drawers. A gilded mirror hangs above the chest and sitting on top, next to a small jar of lavender, is a photo of Baba Ana. Luisa would know those curls and that face anywhere: they have the same photo at home. It's important to put everything behind her, make the most of connecting with her family. But still the question — what if she's pregnant? It hangs over her like a black cloud. Music. She plugs the Walkman buds into her ears and Toni Childs bursts inside her head: 'Don't walk away.' How can you not play mind games with these lyrics? On the wall behind the bed is a plain gold crucifix. Luisa makes the sign of the cross — *Please, God, help me live with myself again. Keep me strong and my secret safe* — but she hasn't been to church for years. Will God still listen? Does He even care?

The door is pushed open and Mare cranes her head around, ping-pong-ball cheeks and a warm smile. Luisa pulls out the earbuds, switches the Walkman off, grateful she had the nous to cover herself up earlier.

'Thought you might be ready for some food,' says Mare. She wears a plain brown house-dress now and a starched white apron splices her squat square-cut figure. Earlier, she'd been hauled out to the street in her dressing gown to help with the luggage. Mare had apologised to Luisa, explaining that she wasn't expecting them until the following day. Luisa was mortified. Now her aunt's cheeks are dusted with powder and she wears a smear of lipstick. Mare carries the tray over to the bedside table then bustles across to take Luisa's hand in hers. That soft skin again, like tissue paper.

'You're still so cold, *Draga*.' Mare draws Luisa back towards the bed. 'Come. Have some soup.'

Luisa concentrates on keeping her face relaxed as she climbs back into bed. 'Thanks. This smells delicious.' She forces a smile and glances up at Mare, busy propping pillows behind her. 'I feel terrible. It's the only time I've been sick in all our travels,' she says, unable to hold Mare's eye.

Mare passes her the tray. There's a bowl of *brudet*, thick tomato-based soup laden with chunks of fish and calamari rings, and a fresh wedge of bread. Luisa still feels wary of her stomach but this soup smells like home. She takes a sip.

'Delicious! Just like Mum's.' She is pleased at how confident she sounds, and that her Croatian isn't as scratchy as she had feared.

Mare rewards her with a smile. 'Eat some bread too,' she says. 'I made it myself. We need to get you strong again.' The way she talks sounds like Mum.

Luisa dips the bread into the soup. She hadn't realised she was so hungry. Mare lingers beside the bed, silent, smiling when Luisa wipes the bowl clean with the last of the bread.

'Join me in the kitchen when you're ready,' says Mare, taking the tray. 'Take your time.'

Luisa takes a last look around the room. Unpacking and arranging her belongings — toiletries, the small stash of cassette tapes, her book — has felt comforting, another positive step forward. The Swiss Army knife, though, is an imposter and she has returned it to the top pocket of her pack. Any clothes that are still clean are stacked in the chest of drawers and a pile of washing sits to the side. She pulls on a fresh top to cover the bruise then plucks up the courage to head downstairs.

The kitchen is small and cosy with a heady mix of garlic, tomato, onion and meat wafting about. There's a sweet smell too, and the lingering aroma of coffee. Mare herds her towards a table by the window which looks out to a small courtyard. The sun bathing the table feels inviting.

'One of Mirjana's,' says Mare, pulling a magazine from a cabinet.

Luisa draws the magazine close. A young woman, flawless skin, impeccable outfit, poses before a backdrop of city buildings and a bridge. Paris, perhaps? Luisa wonders if she'll ever make it there, whether she'll enjoy travelling again. A plate of scrolls on the table release a warm yeasty aroma mixed with sweet cinnamon. Mare attends to something on the stove and Luisa flicks through the magazine, making out she's concentrating, wishing she could feel more relaxed.

'Is Josip still in bed?' she asks, thinking she should make more of an effort to chat. It's just as well Mum kept the language alive at home and made her persevere with the lessons at the club.

'Went down to check on the boat,' says Mare. 'Don't expect him back for a while.' She smiles and goes back to her cooking. Luisa is grateful for her no-nonsense manner.

The aroma from the cinnamon scrolls overrides everything. Having conquered the soup, Luisa reasons that the queasiness she's feeling is what always happens just before her period, or perhaps it's just hunger? Her period's well overdue but she knows how stress affects her cycle. *You'll be fine*, she reassures herself.

There's a noise in the entrance way and Luisa jerks her head up. 'Must be Mirjana, home from work,' says Mare, glancing towards the door.

A young woman stalks into the kitchen. She has the same beanpole frame and olive skin as Luisa. 'They arrived early,' says Mare, responding to Mirjana's surprised look.

Mirjana crosses to the table and Luisa pushes herself to standing. Her cousin is slightly shorter and her face is more angular. It's her striking eyes which distinguish her: little black beads.

'The mystery cousin,' says Mirjana, her thin nose at a tilt. 'Finally, we meet.' She hugs Luisa but it's a brisk rather than warm embrace. Her black hair is sleek and shiny and styled in a short bob, the ends flicking out at chin-level. The way she carries herself, stiff and erect, together with her serious demeanour, makes Luisa think she might have a battery pack strapped to her body keeping her fully charged, that crackles of energy might fly off her.

'Nice to meet you too!' says Luisa, trying to sound relaxed. She feels that she's being sized up and spat out by Mirjana, who offers a half-smile back. *If Bex was here, she'd jump in with some banter to smooth the way.*

'What time did they get here?' Mirjana asks her mum now. 'Wasn't it meant to be tomorrow?'

'Just after you left for work. Poor Luisa's been in bed most of the day. She's not well.'

'Oh? Still sick. What's wrong?' Mirjana fixes Luisa with her piercing eyes.

'Some bug I picked up. That, and a bit of exhaustion.' Luisa swishes her hand as though batting Mirjana's questions away.

'Guess you can't complain. Not with all that travel.'

'You must work close by?' says Luisa, desperate to take the focus off herself. She thinks about her own job and how Mirjana's got it lucky to be getting home so early — she would be at work for at least another couple of hours.

'Why don't you two sit down and get to know each other,' says Mare. 'I'll make some coffee to go with Mirjana's favourites. Do you have the sweet rolls at home, Luisa?'

'Yes. I've been holding myself back to be honest. They smell delicious.' Perhaps food is Mare's language of love too. Mum often says, *Love goes through the stomach,* linking a recipe back to someone from the homeland: *Nada's Mama's brudet,* or *Baba's jabucni strudel,* the dessert she made when apples were plentiful.

Mirjana pulls out a chair opposite. 'Aren't you going to join us?' Luisa asks Mare, thinking how much easier it would be with her at the table too.

Mare pats her shoulder. 'I'll be back over soon, *Draga*. A few jobs first.'

'Let me help,' says Luisa, making to get up, the sudden movement sending a jolt of pain. She winces but doesn't dare look across at Mirjana.

'No. You rest up,' says Mare. 'There'll be plenty of time later for helping.' She's already back at the kitchen bench and Luisa eases herself back down onto her chair.

'You asked about my job,' says Mirjana, fixing on Luisa. 'I'm a paper-shuffler. At the local post office. Not as exciting as being a lawyer, I'm afraid.'

'Don't know about that. Plenty of paper-shuffling in my job too.' Luisa sinks her teeth into a scroll. It's delicious, sticky and still warm. Her stomach does a cartwheel, but she's determined not to let it show on her face. *When will it settle?*

'Worth it, though, when you can afford to travel,' says Mirjana, taking a small bite of her scroll. Mare returns with a pot of coffee and Mirjana pours them both a cup. 'How's the trip been? We've enjoyed getting the odd postcard.'

'It's been amazing. So many cool things.' Luisa is conscious of gushing. 'But honestly, this is the best. I've dreamt of coming here for so long.'

'And what's been your favourite place, Luisa?' Mare calls out from the stove.

'So many highlights. But maybe Turkey? Ephesus was incredible and Anzac Cove is momentous for us Kiwis. Turkey was the country that's surprised me the most, I guess.'

'Macedonia didn't rate up there?' says Mirjana.

Could she be scoffing? Mirjana is probably like Josip and wondering why they even went there. Josip made that very clear: *Damned awful place.*

'Not exactly,' says Luisa. 'Didn't help I got sick there.'

'Tata said you were stressed on the phone. Didn't sound like sickness. Your friend upped and left, didn't she?'

'She did. But these things happen when you're travelling.' The nausea is back and she's desperate to escape upstairs.

'I wish I could travel like you.' This time it doesn't sound accusatory, more a hankering.

'I used to think New Zealand was the most boring country. Sounds like you might feel the same about here?' Luisa feels the weight of privilege again. It hadn't crossed her mind before leaving home, but now she realises how lucky she's been growing up in New Zealand.

'Exactly,' grumbles Mirjana. 'Only difference is, I'll never get out.'

'Macedonia was way behind but I don't know — here it feels different. It's just as I imagined from Mum's stories, but even more beautiful.'

'Shiny on the surface, but a cesspool underneath. There's all sorts of rumblings. But we're used to the conflict. Tito kept things together for a long time, I'll give him that.' Her face twists into a grimace. 'But now it's unravelling, big time.'

Luisa doesn't know how to reply. Her imaginings of her Mum's birthplace had centred on the scenery, the customs and the food, not on how the country was run. In New Zealand she rarely had to worry about politics or how safe the country was. Unless you counted the protests and riots that erupted in Wellington during the Springbok rugby tour in the early Eighties, back when she was seventeen. It would feel trivial admitting to Mirjana that at the time she'd watched Charles and Diana exchange their wedding vows on TV at Niamh's place and how they'd joked about it afterwards. She sips her coffee, wishing she could offer some meaningful comment. The sinking of the *Rainbow Warrior* would be the closest thing. But even that had seemed to brush over quickly.

'Shit happens,' says Mirjana, cutting into Luisa's thoughts, her tone matter-of-fact. 'In this country especially.'

'We don't need that language,' says Mare.

'And it's no way to welcome your tata,' says Josip.

Luisa has been so busy concentrating on saying the right thing that she didn't hear him come in. She takes in his features again as though seeing him for the first time. He seems years older than Mum. Partly it's his lined, weather-beaten face but it's also the way his skin hangs from his cheeks into loose folds around his mouth.

Mirjana laughs. 'Timed to perfection, as always, Tata.'

'Ah, wonderful to see you two getting acquainted. Feeling better now, Luisa?' He stoops to kiss Mirjana on the cheek.

'Much better, thanks,' says Luisa.

Josip is beside her now and leans over to kiss her cheek, the brush of his skin like sandpaper. She's sure he's about to say something about the phone call. 'Aunt Mare's been plying me with food,' she gushes. 'And it's been great meeting my twin cousin finally.' Mirjana rewards her with a smile.

'I called your mama this morning,' says Josip, a concerned expression on his face — a reminder of Mum but with less fire-power. Luisa's head feels full of static. She's desperate to know the outcome but at the same time she doesn't want to hear about it.

'Jesus. How did that go?' says Mirjana, looking flummoxed, an expression Luisa imagines she doesn't wear very often.

'Mirjana!' Mare scolds.

'She says she'll call back,' says Josip, his tone suggesting he doesn't want to discuss it further. 'Not surprisingly she wants to collect her thoughts. She was perfectly civil.' He steps forward and rubs Luisa's shoulder. 'Mostly she was relieved to hear you were alive and well, *Draga.*'

'I'm sorry.' Luisa pushes back her chair. 'I feel so rude but I think I need my bed again. A couple of hours and I've reached my limit.' She needs to escape before she embarrasses herself again.

After brushing past Josip, Mare steps forward, blocking her path to the door. 'From what I can gather the call was short. Gabrijela hung up on Josip. We need to wait now.' Mare's expression softens. 'I hope you sleep well, love. Remember, tomorrow's another day.'

The stairs are Luisa's target. She mumbles a quick goodnight and it's not until she's halfway up that she feels the stiffness. Each step is a reminder. Worse, though, is the wrench she feels for home. Back in her room it takes her last reserves to get ready for bed. The sad weight of her secret churns and sends up another wave of nausea. It's like sea-sickness, striking at the most unexpected times. Easier to deal with when she's alone, when she can reason with herself, parcel it up, and pack it back down. She wonders how long it will be before Mum phones back but even that seems trivial compared to what will be in store if that bastard animal has managed to sow his fetid seed inside her.

SEPTEMBER

SATURDAY

Two days later, and Luisa has never felt so relieved when there's blood on her knickers. One more thing that's gone right, another move in the right direction after all the challenges. She stares at her knickers, at the stain, and despite herself sends up a prayer to thank God.

The previous day she spent holed up in her bedroom to be close to this same toilet. Again and again, the horrors of Macedonia wrested their way to the surface. Kosta using her body. Kosta drilling into her soul. He loomed close even while she was bent over the toilet bowl heaving and retching. In the moments when her body allowed her some rest and she hauled herself back to bed, everything was still impossible, as though she was an empty can, hurtling and twisting along her own muddy river. When she cast her mind away from Macedonia, Mike filled her head. *Will I ever put the pieces of myself back together again? Will I ever feel right again in someone's arms? Making love?*

Mare, bless her, was an angel, seeming to know just the right time to pop her head around the door. Thankfully Mirjana and Josip kept away. Without asking questions Mare draped cool cloths on Luisa's forehead and kept her water glass filled. Later in the day, when it seemed Luisa had nothing more to give, Mare brought dry crackers and a cup of thin chicken broth.

Luisa dresses, making sure to cover her bruise. She stares at herself in the mirror. 'Okay, first step to rebuilding. There's nothing you can do about Mum, that's out of your hands.' Even so, she pauses at the kitchen door before entering.

Mirjana sits at the table with the newspaper spread out front. The remains of breakfast are on the table: a crusty loaf of bread; a jar of pomegranate jam; a platter of fresh fruit that's already been well picked over; and a pot of coffee, still steaming. No Mare or Josip? Crossing to the sink she pours herself a glass of water, still unsure whether her stomach will handle anything to eat.

'Morning,' says Mirjana in English, glancing up as Luisa sits down at the table. 'How're you feeling today?'

Luisa's relieved to give her a genuine answer. 'Much better. Seems I might have turned a corner.'

'That's good,' says Mirjana, turning back to the paper. 'Guess you were sick, after all.' There's something in her tone that implies a question.

'Did Josip and Mare head out?' says Luisa.

'Mass.' Mirjana grins. 'Tata says he needs all the help he can get.'

Luisa's sigh escapes more like a whimper and she hides her face in her hands. 'I feel so bad. Has he heard back from Mum yet?'

'Hasn't said. He'll be fine, though. Think of it as a positive that you've got them back in contact.' Mirjana leans forward, her elbows on the table. 'We have a saying here. *Ne drzite stvari preblizu* — and it seems you're holding things close. When are you going to tell me what happened in Macedonia? And how you lost your friend on the way?'

Luisa groans, her face in her hands. 'Please don't ask me about that.'

'No point letting things fester. It's our way here. Better to get things off your chest.'

'I can't,' says Luisa, her voice a whisper. 'Not yet.'

'Your problems are eating away at you. Then you go and throw them all up, like yesterday.'

'It's nothing,' says Luisa, looking her in the eye. 'Really. People fall out — you must know that.'

'But something happened to change things.' She fixes Luisa with her piercing eyes.

Yes, Luisa thinks, *but what about some respect for my privacy?* But she feels torn. Mirjana seems more open, warmer, and Luisa wants to build on this sense of camaraderie. But then, she thinks, all the problems she and Bex shared made not a scrap of difference.

The front door slams and Josip and Mare's voices fill the small hallway. Josip appears in the doorway. 'Ah, Luisa,' he says, stopping as though stranded.

'Go on, tell her,' says Mare, pushing him from behind. 'Get it over with.'

Josip hesitates. 'Luisa. Your mama rang last night when you were asleep. She's coming in a few weeks. Their flights are booked. Roko's coming too.' He pads across the room and squeezes Luisa's shoulder. 'Everything will be fine, *Draga*, I promise.'

Luisa turns to face him, tears pricking her eyes. Everything feels hopeless, out of her control.

'You are *naša*, Luisa, one of our own, one of our branches. Our home is your home.'

Goosebumps travel down Luisa's spine. Josip has just put into words what she has so often failed to encapsulate herself: why she was so determined to come, to reconnect, to understand her origins and pay tribute. New Zealand will always be Luisa's home but it was in Yugoslavia, Dalmatia, where the roots of her tree first took hold, setting anchor in this inhospitable soil. Even though the limbs of that tree have been far-reaching, she is still one of those branches. This place is what sets her apart.

GABRIJELA, 1958

KORČULA, YUGOSLAVIA

MARCH

There was a whiff of celebration, the unmistakable tang of fresh meat, that greeted me when I wound up the hill towards home. I wondered if our neighbours had been spying, if they had noticed the comings and goings in preparation for our important guest. For me, the clock at Jadranka had ticked at half speed all day, torture after enduring a February that seemed determined not to roll into March. I tiptoed inside the house and the aroma was intense, as though it had wafted through each room to find every nook and crevice to settle in. I huddled in our tiny entrance way, straining my ears, feeling furtive but determined to hear him speak. Mama's laughter filled the house like a song and when his voice finally came it wasn't authoritative or officious, the way I had expected a Party official might sound, but deep and gentle.

I took extra time washing away the sardines before creeping upstairs to change. Meeting my mystery *ujak* was definitely an occasion for a dress and I had laid it out on the bed that morning. March was still too chilly for no sleeves but this was my only dress, discounting my ball dress — a tragedy because most of the beautiful golden colour was now covered by my old grey cardigan. I tried to keep my feet light while descending. Mama was always scolding, *Walk like a lady, not a donkey,* and I wanted to ensure it was me who caught the first glimpse of Uncle Ivan and not the other way around.

'Gabrijela, *moja*, is that you?' Mama called out, before I'd even made it to the bottom step.

I cursed myself as I paused at the kitchen door and smoothed the skirt of my dress. I pushed the door open and peeked around the corner. Uncle Ivan sat in Tata's seat at the head of the table. He glanced across and smiled.

'Ah, *Draga, moja,*' Mama turned and beckoned me over. 'Come. Meet your uncle.'

My first thought was how handsome and important he looked. How his smile was at odds with the stiffness and formality of his uniform.

'Please, call me Ivan,' he said, scrambling to his feet. 'Surely I'm too young to be your uncle?'

He looked so sure of himself and his bright white uniform seemed too stark for the room. Despite all my efforts I felt shabby. His hair was even blonder than Mama's and where her curls were flyaway, his cascaded back in thick waves from his tanned face. I wondered how he'd managed to escape our winter. I shook his hand and he wrapped his other hand around mine. His skin felt soft and smooth not calloused and angry like Tata's from his work at sea. It dawned on me that I had no concept of what a Party official might be required to do. He reminded me of the officers from El Shatt, and Tito himself, men on a pedestal who were not like our local men. Men you implicitly trusted to deal with important matters, whatever they were.

'What a treat to meet you again.' He turned to Mama, 'Our family produces fine-looking women, Ana.'

Mama giggled like a silly schoolgirl. 'The younger generation, at least.'

Ivan's eyes glistened green like shiny olives. I wondered how he saw me. My hand was still in his and time felt suspended. He scrutinised my face. I didn't know what to say or where to look so I glanced at the floor, worried that my embarrassment might be reflected in his polished black shoes or that my stomach might grumble from the smell of the meat.

'The last time you were just a baby,' he said, finally dropping my hand. 'I think you'll be more interesting this time.'

Mama came close and wrapped her arm around my waist. 'Ah, Jela. You were tiny but very noisy.'

'You wouldn't stop screeching,' said Ivan, his grin full of mischief. 'Josip and I nicknamed you "the seagull". We were happy to leave you inside with the adults while we rushed outside to climb trees.'

Why was I so tongue-tied? My armpits felt steamy and I was certain my cheeks were as red as apples. It was infuriating that my body played such rude tricks on me but his youthfulness had caught me off-guard. It seemed inconceivable that he was twelve years older. He might as well have been the same age as Josip, he looked so fresh-faced.

'It's a crime you didn't get to know your baba and dida,' Mama said, squeezing me tight before stepping away and making the sign of the cross. She held her hand to her heart. 'God bless their souls.' Her eyes welled and I worried what Ivan might think.

'A shocking time.' Ivan frowned. 'Ana, I apologise for keeping my distance. It was my way of coping. I realise now how wrong that was. You are all the family I have and I appreciate having a second chance.'

'New beginnings,' said Mama, looking towards the kitchen as though wanting to escape this talk of family. 'Come help me, Gabrijela. And after your long trip, you must want to relax, Ivan. Why not take a bath while we prepare dinner. The water's heating.'

'Exactly what I need,' he said. He followed Mama into the kitchen, his smart black shoes tapping against the tiles like a victory march. When he pulled the door shut I joined Mama in the kitchen, for once not resentful about helping her. I tilted my face over the large pot on the stove that was still steaming. The smell of meat was reason enough to stay put. Stacked at the side, on the butcher's block, was a tray of *njoki*.

My mouth watered again. 'He brought us the meat, Mama?'

'One of the perks of his position.' Mama smiled. 'Hopefully there'll be more in the months to come. Why don't you help me slice these tomatoes. If there's still time, you can use the bath water after Ivan. Apparently he'll be staying at least nine months, plenty of time to get to know him.' She returned her focus to the tomatoes, seeming lost in thought.

I squirmed. I hadn't thought about the downsides of having Ivan to stay. I'd had to make the same adjustments when Mare first came and in the past weeks, since she and Josip had moved out, I'd got accustomed to the luxury of having the first bath. I resigned myself to adapting again.

Later, an air of anticipation intermingled with uneasiness swept through our kitchen and dining room. The preparations for dinner were complete. All that remained was for Ivan to join us. He hadn't re-emerged after taking his bath, and we assumed that he must have important Party business to attend to.

Mama now had a smear of pink on her lips, and she'd changed into the blue blouse and skirt that she always wore to the local dances. Mare had arrived, dressed in her honeymoon outfit — a red skirt and cream blouse — and I was struck by how pretty she looked. Her cheeks were glowing through her powder. I wished I had cosmetics of my own, but Mama insisted I was too young. If Mare had still been living with us she would have powdered my face just like she did before the local dances. Tata and Josip had changed out of their work gear but only into the trousers and shirts they wore on the weekends. They had already started drinking wine. It annoyed me that they could come in from their day at work and relax. For me there was always more work to do.

The table looked festive with its array of water glasses, wine glasses for the men and serving spoons laid out. Mare and I had set it and while we'd managed to find six matching dinner plates that weren't chipped, the cutlery was an eclectic mix. Ivan was likely used to fine silver, and no matter how hard we tried we could never compete with that. Tata had raised his eyebrows at Josip when Mama put a small jar packed with rosemary in the centre of the table, but I was relieved we were making an effort for our important guest.

I hovered close to the stove, ensuring the water for the *njoki* remained at a simmer. Mama wiped the bench for what must have been the tenth time. Mare stood close by, assembling the salad and plugging the awkward silences with conversation.

'Is it nearly time to eat?' Tata called. 'We're close to starving in here.'

'Keep your voice down,' Mama called back. 'You won't die waiting a few more minutes.' She raised her eyebrows as though exasperated. 'Jela, perhaps go knock on Ivan's door. Tell him we're ready.'

I tiptoed up the stairs. It seemed rude rushing him, and I welcomed the chance to duck into my room and brush my hair one more time. I smiled at my reflection: my cheeks held a rosy glow even without cosmetics. Out on the small landing, I raised my hand to knock on what had been Josip's door. It was the exact moment Ivan chose to stride out and I shrieked and jumped back.

'Beware of charging cannon-girls,' he said, backing up against the door and laughing. 'We'll have to get better synchronised. Don't want any injuries.'

I couldn't look as I squeezed past him. My shoulder brushed against his chest. 'I'm sorry,' I spluttered, before racing down the stairs, summoning my willpower to prevent collapsing into a fit of giggles. The tight spaces in our house were impossible. It had been the same when Mare first moved in — always colliding on the landing, or having to squeeze past each other on the stairwell — but that was far less embarrassing than bumping into a man I hardly knew. A Party official, no less.

Back in the kitchen, I popped my head around the corner, raising my finger to my lips to shush Tata. He muttered something under his breath and took another sip of wine. I turned back and Ivan was filling the gap in the doorway, beaming. Out of uniform he was even more handsome. He'd changed into a white open-necked shirt and dark trousers, and a scruff of hair escaped over the top button of his shirt. I felt daring even noticing this, a detail that seemed far too intimate. His hair was still wet from his bath and slicked back, darker now, enhancing his eyes. I was embarrassed that Tata and Josip hadn't made more of an effort.

Mama stepped forward and took Ivan's arm. 'Come and meet Mare, Josip's new wife.'

'It's my pleasure,' he said, crossing to Mare and taking her hand. Both Mama and Mare were like dwarfs alongside him.

'Now, come and join Ante and Josip,' said Mama, herding Ivan past me and through to the dining area. Tata and Josip both stood and slapped Ivan on the back. Ivan was a good half-head taller than both of them and broader too.

'Sit. Please,' said Tata. '*Pošip*? It's been far too long.' He poured Ivan a glass of our local wine.

Mama returned to the kitchen and pulled me over to the stove. 'Make sure you don't take the *njoki* out too soon,' she whispered. 'Wait until they rise and float.'

I stared at her. She knew I was perfectly capable of cooking *njoki*. Mare glanced over from where she was dressing the salad, and raised her eyebrows. Regardless, I didn't take my eyes off those plump parcels dancing in the water, but I strained to hear what Tata was saying. His voice was unusually low and I prayed he wouldn't say anything controversial. Mama placed a large dish beside me and watched closely as I layered the *njoki* into the dish and sprinkled the parcels with olive oil.

'We almost collided on the landing,' I whispered, my hand at my mouth to contain my laughter.

Mama suppressed a giggle too, then just as quickly became business-like, clapping her hands. 'Bring everything through now.' She picked up the bowl of meat sauce.

Mare followed with the salad plate layered with tomato and fresh goat cheese and I held the dish of glistening *njoki*. The three men were clustered around one end of the table. Mare, Mama and I took the other end: Mama at the head, opposite Tata; Mare beside Josip; and me on the seat next to Ivan. I made certain to keep some distance. He seemed so broad and I was conscious of his body heat. It was rare for me to feel small but beside him I felt like a mouse. I was grateful when Tata broke the silence.

'We must thank you for the meat, Ivan. A rare treat for us.' Tata made a show of refilling the men's wine glasses.

'My pleasure,' said Ivan, seeming to straighten a little.

Mama cleared her throat and bowed her head. 'We thank you, Lord, for the food we are about to eat. And especially for the meat brought by Ivan. We thank you for the gift of family. Amen.'

'Amen,' we repeated, making the sign of the cross.

'Oh!' said Mama, her hand at her mouth. 'I should have checked, Ivan. Is it acceptable that we say grace? We don't want to cross the Party.'

'Please,' he replied. 'I'm not here to pass judgement. Do as you always do.'

'I hoped we might get a break,' said Tata, half under his breath.

Mare looked aghast and I stared at my plate. When I dared glance up, Tata was leaning back in his chair and I was surprised at how relaxed he seemed.

'Please,' said Mama, pushing the bowl of *njoki* towards Ivan. 'Enjoy! We could starve listening to this nonsense. Quick, before it gets cold.'

Ivan piled food onto his plate, including two large servings of the meat sauce. I glanced towards Tata, whose eyes had widened. Meat was such a luxury, and the rule was always one spoonful. I took a large sip from my water glass, willing him to hold his tongue while racking my brain for something sensible to say. 'Can you tell us what's involved in the road project? What you want to achieve?'

As soon as my words were out I worried that my question was stupid. Perhaps he wasn't able to talk about official things. His knees brushed against mine as he turned to answer and I shuffled my legs sideways.

'So that cars can drive around the island?' said Josip, rolling his eyes at me. Mare shot him a wary look and nudged him. It infuriated me that Josip could be so brave with me and yet so timid outside the house. I wished that we could be on the same side for once.

'All in good time,' said Ivan, seeming to ignore Josip. 'It's exciting. This country's going from strength to strength. Korčula's roads will be first, and all going well, Hvar will follow. The Party wants roads fit for cars, as well as donkeys and bikes. It'll take a few months — possibly closer to a year. We're hoping to provide the local youth with employment and a wealth of experience.'

'My *dragi*, Branko, might be interested,' I said.

'You have a *dragi*?' Ivan's voice boomed. 'He is lucky, no?'

He sounded surprised and I wondered again how he saw me. I felt as though he was looking right into my soul as his eyes searched my face.

My cheeks flared red hot and I looked away, wishing I could strip off my cardigan.

'They're a couple of lovebirds. So sweet,' said Mare, smiling across at me.

Josip took the attention off me by reaching over for another spoonful of the meat sauce. I was relieved, despite knowing it would end badly. Tata didn't disappoint, batting Josip's hand away.

'The meal is delicious. You are excellent cooks,' said Ivan, seeming not to have noticed.

'It's our pleasure,' said Mama, brushing her hair back from her face and behind her ear.

'Might sign up, as well,' said Josip. 'Could be better than the fishing business.'

Mare looked aghast and I waited for the explosion.

'You'll do nothing of the sort!' said Tata. '*Krešimira*'s where you belong. All this talk of cars — it's boats that make Korčula tick.' He twisted his neck to stare at Ivan.

Mama looked horrified.

'As you say, Ante,' Ivan replied, his voice measured, 'fishing will continue as the lifeblood of this island. But don't close your eyes to modern technology. We must upgrade the roads. Think about transporting food and other products between the towns. How the standard of living will improve for everyone.'

'Only for those who can afford a car, let alone the petrol to run the damn thing.' Tata took a slug of his wine. 'Pity our officials don't ask the people living here.'

'Have some more food, Ivan,' Mama cut in. 'It's there to be eaten.' She glared down the table at Tata.

'It doesn't hurt for our Party officials to know what goes on here,' said Tata, his voice clipped. 'Away from Party headquarters.'

It was infuriating that Tata couldn't see progress when it was right in front of his eyes. He was a pessimist and determined to hold on to the old ways. I thought again about the importance of teachers. How they could help instigate change. Josip was still chewing at his nails and I felt a rush of compassion. It couldn't be easy having to spend so much time with Tata, and perhaps it was no coincidence he was mentioning the desire for change. Tata stared down at his wine glass, frowning, as though it might hold a secret. Mare was unusually quiet but seemed to be wriggling in her seat. I wished Ivan could see our family as united, not so at odds with each other.

'We're very proud of where you've got to in the Party,' said Mama, and I could have hugged her. 'Tell us more about the places you've visited.'

'I've spent a lot of time in Zagreb,' said Ivan. 'And I loved my time on the islands to the north of there. Dubrovnik is my absolute favourite, though.'

I was impressed at the way these places rolled off his tongue, and how smoothly he could move on and dissipate what could have been a tricky situation.

'I would love to see more of our country,' said Mama wistfully.

'Me too,' I said. 'In school we learnt about some of those places. The islands of the Rovinj archipelago sound particularly beautiful.'

'They must be seen to be believed,' said Ivan, smiling. I wondered whether one day he might take our family there. As a member of the Party this might be something he could arrange?

'Keep working at Jadranka,' said Tata, 'and find yourself a good man. Nothing comes without hard work. Your generation will likely have far more opportunity to travel than we ever did.'

He might as well have clamped a boulder to my foot. 'You know I hate that factory!' I clenched my fists. 'I won't be staying long enough to earn my fortune there.'

'You'll do as you're told,' said Tata, thumping the table and leaving me feeling like a small child.

I hated him in that moment. *He wants to make my life difficult.*

'And when the roads are complete there will be other opportunities for employment,' said Ivan. I smiled at him, grateful, although still smarting. 'Mare, you work at the factory too?'

'Yes, although not for much longer as it happens.' She nudged Josip and reached for his hand. 'We've got some exciting news. Early days, but . . . we've got a baby on the way.'

'Oh!' Mama clapped her hands in delight. She leant across the table and patted Mare's hand. 'That's wonderful news, *Draga*.'

'This is cause for celebration,' said Tata, scraping back his chair and slapping Josip's back. 'Wine for everyone!' He made a show of topping my water glass and Mare and Mama's with a dash of wine. He refilled the glasses of the men.

Everyone scrambled to their feet and joined in his toast. 'To new beginnings! *Živjeli!*' Tata tipped back his glass then slammed it on the table.

The room erupted with hugs and kisses and back-slaps. Mama and Tata embraced for the longest time and afterwards Mama kept hold of Tata's hand. It was easy to get caught up in the excitement, to hope this might be a positive sign of change. Of course I was thrilled for Mare and Josip, but it was the last thing I wanted for myself. I dreamed of travelling and seeing more of the progress and change which Ivan talked about, change that I was sure was happening throughout our country under Tito's leadership. I snuck another look at my uncle. Those new roads could be my pathway to escaping Vela Luka, perhaps even to Korčula's old town at the other end of our island.

MAY

I hovered by our kitchen window, desperate to catch my first glimpse. I heard it first, a clattering noise combined with a steady thrum, perhaps as far away as the bottom of our hill. Mama joined me at the window and we both perched up on our toes, tilted forward, peering out. It might have been a swarm of bees trapped inside a tin can. Instead it was Ivan, his driving goggles wedged beneath his peaked Party hat, guiding the motorbike up towards our house. My heart just about missed a beat. Soon I'd be riding on that machine with its round front eye like a searchlight.

I wondered how many of our neighbours had raced from their homes to see what the racket was. A motorbike wasn't a common sight and they might be curious, even frightened. Probably the last time had been during the war when the Germans were in charge. Mama nudged me and I grinned, knowing she felt just as excited as me.

'Lucky girl.' She fussed at my scarf. 'Make sure it's nice and tight. You don't want your hair blowing everywhere.'

'These shoes look stupid.' I scowled down at the heavy black work shoes Ivan had insisted I wear. They were far too hot for May, and besides, they looked out of place with my pretty skirt.

'Don't be ridiculous, *Draga*. It's not a fashion parade.' But Mama's face shone with a warm smile. She rubbed my arm. 'You look fine.'

I hoped so. I had spent all morning deciding. Ivan swung the sleek black machine around, angling it outside our house. He cut the engine and rested his feet on the ground, steadying the bike. Fat tyres encircled an intricate pattern of wheel spokes, and its shiny chrome exhausts stood out against the dull black paintwork. I couldn't drag my eyes away from the empty black seat perched over the rear wheel. I worried about how difficult it would be to balance, how easy it might be to topple off.

Ivan's head was still down, checking the dials perhaps. He was dressed in his Party uniform and his black shoes were polished to a shine. He looked so important, at odds with how I'd come to know him around the house — he no longer felt like a guest and we had even shared the odd joke. That Party hat with its distinctive pale-blue band and gold braiding transformed him back into someone official and much older, someone I had no right to be accompanying. I pulled back from the window. My first instinct had been to run outside; now I felt as though I should wait to be called.

It had been the previous night, over dinner, when Ivan had asked whether I could join him. He said he wanted to show me the progress on the new road. I just about choked on my food while I waited for Tata's refusal. Of course it came, a firm no — there was plenty I could be helping Mama with on my day off — but Mama, bless her, told Tata not to be ridiculous. That I should go and enjoy a day out. *It'll be good for her.* I tried to act as though it was nothing out of the ordinary, but my head spun. I was already imagining myself zipping along, and ever since all I'd been able to think about was how exciting life had become since Ivan's arrival.

I snuck another peek out the window. A crowd of neighbours were gathered. Ivan pushed his goggles over the peak on his cap. He was talking and throwing his arms about, bending over the bike to rev the engine. It sounded like a lion and some of the neighbours stepped back, while others clapped or held their hands to their mouths. My buzz of excitement returned when Ivan leant on the horn and gestured to me.

'Go on, then,' said Mama. 'Don't keep him waiting.'

Even so, I hesitated at the front door.

Our neighbour, Mrs Nola, called out. 'Fancy way to travel, Gabrijela.'

I knew she was jealous, but all I was capable of was nodding. On the one hand, I felt proud and secretly thrilled there would be a crowd to see me off, but closer up, that bike looked huge and I worried about clambering on with my skirt and flashing my underwear. Mama seemed oblivious to my distress, standing behind me, pushing me forward. Ivan's eyes were hidden again behind his goggles: he was transformed into an insect with bulging black eyes. I had to clamp my mouth shut to stop my giggles.

He beckoned me over and patted the rear seat. 'Put one foot here,' he said, pointing to a footrest, 'then swing your leg up and over. Don't worry, I'll hold her steady.'

His voice was so assured that it gave me a jolt of confidence. I hitched my skirt, holding it close to my thighs, then stepped up, swinging my leg out and over the back of the bike. I had no idea whether I flashed or not but once I was safely seated I consoled myself that modesty was a small price to pay. I settled my skirt around me and gave everyone a cheery wave.

'Be careful,' Mama called out.

'You look like a queen,' called Mrs Nola.

Ivan checked back. 'Hold on tight,' he said.

I rested my hands either side of his hips, but he drew them further forward so that I was hugging him tight around his middle. I was sitting so close to him now that my breasts brushed up against his back, and I could feel the warmth coming off him on my face. I inched back.

'Just relax,' said Ivan. 'We don't want to lose you.'

My arms were like sticks and I wriggled them, trying to loosen up. The only time Branko and I got this close was when we danced or when we kissed, but that was only momentarily. I felt frustrated by my inexperience, but at the same time a tingle coursed through me. Most of all I was grateful for Ivan's no-nonsense guidance. There was no time for thinking — Ivan revved the engine and I felt a surge of power under my seat. My breath caught in my chest as we zoomed off, the engine a loud clatter. It was exhilarating but I had to remind myself to look up. I had no sense of whether anyone waved; all I could think about was keeping my arms wrapped tight around Ivan.

We roared off down the street towards the harbour, me shielding my face from the breeze whipping past us, my scarf flapping over my ears like a mini-motor. I was surprised at how quickly I grew accustomed to burrowing in behind Ivan's back, relishing the thrill as we swung around the corners. When I dared peek over his shoulder a few strands of my hair whipped in tangles about my face to catch in my mouth. I tentatively lifted one hand to brush them aside and congratulated myself on being so brave.

The road heading out was hard-packed dirt. When I plucked up the courage to glance behind, Vela Luka was shrouded in a cloud of dust. By now the engine sounded more like a gentle purr. I could taste the dirt at the back of my throat, but it wasn't unpleasant, more a taste of freedom. The sea sparkled on our left, the bluest of blues and icy clear. A good day for fishing. Tata and Josip would likely see the fish running. It would be no consolation for Josip, though. He would be annoyed to be working while I was out on an adventure, and I felt privileged that it was me Ivan had chosen.

Further out from town the road became more rutted. We headed inland, travelling more slowly, winding our way towards Blato. At times Ivan had to swerve around potholes, and I felt self-conscious grasping him tightly again. To our right the hills rolled away, rising up towards the spine of the island. The land around us was now lush with crops and grapevines. I had rarely been this far out of town and I felt as though I was seeing my island through new eyes. Occasionally Ivan turned back, and his face, with those goggles, made me laugh inside. It wasn't just his comical look; it was because I was feeling so carefree. He pointed out landmarks, but I couldn't make out his words. They flew past me, trailing behind to settle in our dust.

When we reached the start of the new stretch of road, Ivan pulled over and cut the engine. The concrete stretched like a pale grey scar through the countryside. Trees and shrubs lay trampled at the sides, a thick layer of dust muting the bright green. In their place were tall thin poles, stuck at intervals, sticks linked by wires.

'Impressive, isn't it?' said Ivan, straddling the bike.

I nodded, but in fact I was thinking how ugly it all looked. The sun perched high in the sky like a watchful eye, beating down on us, searing hot. I thought about the men working in this heat. No wonder Branko complained.

'Piece by piece we'll snake our way through to Lumbarda,' said Ivan, pointing ahead. Then he rubbed his hands together. 'Time to take you on a real ride now.' His look was mischievous. 'Ready?'

I nodded, but then squealed at the rush of speed as we took off. Even so, it amazed me how snugly the bike gripped the new road. When we swept around the corners, Ivan dipped the motorbike low and my skirt flapped around my knees. The sea was a blur, and when I dared glance behind me there was no sign of our tracks, just that same stretch of grey seal, like a bandage covering a wound.

It seemed only minutes before Ivan slowed the bike and we thumped back down onto the dirt again. Up ahead, groups of men, all shapes and sizes, were clustered haphazardly along what appeared to be a scene of chaos and destruction. Ivan pulled the bike to the side.

'Back to walking now,' he said. 'Too many hazards ahead.'

He lowered the bike on an angle and my heart hammered in my chest. It was ridiculous, but having got myself on, I now felt self-conscious getting off it. I was grateful we weren't parked any closer to the men and that Ivan was looking ahead. I edged backwards and scrambled off. Ivan kicked out the bike stand and swung his leg over, making it look so simple. He wrenched his driving goggles off and looped them over the handlebars.

'That's better,' he said, smoothing his hair and running his hand over his shirt and trousers before replacing his hat. The medals on his shirt lapels glistened in the sun. I untied the scarf from my head and shook my hair loose, hoping I might look less frumpy.

Ivan smiled. 'Come on. I'll have to keep my eye on you. You'll cause quite a stir out here.' I felt myself blushing but was pleased all the same. Ivan was already a few steps ahead and I hurried to catch up.

The warning signs were everywhere: *Danger! Slow! Machinery Ahead!* Ivan must have sensed my nervousness because he placed his hand at my back to guide me. The sun beat down and a mix of discordant noises: banging, rattling and chipping — sounds I associated more with Jadranka — filled the air. I cast my mind away from work, shielding my eyes, trying to concentrate on what was ahead. We walked down the centre of a wide stretch of dirt, smoothed out to the same width as the road we had just travelled on, but still rough and uneven. I understood then why Ivan had insisted I wear my clumpy work shoes.

Groups of men lined both road sides. Some dug and shovelled dirt while others raised picks and thumped them into the ground. Ivan explained they were digging trenches to take the pipes for the drainage and preparing edging to hold in the concrete. Most of the men were stripped to the waist and their torsos glistened wet with sweat above their long trousers or baggy shorts. The dust showed up as dark streaks down their bodies, or smeared across their foreheads, or caked on their heavy boots. Some had draped their singlets or shirts over their heads, transporting me for a strange moment back to Egypt and the headgear the Arabs had worn. The men looked up from their work, nudging each other or standing stiffly as we passed. I scanned the faces, looking for Branko, certain I would recognise someone at least, but I was left feeling like an outsider, that I was in some foreign place. Further ahead, large machines like army tanks ran up and down the dirt road. Their tyres were like looped conveyer belts and Ivan explained their job was to smooth out the new road. Still more men worked at the sides, digging trenches. At points along the line, umbrellas cast shade over tables where groups of men, dressed in uniform, some with Party caps, crowded around to pore over large sheets of paper. Ivan waved.

'Great day for a stroll, Captain,' someone called out.

'Who's your young lady?' another said.

I kept my head down, but inside I was bursting with pride that Ivan was my relative and that I was an honoured guest.

Heavy metal pipes, wooden poles and metal grid sheets were stacked at the side, and trucks with tyres as tall as humans, their trays laden with rocks and dirt, worked in the area behind them. They moved backwards and forward, dumping and refilling while cranes with long arms like dinosaurs scooped up whatever had been dumped.

'They're preparing the mix for the concrete,' said Ivan. 'The rocks and sand go into a crushing machine.' Without him I wouldn't have made any sense of what was happening.

I almost missed Branko. He was bent over a trench, pointing out something to a fellow worker, but when he straightened there was no mistaking his shock of black hair standing to attention, like a rooster's comb. It was comforting seeing this familiar sight among all that was so foreign. I wasn't in the least surprised he hadn't covered his head. He took great pride in his hair and wouldn't have wanted to flatten it.

His body was cloaked in sweat and his wiry frame looked far too fine for the shovel he was wielding. No wonder he complained about his aching muscles. I understood why I hadn't seen much of him over the past six weeks. Branko looked shocked to see me but he waved and called out.

'You know this boy?' asked Ivan.

'Branko is my *dragi*. I thought you knew.' I felt stupid having boasted to Branko that I'd helped him get the job. Clearly they were in need of as many workers as they could get.

'Ah, Branko. The special one.' A look of recognition crossed Ivan's face. 'Come. Introduce me.'

We crossed to where Branko was standing. Some men working just along from him wolf-whistled.

'Enough,' Ivan called out sternly. 'Show some respect.' He leant in and whispered behind his hand. 'Told you. This mud and dirt makes a pretty girl stand out even more. Forgive them.'

I didn't have time to feel embarrassed. Branko was looking this way and that. I hung back, wondering whether I should give him a peck on the cheek but I was too self-conscious for that.

'Well, introduce me to your *dragi*,' said Ivan.

I was relieved he'd taken charge. I made the introductions and Ivan shook Branko's hand. Branko still looked as though he wanted to run away and I was embarrassed he was acting so childishly.

'Show me what you've been working on, Branko.' Ivan's hand swished at the trench.

'Preparing for the drainage. It's slow going. These rocks are like boulders.' I was glad he sounded more confident.

Ivan stared at him for what seemed like minutes. I didn't know where to look. Finally he barked, 'The rocks are like boulders. What?'

Branko glanced at me as though I might have an answer. I wanted to climb inside one of the big drainage pipes at the side of the road and hide. I didn't know what else he could say. Ivan's eyes were steely under the bright blue peak of his cap.

'Just that. Hard to move,' Branko said, still looking baffled.

'The. Rocks. Are like boulders. What?' Ivan was talking to Branko as though he was an idiot. I'd never heard him speak this way. It made me feel like a child, too. 'I'm less worried about the hard work, son, and more about your manners. Consider who you are addressing.'

Branko's eyes widened. He snapped his shoulders back and I worried that he might topple into the trench behind. 'The rocks are like boulders, sir. My apologies, sir. I wasn't thinking, sir.' Branko's eyes darted sideways as though looking for a way to escape.

'Better,' said Ivan, his voice snippy. 'Less time talking and thinking, more time working. I wouldn't want to involve your supervisor. We're not here for a picnic, are we, son?'

'No, sir. As you say, sir.' Branko picked up his shovel and thrust it back into the dirt. He didn't look up. I felt so ashamed for him. Our supervisors at Jadranka demanded the same respect, but even they weren't so callous. Ivan strode off and I scuttled after him, not daring to look behind, but feeling Branko's eyes drilling my back as though I was a traitor.

Ivan and I walked in an uncomfortable silence. He seemed to be bristling and I wondered what the other workers thought of Ivan, whether they talked behind his back like we did sometimes about our bosses at the factory. I struggled to reconcile this Ivan with the version I knew from home. Perhaps the real reason Branko had refused to visit our house was because he feared Ivan. Perhaps it wasn't for the reason he claimed, that it would be inappropriate with his boss there.

'Sorry if that was uncomfortable,' Ivan said after what felt like minutes. 'I can't have rules for one and not for others. Without respect, the discipline fails.' He smiled then, and it seemed the old Ivan was back.

'That's okay,' I said, still trying to push away what had just played out.

A dreadful clamour filled the air, a horrendous boom which rattled the earth. I shrieked and grabbed Ivan's arm, my heart pounding, but he burst out laughing. I stepped away, my hand at my chest. The land continued to shake and thick clouds of rubble and dust exploded ahead followed by loud cheers.

Ivan grinned down at me. 'Sorry, I should have warned you.'

'I thought we were being shot at,' I spluttered, collapsing into a fit of giggles, unable to say more.

'Relax. I'm here to protect you.' He took my arm.

It was as though my giggle got strangled inside my throat. I edged away, feeling on display in front of the men, hoping Branko couldn't see me. My fun-loving uncle was back but out there everything seemed at odds.

'What's happening up there?' I asked, trying to divert his attention off me.

'Men are scaling the hillsides and planting sticks of dynamite. We're blasting our way through so the road can more or less go in a straight line.'

'But isn't that dangerous?' I peeked up at him.

'We give the men training. Not everyone's suitable.' His face turned serious again. 'We shouldn't go much closer. In fact, it's probably best that I get you home.'

He strode off and I wondered if I'd said something wrong. I scurried to catch up, thinking how as children we'd been warned to look out for unexploded mines. There were plenty in the caves nestled high in the hills behind Vela Luka, and Branko, Nada, Josip and I had often gone exploring. It was always Josip and Branko's job to go in first, to clear the way before Nada and I were allowed to enter. Branko had a special knack for finding the caves and he prided himself on discovering any secret treasures inside. When we were younger I'd always thought of him as the brave one. I knew how much he would covet that job up ahead and I wished I could tell Ivan. But how could I when Branko had acted like a startled squirrel? I felt embarrassed that the person I loved was not seen as worthy by Ivan. That Branko had failed me by acting like a fool when Ivan had just been doing his job. By the time I caught Ivan, we were passing alongside where Branko was working. I didn't dare look across, didn't say a word.

Perched up behind Ivan on the ride home, I struggled to push my bad thoughts about Branko away. I focused instead on all the new things I'd learnt since Ivan's arrival, how he might change my life, just as Tito's projects were making changes all over Yugoslavia. The wind streamed against my face as the familiar shape of Vela Luka, clustered around the harbour, came into sharper focus. How much did I love Branko? This wasn't the first time that I'd allowed my mind to drift, thinking about the prospect of Ivan introducing me to one of his Party contacts: someone who might show me another side of life; someone who could change my world.

~ ~

I let Branko's hurt settle before seeing him again, waiting until the weekend before calling around. Branko greeted me at the door to their house, his rooster's comb dishevelled. He rubbed at his eyes, which were like saucers in his pale face.

'Been curled up in a sunny spot somewhere?' I said. 'Sorry to interrupt your beauty sleep.' I reached up to touch his cheek but he wrenched back, half-scowling, mangling his hand through his hair.

'Everyone's out. I'm taking my chances when I can,' he said, pouting.

'I'd hoped you might join me for a walk.' I forced a smile and threw my hand towards the street as though inviting the day into the darkened porch. Branko shook his head and I leant in, grabbing him by the shoulders and pecking him on the cheek, desperate to ease the tension and regain some familiar ground.

'Stop trying to dodge it,' said Branko, his face still drawn. 'I've been wondering when you'd show up.'

I felt as though he was chiding me, that it was his way of paying me back, that he was asserting his authority, but I was determined not to start with an argument. 'Come on,' I said. 'Let's go inside and talk things over, away from prying eyes.'

Branko turned on his heel and led me into their front lounge room. He crossed to the sofa that had its back to the window looking out to the street. I left a gap between us when we sat down. Branko seemed determined not to look at me.

'Come on, snap out of it,' I said. 'It wasn't the worst that could happen.'

'Easy for you to say,' he muttered. 'I'm the laughing stock at the site now. All because of your stupid uncle.'

'At least you've got a good job,' I said, feeling a need to defend Ivan. 'Come on, it was just a misunderstanding. It didn't help having me there. He's not that bad, surely?'

'He's an arsehole. I'm sorry, Jela, but everyone thinks so. Pity you can't see it.'

'He's only doing his job!' I said crossly. 'You can't blame him for that.'

Branko folded his arms and turned away. 'What's the point in talking? You'll never see anyway.'

I reached out to touch him but he brushed me away. I realised then that perhaps I owed Branko more loyalty, that I should have felt more torn.

We sat in an uncomfortable silence and I wondered whether this was it for us, the point of no return. It would feel strange after a year of dating, and despite everything I felt nervous about losing what we had. I worried about Nada, how she might react, how it would affect our friendship. She had been the matchmaker, engineering our first date by working on me for weeks, dropping hints about Branko, how he felt about me, insisting that he was too nervous to ask me himself. I relented in the end and later I wondered if Branko had too. In a sense we'd been thrown together and perhaps this was why we'd continued to be so tentative with each other. Maybe our relationship had been slow to progress because he saw me more as a sibling too. Antica was always teasing me, asking if we'd got past first base. Branko and I never discussed it. We'd allowed ourselves to drift into a comfortable pattern, knowing that our families and friends agreed we were well suited. But at that moment, on the sofa, our relationship was thrown into sharp focus. After what seemed an age, Branko turned back and put his arm around me.

'Hey, I'm sorry,' he said, pulling me close. 'I'm being selfish. Of course it's not your fault. I'm just exhausted. I can't even walk in a straight line, let alone think clearly. Let's not argue.'

I scanned his wan face. When I reached up to ruffle his hair, desperate to regain some normality and take the tension away, as always, he smiled. His spiky black hair bristled under my fingers before bouncing back, refusing to lie down. I couldn't help smiling too. What was the point in changing things? Neither of us was putting pressure on the other. There was no reason not to keep the status quo.

'Let's not fight,' I said. 'What you need is a decent rest. How about we go for a swim tomorrow? We can ask Nada and Dinko to join us.'

'Okay. I promise I'll be back to my old self then.' He rubbed his thumb back and forth along my palm as though this was all he had the energy for. 'Thanks for understanding.'

I wondered whether he was also thinking that we had dodged a bullet. I'd been surprised by my confusion. All my secret thoughts about meeting one of Ivan's contacts suddenly felt false, threadbare, an unrealistic dream. Branko was a decent man, one of the better ones around Vela Luka, and Ivan's arrival hadn't changed that. I would be stupid to toss it all away on a whim.

AUGUST

Nada, Antica and I always chose the same rock ledge, out of earshot of where the men congregated. We waited, along with Mama, Mare and little Luci, for the men to file past. It was our annual picnic to honour Josip's birthday at our favourite horseshoe bay cradled at the base of an amphitheatre of rocky ledges on Proizd Island. The men's ledge was halfway down with plenty of room to splay out. Ours was compact but with a bird's-eye view.

'I'll take Luci down with me,' said Mare.

'Are you sure?' asked Antica.

Mare smiled and patted her mounded stomach. 'I need all the practice I can get.'

'I'll join you,' said Mama. 'Leave you three to catch up.' She held out her arms for Luci. 'Come on, *Draga*. Shall we find some waves?'

Antica handed her daughter over and Luci squealed with delight. 'You be good.' She waggled her finger at Luci, who was snuggled into Mama's chest.

Mama and Mare picked their way down, passing Luci between them like a precious parcel at the steep drops. The men were already sprawled, shirts off, a collection of nut-brown bodies strewn on the slate. It was Ivan's first visit here, and all week I'd been anticipating showing him our local jewel. As usual, Dinko and Antica's Marin had joined us. Branko had opted out with an excuse of helping his baba and dida. I knew he was still bitter at Ivan but I'd been half-relieved, not wanting any tension to spoil what had become our favourite annual family event. Over the years I'd come to think of Josip's birthday picnic as my party too; my own birthday fell in mid-January, a miserable time for celebrating, and besides, Josip always invited my friends to bolster his numbers. In Branko's place, or at least that's how it seemed, Josip had invited Stefan, a new acquaintance none of us knew well. He seemed the quiet type, much like Josip.

We had crowded onto *Krešimira* mid-morning under a burning blue sky, with Tata at the helm, to make the half-hour trip across. Our favourite beach was an indent in a coastline of hewn angles, each one another link in the dramatic chain. Even Ivan, who had seen so much, stopped short and whistled. Pin-pricks of pride tingled through me. It was his affirmation that a place I valued, despite my limited world, was also admired by someone of importance who had travelled widely.

Mama and Mare were side by side on the beach, their skirts hitched up and legs outstretched. From our vantage point Mare's taut stomach might have been a ball resting on her thighs. Luci bounced against it, squealing with delight, her legs dancing in and out of the crystal-clear water that lapped onto the shore as though tickling the white pebbles and painting them with foam.

Nada and Antica had already slipped out of their skirts and blouses down to their swimsuits. I followed, squeezing alongside Nada, my stomach flat against the stone, the warmth radiating through me. Perched on that spot we all knew so well, the sun having worked its summer magic to turn our torsos golden, I could almost trick myself that it was like old times. And yet I was struggling to feel enthused. So much had changed in a year. Antica was already a mother and about to get married. Nada was heading in the same direction with Dinko. I felt her criticism, so much so that our friendship had become strained, as though each conversation held a built-in reserve. Ever since my visit to the construction site, and despite our best efforts, Branko and I had become more distant.

It was true that I had veered off course. Ivan's stories about the opportunities for young women like me had rekindled something I hadn't felt since school days, Jadranka having squeezed all the passion out. How could I explain to Antica and Nada that their talk of marriage and babies bored me? Mama and Mare were obsessed too. Lately I'd been left feeling there was nothing to look forward to. When I'd confided in Ivan a few weeks back that I wanted to escape Korčula he said he understood. But deep down I knew my dreams were no more than marbles rattling inside my head, a pinball machine with a deafening clatter. With no money there was little prospect of me ever making a change. I would likely be stuck on Korčula forever. The thought filled me with dread.

'I don't envy Mare,' said Antica, grimacing as if on cue. 'There's worse to come yet.'

'She'll cope,' I said, forcing a smile. 'Everyone does. Even you.'

'Come on, Nada. Funniest memory of the week?' said Antica.

Nada's face transformed into an impish grin and I felt a wash of relief. Some things didn't change; perhaps a visit to Proizd was all we needed.

'Has to be Vinka going for the factory slide,' said Nada, breaking into a fit of giggles.

Antica and I laughed too and it felt liberating. 'She had it coming,' I said. 'Who does she think she is? Firing off orders all day.'

'How perfect she went down by the scaling table.' Nada swiped the tears from her eyes. 'Did you see the scales coating her backside? Serves her right. She's the worst.'

'Yuck! No! What about Sretan Musin?' said Antica, her face scrunched like the inside of a fig. 'He's revolting, how he carries those food scraps in his beard.'

I cringed.

'Every morning's the same,' said Nada, her words muffled behind her fist. 'What does he see in the mirror?'

'Just his good looks,' I said, 'obviously.' I smirked, feeling my frustrations slip away. 'Vinka should focus on him — *that* would be a job worth doing.'

'He'd better watch it.' Antica's face crumpled again. 'I'm so used to cleaning up Luci I might do the same with him.'

'You wouldn't!' I cried. 'But just imagine the look on his face.'

'Don't put it past me,' said Antica, with a wry expression. 'I'm that damned tired, who knows what I might do. There's plenty of things I do now that I don't even realise.'

'No one would let you forget it,' said Nada, lying back and closing her eyes. 'Change the subject. Something nice. I want that horrible man out of my head.'

'All right. New subject,' said Antica, leaning close to the edge to peer down. 'Uncle Ivan.' She turned and flashed me one of her devilish grins.

'What?' I said.

'He's got all the girls talking. The whole factory's swooning. He's Korčula's latest attraction.'

Antica was right. Ivan could have the pick of any girl he wanted, going by the table talk over the past months. Not that he'd shown anyone the eye. I was almost certain of that.

'Can't see what the fuss is about,' said Nada, her eyes still closed.

It seemed she was relishing getting her knife out and twisting the point. I propped up on my side and glared at her.

'You can't be serious?' Antica said, prodding her in the ribs. 'Sit up. Take a proper look, girl. If it wasn't for my Marin, I'd be no different than the rest of them and Jela's handsome uncle wouldn't stand a chance.'

I shot her a warning look. Most conversations had the potential to lead back to Branko.

Nada hauled herself to sitting. 'Looks aren't everything,' she said, her voice prickly.

I hated that she might consider me fickle or unkind, but it had been difficult lately to deny that Branko and I weren't right for each other. From down below came the sounds of scrambling and jeering. We all jostled forward to the ledge. Josip, Ivan and Dinko had stripped to their swimming trunks and were strutting about as though parading.

'Ah, well, even I can't deny that,' said Nada with a sheepish grin. 'Surprising what you can hide under your uniform.'

'Nada!' I said, shocked, but I'd noticed the bulge in Ivan's swimming trunks too.

'Seems your eye's tuned in too,' said Nada, returning my look. 'Hope it wasn't my Dinko you were sizing up.' I could have thumped her.

'What a catch,' said Antica, her eyes twinkling. 'Pity you're related, eh, Jela?'

My ears were burning and I turned away, flipping onto my stomach to rest my head on my arms. 'You're both too much,' I muttered, as a loud splash erupted below.

'Relax,' said Antica. 'We're only joking.'

The heat crept across my face. I'd be the colour of a tomato soon. I was disgusted at myself but there was no denying he was handsome. It was difficult thinking of him as my uncle: he seemed too young and unlike anyone else in my family. I could have just as likely met him on the street and been the same as the other young girls in Luka, throwing him a chaste eye while thinking the exact opposite. A few girls at work had mentioned how they were jealous that I had Ivan living at home. And life had become more interesting since his arrival. Lately he'd started teasing me, like an older brother might, and I was surprised at how quickly I'd adjusted to feeling at ease in his company. Ivan was far more interesting than Josip. I thought of my brother as a delicate flower refusing to unfurl, whereas Ivan was resplendent in full bloom.

There was another loud roar and I glanced up. Antica and Nada were on their feet and I edged back across to the ledge. Marin was below, drumming his barrel of a stomach with his fists.

'Leave some water for us!' Antica yelled.

The men were a row of bobbing heads, wet hair plastered against their faces. I was grateful the attention was off me but the heat still felt too intense. 'I'm getting baked dry. Shall we join them?' I said.

'Excellent idea,' said Antica, already moving away to start the clamber down.

We chose a spot towards the rear of the men's ledge under some shade cast by a gnarly tree. I helped Mama lay out the picnic lunch. Throughout the morning my spirits lifted as we feasted on all the offerings of our crystal-clear playground: jumping off the rocks and ducking down to pierce the aqua depths like arrows; floating weightless like corks, our faces to the sun, then retreating to the rocky ledges to bake our bodies dry again. It was easy to forget my troubles in that place of beauty with the salt a powdery slick on my limbs, a gentle itch, a reminder of the fun times we always had in this place.

Mama had packed the usual staples: bread, goat's cheese, tomatoes, stuffed peppers, and some luxuries too. Over the weeks she had squirrelled away a stash of Ivan's špek and I couldn't wait to see the reaction from the others. It was difficult to pin down, but all morning the men had seemed less relaxed, as though they were skirting around conversations. I wondered if, like me, Mama hoped the atmosphere might shift to one where Ivan felt more accepted. Perhaps our friends were unsure how to address him? It was clear they had plenty of questions but they often seemed forced or unnatural, as though too much time had been spent composing them. I'd felt Nada and Antica's scrutiny too, as though they were judging how I acted around my uncle. I was reminded of that first dinner with Ivan at home.

Mama clapped her hands and called everyone to eat. Tata was there first, filling his plate before claiming a quiet spot at the side. The other men hung back and I wondered why they hesitated. Dinko gestured towards Ivan. 'Visitors first,' he said, but he wasn't looking at Stefan.

I felt embarrassed, knowing that Ivan would hate to be seen as different, but he stepped forward to crouch over the food and fill his plate. He had no sooner moved off than the other men crowded in, filling their plates and spreading themselves around the edges. Stefan went to sit by Ivan.

'Don't wait,' said Mama. 'Eat.'

This surprised me — Mama insisted on grace, even when picnicking, and everyone bar Ivan and Stefan would know this. I shot her a questioning glance and she made an underhand gesture towards Ivan. I realised she was likely trying to defuse any possible tension around our religion, given that Ivan was one of Tito's representatives.

Mama, Mare and I hung back until Antica and Nada had filled their plates.

'What have we here?' said Marin as though unable to contain his delight. He pointed at the špek. 'Same as Christmas, Luci — but where's Santa?'

'Over there.' I pointed across to Ivan, feeling smug that this treat was commonplace.

A general acknowledgement and mutter of 'Thanks' went up from everyone.

'Just as well you left some for us,' said Antica. Luci twisted on her hip, stretching towards the food as though she couldn't wait a moment longer to devour something.

I sat down with my food. Ivan was talking with Nada and Stefan who were sitting close by. I was proud my special relative was showing he wasn't above anyone. I wished Branko was there to see it and hoped Nada would see the fun side of Ivan and report back favourably. But just as in the earlier part of the day the conversation felt a little sparse, as though a hint of hesitation hung in the air, and everyone preferred to focus their attention on eating.

Mama handed around Josip's favourite sweet treat, *fritule,* and Luci grabbed two, stuffing both into her mouth. Antica scolded her, but who could blame Luci when treats were such a rarity, even for children. Our laughter felt cathartic as we watched Luci, her eyes like shiny beads and her cheeks bulging, determined to chew while all the while clapping her hands. Afterwards, when we sang 'Happy Birthday' to Josip, it felt like old times again.

Much later in the afternoon, Dinko called us together for the annual *Trofejni Izazov*, the Challenge Trophy. This was our favourite game, one that had evolved over the years. Dinko explained the rules for Ivan and Stefan's benefit, while the other men made a show of limbering up and flexing their muscles. It felt odd standing next to Ivan wearing only my swimsuit, and I was aware of Nada's piercing stare. I swung my arms then stretched them above my head, trying to appear relaxed while focusing on the *trofej,* the mound-shaped rock about a hundred metres out which never failed to separate the swimmers from the stragglers. When my swimsuit rode up, catching in the crick of my bottom, I glanced towards Ivan, feeling paralysed, willing him to look away.

'Remember, the *Trofejni Izazov* is more than just a swimming race,' Dinko cut in again. 'The winning team is the one who gets all three people onto the *trofej* ledge, at the same time, with the scarf. You can't shout "*Šampions!*" until you are all there and the scarf is raised.' He waved his arms to quieten us. 'And now, Antica and Mare will announce the teams.'

This was my chance. Ivan looked away and I wrenched my swimsuit down.

Dinko and Stefan were in my team; Mama had Ivan and Josip; Nada was with Tata and Marin. Both Antica and Mare had opted out. We all knew Antica hated swimming but she used Luci as her excuse, saying she wanted to settle her for a nap. Mare joked that she'd have an unfair advantage with two motors on board.

'Nothing wrong with double the engine size,' said Marin, patting his stomach.

'No special treatment next year, mind,' said Josip.

'You'll be the one on the sideline then,' Mare retorted, waggling her finger at Josip.

'I'll believe that, when I see it,' said Marin under his breath.

Josip nudged him as though backing him up, but if anyone could change the order of things, it was Mare. The talk at Jadranka was that she coddled Josip, that he should stand up for himself — be a man's man. Mare's pregnancy and Ivan's arrival had cast a spotlight on our family.

Dinko handed each team their coloured scarf. Ours was green. Antica made a show of saluting him when he asked her to start us off. She picked up the two rocks he'd put aside.

'Ready, set, go!' she shouted, clapping the rocks together.

'Quick,' said Dinko, rushing forward. 'Make sure you tie it tight.'

'Get going.' I flicked my arm towards the water. 'Tying a scarf's something I can do. Get!' I was the fastest swimmer of the women and Dinko one of the fastest men; speed was likely our team's best asset whereas the others would have the advantage of strength once they reached the *trofej* ledge.

Josip had already launched, and both Stefan and Dinko dived off to give chase. I checked for Ivan, expecting him to do the same, but Mama was helping him tie the red square around his neck. This was a new tactic. Men were never the scarf carriers.

Nada was busy securing her yellow scarf. I concentrated on tying my knot so that it was secure enough to keep the scarf on, but easy to undo once I reached the *trofej*. Mama slipped off the ledge, making her way by breaststroke so as to keep her head above water. It was an unspoken rule, although there were always exceptions when it came to the *Trofejni Izazov* — no dunking Mama unless absolutely necessary because she hated her curls turning to a frizzle. After a spectacular splash Tata and Marin were on their way too.

'Go, Ante! Go, Tata!' shouted Antica. 'That's your Tata making the big splash, Luci-loo.' Luci squealed and pounded her fist against Antica's chest.

I rushed forward and dived, keeping as shallow as possible to protect my scarf. When I resurfaced there was a swell of unsettled water behind me. I checked that my scarf was still intact and stroked out, finding my rhythm, taking the most direct route. Nada would be using

Mama's tactic, keeping well to the side, out of harm's way. Nada's team was lucky: she might be the easiest to pull off the ledge but she'd made a name for herself over the years at being the most skilled at holding her breath under water. If she timed it right, her teammates could pull her onto the ledge at the last minute.

I was gaining on Tata and Marin's white foam, focusing on keeping my strokes steady. They were out to the side now, treading water. I was angling away to give them a wide berth when a hand clamped over my leg, stopping me short, then dragging me backwards so that I swallowed a mouthful of sea water. I resurfaced, coughing and spluttering, feeling disorientated. There was Ivan, stroking off, a flash of green rotating in and out of the water on his wrist.

'Catch me!' he called from up ahead, waving my scarf high, taunting me.

My legs and arms burnt as I raced out after him, the taste of salt making breathing difficult. This was another level of cunning, to steal a team's scarf before getting to the *trofej* — without it we couldn't win. If I didn't reclaim it I'd be left looking a fool. With each stroke I tried to work on a plan but when my fingers slapped hard against rock I cursed, for being distracted. Stefan, Josip and Dinko were already jostling for space on the *trofej's* ledge; Ivan was nowhere to be seen. Stefan got flipped off and was floundering about just to the side of me, trying to catch his breath. I guessed Ivan must have gone around the back of the *trofej* but time had likely run out for following him. Tata and Marin were already closing in, and Mama was angling in from the side like a cat hunting a bird, biding her time. I knew Nada wouldn't be far behind; she might be hiding at the side already, waiting.

'Charge!' I jerked my head up. The front face of the *trofej* was now Ivan's slide to reach the flat ledge.

'Dinko! Watch out!' I cried. 'Our scarf!' I hauled myself onto the ledge, turned and beckoned to Stefan. 'Come! Quick! Here's our chance.'

Ivan and Josip were on either side of Dinko. Ivan held him in a chest hold and yelled at Josip to take Dinko's legs but Dinko was fighting back, kicking up merry hell.

'Show some courage, Josip!' shouted Ivan, his voice stern as though he was on a battlefield. I thought this was a tactic to scare Dinko. Josip lost hold of Dinko's leg. I saw he was off balance and wasted no time, stepping forward to push Josip from behind. He toppled into the water, arms and legs flaying. Ivan threw up his arm in dismay allowing Dinko to wrestle out of his hold.

'Quick, Dinko, the scarf,' I yelled. 'The scarf!'

Ivan waved the scarf high, out of Dinko's reach. 'For God's sake, Josip!' he yelled, his look of exasperation obvious. 'What are you — man or mouse?'

'Shut your fat arsehole!' retorted Josip, shaking his fist at Ivan, his face streaming with water. 'You're not in the Party now!'

A hush fell over everyone and the game ground to a halt. I'd never seen Josip so furious. Those in the water pedalled their arms and legs, keeping themselves afloat. Mama and Nada clung to the *trofej* at the side and Stefan was suspended on the rock part-way up. Even Dinko and I stood quietly, next to Ivan, as though calling a truce. I was still trying to fathom how our fun game had turned. Ivan leapt high in the air, tucking his knees to his chest and bombing into the water. He landed just to the side of Josip, drenching him with a wash of spray. Josip lunged at Ivan, still shouting obscenities but Ivan was already swimming, fast as a sprat away from the *trofej*.

Josip thumped his fist into the water. '*Boli me kurac!*' he shouted.

Mama gasped, her hand at her mouth. She hated swearing.

'Good on you, son!' Tata yelled. 'Don't let him boss you around!'

'Bravo!' called Marin, punching his fist in the air. 'Good news for us, Ante! May the best team win. You ready, Nada?' He splashed forward, stroking out.

Dinko turned to me. 'Don't know how he can call himself family. You should be just like the rest of us, happy to see him go back to his precious Party.'

I wanted to defend Ivan but I was stunned speechless. 'He won't get away with this,' I said and dived in to give chase.

The game was up for our team but it was a matter of pride and I was determined to retrieve the scarf. Mostly I wanted to escape the cauldron and not have to respond to Dinko's criticisms. I felt sorry for Josip but what had just played out only accentuated what had been happening around home. My already tenuous relationship with my brother had been stretched even thinner. Perhaps my admiration for Ivan had forced Josip to hold up a mirror? Perhaps he too was frustrated by what he saw? Given his explosion maybe I should have felt proud of my brother but instead I felt embarrassed. It seemed Ivan's presence was shining a light on the inadequacies of all our men; it was clear they were jealous. But the person I most worried about was Mama. Ivan was her brother, after all.

Ivan was quite a distance ahead, treading water, taunting me by waving the scrap of green in the air. I was breathless by the time I caught him, all the nervous energy I'd bundled and taken with me from the ledge having leached out during the chase.

'What was that about?' I spluttered, still scrambling to make sense of it all. I swiped at him, any feelings of self-consciousness gone.

'Here.' He grabbed my arm, the dripping rag still out of reach.

'You're an idiot!' I said, making another snatch for it. 'And your dirty tactics have backfired. We'll both lose now. Tata will be unbearable.' I couldn't believe I was talking like this, that I was being so grumpy.

'Wait, Jela,' he said, lowering his arm to pull off my scarf. I grabbed it and made to swim off but he still had hold of my arm, his eyes pleading. 'Jela, I need to ask you something. Don't be angry. Please. I'm sorry I took my stupid plan too far. I wanted to get you alone and when you didn't follow me the first time I got frustrated. This is what I resorted to.'

I checked back to the *trofej,* hoping to put some reality into this strange conversation. Tata and Marin were reaching down to lift Nada onto the ledge. She was raising the yellow scarf in the air. '*Šampions*!' they shouted.

'I'd thought I'd have the chance to ask you,' he said. 'I hadn't realised there's so little privacy here. It's worse than at the house.'

'You're not making sense. What do you mean?' Over at the *trofej* Tata was pumping his fist.

'I wanted to ask if you'll accompany me to the Party ball. It's in Dubrovnik. In six weeks' time.'

I nodded, blinking, wondering if I had heard him right. He was explaining how the organisers had forgotten about the officers posted to Korčula. That he heard only yesterday and needed to respond after the weekend. My mind was doing cartwheels.

'I'll need to ask Ante,' he continued, 'but I wanted to be sure of your answer.' He smiled. 'I know you feel hemmed in. This might be a way to help you out of Korčula. There will be people I can introduce you to. People with connections.'

I wanted to hug him but I didn't dare. Besides, we were still in the middle of the sea. It felt wonderful to know that somebody had taken me seriously. That he understood.

'I'd love to go, of course. But Tata . . .' My excitement drained as though emptying into the sea. 'You know what he'll be like.'

'Perhaps my stupid plan wasn't quite so stupid.' He smiled again and pointed to the *trofej*. 'At least he will be in good spirits. Could work to your advantage.' He winked at me. 'Come on. Let's head back and congratulate them. I've got an apology to make, too.'

~ ~

It wasn't until Monday, over breakfast, that Tata finally gave his consent. All day I'd been giddy with excitement. It had taken all my willpower not to spill my secret to Nada and Antica. After dinner I unlatched the rear gate, my stomach feeling set to burst, anticipation mixed in with a dose of nerves. It was important I tell Branko first. Life had become so dull between us — him so exhausted and me feeling so confined — that I wanted to share something positive, to have him share in my excitement. I hoped it might be a way for us to connect again, that he would view it as the opportunity it was, potentially for both of us.

I tilted my head to peer up at the clear summer night sky. There wasn't an oppressive brooding cloud in sight and the moon was a thin crescent rotated on its back like a smile. Surely Branko would understand? I shuffled my feet to help release my tension and focused on the warm ray of light cast by my oil lantern. I raised it high and picked my way up the pathway of hard-packed dirt. The hills behind Vela Luka were riddled with these narrow trails leading up from the houses. I imagined that if you looked from above, high in the sky, they would appear like tributaries, tiny veins linking with the main track, zigzagging to the top. So many times I'd tapped into this network, climbing higher and higher to escape Tata's small-mindedness when everything got too much. Up high there was always relief. I would gaze at what was beyond, allowing myself the space to breathe.

I reached the main track and strained my ears, lifting my lantern higher. It swung to and fro from its hooked handle, casting light in haphazard angles so the olive trees with their gnarly branches, and the spear-like leaves of the aloes, appeared sinister. Luka was sprawled out below, a collection of amorphous shapes stopping short at the harbour wall and hugging its curve. The lights from the oil lamps scattered among the windows gave some definition. Not that I needed it. Most of the buildings were landmarks for me, their features cemented in my memory. Soon I would have the opportunity to feast my eyes on Dubrovnik, a place that so far existed only in my imagination but which I'd heard so much about. No one else, Nada, Branko, Josip, even Antica, understood how I was able to view the two years spent at El Shatt with any positivity. Granted, there had been terrible times in that place, but it was still an experience, a memory of something outside of my small life here.

I hoped Branko would be there to meet me at the place we had met so many times before, ever since childhood. I moved forward, sticking close to where the path cut into the cliff, keeping clear of the edge, taking care not to stumble on the crush of loose stones. Branko had been opting out so often lately and I had to trust that Nada had stressed how important it was that he come. I rounded the corner and there he was, at the point where his own small pathway met the track. He was leaning back, his oil lamp at his feet, the flickering light playing his shadow like a caricature against the cliff wall. My relief felt like a rush of pride.

'What's taken you so long?' he called, peeling himself away to stand tall.

'Sorry,' I called back, hurrying now. 'Mama kept dishing out jobs.' He held out his hand and I rushed forward, taking it in mine, leaning in to kiss him. When I pulled back I scanned his face. 'I'm glad you came,' I said, bending to set down my lantern. 'I knew you'd be tired.'

'At your service,' he said, saluting. I scanned his face and he smiled. 'You're getting demanding and I'll have to watch myself — can't have people saying you're wearing the pants.'

I leant in and kissed him again, wanting to keep the moment light, to show him how important this was for me. I lingered and realised then how long it had been since we kissed like that, but I couldn't contain my excitement any longer.

'I've got some brilliant news. I wanted you to be the first to know.' I rubbed his arm, hesitating now, my words feeling stuck in my throat.

'So?' he said. 'Been promoted?' He looked worried. 'Or fired? Come on, Jela. What is it? You look set to burst.'

My words scrambled out. 'Uncle Ivan's invited me to the Party ball in Dubrovnik next month.'

His reaction was immediate. 'You must be joking,' he said, dropping my hand and stepping away, bristling. 'Absolutely not!' His voice had a harsh edge. 'Out of the question. What are you thinking, Jela?'

For a moment I was flummoxed. Who did he think he was? My jailer? I'd expected some pull back but not this blatant refusal. 'You're the one who can't be serious,' I said, my voice strong.

'I couldn't be more serious. Why would I allow it? My girl going off, alone, with that arsehole.' He stamped his foot. 'What do you take me for? A fool!'

'Oh for God's sake, Branko! Why are you worried?' I threw my arms in the air. 'That you can't trust me? You don't have the right to tell me what to do! I'm not your property, something you can pick up, and put down, and keep in a box until you're ready to play. All you've done is ignore me lately. Too tired, too busy.'

He stared at me, unmoving. I nearly stepped forward to shove him but the narrow pathway with its rubble of stones stopped me. I bent to retrieve my lantern, desperate to escape.

'I won't let you take my freedom as well!' I shouted, glaring at him, determined to stay strong. The light caught his stony expression. 'This is the chance I've been waiting for, to escape Korčula, even if it's only one night. Why would you crush my fun? You're the same as Tata and all the other men around here. Full of your own importance!'

Branko called out as I stormed off, 'Ah, Jela! You're always looking for more. Never satisfied. If you go, that'll be the end. I'm telling you now. That'll be us. Finished!'

I stopped and turned. 'Is it any wonder I'm not satisfied?' I yelled. 'You're right, Branko. We are finished. I've had enough. I don't need you!' I strode off, stopping just before the corner. 'Good riddance!' I shouted.

'Granted!' he yelled back but I was already around the bend.

With each thump of my footsteps I cursed how men rule the roost and how girls are second best. I pictured myself crushing Branko's small-minded retorts. I'd been a fool. He was too wrapped up in himself and his own tiny dreams to support me. Despite my anger I felt a wash of relief. Branko had been parcelled up and presented to me, back when we were teenagers, with the label 'safe as houses'. I'd been pushing down my fears that he might ask to marry me. Now I was certain. Branko wasn't the one I wanted to share the rest of my life with. He would never be my ticket off this island. I was better off without him.

SEPTEMBER

The shining face of the Luža Square clock tower guided us forward to the Party ball. Ivan and I were among a throng of well-dressed people, a cast of floating fabrics, streaming down Dubrovnik's white stone Stradun towards the Rector's Palace. I had the strangest feeling that I'd shrunk to become a miniature version of myself, and I looped my arm over Ivan's, gripping his forearm, as though the bulk of his jacket might reinstate me to full size. Merry chatter bounced off the limestone walls to meld with the clip, clap, clip of heels on the cobblestones. I worried that the tall buildings might topple and entomb us, exotic butterflies frozen in flight. My fingers scrunched Ivan's coat fabric again, a grasp on reality, while not wanting to escape this dream world or my sense of enthral.

I stared at all the women with their made-up faces. How much could change in six weeks. Again my tongue worried my painted lips. Antica had pressed the cherry-red lipstick into my palm at the ferry that morning. 'It'll help you catch one of those *Kapetanes*,' she'd whispered, her smile wicked. We'd talked of little else over the past weeks. Antica had been my buffer, keeping me sane. Nada hadn't been there for me. Ever since my break-up with Branko we'd been wrenched apart. She'd been snippy, keeping her distance. *Of course I'm fine,* she'd say when I pressed her, *do whatever you want.* I hoped she would forgive me soon.

'Still there,' said Ivan, nudging me and grinning widely. 'You look beautiful, but there'll be no lipstick left soon. Just relax.'

I clamped my lips tight. 'Just checking,' I said, and he patted my arm and winked, leaving me feeling embarrassed as though he was poking fun at me.

I was desperate for him to view me as a young woman, not a child — a confident young woman, worthy of introduction to one of his Party associates. I reminded myself of all that I'd savoured during the day: my initial glimpse of the old town jutting out on the headland, enclosed by its fortified walls; stepping into the foyer of our hotel, never having anticipated I would stay somewhere so grand; the afternoon spent exploring with Ivan, my knowledgeable guide, and how Dubrovnik was just as glamorous as I'd imagined.

Around the perimeter of the plaza the gas lamps cast warm shafts of light onto the buildings. The dome of St Blaise's Cathedral illuminated the night sky like a green trophy on a shelf. I peered up at Orlando, standing erect on his column, his sword raised.

'Remember his name?' Ivan asked, testing me as he'd been insistent on doing all afternoon, checking that I was paying attention.

I looked away, pretending to search for the answer, but really I was forcing those other thoughts down. Secret thoughts which I'd had when Ivan explained the significance of this city's symbol of freedom. My face flushed and I was grateful for the dim light. There were dreams I'd shared openly with Antica — would the Party ball be my first step to escaping Luka? What special person might I meet? Where might they come from? But then there were the other thoughts, the ones I wouldn't dare share: if only that person could be just like Ivan; if only Ivan was my boyfriend and we weren't related.

'Orlando's column,' I stammered, still glancing away.

'Star student.' He took my arm and guided me forward, pointing towards the Rector's Palace at the side of the square. 'There's our building. Remember?'

In the afternoon I'd marvelled at the assortment of curious animal-like creatures and cherubs carved into the tops of the columns. I'd said they were too small to be shouldering the weight of that vaulted ceiling and Ivan had laughed. The columns were decorated with vines now, and above the loggia the row of gothic arches glowed golden either side of the central bell-tower, yet more silhouettes in the night sky. A cacophony of chatter spilled from the main entrance and we joined the procession of people waiting outside.

I gripped Ivan's arm. 'Look after me, won't you?' I whispered, my fears of being stranded in a corner while Ivan was off socialising suddenly terrifying.

His hand was at my back, guiding me into that cauldron of chatter. 'I won't let you out of my sight. Promise.'

A waiter stood like a mannequin inside the entrance holding a tray of wine glasses. Ivan plucked two, a simple gesture which for me felt so significant: I had escaped Tata's clutches and was being invited to partake in a forbidden ritual. I held my glass and inched further inside, my mouth falling open at the grand architecture. The atrium was like a series of giant clam shells thrown open on their hinges. Oil lamps cast a warm glow over the stonework of the arches and columns. Our dances at home were held in a plain room attached to the local hotel and decorated by enthusiastic locals. Until then, I'd thought of them as grand affairs, but I knew they'd be forever tainted, that I would always see past the thin veneer to the small-town tawdriness lurking behind. There must have been hundreds of people jam-packed inside and I wondered how we would ever make our way forward. From the centre of the balcony opposite, an oversized flag bearing the Dubrovnik coat of arms jutted from a long pole and fluttered high above the central space. Music pierced the hubbub but it was nothing like the traditional tunes I was accustomed to.

'The Dubrovnik Symphony Orchestra,' Ivan whispered, pointing to a group of more than a dozen men dressed in dark suits with bow ties. They were mostly seated, some standing, all contained in a tight space at the bell-tower end of the atrium. A lone man, similarly dressed but with coat-tails, stood on a small raised platform with his back to the crowd and directed the musicians with a stick. I had been expecting to see a small group of men gathered in traditional dress like our musicians who played a mix of traditional tunes and more recent songs from America or England. This music was entirely different — complex and measured, serious even — as though it fancied itself as carrying more weight or importance. It made our musicians seem comical, and the music that I'd always found uplifting, childlike.

'Ivan Novak!' boomed a man, coming forward and slapping Ivan on the back. 'Welcome!'

A woman dressed in bright pink squeezed through the crush to plant kisses on Ivan's cheeks. 'Lovely to see you,' she gushed, 'but wherever did they send you? We imagined you lost to civilisation. Puff!' She threw her arms skyward, and her face shone nearly as pink as her dress.

I pulled back, conscious of their stares. They were much older, maybe even Tata and Mama's age. I brushed my fingers down the chiffon layer of my dress trying to muster the confidence I'd felt earlier, back at the hotel, when I'd stood in front of the bathroom mirror and remembered Mama's words: *It'll be new to everyone else so wear it with pride.* I pulled back my shoulders but my tongue was at my lips again. All the colour would surely have vanished by now, I cursed inside.

'What a treat to see you both,' said Ivan, pulling me forward into their huddle. 'Allow me to introduce Gabrijela Surjan. Gabrijela, please meet . . .'

Their names disappeared like the Pink Lady's 'puff'. She leant forward and brushed her lips against my cheek, one, two. Big Man brushed his lips over my hand.

'Jela's been my saving grace on Korčula,' Ivan said.

Pink Lady touched my arm. 'Lucky girl,' she said, drawing me aside. 'Ivan's quite the bachelor. One going places for sure.' She pursed her pink lips as though to add emphasis to her words but sizing me up at the same time. I didn't want to mislead her. Ivan must have had a reason for not explaining we were related.

'He's doing a fine job with the new road project,' I said, relieved my voice didn't waver. 'It's been interesting getting to know him.'

'I bet. Such an entertaining man. We know him from Zagreb. Party headquarters. My husband's got an eye for the up-and-comers.'

I felt a rush of pride that Ivan was considered someone who was going places and searched my mind for something else to say. I was spared. Another woman tapped Pink Lady on the shoulder and she turned away.

I took a sip of my wine, swallowing it at a gulp. I was nervous about drinking too quickly but it was the flavour that caught me off guard. Undiluted, the wine was so strong that I wasn't at all tempted to roll it around in my mouth like I'd seen Tata do. It seemed that all the people crowding the balconies were looking down at me. That a light was shining directly above to highlight my inexperience. I concentrated on the tiled floor laid in intricate patterns, and after what felt like several minutes, challenged myself to take another sip of the wine. This time, although it still tasted unpleasant, I felt more assured. I scanned the room again. Wide staircases, their balustrades carved with pretty flower and grape motifs, curled up either side of the room to the mezzanine balcony. Cliques of people gathered there, some leaning out through the gaps in the arches. I had been certain I was the centre of their attention, but it seemed no one was looking. I took a deep breath and concentrated on the gothic arches forming the outer walls of the balconies. I wanted to climb those stairs too and take everything in from that bird's-eye view.

'You two young things run off and dance,' said Big Man, touching my arm. I worried that he thought me rude but he was slapping Ivan on the back. 'Don't let us hold you back. Fabulous to see you again.'

Pink Lady turned and leant forward to kiss Ivan. 'Such a treat, *Dragi*. Lovely to meet you, *Draga*.' She fluttered her hand as though dismissing an insect then went back to her conversation. Big Man threw me an apologetic look.

We moved off and Ivan wrapped his arm around my shoulder to pull me closer. 'Those two have been like a second family,' he said. 'I'm pleased I got the chance to introduce you.'

I pulled back. 'But why didn't you say we were related?'

'Who needs to know?' I tried to read his face, still baffled. 'Ah, Jela. Why bother explaining the complicated relationship? There's not many who know my family story. It doesn't worry you, does it?' He winked, as though we were sharing a private joke.

'If you say so,' I said, still uncertain.

'Come on,' he said. 'I need another drink.' He raised his empty wineglass and pointed across the room to a bar. On the way we must have been stopped by at least ten different people — just enough time for Ivan to say a quick hello, plant a kiss on a cheek or shake someone's hand — he didn't bother to introduce me, and I was relieved to be saved from further confusion. At the bar I hung back, just to the side. The woman serving laughed at something Ivan said and I wished I had his self-assurance, which at times during the day had left me feeling confused and wondering if he was flirting — when his hand lingered close as though wanting to hold mine while we wandered around the battlements, or that look which I'd felt sure was tender when I was dressed and ready for the ball. My spine tingled — imagine if he had secret thoughts too! *But this is impossible*, I cautioned myself.

Ivan was my uncle and I was here to meet someone special. I set my first glass down on a small table. I hadn't drained it but I was petrified of feeling the alcohol's effect and making a fool of myself. Ivan returned and handed me another glass of white wine.

'Good health!' he said, clinking our glasses. 'It's been a fun day, no?'

I took another sip and dragged my eyes to the floor. In that room full of strangers, combined with my tangle of thoughts, I felt self-conscious being alone with him. What would Tata say? He would surely have imagined me as part of a large group, like the dances at home.

'Did Tata know about the hotel?' I blurted.

'Relax, Jela.' He looked amused and I wished that I could swallow back my stupid words. 'You know I wouldn't cross your Tata. Nothing's worth that. But you're not a child — you have your own mind, and I know you love to use it. Come on, treat yourself. Have some fun.'

Ivan was right. I sipped at my wine trying to recapture all the precious moments of freedom I'd felt and my sense of self-confidence. Of course I wanted to live my own life, but it was hard to shake off Tata. He was always close by, sitting on my shoulder, judging my every move. A woman called from the balcony, waving her hand through one of the gaps in the stone work. Ivan glanced up and waved back.

'How about I introduce you to some of my younger friends?' he said.

I nodded, my buzz of excitement rekindled. *This might be the moment.* We climbed the curved stairway and a tall, thin man with a baby face beckoned us over.

Ivan paused on the top step. 'I'm warning you,' he whispered. 'You'll be fending off the dance invitations now.'

My spine tingled as we moved towards the group. There were two women, one dressed in silver and the other in black, and four men who, like Ivan, were in Party uniform. 'Meet Gabrijela,' Ivan said, pulling me forward. 'The most beautiful girl on Korčula, who also happens to be my niece.' My cheeks coloured but I was relieved he had taken me seriously.

'Lucky you, Ivan,' one man said. I'm not sure who, because I was looking at the floor.

'Always the charmer.' The woman in the chic black dress had stepped forward and was kissing Ivan on the cheek. 'It's been a while. How've you been?' She manoeuvred herself to stand in front of me, blocking me from their conversation.

I inched back, my heart like a clock in my chest, but grateful there could be no misunderstandings. A solidly built man, his head perched like a square block on his wide shoulders, touched my elbow. 'Welcome,' he said, his smile kind. 'First time at one of these fancy parties?'

'Yes,' I said, smiling back, entranced by the row of gleaming medals adorning his lapels. I wanted to ask how he'd earned them but I worried that it might be rude to ask.

'Have you eaten yet?' he said, and I shook my head. 'Why not join us? We were saying it was time.' He waved his hand at a row of tables groaning with platters of food. 'Would be a shame to see it all go to waste, no?' He signalled to Ivan that he was taking me off.

'We'll join you shortly,' said Ivan, waving at me.

As I walked towards the tables with this strange man, my sense of freedom returned.

'My apologies, I didn't catch your name. I'm Matē,' he said, holding out his hand.

'Gabrijela. But everyone calls me Jela.' I took his hand and he brushed his lips across my fingers, his eyes smiling.

'It's a beautiful name. And tell me, have you enjoyed having that rascal uncle around?'

'It's been wonderful. He's like another brother.' I swallowed hard and scanned the bounty of food, wondering how I would even begin to choose. My stomach felt like a knot. Tata was back in my head. I imagined how scathing he would be of this extravagance.

'We can start here,' Matē said, pointing to a platter of seafood, 'and then work our way down.'

There was every conceivable type of food: some of the seafood I recognised — squid, octopus, scampi and grilled sardines — but other varieties I'd never seen before. Platters of meat — skewers, a leg of lamb smothered with herbs, breaded schnitzel, a stew which looked like *pašticada,* cured ham slices, pancetta, and *špek*. Vegetable dishes were further along — sauerkraut, tomatoes, bean stew, dishes of *njoki* and polenta, and baskets of *pogača* bread. At the far end were sweet treats, slices of *štrudel, kroštule* piled high, and parcels of ravioli. How could there be so much food in one place when at home we had so little? My stomach clenched again.

I chose a few pieces of seafood, a meat skewer and a small spoonful of each of the vegetable dishes. I didn't want to appear greedy, and I doubted my stomach would handle the richness. Matē, however, piled his plate high. I thought how Ivan, being accustomed to all this, must have thought us such peasants. Matē directed me towards a round table set up at the far end of the balcony. I could only pick at my food whereas Matē wolfed his down. I couldn't help drawing comparisons between him and Ivan. Matē seemed serious, older than his years. I scanned the room looking for Ivan, already missing his ease and fun-loving nature.

'Let me guess,' Matē said, still chewing. 'You must have an important job on Korčula. As Ivan's niece I'm sure you're making a fine contribution to our country.' He scanned my face and I squirmed in my seat. 'Perhaps you're a nurse?'

'I wish that were true,' I said, flattered that he thought me capable. 'Like most of the local girls I work at the sardine factory.' I scrunched my face. 'My dream is to be a teacher.'

'Never too late,' said Matē, wiping his mouth with a cloth serviette. 'Our country's in need of good teachers. I'm sure something could be arranged. I've got some contacts. Get Ivan to talk to me some time.' He stared at me as though wondering where in the country he might send me.

'That would be wonderful!' I said, feeling like cheering.

Ivan and the others joined us. Ivan's plate was laden too. I was bursting to talk to him but Baby-face took the spare seat beside me. Ivan sat directly opposite. Baby-face seemed to find it difficult sitting still. I tried to catch Ivan's eye but he was engrossed in conversation with the woman in black beside him. Silver woman sat on Ivan's other side, and a portly man, Silver's husband maybe, had his arm draped across the back of her seat as though claiming her. A handsome man with dark curly hair sat between the woman in black, and Baby-face beside me. I sensed he was quiet and I couldn't work out who he was with. Woman in black? Perhaps he was annoyed. I wished I felt brave enough to enquire and find out more about these people. I concentrated instead on eating small mouthfuls of food.

A clash of cymbals erupted from the far end of the room and the orchestra began a fast-paced tune. I twisted in my seat to check through the gaps down to the atrium. A large area had been cleared for dancing and couples were already moving forward to crowd the space. As a waiter approached to refill our wine glasses Baby-face turned to me. 'I'm Jure, by the way.' His brown eyes twinkled as he shuffled about. 'Now tell me, Gabrijela, beautiful niece of Ivan, I'm sure you enjoy the dancing.' I could only nod yes. 'Would you treat me to the first dance?' He gave a beaming smile, and I guessed he might have a cheeky sense of humour as well as boundless energy. I glanced across at Ivan. He was still talking to the lady in black.

'I'd love that. Thank you,' I said, bursting with a new-found confidence. Perhaps this was the moment when my dreams and scheming with Antica might really come true and I could bury those other thoughts once and for all.

Matē leaned forward, peering past me towards Jure. He waggled his forefinger. 'Watch these fast movers, Jela,' he said, catching my eye. 'Seems I'll have to play second fiddle.' He stared hard at Jure. 'You know what they say? Youth pales beside experience.'

I couldn't tell if Matē was serious. Jure tipped back his head and roared with laughter. 'They say many things, comrade. Not all of them true.'

Ivan looked across and raised his glass. His eyes seemed to say, *Are you happy?*

'Very happy,' I mouthed back.

For a while we stayed around the table, everyone finishing their meal, some making a second visit, most of us treating ourselves to the sweets. Waiters hovered at the ready to refill our wine glasses. I was careful to take only occasional sips but I'd lost track of how much I'd drunk. Matē and Jure had me in fits of laughter with their banter. I learnt that Jure was a mechanic for the Party and that recently he'd been responsible for Tito's fleet of vehicles at his summer house. Matē assured me again about a teaching job. He had a friend in Split who oversaw a number of schools. Both men seemed full of confidence about our country: nothing seemed impossible.

When the music started up again Jure stood and held out his hand. 'You can't possibly keep me waiting any longer,' he said. I cast a glance towards Ivan but he seemed intent on Silver, and she on him, as he recounted some story. Jure led me down the stairs to the dance floor and I concentrated on staying steady on my feet. Couples twirled around the floor and with Jure's hand at my back we blended into the melee, my feet managing to behave most of the time despite me not recognising the tune. When we did trip, or if I moved the wrong way, we laughed and I felt heady with the excitement of it all.

Over the evening I danced countless times, Matē and Jure taking turns to cut in. Both were charming partners but I felt most relaxed with Jure. I couldn't resist sneaking the odd glance at Ivan to see who he was holding in his arms. Our eyes had met a number of times and he'd raised his eyebrows and smiled as though saying, *Isn't this fun?* There seemed to be no shortage of different women on his arm, and I thought how privileged I was to have accompanied him.

'If I'm honest, you've worn me out, Jela,' Matē said, after what must have been our tenth dance. His cheeks were red circles and he seemed to be struggling for breath. 'Would you care to sit down for a while? We can chat before Jure pushes in again.'

I had no idea how much time had passed but I didn't want to sit down. There was no chance to answer because Ivan was alongside, tapping Matē's shoulder. 'Must be time *I'm* allowed to dance with my date,' he said, winking at me.

Matē gave me a resigned look and waved his arms like a toreador, as though passing me over.

Ivan pulled me close. 'Finally,' he whispered. 'It's time for *us* to have some fun now.' His breath was a hot wind against my ear, and his lips brushed so close that a tingle swept through me. For a moment I wondered if he'd kissed me and I pulled back, flustered by his familiarity, my cheeks burning.

'This music sounds familiar,' I said, despite not having a clue. 'Do you know it?' I forced myself to breathe.

'Strauss,' he answered, matter-of-factly, drawing me close, much closer than I'd been held by either Jure or Matē. I thought about when Branko and I had danced like this. How the moment had always been tinged by me trying to relax and convince myself that everything felt right.

We waltzed, his hand at the small of my back; we might have been gliding. My feet felt so light that it seemed we were moving as one. The music was complex, and I had to concentrate, but with Ivan my feet seemed to know where to go. I relaxed in his arms; it was as though we were floating around the floor.

'That was fabulous,' I said when the music stopped. I felt breathless but every fibre in my body wanted to continue, to feel the warmth of his arms, to be held so intimately again.

'I didn't know you were such an expert,' he said. 'You should have warned me.' I smiled up at him, swelling with pride and feeling light-headed. 'For the rest of the night you must give me lessons. No more time-wasting on those other slow learners.'

And for the rest of the evening Ivan was true to his word, not letting me out of his sight. When Matē or Jure tapped him on the shoulder, he waved them away saying, 'Go and find someone else.' Part of me wanted to protest, but mostly I felt flattered, as though I'd been thrust high onto a pedestal. On the dance floor with Ivan I felt like a princess, the way I'd felt in the afternoon while climbing the city walls, where with each twist and turn I'd had a glimpse into another world, privileged views of the bustling piazzas and courtyards below, and magnificent vistas over the terracotta roof tiles. A feeling that I was already far away from Vela Luka, embarking on another life.

It was past midnight when we arrived back at our hotel but the lights were still glowing. A porter swung the huge glass door open, bowing and waving us into the foyer. Rather than feeling intimidated as I had earlier in the day, I felt carefree, as though I was walking on air. The hotel still had a grand allure but I felt comfortable now, just like the people lounging about on the chairs and plush sofas in the lobby.

A man bustled forward from behind the front desk. 'Good evening, sir,' he said, extending his hand. 'It's our pleasure to have you stay.' His head bobbed up and down.

'Thank you, Pavle. Always a pleasure to be back.'

The man continued to nod as though his head was attached by a spring to his neck. 'And welcome, madam.' Nod, bobble, nod. 'It's our pleasure to have your company tonight.'

I smiled, all the while drinking in the opulence, the lustrous floor and wall tiles, shades of pearl and cream enriched by the oversized chandeliers blazing with candles. I glanced at the curved staircase that wound up from the lobby with its shiny wooden banister, and carpet the most intense shade of royal blue, cringing at my naivety from earlier in the day when I'd climbed that staircase and walked along the wide passageway lined with doors. How my anticipation had been tinged with shock when I realised we were to share a room. Luckily Ivan seemed not to notice. I'd chided myself afterwards — there were two beds, and having two rooms would be excessive in this luxurious place paid for by the Party.

Ivan guided me towards the staircase. I tried to regather my sense of excitement, imagining the people below as a crowd of admirers whispering, *Such a glamorous couple.* I inched up the stairs, my hand dragging behind on the polished railing. Ivan was ahead now, waiting on the landing. My stomach churned as he led me down the hallway, catapulting me out of my dream world again.

'Home,' he said, pushing the door to our room open and waving his hand. 'After you, madam.'

Someone had been in to prepare the room for the night. The mulberry curtains were drawn, creating a velveteen backdrop behind the two armchairs in the sitting area. Two oil lamps were lit, one on the small table between the armchairs and one between the beds. My feet buzzed with a tired ache and I collapsed into one of the chairs, flicking off my black pumps, trying to appear at ease. I glanced over to the beds. The quilted bed-covers, collisions of marshmallow pink and muted brown tones, were now folded back at the foot of each bed. The white linen looked far too smart to climb into. I looked towards the bathroom, remembering the luxury of my afternoon bath. My stomach cartwheeled as I wondered how it might work getting ready for bed.

Ivan came to stand beside my chair and rested his hand on my shoulder. 'Why don't you use the bathroom first and I'll follow afterwards. You can get changed in there.' I could have hugged him for taking charge. He collapsed into the other chair. 'Take your time. I'm in no hurry.'

I gathered up my things and scuttled past into the small black-and-white tiled bathroom that we didn't have to share with other guests, where maids could be summoned at the click of a finger to fill the bathtub. I relived the childish pleasure of my afternoon soak, wishing I could lose myself in that steaming water again. An elegant bottle filled with soft pink cubes, *Roses after Rain,* beckoned from the shelf on the wash-stand. Those bath salts epitomised the sheer indulgence of my day.

At the basin, oil lamps flickered either side of the large gilt-framed mirror. They enhanced the green glimmer in my eyes, making me seem a little wicked, as though acknowledging that I had finally stepped over an invisible line and shaken Tata from my shoulder. I undressed as brazen thoughts skipped through my mind — the possibility of Ivan pushing the bathroom door open and seeing me naked. I wrenched my nightdress down over my head and stared hard at the mirror, shaking my head to clear away the giddy feeling. I peered close, willing my sensible self to stay, and when I brushed out my hair, *don't be a fool* batted from one side of my head to the other with every stroke. I paused in front of the closed door, my hand on my chest, trying to calm myself. What was happening to me? Nothing felt real. I turned the handle and pushed open the door.

'Something to help me sleep,' said Ivan, still lounging in the armchair, shoes off, legs stretched out. He raised his glass and swirled the last of the amber liquid around its base.

I passed by him, conscious of my breasts swinging freely and pushing up against the thin cotton of my nightdress, excruciating, as though I was walking naked. I hurried to climb into one of the beds, pulling the covers close around my chin and shutting my eyes.

'Good night, Ivan,' I murmured, trying to sound my sleepiest.

'Sleep well. I won't be much longer,' he replied.

If only I'd blown out the lamp between the beds. It was too bright even with my eyes squeezed shut, but I didn't want to draw further attention to myself, or disturb him while he was relaxing. How long would it be before he climbed into the other bed? Would he want to talk more? I focused on my breathing, recalling how relaxed we had been together on the dance floor.

His chair creaked. He extinguished the table lamp then padded towards the bathroom. The door clicked shut and my eyes sprang open. A thread of warm light filtered under the crack of the bathroom door. Ivan was humming but I didn't recognise the tune. When the door opened again I snapped my eyes shut. His footsteps were heavy as he shambled towards his bed, and it groaned when he climbed in. I lay frozen, too self-conscious to say anything. His bed creaked again when he blew out the bedside lamp and rustled about.

'Jela, are you asleep yet?' he whispered after a short time.

For a moment I was speechless. 'No,' I finally managed, my heart like a hammer in my chest. 'This bed feels strange.'

'Imagine we're still sleeping across the landing, only a little closer now.' I pictured the grin creeping across his face, and I was transported back to the end of the evening when I'd felt so carefree and sure of myself. 'It's nice, no? If it helps, it's strange for me too. I had a wonderful time tonight. You're an enchanting partner.' His words were like syrup pouring off a spoon, reassuring me, helping to calm my churning stomach. 'Jela,' he whispered again, 'would a cuddle help? It might help you relax, no?'

At that moment all I wanted was to be cradled in his arms and to return to my fairy-tale world. The world I'd pictured myself in so often over the past months that had finally felt real. A world far away from everyone who looked at me in disbelief when I talked about my dreams. No one seemed to understand me like Ivan.

'I think it might help. Yes,' I said, surprised at how steady my voice was, how quickly my words spilled out. I turned to face his bed and pulled back my covers.

He climbed in beside me and I gasped at the warmth of him, then realised he was naked. There was no time to think.

'*Draga,*' he whispered, pulling me close and wrapping his arms around me. 'You have no idea how much I've wanted this. But I think you know it too.' He kissed the top of my head.

My mind was too muddled to speak. I felt trapped. How could I tell him that all I'd wanted was to be held by him? For it to be the perfect end to my fairy-tale day. I buried my head beneath his chin, trying to order my thoughts, crazy thoughts of Antica and little Luci, and Mama's warnings, all racing through my head. His chest rose and fell under my ear, his hairs tickling my face and in spite of myself I giggled.

'This is fun, no?' he said. 'Much easier to relax.' He squeezed me again and his body felt like fire.

I burrowed my head further down against his chest as though hiding from my nervousness. I tried stretching my arm across, willing him not to sense my discomfort. My hand brushed his stomach and I reached out further to lay my palm on the cool, crisp sheet to the side.

'Why not put it here,' he said, his voice a little stern, lifting my hand. 'Where it'll be comfortable,' he added, as though to mask the edge of authority that had crept into his voice.

I had no time to think. I was too focused on swallowing my gasp. My hand was now covering his rock-hard penis. It wasn't the woodenness of his erection but the heat of him that was so surprising. In my imaginings of sex I'd transitioned the penis from limp to erect, but I'd somehow disconnected it from being a body part. I'd thought of it more like a stick, a non-living thing, not something that pulsed and throbbed. Absurd images crowded my mind: me noticing him in his swimming trunks on Proizd; Branko and me and our friends at dancing lessons with Zlata, our golden-haired teacher; Zlata tapping us on the shoulder to rescue us — S*ix inches apart, let the holy spirit breathe* — and how we sprang apart, smirks on our faces; the cloakroom chatter, all the girls boasting about the bulges in the boys' trousers, *snakes in their pants.* Lying there beside Ivan, I would have given anything for Zlata and her six-inch buffer, anything to lessen the immediacy of that thriving dynamo under my hand. I edged up onto my elbow but Ivan reached for me again, pulling me closer.

'Ah, Jela.' His mouth seemed attached to my ear. 'You know what hangs between our legs. It loves to play sometimes. It will be fun for you too, no? Come on. Put your hand back. Don't be a naughty spoilsport.'

'It doesn't feel right,' I said, hating that my voice sounded panicked. 'Can we stop?'

What would Antica say if she knew I was lying with my uncle, and not our imagined *Kapetane?* How had I even allowed myself to think of Ivan in this way? I should have stopped my thoughts before they'd even had a chance to form.

'You've got me going, Jela. Come on, feel me again. You shouldn't have been such a tease.'

The timbre of his voice took me back to the construction site and his reaction to Josip at the *trofej*. This was my fault. I had led him on, and this was the consequence. It was exactly what Tata and Mama had warned me about when they'd first heard about Antica. *Soiled goods.*

'Let's start with these,' said Ivan, hitching up my nightdress and pulling down my underwear, peeling them off me, then using his foot to disentangle them from my ankles, flicking them off.

Everything was happening in slow motion. I wished he could see my face, to know how frightened and disorientated I was. I reassured myself that he wouldn't do anything to hurt me.

'That's right. Just relax,' Ivan said. I focused on calming my breathing, his voice syrup-like again as he caressed my legs and stomach. 'Come on, you can play too, you know.' He tickled me and it seemed the old Ivan was back.

My face was burning up. 'I'm not sure what to do,' I admitted, my voice small.

'Let's start here,' he said, putting his hand between my legs and caressing me in my most private place. I closed my eyes and a ripple of warmth coursed through my body. He kissed me then, a long slow kiss, a delicious kiss, and it felt right. I rubbed my hands down the length of his back and when he groaned my confidence soared.

'Don't be frightened,' he whispered, his breath like fire in my ear. 'It's something we can enjoy together. I think you're ready to be a woman now — to taste the icing on the cake.'

He knelt over me, pushing my nightdress higher and running his hands over my body, cupping my breasts and tweaking my nipples. I arched my back, the sensation so unexpected, as though I had pins and needles coursing through me. I reached up to pull him closer, wanting him to kiss me again but instead he groaned, and whispered something that I couldn't make out, raising his body as though to hover over me. His arms were now two stiff levers at my side and his breathing came short and fast. And then I was lost, everything was out of control. He pushed down on me, harder, again and again, urgent and groaning, until with a rush he had pushed inside me. I yelped at the sharp pain, a small animal sound.

'Ah! Ah!' he cried, as though oblivious, moaning but continuing to thrust.

It had happened too quickly. He was hurting me and I wanted him to stop, but he seemed lost in his own world, as though he'd forgotten me, as though I'd become something for him to push into, faster and with an urgency that I had no control over.

'Ah! Jela, *Draga.*' He collapsed with all his weight on me then lay there for what seemed like the longest time. I felt dirty and still in disbelief at what just happened. I didn't know whether I should say something. He'd gone so quiet.

When he eventually rolled off me, he pulled me close and planted a succession of kisses on my cheek. 'Ah, wonderful, wonderful.' His words were like a sigh. 'I think you enjoyed your first time too, no?' He stroked my cheek. 'I'm a lucky man to have picked your flower.'

I couldn't speak, couldn't say I was disappointed by my first experience. Instead, I kissed him on the cheek and within moments his breathing became slow and rhythmical. I waited until I was certain he was in a deep sleep before shrugging my nightdress down and tucking it firmly around me. I wanted to clean away the stickiness but I felt paralysed. Antica and little Luci were back in my mind and my eyes welled with tears. For the longest time all I felt was shame but then I crept closer to his warmth, and even in his sleep Ivan slung his arm across me to draw me in close.

OCTOBER

The last of the stolen bath salts slipped through my fingers. I watched the pink petals of *Roses after Rain* fizz and foam and shivered. My anticipation for this, my last luxurious bath, was tinged with guilt. Mama, Mare, Antica and Nada would all have loved just one bubble bath, and yet I hadn't shared any. Instead I'd pampered myself, eking out my stash over the past three weeks. I stepped into the water and slid down low, leaning back to capture the warmth. The bubbles tickling my shoulders were an airy cushion. It wasn't like me to be selfish, but I was too wary of the questions that would be stirred up. I'd given nothing away, not even to Antica, about sharing a room and I'd toned down my description of the hotel. These luxurious baths were my way of celebrating, given that I still had to downplay all that was new and exciting in my life.

It amazed me that Mama and Tata hadn't noticed the energy sparking off Ivan and me. Whenever we exchanged a glance or brushed against each other, I was certain there was a frisson of energy surrounding us. But baby Jakob's arrival, the week after Ivan and I returned, had shifted the focus promptly away from the ball and onto him, our latest family addition. Mama and Tata were so preoccupied with their new grandson that I felt invisible. Just as well Ivan's attention allowed me to soar above the minutiae. For me, the excitement of baby Jakob paled in comparison to my budding romance, which had become my sole focus, the meaning for my existence. My ticket to escape.

I was terrified I might let my secret slip. I'd spun more lies to Antica, concocting a story about a handsome *Kapetane* who had kissed me at the ball, hoping that this might account for some of my excitement. I was dying to tell her the truth, to share that I'd lost my virginity, but the risk was still too great. I had sworn her to secrecy. Even though Nada had thawed we were still walking a tenuous line and I was determined not to let anything endanger that.

I lifted my leg from the water, pointing my toe like a ballerina. The bubbles perched like dandelion puffs and I gathered them up, squeezing them between my palms, so that they frothed over my fingertips. Would my handsome lover creep into my bedroom later? The syllables rolled around in my mouth, the shape of them sliding off my tongue. My smile pinched my cheeks. How sophisticated. Me with a *lover*. It was only when my period came in the week after our return that he'd refrained. He'd kissed me and whispered in my ear, 'Abstinence is good for the appetite. Now's your time for beauty sleep.' He was always flattering me, complimenting me on my *beautiful smile* or *pretty eyes*.

I stepped out of the bathtub and wrapped myself in my towel, forcing my mind away from lingering doubts, picturing instead him kissing my soft skin and imagining the fragrance of roses still lingering. I pulled on my nightdress and remembered back to our first night in the hotel, how naive I'd been then. We'd laughed about it since and Ivan reassured me that it was natural, that everyone had to learn. Since then he'd taught me so much. He never boasted, and we never discussed it, but I wasn't silly enough to think that he hadn't enjoyed himself with other women. Perhaps this was the one thing holding me back from being completely honest with him.

The house was in darkness and I raised my oil lamp high, glad of its warm glow, but as I climbed the stairs my doubts returned. Ivan had seemed preoccupied and off-hand over dinner and I suspected he too was finding our subterfuge stifling. I paused on the landing, half-tempted to tap on his door, but this was something he'd made clear: I wasn't to disturb him because often he had important work to complete. But that closed door was a reminder, an obstacle to making things right with him. I left my own door slightly ajar, hoping that he wouldn't keep me waiting too long. It was always difficult snapping out of my hazy state if I happened to doze off.

Despite my good intentions, I started when Ivan tapped me on the shoulder. I pulled back my covers in what was now an automatic response, forcing my eyes open. He slid in beside me and I wasn't surprised that he was already hard for me. I reached for the condom enclosed in his hand, trying to beat away my grogginess. He'd first produced the small silver packs in Dubrovnik. I'd woken in his arms and he'd apologised that he'd been taken by surprise, *a beautiful surprise.* He'd shown me how the condom worked, another perk of the Party, he'd joked, turning what might have felt embarrassing into a natural part of our love-making. When I worried how safe it was he brushed off my fears, assuring me he was extra careful. Even so, I was counting down the days to my next period.

I pushed myself to my knees and took his penis in my hand, smiling at his familiar groan of pleasure when I rolled down the rubber sheath. My heart sank, however, when he wasted no time to pull me on top of him. I was still fighting against my sleepiness, trying my best to focus, but he seemed intent on moving quickly to his climax. Again it was over too quickly. This was the cloud hanging over me, the subject I didn't know how to broach. I was nervous he might think I was judging him, I was too critical, or needy, or I expected too much. He was always tender but I was yet to experience the 'thunderclap moment' Antica described. Over the weeks I'd reassured myself that the next time would be better, that I was still inexperienced, but again I felt I'd failed. I blinked away my tears as I lay down beside him. Ivan turned and pulled me close.

'Ah, *Draga*, what a dream you are. You enjoyed it too, no?'

I clenched my hands, annoyed that he hadn't even taken the time to savour my delicious scent of roses. For the first time ever I turned my back on him and faced the wall.

'You okay?' Ivan murmured after what seemed like an eternity. 'It's late, Jela. I should go.' When I didn't respond, he tapped me on my shoulder. '*Draga,* what's the matter, my beautiful?'

I turned to him, willing him to caress my cheek and feel the dampness. 'It's just . . . you seemed distant over dinner. I know you think it's best we keep things a secret but I want to be open with Mama and Tata. Make them see.'

'Ah, Jela. Not now.' Even though he was whispering I heard his exasperated tone. 'I've got too much on my mind already. You're too impatient. Trust me. I know what's best.' He flipped onto his back, and his arm was like a stick at my side.

I pitched up on my elbow. 'But I love you and I want *them* to know that. Why hide my feelings? They should know how you feel about me too.' I tickled his side in that place I knew he found impossible, desperate to lighten the mood. 'I know them best, remember.'

He grunted and shifted from my touch, turning his back on me. I worried that I'd sounded like a whining child and I swallowed back my tears, hating our silence.

'Come on, Jela. We've talked about this. They're not ready.'

'But you can explain.' I leaned over his shoulder to kiss his cheek. 'You're always saying how we're not directly related, how you and Mama are only step-relatives with your different tatas. And besides, there's years between you and Mama. I'm positive they'll see it from our side.'

'Jela, they're so caught up in baby Jakob, they won't see anything clearly.'

'But I want more!' I whispered as loudly as I dared. 'I hate going behind their backs. And what if Nada and Antica find out?'

He turned towards me. 'We need to bide our time. Be patient. Nothing would be worse than rushing and risking everything.' He ran his finger down my cheek. 'Come on, you know this.'

He swung his legs out of my bed then sat with his back to me attending to the condom. It was his habit to leave it on the chest of drawers beside my bed, on top of the empty foil package. He stood, leaning to tuck the covers around me and kiss me on the cheek.

'Go to sleep.' He ruffled my hair. 'Everything will seem better in the morning, *Draga.*'

He padded back to his room. I lay awake for the longest time, still unsettled and grumpy. Of course we were in love, and I wanted to believe in his judgement, his assurance that once the roading project finished he would take me away. But at the same time I felt confident that Mama would understand, that she would bring Tata around too. Surely Tata could look past the complicating factors and see we were a good match.

I edged across to lean over the side of my bed and hunt for the squares of paper I'd squirreled away in the bottom drawer. Rather than feeling a small thrill as I had in the first weeks when wrapping the used condom, it felt more like dirty women's work. I shoved the illicit parcel under my bed and lay back down, staring at the ceiling. I wanted so much to experience that moment of ecstasy myself, and yet how could I when I was always worried Mama or Tata might hear us?

~ ~

The next morning, I rapped on Mare's door and let myself in, heading first for her kitchen to dump the bag of pomegranates I'd picked that morning from our tree. It was my day off work but Mare had begged me to come and help her out. 'Is that you, Jela?' she called. 'I'm in the lounge.'

She was sitting in one of the brown armchairs, her black housedress unbuttoned to her waist, nursing baby Jakob. He was wrapped up tightly in a knitted shawl. The morning sun had worked its magic, lending a cheerful glow and warming the small lounge. Mare and Josip had moved into the tiny house three months back and she had made it homely with their few possessions. She had a knack, small details like the lace cloth draped over a low wooden box to transform it into a table between the lounge furniture, and a small jar of lavender placed on the mantelpiece above the fireplace.

'Have a seat.' She nodded towards the armchair opposite. 'Had a sleep-in? Lucky you.'

I wondered when she'd last washed her hair. It looked lank and Mare was usually so fastidious. No wonder she looked exhausted. Jakob had grown so much, and Mare's milk was his only source of food.

'Took a walk to the harbour first,' I said. 'It's such a beautiful morning.' I thought how the package I'd just disposed of was saving me from this same fate — breast exposed, baby attached.

'Does it hurt?' I sat down with a shiver running through me. 'Looks like he's eating you.'

Mare laughed. 'It's not that bad, Jela!' She tickled Jakob under his chin. 'Had to learn a few tricks, though, didn't we little man?'

'Seems like you're doing a great job,' I said.

'I worry there's not enough milk sometimes. You're such a hungry boy, aren't you, Jakob mine.' Her smile seemed resigned. 'If I can do it with these pimples, you'll have no problems.'

I picked at the threadbare armrests and closed my eyes. The sun felt luxurious on my face, autumn having leached out the intensity. I'd been determined to get rid of the package before coming to help. I was petrified Mare might smell it or, worse, that the contents might leak and stain my bag. I gazed out the window, shielding my eyes against the sun streaming in. Jakob finished suckling and Mare lifted him so he was upright against her shoulder.

'Come on, let that wind out, little man,' she said, rubbing his back using small circular movements. 'This will be you one day, Jela.'

My stomach turned. 'One day,' I replied. 'All in good time.' I had an impulse to run. The memory of that stickiness I'd felt back in Dubrovnik still taunted me. There was always the chance that a condom might leak inside me.

Jakob let out a mini-explosion. 'Oh, clever boy!' said Mare, her face like an open book. 'Wait for it . . . Honestly, *Dragi*, you're as predictable as your tata!' She pinched her nose and scrambled from her seat. 'You need changing before a cuddle. We can't be putting *Teta* off, can we.'

She bustled out of the room. I eased back in my chair but still felt on edge. Mare hummed in the bedroom, just off the lounge. I wanted to feel happy too. I was in love and my life was about to change for the better — but the subterfuge was killing me.

'Will you hold him for me?' said Mare, returning to the room, cradling Jakob. 'I've some jobs in the kitchen. Are you okay? You seem distracted.'

I held out my arms. 'I'm fine. And of course I don't mind. I'm just tired, that's all.'

'There,' said Mare, laying Jakob in my arms. 'Now you two can get to know each other. It's such a help. You wouldn't believe how much time he takes.'

'You go,' I said. 'We'll be fine.'

Jakob stared up at me from his tiny wrinkled face. He wriggled his arms free to reach up and wrap his hand around my little finger, tight as a clamp. I had been tiny once and Mama would have gazed down on me, knowing it was her responsibility to protect me. I remembered her in El Shatt, whispering assurances in the tent, *Family is the most important — we help each other through the tough times.* It was no wonder Ivan downplayed family, given the shock of losing both his parents as a teenager. I thought about Tata holding Jakob, how he seemed a changed man, softened around the edges. Mama would understand — she would convince Tata.

With Jakob still staring up at me I knew it was time to take matters into my own hands. In this instance, *I* knew best.

I left Mare's place just before midday feeling much lighter, but the closer I got to home the more my sense of conviction faded. I pushed myself forward, trying not to dwell on the negatives. Mama was in the bathroom, leaning over the bathtub scrubbing at one of Tata's shirts on the wooden washboard. The water was a dirty sludge and my guilt felt like a heavy cloak when I remembered my luxurious bath the night before. Mama was so engrossed she didn't hear me approach.

'Mama?' I tapped her on the shoulder and she turned back, her face set in deep concentration.

'Ah, Jela,' she said, pushing her damp curls from her forehead. 'Perfect timing. I need a break. How's my Jakob doing today?'

'Fine, and feeding beautifully.' My voice wavered and Mama looked at me, concerned.

'Mare's doing a great job, it's not easy,' she said. 'But, whatever's the matter?' She pushed against the bathtub, dragging herself to her feet.

My tears were streaming. I felt sick. All my self-assurances were crumbling like lies.

'Come.' Mama pulled me to sit on the edge of the bathtub beside her. 'Tell me what's wrong. Nothing's that bad, surely.'

I couldn't look at her. All my bravado disappeared and I couldn't control my sobs. I wrung my hands, feeling as dirty as that bath sludge.

Mama squeezed my shoulder. 'Now stop it. Listen,' she said, firmly. 'Tell me what the matter is.'

'It's Ivan,' I managed to splutter.

'Have you heard something? Is he hurt?' She sounded desperate. I'd gone too far now.

'No, Mama. No. He's not hurt. It's . . . we're in love. I thought it was obvious after Dubrovnik.'

I blinked away my tears, searching her face for affirmation. Mama closed her eyes and looked away. When she turned back her face was pale and drawn. I'd never seen her look so serious. 'You must tell me the truth now, *Draga*. The whole truth.' Mama rubbed my back.

I began at the ball and from there my secrets tumbled out.

'Enough!' Mama said, edging away as though I was contaminated, 'I've heard enough.' She thumped her fist on her leg. 'This can't go on. How could I have been so blind? My own brother. And under my own roof!' Her eyes filled with tears.

'Mama! We can work this out. He loves me. We'll find a way.'

Mama took a deep breath and shook her head. 'Gabrijela. Listen. This can't continue. First I must speak to your tata.' She was like a cornered animal, the way she shrank back, the frightened look in her eye. 'Leave me. I need time to think.'

I stood and shuffled past her, pausing at the doorway, desperate for her to beckon me back, for her to take me in her arms and reassure me that everything would work out. But instead she stared without seeing me and everything felt wrong. As I climbed the stairs to my room each step felt leaden. All that had felt possible now felt impossible.

For the entire afternoon I waited. Mostly I prayed, my fingers working through the decades on my rosary beads. Mama remained downstairs. I'd expected her to relent, to call out for me to come and help with the dinner preparations, but the house remained eerily silent. My prayers were a foil to stave off my other thoughts but at times my fingers worried the same bead, over and over, my traditional prayers replaced by thoughts with no structure: *What have I done? I should have known better. How will this end? Lord, help me.* I'd force my fingers onwards: *Hail Mary, full of Grace, the Lord is with thee.* This wasn't the time for tears. I would need all my reserves and energy for what was to come. One of Mama's sayings haunted me, *nevolja nikad ne dolazi sama —* misfortune never comes alone.

The front door opened. Tata cursed and I heard the familiar thump of his boots as he pulled them off. Mama's voice was there too, her urgent voice. The kitchen door clicked shut and I paced my room, heart pounding, feeling lightheaded. If this was like most nights, Ivan wouldn't be far behind. I didn't have to wait long. Ivan must have barely been over the hearth before Tata was yelling. I covered my ears.

Moments later Mama was banging on my door, pushing it open. Her face was panic-stricken. 'We should wait here. Let your tata deal with this.'

It came like an explosion, *'Boli me kurac!'* Tata's voice hurtled through my floor boards, followed by crashing and banging. Something large smashed and I wrenched away from Mama, charging for the door. I had to stop Tata, and Ivan needed my support.

'Jela! No!' Mama cried. 'We can't trust either of them!' A wave of guilt washed over me as Mama rushed forward and tugged at my sleeve. 'Let me.' She pushed past as another round of swearing erupted from below.

I shadowed Mama's frail back down the stairs. The noise was deafening. We pushed through into the kitchen and I craned my neck around the corner, to the small sitting area where all the shoving and yelling was coming from. I wanted to scream, 'Stop it! We can fix this!' But my words pounded in my chest and refused to escape. Mama steadied herself at the dining room table, gripping one of the chair backs. I sheltered behind her, peering over her shoulder.

Ivan and Tata were tussling in the middle of the small sitting room which was now a scene of carnage. Ivan was in his Party uniform but his hat lay trampled to the side, the top flattened and the peak ripped away. Mama's favourite vase lay in jagged wedges, smaller shards of the aqua porcelain scattered about, some lying close to Mama's feet. My eyes filled with tears. The vase had belonged to Baba, Mama and Ivan's mother. It always sat on the small table next to the sofa but this was smashed too, one of its thin legs at an impossible angle. Ivan swung around to face us, blood streaming from a gash on his temple. I gasped, feeling nauseated. He grabbed a fistful of Tata's checkered shirt and was struggling to keep him at arm's length, pushing Tata backwards. I worried Tata would slip in his thick woollen socks and cut himself.

Mama's hand was at her mouth and I edged up to stand beside her. 'Stop it!' I shouted, surprised at the strength of my voice.

'You stupid girl!' yelled Tata, turning and shaking his fist at me. 'You've brought shame on our family!' He swung a punch but Ivan intercepted his arm. 'Get your filthy hands off me, you bastard black sheep!' Tata bellowed, twisting and trying to shake off Ivan's hold. I shrank backwards again, Mama too.

'Calm down, Ante,' said Ivan, sounding irritated. He still had hold of Tata's shirt. He jerked his head around to stare at me. 'Why not let Jela speak for herself? She's had a part to play.'

I waited for Ivan to say the words. To tell Tata that he loved me. Those same words felt crushed inside my chest but somehow the silence forced them out.

'Tata, I love him. We love each other. Hear Ivan out. Please.'

Balls of fire were behind my cheeks and my hands were a trembling mess. Mama reached out and pulled me close but her embrace felt stiff. I stared straight ahead, scared to look sideways. Both Tata and Ivan were still for a moment.

'I've heard enough of your filth!' Tata said, glaring at me. He turned and sent a glob of spittle towards Ivan's shoes. 'There's what I think of you!'

Ivan roared and kicked out his leg. Mama and I leapt back, knocking a dining chair and sending it crashing to the ground. Ivan was frog-marching Tata backwards. A few steps more and Tata would trip over the broken side table.

Mama rushed forward and tugged on Ivan's jacket. 'Ante! Ivan! Enough! Move away now. Both of you.'

To my surprise, Ivan released his hold on Tata and they both retreated a few steps, still bristling. Mama stood to the side while they faced off, pacing like caged animals, back and forth, shaking their fists at each other.

Mama pushed the flat of her palm towards Ivan. 'Go and pack your things.' Her voice was as hard as stone and she pointed towards the door. 'Let him past, Ante.' She motioned for me. 'Gabrijela. Come.'

I skittered over to stand beside her, looking down at my feet.

'Open your mind, Ante. You're a fool!' Ivan said, and I jerked my head up. 'Can't you see Jela wants more? That you're killing her spirit.'

I searched Ivan's face, aching for his smile, for his look of assurance, but he stormed towards the kitchen door. His shoes clicked against the tiles as if he was marching.

'Jela took a chance,' he said, turning back at the door. 'You've ruined all that. Frankly, you disgust me.'

I snuck a glance at Tata. He was still glaring after Ivan as his footsteps pounded up the stairs. I reached for Mama's hand. 'Mama, Tata. I love Ivan. I need to talk to him before it's too late.'

'You're going nowhere!' yelled Tata. 'You'll never speak to him again. Ever! Understood? He's not family. He never was. And you . . . You're *zamazan!* Soiled goods! Who will have you now?' He shook his head as though he couldn't stand the sight of me.

'Stay,' said Mama, clenching my hand tighter. 'Let him go.'

'But I want him, Tata. We want to be together!' My tears were streaming and my words sounded like muffled gulps of air.

'Can't you see? You're a fool, Jela.' Tata shook his head as though all the answers had deserted him. He stalked past me and slumped down at the dining table, cradling his head in his hands.

'Come,' said Mama, leading me towards the sofa. We picked our way through the debris and Mama sat me down. I stared into that room that was so familiar without seeing a thing. Ivan's footsteps crashed down the stairs and the front door slammed.

DECEMBER

When anyone asked, we told them Ivan had moved to Lumbarda to be closer to the business end of the project. Somehow I had made my way through the weeks, one foot in front of the other, *polako, polako,* disguising my sadness in the form of another lie: my *Kapetane* hadn't contacted me and I'd been taken for a fool. I shared this with Nada and having to endure her smugness was a kind of penance. 1 was consumed by thoughts of Ivan. His absence was such a wrench that I questioned whether I could go on. My body ached for his touch. I felt mortified knowing I had ruined everything, but mostly I was disgusted at the reaction of my parents. How they had failed me. That they didn't want the best for me. That they wanted me to suffer.

Three weeks after Ivan's departure Nada and I were leaving Jadranka when a shrill whistle came from somewhere close to the building, startling us. It was twilight, that point in the evening when the shadows have lengthened but night hasn't yet claimed all of the light as its own.

'Jela! Can I have a word? Alone.'

I peered into the shadows. Stefan, Josip's new friend, was sitting on an upturned fish crate pushed up close to the factory wall, his black beret and slate-coloured jacket a perfect camouflage. Nada threw me a look that seemed to say, *Is this what you've resorted to now?*

'You head on up,' I said to her. 'Maybe I'll catch you afterwards.'

'Watch yourself,' she said under her breath, before striding off.

I walked across. Stefan was standing, hands in his pockets, head down. 'Hi,' I said. 'This is a surprise.'

'Um, your uncle.' He dug in his pocket and pulled out an envelope. 'Here. He asked me to find you.'

I hadn't seen Stefan since Proizd Island but Ivan had told me he'd enlisted for work shortly after the picnic. 'Thanks,' I said, making out that this was nothing out of the ordinary. Inside my heart was beating to a different rhythm. Stefan still seemed jittery. 'How's the new job?'

He shuffled from side to side. 'Good,' he said. 'Tough at first but I'm a quick learner.'

'One day at a time,' I said, holding up the letter. 'Thanks for this. Much appreciated. I'd best be off.' I made to leave then stopped. 'Stefan? If our family needs to get a message to Ivan, could you help? It's tricky now I've broken up with Branko.'

'Sure,' he said, seeming to come to life. 'A truck picks us up at eight each morning outside the hotel where the dances are. I'll keep a look out, make sure Branko doesn't see.'

I could have hugged him. 'Thanks. I might see you tomorrow,' I said, ensuring my voice didn't betray my emotion. 'I know Mama's keen to get him a message.'

I strode off, thinking about how Stefan was such an unlikely saviour. The letter was like an itch on my palm. I slowed when I rounded the corner from the port to walk along the waterfront. Nada was up ahead, yet to turn up the hill for home. I darted into a side street and leant against the limestone wall of the Luka Posta, tearing the envelope open, my hands trembling. I lifted the half-sheet of notepaper out and held it to my lips. He'd written it by hand and I had to peer closely to make out his words in the dim light.

Draga, please don't be angry.
I've tormented myself wondering what I could have done differently. I'm sure you have too. I had no choice but to leave and now we must be patient. You mustn't anger your tata. I know this is possible, that you can be strong, it's one of the qualities I admire most in you — as well as your beautiful eyes and smile, of course. I miss you so much, Jela, but I trust Stefan may prove a useful go-between. Can you see a way for us to meet again? There is talk they may send me back to Zagreb and so we may not have long. I long for your reply and to hold you again.

Yours, Ivan.

I returned the letter to its envelope and tucked it inside my coat pocket. When I walked up the hill towards home I felt both confused and thrilled. Of course I had to see him again, but what would it mean for us if he was sent away? I had to put my faith in him. He had succeeded in getting a message to me, and he would know what to do.

Tata, Mama and I sat around the dinner table in silence. Tata was business-like as usual, speaking to me only when required. I offered him little in return. We had been cohabiting like strangers over the past weeks and he seemed happiest avoiding me. Mama had retreated inside herself, but she at least would make small efforts to reconnect. At times I would let her in and for the briefest moment life would seem as it had been before. On the few times Josip and Mare joined us for a meal, Tata, Mama and I put on our best faces. Baby Jakob became our foil for all that rumbled beneath the surface, a bit-part player who innocently stole the limelight. We never told them the real reason for Ivan's departure. They were fed the same story we told everyone else.

'Caught up with Stipan Tomić from New Zealand today,' said Tata, and I almost choked on my fish stew. He sounded almost cheerful and I jerked my head up, oblivious to who he was talking about. 'Amazing how some things don't change. You remember him?' He was focused on Mama at the opposite end of the table. 'My old school friend.'

I closed my eyes trying to block out Tata and remember who this person might be. The letter was in the pocket of my skirt and I imagined it as Ivan's hand resting on my thigh.

'So, neither of you have aged?' said Mama, making an effort to sound cheerful too, wringing out this moment of connection.

'Pity he couldn't make contact earlier,' said Tata. 'They've been busy catching up with everyone. Thirty years now. Incredible.'

'And our Marta?' asked Mama, with what sounded like an edge to her voice.

'You've been let off the hook,' said Tata.

Mama's laugh came like a tiny explosion, her hand covering her mouth.

Tata continued, serious again. 'Stipan sends his apologies but Marta's mama's not been well. Marta's spent most of her time there, apparently.'

'Oh, that's no good,' said Mama. 'Times like this she must feel a long way from home.'

'It's been tough, Stipan says.'

I chewed my food, concentrating on my plate. When Tata reached across and touched my arm I lurched back as though he'd branded me with a fire poker. 'Stipan asked something specific,' said Tata, frowning. He held my eye as I glared at him. 'He could do with our help. His son needs a housekeeper. I told him we'd take him up on his offer.'

My mind reeled, trying to make sense of what he was saying.

'What are you talking about, Ante?' said Mama, looking horrified.

'They need someone over in New Zealand. They can sponsor Jela. It will be an opportunity. A way to escape. A right for all her wrongs.'

My mouth went dry. It was impossible to swallow. Mama's face looked drained of all colour but Tata continued, oblivious. 'They live in Auckland, the largest city. Beautiful, so Stipan says. There's a harbour just like here and a community of our own people. He's made a life for himself. You could do the same, Gabrijela.'

'No!' I said. 'I won't! You can't make me!'

'Ante,' said Mama. 'We need to talk.'

'The decision's made. We'd be fools not to take him up on it.'

'This is too much,' said Mama, shaking her head.

'*Draga*, I couldn't be more serious,' he said, fixing Mama with a stare. He banged his fist on the table and Mama and I both jumped. 'Jela's chosen to make her bed, and now she must lie in it. She should count herself lucky.' He scraped back his chair. 'We all should!' He marched from the room and up the stairs.

I couldn't stop shaking. How could he have looked straight through me? Mama came to sit beside me and wrapped me in a hug. 'I'll speak with him, *Draga*. We'll find a way.'

I hated that her voice wavered and her face seemed painted with fear.

Ivan enlisting Stefan as a courier had been a stroke of genius — five days later the arrangements were in place. Our goats lay side by side under the pomegranate tree, the centrepiece of our small back garden. I used the excuse of taking the goats up to the hills to feed. The older goat hefted itself up and came towards me, its bell singing. It butted me with its head. They were just two of a long string of goats we'd had over the years. When I was much younger I'd given them names and thought of them as pets but the very act of naming forged a connection that inevitably ended in heartbreak. Now I just thought of them as goats.

'Come on you,' I said to the younger one, slapping my thigh to try and startle it into action. 'Time to go.' Why was it that on days when you had no time to waste these animals thought they had all day? I waited at the back gate and the older goat butted me again. 'Lunch time, lazy,' I called to the younger one, opening the gate. At last, the sound of its bell as it scrambled to its feet and followed me.

We picked our way up the narrow path, the goats following, their bells clanging. When we reached the main track they skipped ahead, stopping at every opportunity to sample the shoots which had pushed their way through the rock crevices. I hoped Ivan wouldn't have trouble finding the cave I'd described. He'd only been there once, well before Dubrovnik, when I took him for a walk to show him where we'd played as children. It was the biggest cave, about half way up the hill but far enough away from prying eyes.

I didn't notice the steep climb. My body ached for Ivan's touch, his caress, what we'd shared. Our enforced separation and our letters had only intensified these feelings. My guilt over what I'd done, how I'd ruined everything, was there like a wriggling worm but rather than despairing I was confident that Ivan would be able to stop Tata's nonsense plan of sending me to New Zealand, that he was the one who could help me break free from Tata's shackles.

We reached the cave and I tethered the goats, who seemed happy munching their way through the lower leaves of an olive tree. I perched on the rock ledge to the side of the cave's entrance. My senses were on high alert but what I gazed out on looked dreary. The sky was a grey cloak and even the sea, usually the sky's vibrant petticoat, seemed washed out as though the colour had faded. I peered hard across the ocean, wondering where *Nova Zelanda* was. It seemed impossible that at the furthest point on the horizon there were places tucked in behind. Another world. I imagined those places clinging on from underneath. Would it be possible to lose your grip? I didn't have to worry about such things, I reassured myself. Ivan would have a plan.

One of the goats pricked up its ears and stopped grazing. My heart went crazy, but I hoped it was Ivan and not someone else choosing to take a stroll. It was impossible to see because the hillside was so steep that the path snaked up in hairpin bends. He rounded the corner and I was already racing towards him. It was odd that he wasn't in uniform. I had thought it was a work day. Instead, he wore a dark-grey sleeveless vest over a light grey shirt and trousers.

'Don't be angry,' I said, flinging myself into his arms. My words muffled against the thick wool of his vest.

He lifted my chin with his finger, holding it underneath so that I was forced to look him in the eye. 'Jela, of course I'm not angry. You did what you thought was right. You couldn't know he'd react like that. I know you hoped for better.' His eyes searched mine and I felt a rush of relief.

'I didn't want us to be a secret,' I said.

'I know. But now you must be patient. Until we can be together again.'

'But he wants to send me away! Far away. To New Zealand!'

'Shush.' He placed his finger on my lips. 'We've more important things first.' He wrapped me in his arms and kissed me and all my worries disappeared. He took my hand and pulled me towards the tangled curtain of green floating across the semi-circular cave entrance like a veil. 'After you, *Draga*,' he said, parting it and holding it back.

I gathered up my skirt and ducked to squeeze through the opening, beginning my crawl along the low passage. The packed earth felt gritty beneath my hands and knees and the air smelt like Tata and Josip's woollen socks after a day on the boat. A steady stream of drops made a hollow echo from somewhere towards the rear of the cave. Plink, plink, plink, as if the drops were ricocheting off and landing in a puddle. I edged forward, one hand against the ceiling, searching for the point where the tunnel opened up, where you could stand at full height inside the cave. Ivan was behind me, his hand sometimes grazing my ankle as he reached forward too.

'Are we nearly there?' he whispered, as though someone might be listening.

'Nearly,' I whispered back. My hand gripped the edge where the rock face swept upwards and I edged forward, ensuring I was well clear of the tunnel before unwinding myself to stand tall. I blinked and twisted my head this way and that, waiting for my eyes to adjust. Tiny cracks of light slanted through the fissures in the cave's ceiling and the rear wall of rocks loomed clearer. The dripping sounded louder too, a plunk more than a plink. Ivan pushed to stand beside me, taking my hand. I waited for his eyes to adjust.

'Ah, Jela. I've missed you so much,' he said, no longer whispering. He pulled me into his arms and wrenched my cardigan free from my shoulders, leaning in to kiss the crook of my neck, slipping the coarse wool further down. I freed my arms and his fingers traced the length of them. Undressing each other had never been part of our love-making before and all my nerve endings were jangling. I felt emboldened and looped my hands under his vest, tugging at his shirt to pull it free from his trousers, pressing my hands against his chest. It felt like a furnace. Ivan removed my skirt and then scrambled out of his vest while I unbuttoned his trousers. I took his penis in my hand, conscious of the dampness in my underwear. I pulled them down and stepped out, feeling brazen.

'Only the very best for you, my princess,' he whispered, pulling me onto the ground and cushioning his vest at my back. His fingers sought out mine and he passed me the condom. 'Take your time, *Draga*. There's no one to hear us.'

And in that cave, high above Luka, I experienced what I'd missed before. It was a beautiful surprise, reaffirmed as my echo resonated with his before softening and fading away.

Afterwards, as we lay cradled together, Ivan reached across for our clothes, draping them over us like a blanket. I didn't want to move. Didn't want to talk about the trouble I'd caused, how much I'd lost by telling the truth. 'What can we do?' I said, the cold creeping into my bones. 'How can we stop Tata sending me away?'

Ivan pulled me closer. 'Jela, he's already spoken with me. I'm sorry, I had no choice.' His words batted against my chest. 'He came to see me the day your letter arrived. I agreed to cut a deal. It was the best I could do.'

'What do you mean, no choice?' I squeezed my eyes shut, as though this might block out his words. Ivan stroked my neck but it felt like a weak apology now.

'If I help with your paperwork and the money for your fare, he'll keep quiet about us. I can't risk him talking to my superiors, Jela. My position would be at stake. They've offered me a promotion, signed me off from the road project. I'm leaving on the weekend for Zagreb.'

So that's why he wasn't in uniform. 'No!' I sobbed, thumping at the ground and turning my back on him. 'How could you? What about me?' I stared into the blackness, biting on my lip to hold back my tears.

'You have to understand, *Draga*,' he said, his voice a whisper again. 'It would be curtains for my career if I didn't agree.' He leaned over and caressed the side of my face. 'The higher up I go in the Party, the easier it will be for both of us. Surely you must know this.'

'But you must be able to do more!' I cried, my echo sounding sharp, desperate. 'You're abandoning me! Surely I'm more important than your stupid job!'

He sat up and the blanket of clothes slid off me. 'That's enough, *Draga.*' His tone suggested the matter was closed. 'You must be brave now, and patient. I promise I'll come for you when I can.'

I curled myself into a tight ball, unable to stop the tears. He pulled his clothes on with sharp movements, like a knife cutting the air. All I was capable of was creeping further into my huddle of disbelief.

'Here. You'll catch a cold.' I flinched at his touch but he pulled me to standing, passing my clothes across in a bundle. 'Come on, don't be silly. There's always letters.'

He drew me close again but I held myself stiff then pulled back to start dressing. My limbs felt heavy and the sounds of the cave ominous as I dressed in silence. All my energy had drained out of me. What had felt so natural now felt awkward and wrong.

'I want you to have this,' he said, reaching for my hand and wrapping my fingers around what felt like a letter. 'It's a photo, and my new address. The photo's not the best, I'm afraid. It was taken years ago, but hopefully you'll still see the resemblance.'

Everything felt wrong. I needed more time. 'But I have nothing for you,' I said, a stupid thing to say since this wasn't meant to be a farewell. It was as though I was playing a game where I didn't know the rules. I was being polite when all I wanted to do was scream.

'You've given me so much. How could I forget you?' He kissed me on the cheek. 'Jela, I have to go. My bosses are expecting me to make the last of the arrangements. Wait ten minutes and there won't be a risk of us being seen together. I'll take the long way into town to avoid the house.' He was already on his hands and knees, making his way back towards the entrance.

I felt in a daze, still denying this was happening. He called back part-way along, 'Remember that I love you, Jela. That's the most important thing. To hell with the rest of them.'

I wrapped my arms close trying to capture those last words and hold them tight. They were all I had left, that and his photo. There was a flash of light as he parted the foliage to push through the opening — and then he was gone and I was left in the darkness, numb.

The goats bleated their farewell from somewhere outside. For the longest time I couldn't bring myself to move. When I did, my foot brushed up against something soft on the floor and I reached down to retrieve his vest. I held it to my face to drink in the smell of him again, reassuring myself of his promise. This would give me the strength for what lay ahead.

Outside, I hid his vest inside my cardigan then trudged off home, my mind a blur. When I reached our gate my eyes stung with tears. There was our pomegranate tree, now stripped of fruit. Would this have been my last year for witnessing our family's annual entertainment — our game of who would get to the fruit first, us or the goats? From October, it was always our challenge to remove any object lying close enough for the goats to climb onto; they relished nothing more than to crane their necks and pluck the ruby ripe fruit. There were so many things I realised now I would miss, so many things I wished I had paid more attention to over the past year. The goats crowded close and I patted their soft pelts, pushing my tears away. Ivan was all that I had. I had to trust in his judgement.

It wasn't until I was back in my bedroom that I remembered the condom. Ivan wouldn't have taken it but I couldn't bear to return. Just as those caves had harboured secrets which Branko, Josip, Nada and I had discovered as children, that condom might also become a wicked find for some other child, a source of speculation and wonder. I was certain, though, that no matter how imaginative the finders might be, they could never concoct a story that would even come close to the truth.

LUISA, 1989

KORČULA, YUGOSLAVIA

SEPTEMBER

Luisa starts and turns back from gazing out her bedroom window as Mirjana barges in.

'They've been staring at me all day,' says Mirjana, breathless, thrusting two aerogrammes at Luisa. 'As soon as I saw the New Zealand stamps I knew they were yours.'

It takes a moment for Luisa to register. There's a letter from Mum but the second one's from Bex. Her reaction is immediate. She crosses to the bedside table and tosses Bex's letter down.

'That one from your *friend*?' says Mirjana, standing back, watching.

Luisa ignores the jibe and waves the other letter. 'Mum will be here in person soon.' She shakes her head. 'Why would she bother?'

'Who knows?' says Mirjana, waving her hands like a conductor while backing towards the door. 'But all day they've been staring at me. I'll leave you to it but let me know everything's okay. Don't want you going into meltdown again. That toilet's seen quite enough of you.'

'Yep. Been there, done that,' says Luisa, giving Mirjana her best pained expression. 'Thanks. I'll let you know.'

When Mirjana's gone Luisa collapses onto her bed and stares at the thin blue letter bearing Mum's scrawl. She can't help herself though, Bex's letter is like a magnet. She places Mum's letter on the bed and leans across to pick up the other one, turning it over in her hands as though by looking at it from all angles she might make the best decision. The New Zealand stamp is intriguing. Bex must have gone home? Luisa's curiosity gets the better of her and she tears it open.

September 3rd

Dear Luisa,
I'm determined not to fail this time. I need to apologise, but it's also time for me to confess. When I left you at the airport in Skopje, just like all the other times, I was running away from myself, only this time I couldn't escape. I didn't stay in London. Couldn't. I went straight back to New Zealand to try and sort my shit out. I'm determined not to give up this time and this letter has to be the first step if I have any chance of healing. There's no easy way to say this. I was to blame for what happened. It wasn't just that I slept with Nikola and left you on your own. I did something far worse.
It was when we were playing cards, after you'd gone to bed. I made a stupid throwaway comment to Kosta, a terrible thing. I said that you'd been uptight since breaking up with your boyfriend and perhaps all you needed was a decent shag. The next morning I blamed the alcohol but of course that was no excuse.
Those same words have been churning inside me ever since. You had to live through the most horrific trauma imaginable and afterwards I treated you so badly. I didn't even have the guts to admit what I'd done.
All I can offer is my deepest apologies and hope this gives you some explanation for the way I acted. Rightly, you felt abandoned when I was so busy hiding from myself. You had

*been so good to me, so understanding when I was trying to
stand on my own two feet. I didn't deserve your kindness and I
don't expect your forgiveness now. Please trust that I won't
make contact ever again, but I want you to know how much I
value the time we did spend together. I admire your strength
and your resilience, and it's my hope that I can try and draw
from what you've taught me.
I hope with all my heart that you will heal, and that your
Croatian family have surrounded you with the love you deserve.*

Bex

Luisa's trauma rises without warning, the taste of bile a sordid
reminder. Her hands are a shaking mess, but still she manages to twist
and mangle the flimsy sheet of paper into a golf-ball sized missile to
fire across the room. The ball of blue ricochets off the skirting board,
coming to rest on the tiles just in front of the chest of drawers. For the
longest time Luisa gazes into space, unseeing, unable to focus. It feels
like another scab's been knocked off her wound. Eventually, her
attention turns to her hands and she stills them, stops the wringing,
bringing some illusion of control. Again she tries to rationalise her
thoughts but there are no answers. *Is that what Bex really thought of
me? How can Bex think that a letter might absolve what she did?*

Luisa feels compelled to stand as though by touching solid ground the
answer might become clear. Her hand brushes against the other letter.
Mum's letter. This feels like a gift now, a chance to escape what's just
played out and to reconnect with her former self. When she opens the
aerogramme a separate piece of paper floats to the floor and Luisa
gathers this up, smiling, in spite of herself. *Mum's never been known
for her succinctness.* She begins to read.

1st September, 1989

My darling girl,

*There are moments in life when you are forced to look back on
your past, and face the decisions you've made. For me, this
began when you were preparing to leave for your overseas trip
and ended when Josip phoned me last night. For so long, I've
swallowed my secret. It's partly the reason I fell out with Josip
and I fear that if I continue to hold it close, it will cause
problems between the two of us. Josip was concerned you were
holding something back — like mother, like daughter, he said —
which stung me to my core. Being a shut book cost me the
chance to return to Korčula. I never made my peace with Tata,
and worse, I never held Mama in my arms before she passed
away. The truth of this still rips at my heart and I would hate it
if whatever you are holding close worked its way between us.
Perhaps you might choose to stay on in Yugoslavia, or
somewhere else far away. It might seem an easier option. I
want you to know it's not the only way.*
*I'm not one to look back with a sour face, but I think you know
life wasn't the easiest for me growing up. Tata wasn't what
you'd call a doting father. Josip might view this differently, but
then he was the boy. But, of course, this wasn't why we fell out.*

Mum's story tumbles out and Luisa is drawn in. It's as though Mum is
sitting next to her, talking with an honesty they've never shared before.
Not through any of the often heated discussions they've had. Perhaps
Mum felt if she was to safeguard her secret that she had no other
choice than to toe the parent-party line. Luisa had never felt Mum
could relate to her world, that their realms of experience might ever be
the same. Rather than feeling disgusted, Luisa is proud of the way
Mum coped. That Uncle Ivan should be castrated! How could he live

with himself? Luisa's hands start to tremble again. She swallows hard and grabs at the second part of the letter, scrambling to turn her attention to something tangible, anything to clear away those other pictures crowding her mind.

Even though now you will likely think of me in disgust, I hope you can also understand why I kept my secret close. What I'd done felt so shameful that I couldn't face being exposed again. How could I have thought it was acceptable to be with my uncle, even a half-strength one in this way? Looking back, I was a silly young girl, totally entranced by the attention of an older man. But at the time I thought he was in love with me and that he could whisk me away to a better life. With wiser shoulders I realise he was simply taking advantage and using his power to abuse me.

When Mama tried to reconcile the rift between Tata and me, she said I was too stubborn, like a mule. Tata was the same. For his part, I think he found it easier to forget me. Ivan was as much to blame, but of course in Tata's eyes I should have been stronger. It was the way things were with the men. Mama, bless her, was the one who suffered. How could we bridge the gap between our two families so far apart? She missed out on the joy of being Baba to you, Anita and Marko. She missed out on seeing you grow. This makes my heart break if I think of it too long.

I will leave you with the thought of how much I love you. When you feel the moment is right, and before I arrive, please share the first part of this letter with Josip and Mare. It is time. With regard to your own secret, only you will know when the telling time is right. While I'm no shining example, I hope this letter provides some perspective. Your tata was the only person I shared my secret with. At the time we were both young and guilty of diluting the details. He didn't push me to explain my hurt, or take the time to ask more questions, to understand how deeply Ivan's abuse had affected me. I convinced myself that what mattered most was him accepting that I wasn't a virgin so that we could make our marriage work. Being young and so far from home, it was easier for me to remain silent, to not explore my other feelings, to bury my hurt. When I showed this letter to your tata he couldn't hold back his tears. I hadn't appreciated how much my secret had cost him. How it created some distance between us by nibbling away at our relationship and making jagged edges at times. Worst of all, your tata was forced to push aside his dream to visit our homeland.

Draga, our secrets are no more than scars — part of us, but they mustn't be allowed to define us. For me, my scars catapulted me on a journey across the world and I experienced so much more than I might have otherwise. I will leave you with this thought. It's only when we reveal our secrets that we allow ourselves the freedom to become our true selves. Only you will know when your moment is right. Please know that I won't force you, and whatever you decide, my love will always surround you. I know as well as anyone that some things take time.

Dad and I can't wait to see you.

All my love,

Mum xx

Luisa rereads every last word of the letter, blinking away her tears. It's Mum's final words that stare back at her. Sharing what happened in Macedonia won't miraculously heal her, but rebuilding relationships is a two-way thing. She came to Korčula for a reason, and if she's to connect with her family she has to trust. She goes to find Mirjana.

'Good news?' says Mirjana, looking up from where she's sitting on her bed. Her look of surprise quickly changes to concern when Luisa sits down, gripping Mum's letter tight.

'Jesus, you're like a ghost. What's wrong?' Mirjana says, reaching for Luisa's hand.

Luisa understands Mirjana's reaction. Her circulation might as well have been switched off, her hands look so white. Even thinking about what she's about to tell Mirjana makes her want to throw up.

'I was raped,' she says, forcing herself to turn back to Mirjana once the vile words have escaped.

Mirjana's jaw drops. Luisa can't believe how matter-of-fact she just sounded. She pulls Luisa into a hug. 'Oh my God! And you've been carrying that around all this time? I thought you were just being precious about a tiff with your friend.'

Luisa winces and pushes her sleeve up against her eyes. Mirjana squeezes her, pulling her closer. 'I was hoping that by not telling, I might be able to forget,' says Luisa, her voice small. 'But it keeps following me around.'

Mirjana reaches across to pull a handkerchief from her bedside cabinet, passing it to Luisa. 'Did you report it to the police? How could your friend have deserted you?'

'We did report it, but the doctor . . .' Luisa shudders and her words stick in her throat. 'He barely qualified as a human.' Mirjana pulls back, but Luisa can't meet her eye as she continues telling her the story, omitting only the very latest details from Bex.

'I'm so ashamed of our country,' says Mirjana. 'That you were treated like this. What's more, that bastard's unlikely to face any consequences.' She shakes her head. 'That republic. Our country. There's too many issues.'

For a while they sit in silence, Mirjana rubbing Luisa's back. Now that she's voiced it aloud there is some relief, a weight lifted, even if it's just that her cousin has some context for the way she's been acting since her arrival.

'I'm not sure I want to say anything to Josip and Mare,' says Luisa. 'Not yet. There's something more important to tell you all over dinner.' She waves the letter. 'It's about Mum, and that will be enough for everyone to take in. What's happened to me can wait, and it may be something I never share. But I wanted you to know.'

Mirjana nods, her eyes glassy.

'I need a bit more time to get my head straight. Okay? I promise I won't go back to my old tricks but it's so clear to me now why some women never report rape.'

'Of course,' says Mirjana, pulling Luisa close again. 'Come down when you're ready. And thanks. I feel terrible for judging you. For so long I've been jealous, wishing that Tata had been more like your mama, that he had escaped this place too.'

Luisa can't help herself, turning back at the door. 'In the letter Mum mentioned Uncle Ivan. Do you know him? It's the first I've heard of him.'

'The family's mystery uncle,' says Mirjana, her expression questioning. 'How weird. He was the one who helped get your mama out. Maybe she didn't want to let on that she'd gone behind Dida's back? Dida was furious at the two of them, apparently, but I've always admired your mama for being brave enough. Even as a child I knew not to cross Dida Ante. She was obviously smart — after all, Uncle Ivan had all the contacts, and from what I understand he organised the paperwork and helped with her fare. If only Tata had been more gutsy and seen the same opportunity, I wouldn't be stuck here still.'

Luisa grips the doorframe. How could Mum's story have got so far twisted from the truth? 'But you've never met him? What happened to him?'

'His name's in the paper sometimes. He's high up in the Party, one of the generals. I can't tell you the number of times I've fantasised about tracking him down. He'll be in a mansion somewhere, living the life. For sure he'd have known when to jump well before Tito died.'

It takes all Luisa's self-control not to burst Mirjana's bubble. That will happen later, tonight, when she can speak with them all together.

'We'll have to work on our own plan to get you to New Zealand once Mum and Dad get here,' Luisa says. 'I'll catch you at dinnertime. Hey, thanks, I feel better for sharing.'

Back in her own bedroom thoughts whirl in Luisa's head. *It's outrageous that disgusting man got away with this, that he's been put on a pedestal.* She stares at the ceiling, desperate to calm her thoughts. *Even though Bex has admitted blame it's Kosta who is the guilty one, not Bex.* Mum's words push back. What's important now will be moving forward, one day at a time, and trusting that her pain will lessen. Luisa smiles. She can't wait to see Mum now, and Dad. To embrace that familiarity, the certainty that comes from years spent together. She's been lucky with the people who have helped her so far. Her family here, and Helena. She thinks about that piece of paper Helena handed her with her address. With all that's happened, perhaps a miracle is possible. Being passive goes against her whole being; it might help to do something positive. With Mirjana's help maybe she could make contact again, follow up with Nikola? Find out what happened to that bastard Kosta and use her legal nous to force a prosecution.

But these are likely just wild thoughts, and she can't think about them now. What's most important is preparing to welcome Mum home. To pave the way by sharing her story. To put things right.

ACKNOWLEDGMENTS

At times when writing this novel, *The Absent Time* felt more apt as a title. My heart goes out to John McKay, my love, for your enduring faith in this novel, your encouragement when doubts crept in, and for your astute eye and patience when reading yet another draft. Had I realised what was ahead on this journey I may never have embarked on it. Knowing now what I have gained, I am grateful that hindsight is never a luxury at the start of a journey, and that your support was always there to carry me through. Thank you too, Cam, Alex, and Hamish for your understanding — just like teenagers, a distracted Mum was no doubt infuriating at times.

Stephen Stratford, thank you for working your editing magic. Your scrupulous eye for detail was impressive and my words have benefited from your professionalism.

To my parents, Sue and Ron Lamont, your love and support has always been a surety. You were a wealth of information about life in the 1950's as young adults. Thank you for sharing your stories and in particular, Mum, thanks for the spark of inspiration when writer's block set in. Your recollection of that day at the Feilding races, when

Red Glare romped in as a rank outsider, was the inspiration to take Gabrijela to the Ellerslie racecourse.

Louise Marinovich, you have been part of this project from the start, on walks and over wine. Thank you for regaling me with your stories and insights into life growing up as a *Croatian* Kiwi. I could always count on you to cast my curly questions wider to your parents, Paul and Tonka Marinovich, and your extended family.

Antoinette Van der Sande, and Louise and Marin Matulovic, thank you for sharing your personal stories. Your introductions to family and friends at the Dalmatian Society allowed me to glean yet more stories and experiences to inform this novel. I am indebted to Zlata Ozanich, for checking my use of Croatian throughout the novel.

I first met Dr Paula Morris when I was accepted for the Auckland University Masters of Creative Writing class of 2017. Paula, you have been influential as my mentor. Thank you for your insight and insistence that Gabrijela's story must be told — even at such a late stage in the programme — and for believing in me and championing this story. Your contribution to New Zealand literature and new writers is nothing short of exceptional.

I am fortunate to have the support of the MCW cohort, a talented group of writers who are both generous with feedback and encouragement. Thanks in particular to: Rosetta Allan, Rose Carlyle, Amy McDaid, Heidi North, Kirsteen Ure and Sonya Wilson, for your friendship. Caroline Barron, although we have only met recently you have inspired me in so many ways.

My inspiration to start this novel came from signing up to an introductory course at the Creative Hub six years ago. Special thanks to Carol Painter for your continued support.

Michelle Vollemaere, thank you for your sharp eye for detail in the early stages and for your encouragement and willingness to assist as the novel progressed.

Pam Marks, I count myself fortunate to have a well-read friend who was happy to take my very first draft and provide thoughtful feedback.

I am grateful for the generous support of Creative New Zealand, and the NZSA, in awarding me a Complete Manuscript Assessment award. Thank you Barbara Else, for providing the requisite honesty and direction that pushed me to continue crafting this novel to the next stage.

Dr Nina Nola, thank you for reading and evaluating my second draft at what I know was a frenetic time for you and your family. I appreciate your moral support, wise counsel, and your many suggestions of books and films that are central to the culture you hold so dear.

Claire O'Connell, you took me under your wing and have gone above and beyond your brief.

Deborah Darling, thanks for being my travel mate all those years ago!

To my fellow WINOTS and other close friends, especially Fiona Boyle and Julie Sinclair. And to my siblings and their family's, you have all played your part by carrying me through with laughter and a dogged belief that the end-goal was in sight — champagne is now obligatory.

I am fortunate to be a member of one of the best book groups in town who read my final draft (within the tightest of timeframes) and were generous with their astute evaluation and discussion. I am indebted to: Nicki Boswell, Rebecca Washer, Paula Mooney, Lisa Powlesland, Julie Fitzgerald, Emma Malloy, Virginia Van Schaijk, Belinda Law, Suzanne Wilson, Georgina Burt, Kerrie Barclay and Julie Chadwick.

Catherine Farquhar, my talented friend and cover artist, we met for a reason on Pauanui mountain. Thank you for taking my vision and using your own exceptional talents to transform this onto the canvas, the end result is stunning. And Laura Becker, you stepped in with your design skills at just the right time, what an inspiration you are, your talents will carry you far.

And lastly, thank you, reader, for spending time with this story and for being an integral part of the journey. It is satisfying to know that my words, first penned all those years ago, *polako, polako,* have finally reached their destination.

ABOUT THE AUTHOR

Pip McKay's travels through the former Yugoslavia informed *The Telling Time*, however the connections she forged within the local Croatian community while researching stories of New Zealand's Croatian immigrants, have been inspirational. Pip holds a Masters in Creative Writing from the University of Auckland (2017) and in 2018, was awarded a Creative New Zealand/NZSA Complete Manuscript Assessment award for the manuscript.

The Telling Time was shortlisted for the 2020 NZSA New Zealand Heritage Literary Award and the novel's opening won the 2020 First Pages Prize, judged by an international panel and Sebastian Faulks, OBE.

Kia ora. It has been my privilege to have you read this novel. Let's stay connected. Please take the opportunity to visit my website and sign up for my mailing list.

And finally, leaving an honest review on your chosen platform: Goodreads; your e-book store; and/or your social media platform is both helpful and wholeheartedly appreciated. Nga mihi.

www.pjmckayauthor.com

facebook.com/pjmckaynzauthor
instagram.com/pj_mckay_author

NOTE ON SOURCES

Whilst *The Telling Time* is a work of fiction, this novel is informed by many sources including my own backpacking adventures in 1989 through the former Yugoslavia. I researched many books and websites dealing with the Croatian experience during the second world war and the Dalmatian immigration experience in New Zealand. My journey transported me on both a visual and political journey to 1950's and 1980's New Zealand. The following sources were particularly helpful.

Amelia Batistich. *An Olive Tree in Dalmatia*. Longman Paul, 1963.
Amelia Batistich. *Never Lost for Words*. Auckland University Press, 2001.
Stephen A. Jelicich. *From Distant Villages — the lives and times of Croatian settlers in New Zealand, 1858-1958*. Pharos Publications, 2008.
A Compilation of Short Stories. The Dalmatian Genealogical and Historical Society, 2008.
Florida Vela. *Croatia Mine*. Quoin Press Ltd, 1997.
Carl Walrond. *Dalmatians — Facts and Figures*. Te Ara — The Encyclopaedia of New Zealand. http://www.TeAra.govt.nz/en/dalmatians/pages 1-8.

Bronwyn Labrum. *Real Modern — Everyday New Zealand in the 1950's and 1960's.* Te Papa Press, 2015.
Bee Dawson. *The New Zealand Woman — 80 glorious years of fashion, food and friendship from the pages of the New Zealand Woman's Weekly.* Whitcoulls, 2012.
Helen Leach. *Kitchens — The New Zealand Kitchen in the 20th Century.* Otago University Press, 2014.

YouTube videos:

Jadranka Sardine Canning Factory. https://www.korculainfo.com/sardine-canning-factory/
Here to Stay. https://www.nzonscreen.com/title/here-to-stay-2007/
Encounter — I think I go to New Zealand. https://www.nzonscreen.com/title/encounter-I-think-i-go-to-nz-1976
An immigrant Nation. https://www.nzonscreen.com/title/dalmatian-at-heart-1994

Additionally, the library and museum at the Dalmatian Cultural Society were invaluable as sources of information. I pay tribute to the dedication and care of the voluntary committee who maintain this fabulous resource.

And Leonard Cohen, always inspirational. Gabrijela took license when writing her letter to weave in your beautiful sentiment about secrets and scars.

BOOK CLUB DISCUSSION NOTES

The author describes this novel as one that shines light on that fraught period in life when we identify as 'young adults'. Regardless of the era, it's a time when life-changing decisions are made, often based on little or no experience or information, bravado is required and especially resilience.

How successful has the novel been in embracing this theme?

How relatable in today's world are the decisions both Gabrijela and Luisa are called on to make?
Are these decisions easier for our 'young adults' today?
What if anything is different for our 'young adults' today?

Gabrijela:

1. Regardless of where you live in the world, how aware were you of the Croatian/Dally immigrant story? Does the novel highlight anything you didn't previously know about this immigrant group? What aspects of the story might be transferred to any cultural group making their home in a new country?

2. Gabrijela is exiled to New Zealand by her father — sent away in disgrace. How realistic do you think Gabrijela's plight would have been in the 1950's? Can you imagine the same happening in today's world?

3. Is it realistic that Gabrijela held on to her secret for so long? What are the barriers today to disclosing such secrets and has the #MeToo movement helped this?

4. Why do you think Gabrijela was attracted to Ivan? Was this believable?

5. When Gabrijela finally realises she has been duped by Ivan why do you think that deep down she still held out hope?

6. Joy was a shining light for Gabrijela. How welcoming are we to new immigrants? Could we do more? What are the stumbling blocks/barriers to making new immigrants feel welcome/at home?

7. When looking back, Gabrijela describes her marriage to Roko as having jagged edges at times – what do you think she means by this?

8. How do you feel Gabrijela's experiences would have influenced the way she parented Luisa and her siblings?

9. Luisa inferred that even years later, Gabrijela never considered herself an equal to the other Dally women at the club. Do you think this might be a common feeling or one that is unique to Gabrijela?

Luisa:

1. Luisa is proud to call herself a Croatian Kiwi even though she is disparaging of many of the old ways. How typical do you think this is for the second generation offspring of immigrants?

2. Luisa is an intelligent young woman and yet she placed herself in a risky situation. How believable is this? Was it any different for young women in the 1980's than it is today?

3. Do you recall stories of the Moonies? What are the dangers/challenges facing our young adults today when setting off on travels? Are our young people any wiser today? Why/why not?

4. Did the novel transport anyone back to their own backpacking adventures? Anyone keen to share stories?

5. How realistic was Luisa's reaction to her trauma? Why did she keep her secret close and why was it important for her not to disclose what had happened when she met her relatives?

6. If you were Luisa could you forgive Bex? Can you understand Bex's reaction/actions after Luisa's trauma.

7. Why do you think Luisa found it so hard to move on from Mike? Did this fit with her personality?

8. How would you describe Luisa's relationship with her mum?

9. How do you think Luisa's reunion with her Mum would have played out?

Printed in Great Britain
by Amazon

17011958R00212